Praise for
THE BIOMASS REVOLUTION

"*The Biomass Revolution* is an exciting escapist adventure set in the world of Tisaia—mankind's last bastion of technology and civilization."
~Arthur Bradley, Bestselling Author of *The Survivalist*

"A modern day 1984: This book is on the same level of George Orwell's *1984*. That might be a bold claim, but the Biomass Revolution rates that well."
~Richard Stephenson, Bestselling Author of *Collapse*

"A sumptuous novel of epic proportions that left me wanting seconds. Nicholas Smith has delivered a fresh vision in a well-worn genre."
~Michael Flanagan, The Lazy Book Reviewer Blog

"Set in a not too distance future, *The Biomass Revolution* gives us a daring look at a possible power-drive apocalypse."
~Noah Fregger, Author of *Gabriel's Watch*

Also by Nicholas Sansbury Smith

From THE TISAIAN CHRONICLES:

Book I: The Biomass Revolution

Book II: Into the Gray Wastelands
(Coming Winter 2013)

Prequel 1 - Squad 19

Prequel 2 - A Royal Knight

Other Collections:

Orbs (Coming Fall 2013)

The Singularity (short story)

THE BIOMASS REVOLUTION

BOOK ONE OF THE TISAIAN CHRONICLES

Nicholas Sansbury Smith

Donna,
I hope you like this one!

Best wishes,

THE BIOMASS REVOLUTION

BOOK ONE OF THE TISAIAN CHRONICLES

Nicholas Sansbury Smith

nicholassansbury.com

———

Edited by Michelle Brown

Artwork by Phoebe Smithers

ISBN 13: 978-0-9892447-0-1

Copyright © 2013 Nicholas Sansbury Smith

Great Wave Ink Publishing

To my parents who have always believed in me,
supported me and loved me unconditionally.
I love you both more than you know.

ACKNOWLEDGEMENTS

Parts of this book date back to 2006, when I first began working for the State of Iowa. It was then I first became fascinated with the idea of a dystopic future. And while this book is a work of fiction, it contains elements and ideas based on the status quo.

The world of Tisaia may seem like nothing more than another dystopian look into the future, but it's a glimpse into a crystal ball revealing where we're headed—both as a nation and a global community. Fossil fuels, immigration, food shortages, water rights, and nuclear weapons are a few of many issues we face. Without a global response, Tisaia may someday not just be a work of fiction, but reality.

However, before I scare you too badly, I want to thank all of the people who have helped me create this world.

First and foremost, I'd like to thank beautiful Andrea Thompson, who has never stopped pushing me to work harder in all aspects of my life since the day I met her. Your support means everything to me.

My editors Michelle Browne, Haley Thompson, Caroline Morse and Laura Riordan Berardi helped tremendously in preparing this story for publication.

Several honorable men also played a significant role in developing The Biomass Revolution. Mat Noble and Dean Ibsen were two of the first to delve into this world. Former Reconnaissance Marine Steve Oberbroeckling shared his military expertise and experience as a recon scout. Author Sean Fisher helped inspire me through his own work and provided brilliant advice for this debut book. My twin brother, Zach Smith also played a pivotal role in the development of this story.

I owe you all very much.

I'd also be remiss if I did not offer my sincere gratitude to artist Phoebe Smithers, who brought The Biomass Revolution and the world of Tisaia to life through her amazing artwork. I'm truly indebted to you.

Finally, I have to thank my pup, Bella. She has spent years curled up in the back of my aging office chair.

To all of those I have left out please know your support is appreciated. Words can't express how special this book is to me. Being able to share this story is an honor. It's a world I have been working on for so long. And truthfully, a world I hope never becomes reality.

"War does not determine who is right—only who is left."

~Bertrand Russell

TABLE OF CONTENTS

PROLOGUE

Time: 7:14 a.m. January 10, 2071
Location: The Dead Forest. Tisaia

Darkness always made Evandish uneasy. Even after spending most of his adult life scouting the tunnels for the resistance, he never became accustomed to it. He heard some of the younger scouts refer to the tunnels as their homes, but for him they were a place to hide, a place to survive.

Decades had passed since the nuclear fires rained down on the cities in the old world. The fires had consumed everything in their path; it was only by chance he'd survived, seeking refuge with his family in a subway station. The heat, darkness and fear of those first few days would never leave him, seared in his memory like a brand on his skin. There were other memories too, some so vivid they would still slip effortlessly into his mind at arbitrary times.

He recalled the first several months after the bombs dropped. Combing the catacombs of tunnels, looking for shelter and food with his family and the other survivors. Waiting for help his parents said would inevitably come.

The military will mobilize, they said. The Red Cross too, maybe even other countries would send help. As the months slowly passed, the survivors perished one by one. Help never came. Their food supplies dwindled. The remaining survivors became desperate, their last strands of dignity gone.

No child should remember their parents' last moments the way he was forced to. His mother's eyes, wild with fear, peeking out from behind his father's back. His father waving a burning torch as three men, covered in dirt, ash and blood, devoid of their humanity approached them. Words were needless to reveal their intentions; the desperation in their eyes gave it away. They wanted what little food his family had left. The can of peaches, a liter of water and a half jar of peanut butter. It was all his parents' lives ended up being worth. In the end, a single meal became worth a life.

A tear streaked down his face as he tried to shake the memories, the sharp cold of morning finally wiping them out of his fatigued mind. His eyes instantly searched for the garish fire that had kept him warm through the night. The warmth was gone; the light which had cast a vivid glow over his camp had disappeared. His eyes came to rest on the vanishing coals.

He shivered as an indiscriminate blast of frozen wind whipped against his face. The soldier threw his coat around his shoulders and hovered over the dying embers—blowing on them to revive them. He had been in the dead forest for over three days now, scouting out the trolley tracks. His mission was to sabotage the resupply line of the Biomass trolleys traveling to refuel the great city of Lunia.

The ash gray tint of the dead forest had already taken its toll on him. Being a scout he grew to know loneliness; to accept it, embrace it. And normally he would jump at the chance to spend time above ground, out of the darkness of the tunnels. But the forest reminded him of what the world had once been. Unlike many of the younger soldiers born after the bombs dropped, Evandish could remember life before the war, before the destruction. He could recall the bright green leaves sprouting off the limbs of trees reaching towards the vibrant crystal blue skies. He could remember the changing seasons and the rainbow of colors in the fall, when the green leaves would turn to red before the first snow fell.

Another flare of wind grazed his bare skin, bringing him back to the harsh reality of his world. He peered up at the never ending hazy sky, rays of sunlight desperately trying to peek through the thick poisoned clouds. He turned to see the skeletons of trees, long absent of the leaves now turned to ash on the ground below.

The snort of his horse finally distracted him. Evandish turned to make sure Ralli was okay, satisfied to see she was nibbling on some oats he had thrown down for her in the snow.

"How are you doing, girl?" he asked, patting her mane as she ate. They had been together for a year now, scouting the tracks on missions above ground. She was one of the last of her kind, captured by the resistance at the beginning of the war. The world was not a place for beasts anymore. She was a reminder of the innocence lost in decades of war and blood.

He turned his attention back to the fire, blowing slowly into the red ashes. Within minutes the coals glowed orange and he rushed to his knapsack for some kindling.

Ralli watched him kneel and scatter the small twigs onto the flames, before losing interest and turning back to her oats. In the distance, Evandish could hear a faint sound emerging over the intermittent wind. Ralli heard it too, her ears perking up as she sensed danger.

The wind picked up again, draining out the faint sound. He shrugged and diverted his attention back to the flames, his mind preoccupied with the warmth of the fire on his bare hands. Less than an hour of exposure was all it took to get frost bite, something he had no way of treating once it set in.

For a second the wind lapsed again and the mechanical groan of a train emerged in the distance. His head instantly shot up, forgetting the warmth of the flames on his hands.

"Oh no," he said, quickly stomping on the fire.

He stiffened as the treacherous scream of a Biomass train broke through the howling wind.

"There isn't supposed to be a train for another day," he said, his voice raised but calm. He didn't want to alert Ralli anymore than she already was.

He turned, watching as she paced back and forth nervously, pulling at the rope tied to the dead bark of an old oak tree. She could sense the danger.

Evandish searched desperately for an escape route, jumping from the tracks a few yards away to the trail leading from their camp into the forest.

Nowhere to hide, nowhere to run.

The soldier hopped to his feet, ignoring the smoke rising from the ashes. If there were Knights on the train, their infrared equipment had already picked up his location.

Quickly, he scrambled to gather his belongings, tucking them into a small pack on Ralli's back. For a moment he caught her gaze, recognizing the undeniable fear in her dark brown eyes.

The sound of the train cut through the thick wind as he rushed to untie her from the tree. Within seconds they were racing through the frozen branches of the forest, tearing through snow covered bushes and over fallen logs. The lifeless branches snapped under the weight of her hooves as they continued through the graveyard of dead trees.

A cloud of breath exploded from her open mouth as she lumbered on through the forest, her hooves following a path not used for decades. Evandish kicked her convincingly in the ribs to keep her going. The train, which Evandish could now see out of the corner of his eye, was racing towards him, quickly gaining in speed.

The path lay on the edge of the dead forest, following the tracks for another quarter mile before diverting into a valley. They had no choice but to follow it as the forest was too dense to navigate. Their only chance of escape was to make it to the valley, away from the reaches of the Knights' machine guns.

The horn of the train rang out again, causing Ralli to snort another cloud of breath into the air. His heartbeat, elevated, pounded on his ribcage as if it were trying to escape its white jail cell. It knew what his brain was trying to deny—within moments, the train would be on top of them.

"Almost there! Come on girl!" he yelled, kicking her in the ribs again. "A few more seconds and we're there!"

He turned quickly to see the sleek metal train, the flaming torch symbol of Tisaia inscribed in vibrant red on the side. As he suspected, on the top of the engine rested a crow's nest manned by two Knights. He watched the cool blue glow from their night vision goggles staring down on him.

The image sent a shiver down his back and he turned back to the path, kicking Ralli again. "Come on!" he yelled, fear growing in his deep voice.

He tried desperately to hold onto her reins, his frozen hands shaking violently, Ralli galloping faster beneath him.

"Crack! Crack! Crack!"

The gunfire tore through the silence of the dead forest, ringing in Evandishs' ears. Ralli panted on, undeterred, the muscles in her old legs holding strong.

"Faster Ralli!" Evandish shouted over the barrage of machine gun fire. He watched the bullets tear by them, peppering the frozen ground and sending chunks of snow and earth raining down.

Ralli raced in and out of the spray and for a split second, everything slowed down. A bullet whizzed past Evandish's ear. He yanked on her reins, his eyes fixated on the path, hope slowly building inside him. They were almost to the safety of the valley. But Ralli's legs were old and strained. She was not as fast as she had once been and was no match for the speed of the train.

Evandish was foolish to have hope, learning over the years there was no room for it in Tisaia. He cowered in fear, gripping the reigns tightly as the train bellowed down on top of them at the last minute. And before Evandish knew it he was in the air, fumbling for the reigns, Ralli tumbling beneath him. He watched helplessly as the bullets tore into her beautiful dark skin, her eyes wild with fear. They hit the ground simultaneously, arms and legs flailing powerlessly about.

The two companions came to a stop at the crossroads of the trails, their bodies broken and silent. The train hammered on, its horn blaring through the cold wind. Evandish caught one last glimpse of the Knights who turned their focus back on the tracks, ignoring him like nothing had happened, the cold blue glow from their goggles fading in the distance. His gaze fell upon Ralli, who was lying lifelessly to his side, before he too closed his eyes for the last time—a look of horror frozen on his face.

CHAPTER 1: THE PAST UNVEILED

"Reality is only an illusion, albeit a very persistent one."
~Albert Einstein

Time: 10:14 a.m. January 19, 2071
Location: Sector of Governmental Services. Lunia, Tisaia

I t was mid-morning and Spurious Timur sat in his cubicle, staring at his goldfish, Archie. Slowly the small fish fluttered his fins and swam about the bowl. Sporadically, he peered through the glass with interest at the outside world, a place so large the small fish could never comprehend its complexity. And yet, the goldfish stared back at him, his gills puffing in and out, as if he was trying to understand what lay beyond his glass walls.

Ironically, Spurious lived primarily in a space equivalent to that of Archie's. The only difference was the young man was surrounded by four white walls connected to form a cubicle, where he worked 10 hours a day, 60 hours a week.

Archie darted towards the surface of his glass home as Spurious reached over and dropped a pinch of food in the water. He smiled, watching his fish peck aggressively at the small morsels.

"So that's what you wanted. No wonder you were staring at me. I bet you were pretty hungry," Spurious whispered, too quietly for other pods to hear.

Forgetting his small friend, he turned and faced his blue screen, slouching in his plush chair. The scent of bleach and paper prompted him to sneeze. The odor was something he had never gotten used to, even after his five years of working in the same place. There were always service workers in their ocean blue uniforms, cleaning the work spaces with bleach in hope of preventing germs from spreading.

The smell never ceased to remind him of his first day at SGS. He could still remember the floors of windowless rooms with artificial light and the stuffy tunnels below the building—their twisted pipes lining the thick concrete walls like synthetic veins. And he certainly would never forget the first time he entered his office, sitting down only to see the web of ventilation above like bars on a holding cell. It was then he knew his cubicle wasn't a work station—it was a prison.

The clock struck 10:15 a.m. and Remus, a service worker, showed up with his small cordless vacuum cleaner.

"Good morning Spurious," he smiled, pushing his tiny vacuum into Spurious' workstation.

"Do you mind if I vacuum in here right now?"

Spurious didn't need to look up to see the crooked grin painted across Remus' face. It was the same grin he saw every morning, a grin that repeated itself day after day like everything else. He simply nodded and motioned Remus into his cubicle.

Remus, like many of the other service workers, was developmentally disabled. In fact, most of the service workers employed at his office suffered from some condition preventing them from obtaining other work. Their attitudes, however, did not reflect their miserable jobs.

The only thing Remus and Spurious seemed to have in common was their unique family stories. Both of their parents were killed by a bomb during the early years of the Biomass Revolution. And every day Spurious saw the young service worker's crooked grin he was reminded of it.

"All done, Spurious; you have a good day now, you hear?"

"You too Remus, see you tomorrow."

Spurious watched Remus drag his vacuum down the hall

towards the paper stations. He stopped to replace the disappearing stacks of yellowed paper with more stacks, reminding Spurious of his aging childhood book that survived the wars.

"Good morning Remus," chirped Zaria, a secretary that worked just down the hall from Spurious.

"Well hey there, Zaria, how are you doing? Did you watch the last fight at the dome? I heard the Samoan warrior put on a great show," Remus said, putting a stack of papers back onto the table.

"No. I couldn't make it, but I have heard a few people discussing his victory this morning. I overheard he has won the past four fights and if he wins the next one, he will gain his freedom. Is that true?"

"Get back to work, Remus! Don't bother other employees," shouted his supervisor, Mr. Sturm.

Remus looked back down at the carpet and pushed his vacuum cleaner out of Zaria's office, acknowledging his supervisor's request with a simple nod.

Sturm followed Remus and the other service workers everywhere, hunting them with a clipboard and checking off the tasks they performed with the same methodical stroke of his pen.

Spurious never heard anyone call him by his first name, and all of the service workers referred to him specifically as Mr. Sturm. Some days he wondered if Sturm wanted them to suffer.

The slow tick from a nearby clock echoed in his ear, reminding him of how structured his life had become. Having lived his entire life in Tisaia, Spurious knew nothing else. The world beyond the great steel walls was as foreign to him now as it was when he was a child. Like other State workers, he only knew what the State taught him and what he saw with his own eyes.

He could remember only a few things about his childhood. He knew his father was a factory worker in one of the first Biomass factories. His mother was a boarding school teacher for immigrant children before the State had passed Law 99 in 2051. The law deemed any immigrant taken in through the gates of Tisaia in the last decade to be an illegal citizen. The result was deportation back into the Wastelands—a virtual death sentence. A Justice committee was established and a squad of Royal Knights was dispatched throughout Tisaia to find all illegal immigrants and transport them to the camps to process them for deportation. After Law 99 his mother had been out of work.

Spurious frowned, reminded that he could scarcely remember his parents faces. It wasn't the only thing he had forgotten. It seemed he could not recall what it was like to be happy; his purpose was only to provide administrative support to his superiors. Over the years he had come to accept his fate, but deep down he had always wished there was something more to his life.

Spurious swiped at his holographic blue screen to transfer data from a file he received to a spreadsheet. As he finished up his report, the crystal blue screen began to pulsate, indicating he had a new message. He swiped the screen with his index finger to unlock the incoming message, watching the blue background fade and a white screen emerge. "Sound," he commanded.

"Spurious,

We have gotten an influx of new tunnel projects—priority red. I'll need you to get started on mapping them as soon as possible. Make no mistake, this comes from the top.

Regards,

Miria"

"Beats the plumbing projects," Spurious said, quietly. With another swipe from his finger, a 3D image of the tunnels underneath Lunia emerged from a tiny opening in his desk. He rotated his chair, and began to study the red holographic lines snaking their way across his table.

The tunnels had always interested him. They were the grand engineering marvels from the early 21st century. And there were so many of them, like the never-ending entrails of a snake, winding their way deeper and deeper beneath the city. What little he knew came from what his father had told him when he was just a child—a fascinating story about the old world. It was a tale about how things once were; when governments sent their emissaries to meetings where they discussed solutions to the laundry list of problems the world faced. They talked about the dwindling supply of oil, global climate change and rising sea levels, but the talks never materialized. Temperatures rose, oil disappeared and the polar ice caps slowly melted. In a last ditch chance to protect cities from the scorching sun and gamma rays, the United States embarked on an engineering feat not seen since the creation of the New Deal and the building of the Panama Canal. They created new cities, completely underground.

Spurious thumbed through the holographic lines and enlarged a section of tunnel underneath Rohania, a suburb of Lunia. It was here, where he was born, that the tunnels were the deepest. It was going to be a daunting mission to map them all—a mission that supposedly came from the top.

He stared at the contours, watching them snake deeper into the ground. What was so important about the tunnels? Why were his superiors so interested in what lay beneath the city streets?

Spurious shook the curious thoughts out of his mind and continued to study the holographic lines crawling across his desk. He knew not to question his work. Mapping the tunnels was going to be overwhelming, but it was his job.

By the time he was done analyzing the new data, it was time for lunch. He looked down at Archie, who peered back with his oversized eyes, his small gills flexing in and out.

It's pretty amazing that I can't breathe in there, and you can't breathe out here.

Spurious smiled at his small companion and stood, stretching with a long groan before shutting off his blue screen and heading to the cafeteria.

Saving energy had become law in the year 2061. The State

rarely arrested workers for small offenses. More likely, were write-ups which could cost an employee a promotion. He'd seen it happen to his old pod mate, Paulo.

Spurious thought of his old friend as he made his way through the corridor of cubicles. One after another, the white structures of cubicles lined the walls. All cages, housing people just like him. He never liked to peer into these work stations as he passed, hoping others would respect his privacy as he respected theirs. There was one cubicle he could not restrain himself from looking in. It was that of Lana Padilla, a 25 year old dark-haired secretary with piercing brown eyes. Spurious heard the only reason she was given the prestigious and well paying job was because of her beauty. This was one situation where resumes, experience and name dropping didn't matter. There had been only one interview before her supervisor, Varius, hired her as his assistant.

Spurious paused for a moment as he passed the manager's office. He was a disgusting man, sitting in his plush chair, his gut hanging over the same pair of desert tan khakis he wore every day. And then there were his glasses. They were as thick as a magnifying glass, the rims coated with dandruff flaking off his receding and graying hair.

Spurious frowned and continued down the hall towards the cafeteria, his head down, while he contemplated what he would say to Lana. As her workspace came into view, he brushed a strand of his brown hair back into position and cracked his unmistakable half smile. "Hey Lana…" he said, his voice trailing off as the quiet tick of a clock filled his ears.

He craned his neck further into the office to see it was empty. The only explanation he could gather was she was at home with a cold. There was a virus going around the office—a virus not even the gallons of bleach had been able to prevent.

Spurious shrugged her absence off and continued down the hall towards the scent of food, trying to conceal his disappointment.

The cafeteria was busy for a Wednesday. Most people brought

their lunch from home to save credits, but today the dining hall was doing well.

There were two lines: one for deli sandwiches, and the other for salad and porridge. These were some of the only foods the State deemed healthy enough for employees to eat. The entire list could be found in Law 204. It was yet another edict on state workers he had memorized.

Spurious got sick of having the same thing every day, but it was better than what those trying to survive outside the protection of the great Tisaian walls had to eat.

He approached the white, shiny counter, blinded momentarily by the reflection of a metal tray. His vision quickly came back into focus and the toothless grin of one of the cafeteria assistants came into view.

"Hey there, Spurious, what's it going to be today?" she asked.

He gritted his teeth and tried to hide his disgust. "I think I'm just going to have my usual."

"All right. One tuna salad on white, with one slice of cheese and tomato."

"You know me too well," Spurious said, with a smile, grabbing the tray from her.

The pungent smell of tuna entered his nostrils, reminding him of the smell of bleach. These were two smells he would never escape; another two pieces of the monotonous puzzle making up his life.

He stared down at the sandwich, realizing over the years tuna was almost tasteless to him. Sometimes he even wondered if it was really tuna, having never seen one in his life. Ever since the Biomass Wars ended, the boundaries around Tisaia were fortified. No one was allowed to leave and no one was allowed in. He knew it was impossible for the State to ship tuna in from the ocean. The only explanation he could deduce was the State had massive stockpiles of canned goods stored away in vaults underground. Like many State workers, he had heard of these vaults, but never seen one in person, or in any of the engineering design work he analyzed.

"Over here, Spurious," yelled Paulo.

Spurious made his way down the armada of white tables filled with his co-workers. He spotted Paulo and his best friend Ing at a table at the far edge of the cafeteria. After wading through the lines of SGS employees, Spurious finally sat down with his friends.

"What's going on?" Ing asked, as Spurious took a seat.

Spurious sighed. "I've spent the majority of my day staring at holographic images of the tunnels. Pretty exciting stuff," he lied.

Ing leaned closer to Spurious and whispered across the table.

"Oh yeah? What can you tell us? Anything secretive going on?"

Spurious cracked a half smile and shot Ing a quick glance before taking a large bite out of his sandwich.

He chewed loudly while he spoke. "You know I'm not at liberty to say, but…"

"But what Spurious?"

Spurious shook his head. "It's nothing, nothing important."

Ing rolled his eyes before staring at his porridge. "You get to see all the neat stuff," he said, swirling his spoon playfully in the creamy soup.

"I wish I had something to keep me busy. I don't know if I can wait another five years to get out of this place. It really is a nightmare, doing the same old thing day in and day out. Maybe I should get a fish to stare at, too," Paulo said, frowning.

"Five years isn't that long. You've been here for how long? Twenty years? Another five isn't going to kill you," Spurious reassured his friend.

Paulo looked down at his small bowl of browning cabbage. His eyes were rimmed with creases and his eyes were dull. Strands of receding blonde hair crept down his forehead and crawled down his thick sideburns like a vine down a tree. Ing looked at Spurious, blatantly concerned.

Ever since Paulo lost his promotion, things had changed. After waiting five years for a transfer to the Sector of the Treasury, Paulo was to be promoted to Bureau Chief of Insurance Claims, which also marked quite the raise in salary. If he played his cards right, he might have been able to move out of government housing and buy a small condominium outside the Commons, where the rest of the workers lived. That dream ended one day when Paulo forgot to turn off his computer, lamp, and office light before going home from work for the third time. His penalty was a write-up, costing him his promotion.

The once articulate and outspoken man seemed broken and aged. Ing and Spurious knew they had to continue and try to motivate their old friend. With his golden years ahead, he should be managing a group of young people Spurious' age, but due to a small mistake, his life was put on hold for at least another five years, if not indefinitely.

Spurious took one last bite out of his sandwich before he turned to Paulo, attempting to cheer him up. "Tell us about the time you did an audit at the Biomass factory outside the city limits. I've been hearing rumors they are creating an even more efficient Biomass."

The old man blinked a few times, as if he was trying to remember. "Oh yes, the one I traveled to a year or so ago. It was a magnificent facility. The factory floor was lined with circular fuel tanks that rose hundreds of meters into the air. Workers in blood red uniforms raced about, checking the blue screens on each individual tank. It was quite the operation."

For a moment Spurious thought of his father who had worked in a similar facility, long after the State assumed operations from the private company that controlled the Biomass.

"Do you remember the Tisaian Corporation?" Spurious asked.

Paulo nodded quickly in between bites. "How could I forget? Those bastards were the first to use the hybrid soybean seeds that created Biomass."

"Those bastards?" Ing interrupted. "The Tisaian Corporation solved the world's fuel problems practically overnight. Why do you think they named Tisaia after them? They are heroes."

"And they also sparked WWIII when they did. Heroes don't create wars. They end them." Paulo fired back. "Oh that's right you are too young to remember The Biomass Wars. When nations fought over the rights for the seeds. And you probably wouldn't remember these *seeds* can only be grown in fertile top soil—top soil found in only a few locations after 21st century farming destroyed most of it."

Spurious interrupted the brewing argument with a cough. "You guys. Stop arguing. It doesn't matter who created Biomass. All that matters is whether the State can create enough to share it with the outside world."

"That will never happen, Spurious. I don't understand why the government wants to hoard the Biomass, but they do." Paulo mumbled between bites of his cabbage.

Ing laughed. "Well your memory clearly goes back longer than mine, but I'm willing to guess it's because there isn't anyone left in the world to share it with."

Paulo looked up, half way between his next bite. "Then the State has already succeeded in making you believe what they want you to believe." He glanced over at Spurious for a split second. "Remember, what we're led to believe is not always the truth."

"It bothers you that the State denies the existence of other governments?" Spurious asked.

"It doesn't bother you?" Paulo said, running a hand through his thinning hair.

"Well it's simply not true, guys. If there's any government left we would know about it. There would be evidence," Ing piped in.

Paulo snickered. "Ah, what it would be like to be young and ignorant again," he said, rising from his seat. "I'll see you two later. Clearly I'm not going to get through to you today."

Lunch ended as abruptly as Paulo had lost his promotion. It was becoming a common occurrence. Spurious or Ing would say something that upset him and the next thing they knew he would be headed back to his cube. Today was no different, but for some reason Spurious felt a sense of excitement. Not because he had upset Paulo, but because regardless of who was right, this was truly an exciting time for humanity. If this new Biomass was capable of what he had heard, then perhaps things would begin to change. Perhaps things would go back to the way they were in the old world—the world his father used to tell him stories about.

Time: 7:18 p.m. January 19, 2071
Location: Commons Building 21, Apt 44. Lunia, Tisaia

A freezing rain punished Spurious as he rushed down the cobblestone walkway towards his housing complex. The silhouettes of destroyed skyscrapers towered above in the distance, appearing oblique in the darkness. They were now nothing more than artifacts from the past, like the pyramids he had read about as a child.

He pulled his eyes away from the eerie structures, tugging his hood over his head to cover his chapped face, protecting his eyes from the cold, unforgiving wind and rain. A row of street lights glowed within the protection of their glass cases, illuminating the archaic brick walkway below. A strained power line whined in the wind as it carried the Biomass life source to the commons buildings, like blood through a vein.

Spurious continued down the path, nuzzling his face into the collar of his coat. He had taken the six o'clock underground trolley home tonight, opting from walking the near five miles from his office to his apartment due to the freezing rain. He clutched the copper railing tightly, the metal stained green like the rooftop above. A radiant orange glow from several lights guided him to the fourth floor, where he pulled open a massive oak door revealing a hallway lined with blood red doors. His apartment was at the far end, the last door on the right. He slugged down the creaky wooden floor and inserted his key into the lock with a mechanical click.

Dwarfed by the skyscrapers in the distance, the commons buildings were small and cramped for large families. The architecture was late 20th century, defined by pointed arc windows, steep gables, and stone veneer. Before the Biomass Wars, they were used to house distinguished politicians who traveled to the capitol city once a year for a three month legislative session. After the war ended, the common buildings had been rebuilt on a massive scale to house all State workers. It was one of the few perks these workers shared. The citizens living outside Lunia enjoyed far less luxury, often squatting in the metal intestines of destroyed skyscrapers, or congregating in stone buildings constructed hastily in Rohania.

Inside the apartment Spurious was greeted with the familiar sound of Anya's voice. She was the artificial intelligence his flat was equipped with.

"Good evening, sir, what can I do for you?" she asked.

While Anya was nothing more than a hologram appearing on a stand in each corner of the square room he called home, she had the capability of fixing him dinner, turning on his favorite program on the blue screen, regulating the water temperature in his rain room and explaining any new laws the legislature passed.

Spurious set his bag down on the ground. "Would you warm up a cup of tea for me please?" he replied.

"Certainly sir. Is there anything else?"

"Any news about the new Biomass factory?" he asked.

Anya's image jumped from one stand to another as he walked through his small apartment towards the kitchen.

"No news yet, but let me check the mainframe. Give me 31 seconds."

Spurious smiled, grabbing a full mug of warm tea from the automatic food processing counter. He admired her attention to detail, something programmed in her years ago. She was connected to the same system as all the other AIs and held considerable power. Her intelligence was remarkable. She was the ultimate multi-tasking machine. In a millisecond she could be warming up his tea while combing through a massive database of information. It was, in a way, frightening to Spurious. On the one hand she catered to his every need, but if he broke any State law she could report him through the system immediately, prompting a visit from a Royal Knight.

The thought sent a chill up his spine as he made his way to the loft nestled against the east wall of the apartment. Beneath the bed was a leather couch with a perfect view of the blue screen protruding out of the wooden floor in the center of the apartment. He sat the mug down on a table and headed for the marble rain room jutting out of the north wall of the room.

"How was your day, Anya?" Spurious asked, running his hand through his wet hair.

"It was the same as any other day; I downloaded new updates from the State system and read the latest legislation up for debate at the Capitol building. Shall I prepare the rain room for you?"

"I'd appreciate that very much, Anya, please set at 88 degrees. And while you're at it, why don't you describe some of the interesting pieces of legislation to me. What type of laws are they going to impose on us this session?"

"Sir your tone would not be looked upon positively by Council of Royal Knights. I think you should…"

Spurious quickly interrupted her. "You aren't going to contact them, are you?" Spurious asked sarcastically, as he walked towards his rain room, still shaking from the cold.

"As you know, my loyalties are first and foremost to the State, but as you may know I'm programmed to keep you happy, clean and well fed. A quandary, isn't it? So technically it would go against the purpose of my very existence to turn you in to the CRK."

"And don't ever forget that, Anya," Spurious said, smiling, as he stripped out of his work clothes and entered the rain room.

He crouched and sat on the marble floor, resting his back on one of the stone walls. The warm liquid poured down his dark hair, matting it to his head as steam rose around him. Instant relief rushed through his body as he finally began to warm up. His feet tingled as the blood rushed back into his toes. Closing his eyes, he drifted off to sleep as the water massaged his anxiety-riddled body.

Time: 7:50 a.m. January 23, 2071
Location: Sector of Governmental Services. Lunia, Tisaia

Spurious approached the gates of the SGS building, nodding at the two fully-armed guards who stood motionless at each side of the stone entrance. The blue glow from the soldiers' goggles followed him as he walked towards the offices. For a second he paused to check his watch, stealing a glance at the Knights' shiny armor suits.

Tin Cans. It's what the rebels called them on occasion. But Spurious knew they were nothing like the tin cans his tuna salad came from. Their armor was made of a material called gmetal. It was bullet proof, in most cases, and covered their bodies from head to toe. Their armor, combined with the blue night vision goggles attached to their helmets, allowed them to fight in the most extreme conditions.

Spurious forced a smile at the two Knights and continued forward until he reached the gates. It took only a few seconds for the laser to scan his identification card, prompting the gate to swing open. He cringed as the metallic entrance whined and creaked.

Slowly he passed through the stone square surrounding the massive SGS offices on all sides. Leafless trees extended out of the frozen ground, their naked branches reaching towards the gray brick walls of the building.

The office itself was four stories tall and housed about two hundred workers total. The windows were replaced after a sniper killed a worker a few years back. The glass was removed and in its place, the SGS insignia had been edged into the brick.

The top of the office had a copper dome roof tinted dark green with age. All four outside walls had been overtaken with massive vines crawling like bloated veins across the brick exterior.

Spurious entered the first floor of the building, relieved to be out of the cold. He took off his wool beret and tucked it under his armpit, continuing down the hall lined with cubicles on both sides.

His office was on the third floor and could be accessed only by stairs. The elevators had been shut down after another law restricting energy use was passed a few years back. The floor was unusually busy and he shuffled through the crowd of employees to his cubicle, quickly peering into Lana's work station, which still remained empty. She had now been gone for three days straight, and he was beginning to worry.

He took off his thick coat, dressing the back of the chair. The first part of his day was always the worst, but he found ways to pretend he was not at the office. Sometimes he imagined he was at his apartment listening to his pirated copies of old industrial music by DJs from the early 21st century. Other times he imagined he was reading one of the philosophy or history books from his freshman year in college. Mostly though, he just imagined he wasn't at the office, and was perhaps strolling through the beautiful State courtyards and admiring the fountains. These modern gardens had been constructed by the State for that very reason, to remind the citizen they lived in a world of relative safety and abundance, much different than the world outside the great walls.

As he settled into his desk he noticed his blue screen was glowing again. He swiped the message button.

Urgent – Open At Once.

His heart stopped and a wave of anxiety rushed over him as he scanned the title of the message once again.

He sat down to examine it closer. It was from an anonymous source. Typically, messages like these were quarantined by the technology workers, but somehow this one had made it through their constant scans.

Should I open it?

Without thinking, his index finger clicked on the holographic blue screen. The message instantly appeared.

Spurious: Meet me at the Ale House tonight. Don't be later than midnight. Come alone.

As soon as it appeared the message was gone. The burning uneasiness rushed through him again, intensifying. His heart began to race, and his breathing became labored.

Spurious tried to calm himself, wiping a bead of sweat from his forehead. It wasn't every day he received an urgent message asking him to meet an anonymous person outside of work. He stared blankly at his cubicle wall, his mind beginning to race. Whoever it was from, he had all day to make a decision on whether he would meet them.

Time: 11:33 p.m. January 23, 2071
Location: The Ale House. Lunia, Tisaia

A mist rose a few feet above the damp city streets. Spurious placed his gloved hands in the pockets of his coat, wading through the thick fog, and making his way down the brick street.

Against his better judgment, he decided to meet Paulo and Ing at The Ale House located in the East Village about five blocks east of the Commons Buildings. Spurious was already 30 minutes late, having fallen asleep after coming home from work.

He took in a large breath and exhaled a puff of visible air into the night, realizing how unusually excited he was. For some reason, he had a burning desire to know who this person was, regardless of what danger was associated with them.

He stopped to peer into the window of one of his favorite stores. The wood sign hanging above the window read, *The Magician*. Several candles in the windowsill gave off a warm glow, illuminating a shelf full of antiques lined with items from the past.

He had picked up a few trinkets here—a wooden cross the owner had explained held significant spiritual value and a small handheld device with a tiny apple engraved on the back that read, *iPod.* They were artifacts from the old world, where technology and spirituality were both meant to comfort. But those days were long gone. Religions of the past had all but been forgotten—religion was now the State. God was no longer a being, it was the government.

The East Village was one of the only places left in Tisaia that wasn't State subsidized. These small businesses consisted of bakeries, taverns, boutique stores, and bars. They were the last of their kind, a haven for the curious State worker who wanted a glimpse into the world as it once was.

Spurious knew the unfortunate truth—the shop's days were numbered. With more and more of these businesses forced to close their doors each year as the State passed laws banning their products. It was only a matter of time before they were all closed. Some of them broke health laws while others sold illegal electronic devices that wouldn't pass energy audits.

Fortunately, the State did not have the time or the resources to enforce their laundry list of laws, and while his superiors constantly advised him and his co-workers to stay out of the East Village, most of them never listened.

In the distance, Spurious could see a line of citizens waiting to enter The Ale House. He cracked a half smile and dug his hands deeper into the warmth of his pockets.

The State has a long way to go from shutting this place down.

He entered the back of the line and kept his face nuzzled in his collar, inching forward with the mass of citizens. Within minutes he was inside.

"There he is!" Ing shouted over the noise of the growing crowd. Paulo and Ing had been lucky and found the first wooden table in the bar.

The Ale House was small for an eatery, consisting of only two floors. The first floor was built with rich cedar, salvaged from before the Biomass Wars. The walls were lined with framed magazine articles and newspaper pages also from the past, long before the *Lunia Post* existed.

The first floor was reserved for tables and patrons ordering food and ale. The underground floor added to the charm of The Ale House. It was made completely of stone and was used mostly as a dance floor, although there was also a bar downstairs. This area was known as "The Cave" and had a rich history. It was supposedly a hide out for the rebels during the first stages of the ongoing Biomass Revolution. It was said that the first rebel leaders of the Tisaian Democratic Union were betrayed by one of their own and ambushed there not two years ago. The Cave was also rumored to have several underground passages leading into the tunnel system.

Spurious raised his hand to summon a bar maid and glanced over at Ing. "Sorry I'm late. I fell asleep in my rain room again when I got off work. I just can't seem to get enough of it lately."

"What's with the naps, man? You sure do sleep a lot," Ing replied.

Spurious shrugged. "Work has been really stressful lately," he said, grabbing a tavern chip from a basket in the middle of the table.

"It isn't a big deal. Just seems like when you aren't at work, you're sleeping in your rain room."

"Consider it a hobby of mine," Spurious said, laughing.

"Beats what I do after work," Paulo chipped in. "I'm always exhausted after I manage to get out of the office. I usually don't make it past my couch. At least Spurious gets to the rain room."

Ing rolled his eyes. "When did you guys become so boring?"

"So if we're so boring, why don't you explain what you do after work?" Spurious said, irritably.

Ing took a long swig of his ale. "You know, stuff. I watch the blue screen and come here."

"Sounds pretty exciting," Paulo sneered.

"Just in time!" Spurious exclaimed, ignoring Paulo and reaching for a pint of ale the bar maid carried towards their table.

"Thanks," he said, rubbing his hands together and grabbing the cold mug. He took a long swig of the ale and then stole a glance over his shoulder to mentally map out the bar. There were a few familiar faces, other State employees he had seen before, but no one out of the ordinary.

He turned his attention back to his friends. "What's the plan tonight, gentleman?"

"Actually, we were hoping you could tell us why you invited us here. This isn't like you. What's the occasion?" Paulo asked.

Spurious avoided the question. "Does anyone want to check out The Cave later?"

"My old bones could use some dancing, I suppose," Paulo said with a smile.

Spurious laughed. "I'd love to see that."

"You know I have been dancing longer than you both have been alive. In my home country of Brazil, dancing was taught at a young age. Growing up, we were so poor it was one of the only things to do for fun."

Ing cringed. "Dancing, fun? If you say so, old man."

"Ing, you're proving you have the mind of a child." Paulo muttered. "I thought I taught you more than this."

That's Paulo! Spurious thought, sitting back and watching his old friend emerge.

"I have the mind of a child because I don't believe in conspiracy theories? Did you stop to think maybe I just don't care? Did you think maybe the reason I don't ask questions is because I don't want to end up being visited by the Knights?" Ing shot back.

Spurious frowned and ordered another pint from a young barmaid. Her face lit up as he dropped a credit on her tray.

"That's to keep the ale flowing," he shouted.

A loud beat of electronic music exploded out of the entrance to The Cave, drowning out his arguing friends. He wiped away a few beads of sweat forming on his forehead and watched the tavern fill with patrons. One by one he scanned their faces, searching desperately for whoever may have sent him the message.

Slowly intoxication gripped him and he found himself staring at the bar, admiring the waterfall creeping down the granite.

"You better slow down there, Spurious. You don't want to get lost on your way home tonight. I heard the Knights have been snatching State workers up in the middle of the night," Paulo said with a grin.

Spurious cast Paulo a quick glare while he took another swig of his ale. A few strands of hair fell down his sweaty forehead, but he quickly brushed them back into place. He knew he should keep his wits, but the anonymous message earlier in the day brought on a wave of anxiety only ale could relieve.

"Ah, I don't worry about that anymore," he lied.

"Shit, Paulo, why do you have to dampen the night with some of that crap. I just want to stare at some ladies I'll never sleep with, get incredibly drunk, fail miserably while asking one of them to dance and finally go home and pass out," Ing replied. "Is that too much to freaking ask?"

"Come on Paulo, you know just as well as I do those stories are bull shit and are supposed to keep us out of places like this," Spurious said.

Paulo's grin faded and his aged face turned stern. He rested his mug on the table and looked away from the crowd, staring at his two friends. "Remember our conversation about the new type of Biomass the other day? When I told you that not everything is as it may seem… Well, there is much you two young men don't know. Much I haven't told you." Paulo turned and quickly scanned the crowd to make sure no one was listening.

"Truth is, when I was written up at work, it wasn't just because I failed to turn off my lights a few times. My supervisor accused me of spreading negative rhetoric about the State."

Ing raised an eyebrow. "What kind of rhetoric?"

"The type that gets you locked up. Luckily, the case never made it to the Knights. My supervisor dropped it when his boss got involved. It was blackmail. He wanted the position I had been hired for. So he accused me of spreading lies about the State. The truth, however, is more complicated. I had been discussing many theories about the State with another co-worker. This man told me he was getting info from the TDU. He disappeared a couple months ago." Paulo paused and took a short swig from his mug.

"I'd be locked up for telling you both, but I don't care anymore. I have nothing to lose. The State isn't what it's cracked up to be, boys. This life as a State worker, it's all a facade. We're told lies to hide what is really going on. Do you really think there aren't survivors in the Wastelands, or in the skeletons of what used to be cities?"

Ing raised his hand to stop Paulo before he could go on any further. "What you're saying is bordering on treason. You do realize this, right?"

"And I don't care, Ing. I'm telling you this because my life is over anyways."

"Let him talk," Spurious barked. Ing looked over at his normally quiet friend and quickly nodded.

"Go on Paulo. I'm listening," Spurious said.

"I know there are survivors because I have heard the transmissions. I've heard the broadcasts, people on the two-way channels that are asking for help," Paulo exclaimed.

"Try and keep it down a bit," Spurious interrupted. "We don't know who is listening."

"Radio transmissions? Come on, that's a bunch of shit. How do you know this?" Ing asked.

"I know because I have a two-way radio. The co-worker gave it to me before he disappeared. He was getting paranoid and said he needed a safe place to keep it, so I stashed it under my mattress in a metal box that blocks signals from being traced. And at night, I take it into my bathroom, where my AI can't hear the transmissions."

Ing slammed his mug down on the wooden surface of the table, which was already covered in empty glasses. "Man, this is ludicrous. You're going to end up in prison, or worse, dead! And I could end up there with you, just for listening. Forget this. I'm finding myself a female, and will pretend I never heard this conversation."

Paulo stood up to stop Ing as he made his way into the crowd.

"Let him go. Let's move to a leather booth. Over there," Spurious pointed.

Reluctantly, Paulo obliged and they moved across the room to a booth in the corner. It wasn't long before Spurious realized he had all but forgotten the message. He sat down in the plush booth, sinking deeper into the comfort of the aged leather. His curiosity was getting the best of him tonight; first the message, and now Paulo's stories. After living with such a monotonous routine, it was finally good to have some stimulation, even if there was a risk.

"What type of transmissions are you hearing?" Spurious asked.

Paulo looked down at his drink and picked at the wooden table nervously. "Perhaps Ing is right. Perhaps I should not bring you two into this."

"Ing just doesn't care about anyone but himself."

"That maybe so, but it's selfish of me to put you two at risk. You don't know what the State is capable of. What the Knights are capable of." Paulo paused and picked at the table some more, before his drunken eyes turned back to Spurious. "I don't know what I would do if I lost you two."

"It's going to be all right, you know that, Paulo?" Spurious said, reaching over and patting his friend on the back.

Paulo smiled, revealing a set of perfectly aligned white teeth. "No it won't. My life is over. I have nothing left to look forward to, but you...You have so much!"

Spurious raised his glass to his mouth, gulping down another swig of the sweet nectar. "You're right. I do have a lot to look forward to. Many years of working for the State," he said laughing.

"I guess I will drink to that," Paulo chuckled, polishing off the last of his pint.

As the night wore on and the crowd began to dissipate, Spurious caught a side view of a young woman dancing across the wooden floor. His eyes followed her, watching her graceful moves. She swung her arms through the air, gently tossing her long dark hair up and around her face. When the young woman smiled he instantly recognized her. It was Lana.

Shocked into motion, Spurious slid out of his booth, patting Paulo on the back once more, and placing his half-full mug on the table. He pushed through the mob of customers, thrusting his way through them before losing sight of her at the entrance of The Cave.

For a split second, he saw Ing out of the corner of his eye, and he paused to watch his friend flirt with a woman wearing bright red lipstick. A smile curled across his face before he continued on.

The Cave was dim, save for a few candles burning violently, their white wax bleeding down the stone walls. The music was piercingly loud, the echo of bass pounding in his ears. He rested his back against the rough edge of stone, scanning the room for Lana and watching intoxicated patrons grinding against one another. His eyes stopped on a pair of women kissing in the corner, nothing but the shadows covering his eyes.

And then he saw her, dancing in the middle of the room with two of her friends. He froze, watching her as she threw her hands into the air, laughing, while her friends danced around her. He smiled as one of her friends softly bumped into her, throwing her off balance.

A short break in the music revealed the sound of his heart beating rapidly, the pulse pounding in his skull. He wiped a bead of sweat off his flushed face and brushed his hair back into place before making his way towards her.

With a half smile, he grabbed her softly by the wrist. She paused, turning as her eyes locked with his. Instantly she recognized him. "Spurious, it's so good to see you!" she yelled. "I didn't think you would come."

"Come?" he asked, a puzzled look on his clearly intoxicated face. "Wait, you sent me that message at work?"

Lana smiled playfully. "I did, but for now, let's dance," she yelled, grabbing him by his hand and pulling him further out on the dance floor.

"It's so good to see you. I missed you at work this week. Where have you been?" he asked, shouting over the loud music.

He couldn't stop staring at her. For a moment everything seemed to slow to a stop. The music went silent and the room emptied; in his mind it was just the two of them, shrouded in darkness. It was then he knew that she wanted him just as badly as he wanted her. "Come on, dance, Spurious!" she yelled, pulling him back into reality and leading him into the crowd. She wrapped her arms around his neck and began to move her breasts against his body. Lana kissed him softly on his cheek and looked at him. "I can't go back there, Spurious, I just can't," she said, in his ear. Spurious looked at her, recognizing the fear in her face.

"What is it? Why can't you go back?"

Lana looked at her feet.

"I can't…"

Spurious stopped dancing and nudged her chin up with his fingers so he could see her eyes. "You can't what Lana?"

"I can't tell you. Not here."

"All right, let's get out of here then," he said, as he led her out of the darkness.

Time: 2:35 a.m. January 24, 2071
Location: Commons Courtyard. Lunia, Tisaia

A soft blanket of snow covered the stone ground of the courtyard outside the Commons Buildings. The enclosure was built in the shape of a rectangle. Each of the four corners represented a stone statue of the burning flame, the symbol of Tisaia's life blood—

Biomass.

At the front gate a single Knight stood guard, his goggles a cool blue into the darkness. From his viewpoint the courtyard appeared completely empty. Spurious and Lana had evaded his detection by entering the park from the back and sat huddled together on a park bench, facing the memorial fountain. The water was completely frozen over, but the fountain still attempted to work, with the occasional spurt of water exploding into the frothy air.

Spurious held Lana in his arms. For what seemed like an hour the two of them remained there, shivering. Spurious wasn't worried about the cold, nor was he worried about being caught in the park after hours. His only concern was what Lana wanted to tell him at The Ale House a few hours earlier.

"What is it, Lana?" Spurious whispered in her ear. She looked up at him with tears in her eyes.

"I can't tell you, Spurious. I just can't. You'll never understand and will lose all respect for me."

Spurious reached over and wiped a tear from her cheek. "I'd never lose respect for you. Not under any circumstance. Why would you think that I would?"

Lana sniffled, wiping her nose with a quick brush of her hand. "You'll lose respect because I should have told someone a long time ago."

"Lana, trust me, I know what you mean. There are things I have kept in for years—things no one knows and probably never will. I just hope you know you can trust me."

"Okay, but what I'm about to tell you is something you can't share with anyone. Promise me!"

Spurious nodded. "I promise, Lana."

Lana took a deep breath. "For two years Varius has treated me like a slave and I have completed every project for him. Lately, he has become even more demanding. He touches me when no one is looking, and gropes me when no one is around. Worst of all, he's demanded that I sleep with him. He said, if I don't, he will have me fired."A pair of tears raced down her cheeks as she pulled her collar down, revealing a dark purple bruise lining her neck.

"Oh my God..." Spurious said, choking on his words while imagining the abuse she suffered at the hands of Varius.

"I can't go back," she said, sobbing.

"That bastard, he isn't going to get away with this," Spurious whispered, sliding back on the bench and pulling Lana up from his lap. He wiped another tear from her face. "You must turn him in, Lana. You know you must."

"He told me he would fire me if I didn't sleep with him, and he said he would kill me if I told anyone," she whimpered. "I don't know what to do, Spurious. Now that I told you, he'll kill me for sure."

Spurious glanced over at her, his mouth quivering, before he dropped his head into his hands, unable to speak. He ran his fingers through his thick brown hair, raising it into a spike.

"He will never lay another hand on you again, Lana; I can assure you of this. This is what you're going to do. For now, you need to stay home until you're fully healed. Do not go out. Don't risk being seen," Spurious frowned. "What were you thinking, going to The Ale House tonight?"

"I wanted to see you," she quickly replied.

"What if someone from work had seen you there? You need to think about the repercussions. Varius is a dangerous man and is well connected."

Lana looked back up at him, nodding. "I know. I know. It was stupid of me to try and meet with you, but I had to tell you. I don't know who else to trust."

"It's okay. Don't worry about that now," Spurious reassured her. "It's obvious he's infatuated with you, and if you tell him you're sick, he will more than likely let you stay at home to rest for a few days, am I right?"

Lana nodded again.

"Okay," Spurious replied. "In the meantime I want to see you. We'll have to do it secretly, but I need to see you, Lana. I need to know there is something more to life than the work we perform every day and the revolution. This war, the death, the pain... sometimes it's too much to handle alone. I need to know hope can exist."

Did he know what he was saying? Seeing her could mean a visit from the Justice Knights and his job, but something about it felt convincingly right. He wrapped his arms tighter around her, and for a few moments he felt safe, their hearts beating in unison.

Love was an emotion he hadn't known since the death of his parents. And he knew how fragile love could be in Tisaia. He had seen it ripped from the hands of so many others—had it ripped from his own hands as a child.

Spurious squeezed Lana closer. His heart began to pound faster, deeper in his chest. He wouldn't let anyone come between them, not even a Justice Knight would take her from him. He wasn't going to lose her like he lost his parents.

Time: 9:03 a.m. January 25, 2071
Location: Rohania, Tisaia

Spurious strolled through the streets of the Rohania market area, his head tucked tightly into the breast of his collar. He wasn't even sure what had compelled him to get out of bed; usually he would have slept in until at least nine, especially on a day as gloomy as this one. Yet he had risen, showered and forced himself to explore the streets.

Something had encouraged him to come to the area that was off-limits to State workers—something had driven him to take the risk. So he told Anya he was working overtime and he took the underground trolley to the last stop; where he promptly got off and headed for Rohania, combing his way through old stone alleyways and ducking under a barbed wire fence. He knew all the portals linking the east and west together, some consisting of nothing more than idle storm drains or broken chain link fences.

He pushed the thoughts of Lana and Varius out of his mind. Today his goal was to find something; he just wasn't sure what it was yet.

As he walked, he kept his eyes fixed on the aging brick street, the suspicious eyes of the impoverished following him. He was out of place; his dark black pea coat was new and expensive, not one easily purchased in the area.

Fortunately, there really wasn't as much security guarding the border as there used to be. State employees rarely risked venturing to Rohania, and the Rohanians generally kept to their side of the city. Most people in Rohania knew their place. And the CRK had been forceful enough in the past to deter any citizens from Rohania from trying anything in the commons area. Thieves did risk burglaries in Lunia from time to time, but when the State made it a crime punishable by death, the number dramatically decreased.

A shiver crawled down his spine as he approached the neighborhood he grew up in, the same wooden welcome sign creaking back and forth in the chilly breeze.

He stiffened and tucked his head deeper into his collar, scanning the copper roof tops stained perpetually with white pigeon droppings. The past decade had camouflaged the shops and apartments with vines and fading paint. Most of the windows were cracked and boarded up, empty except for the face of a child peering down at him like a ghost from the past.

Slowly he made his way through the old town square, the heart of Rohania, and saw the boarding school he was educated in before the revolution began. The four pillars holding up its white stone roof were now cracked and broken, one of the pillars nothing more than a pile of broken white stone. A rusty sign hung loosely off the front of the building, peppered with bullet holes, but Spurious could still make out the name – The Rohanian Boarding School for

Boys.

Spurious slid his hands into his pocket and gazed at the sign, tucking his face back into his collar just in time to shield himself from a cold blast of wind. He shuddered, freezing, but did not move, his eyes locked on the old school house. The last time he heard the voice of his parents was also the last day he saw this place.

He could vividly remember his teacher Elma, a little old demon of a woman with deep wrinkles and a nasty cough, coming to retrieve him from class and take him to the office of Superintendent Angelo. It was there, in that dimly lit room, he was informed half-heartedly of the untimely death of his parents. The next day he was shipped off to the Tisaian Academy for Youth. He had thought The Rohanian Boarding School for Boys was hell, but it wasn't until he entered TAFY he truly understood what it meant to be miserable.

Another gust of wind shook Spurious out of his trance. He was exhausted, freezing and petrified he would be caught, but now he knew he was close to his old apartment. Tucking his head back into his collar he pressed on, his walk turning into a jog down the narrow brick street.

He pushed his way through the citizens, ignoring their gloomy faces and disregarding the smell of broiled cabbage filling his nostrils with every step. In the distance he could make out a market area where vendors displayed vegetables and fruits grown on rooftops and community gardens.

Spurious continued on, paying little attention to the shouts of the vendors who desperately tried to sell their goods. He would not let the noise of the crowd distract him from his mission of finding the place he once called home.

The state of the buildings could not help but remind him of the refugee camp he visited less than a year ago. The camp was called Halo by the State, but was known by the locals as The Inferno. Its purpose was to house all immigrants captured and awaiting deportation. The conditions at Halo were atrocious, and the State purposely built the camps far from Lunia, hiding the view from the State employees. Spurious had toured the camp to become familiar with the plumbing upgrades the State had commissioned to help mitigate the stench the camps created.

He knew comparing Rohania to Halo was a considerable exaggeration, but he also knew many of the residents, especially those dwelling in the Boondocks, were not living to see the age of fifty. He'd seen the statistics himself in a report a few months ago. These few notorious blocks were a black hole, and he was being extra cautious not to drift into their dark alleyways.

By mid-afternoon he was exhausted, struggling to make his way down the winding cobblestone streets. It seemed like he was traveling in circles.

Shaking his head, he veered down one last street he hadn't seen before, realizing he might never find his old flat where he had spent his youth.

He tucked his hands deep in his pockets, and surveyed the new alley for a sign from the past. And right when he thought about giving up he saw it — a metal door covered in two-by-fours.

His calm stride transitioned into a jog as he made his way towards the door. Seconds later two gargoyle faces carved into the thick wood came into focus, their ugly faces barely recognizable behind the wooden boards imprisoning them.

Spurious stopped as he reached the door, raising his hand to the soft wood exterior and running his fingers across the incredibly smooth impressions of the gargoyle's faces. He remembered this place. It was the door he used to sneak out of when his mother had chores for him to do.

Finally, I've found it!

He paused, overcome with nostalgia. Moments later, he was rushing back down the alley towards the front entrance, quickly noticing the red brick wall ended where he remembered the front of the building used to be. It was here a wall of white stone had been constructed and connected to the red brick of the old building.

Puzzled, he took his first right onto a sidewalk, and looked up at what should have been the entrance to his old building. Instead, the same white stone wall towered over him; no door or windows, just stone.

His eyes scanned the exterior of the building, stopping on the remnants of an old CRK poster flailing loosely in the wind. The ghostly blue glow of a Knight's goggles stared back at him. It was the same image posted throughout Rohania and Lunia, one he was accustomed to seeing on a daily basis, but he read the words he had memorized nonetheless.

Do It for Your Future! Secure Your Spot in the World's Last Honorable Army – Sign up for the CRK Today.

The poster, riddled with bullet holes, was in the wrong neighborhood. And its frayed edges implied it had been there some time. He shuddered at the propaganda, his eyes fixating back on the stone wall.

What was the State hiding? The white stone appeared new, smooth and almost polished, like weathered bones. It was a clear error by whoever designed it, if their intent was to hide something. Or, it was a warning to keep away. Spurious wasn't sure, but as he examined the exterior of the wall closely, he realized the material did not match anything he had seen in Rohania, which meant the State had hired a contractor to come in and build the wall to cover up the building.

Spurious plopped down on a park bench across the street, studying the building, while questions raced through his head. He sat for what seemed like an hour, the urge to find a way into the building growing inside him. And yet he stayed, contemplating his past and watching the faces of strangers pass.

Ten years ago he would have recognized nearly every face, but now they were no different than the faceless Knights. He realized it had been over ten years since he last saw Rohania. Up until today, he had no desire to remember the past, and especially not to revisit it. Yet for some reason, his conversation with Lana compelled him to seek answers to questions suppressed for years.

A group of children ran by him, their laughter distracting him momentarily, and for the first time in the day he smiled. He remembered what it was like to be a child; to run and play and not have worries, and above all, to be free. The last time he felt any of those things he was living in the building across the street from where he sat, a building now covered by a mysterious stone wall.

A small piece of paper caught his eye as he looked down at the brick street. His eyes followed it as it floated in the breeze, until it came to a stop next to his left boot. He reached down to pick it up, frowning as he realized it was just another advertisement for the CRK. In fact, it was the same image posted to the stone wall across the street from him. The only difference was the last sentence read "*Become a foot soldier.*"

The unmistakable sound of a loud speaker broke out in the distance, shocking Spurious from the bench. He instantly followed the noise, curious about the source. Carefully he maneuvered his way back into the crowd. He pushed through the patrons, catching the occasional sound of the loudspeaker in the distance. Standing on his toes, he tried to see over the heads of the people in front of him, but to no avail. A block later he came to the market area where his mother used to hunt for cheap food.

In the center of the cobblestone plaza, a growing crowd gathered around a black truck bearing a CRK logo across its midsection. In the bed were two heavily armed soldiers, their machine guns pointed at the growing crowd. Between the two guards, a man dressed in military fatigues handed out the same yellow flyers Spurious held tightly in his hand.

Spurious stood on his toes again, listening to the rhetoric spewing out of a loudspeaker mounted to the roof of the truck and into the desperate ears of the commoners. The CRK never recruited in Rohania. At least not that he was aware of. If they needed soldiers then the war with the TDU wasn't going as well as reported.

Spurious ducked behind a wooden trailer full to the brim with tomatoes, realizing there could be Knights disguised as Rohanians combing the crowd for dissidents and State workers.

And yet he stayed, partly hidden from view, peeking out from the protection of the trailer. His curious eyes followed the young men, who looked desperately in need of work, file into a line one by one.

"Sign up for the world's last honorable army!" the man from the pickup yelled into his mic. "Good pay. Time off. And food for you and your family," he continued.

Within minutes Spurious had seen enough to realize Paulo was right. The State was lying to them about more than just the Wastelands. They were lying about the Biomass Revolution.

He turned to head back the way he came, tucking his chin back into his collar and diverting his eyes to the street. Everywhere he walked, he felt the eyes of curious observers burning into his back. And to make things worse he felt the sensation of someone following him. His suspicion intensified when he noticed a scruffy old man clearly on his trail.

Spurious rounded a corner, cocking his head just long enough to catch a glimpse of his follower. He looked to be about 60 years old, with a light grey beard latched to his face like a cobweb. He wore a ragged old blue coat riddled with holes.

At least I know this guy isn't a CRK agent.

Relieved, he began to plan a route back to his apartment away from his new stalker. An hour passed and Spurious was still making his way quietly through Rohania. He checked the street number and saw he was almost back to the border. When he rounded the next corner he turned to see the same man discreetly hugging the walls of a building.

"Damn, this guy doesn't give up."

It was getting late and Spurious knew if he wasn't back in a few hours Anya would send an alert to the CRK. And the last thing he needed was a visit from a Knight.

Overhead, the distant sun began to disappear in the gray sky. Spurious pulled his chin out of his collar and gazed up at the tint of orange streaked across the horizon. He paused to catch his breath, watching a pair of birds hug the gray cloud line like dolphins catching a wave in the ocean.

He shook his head, mindful not to let a distraction slow him down. At the end of the street he could see the alleyway he used to enter Rohania. He glanced over his shoulder and quickly scanned the street. His follower was nowhere to be seen.

A smile of relief crawled across his face, happy the man had lost interest. He hurried towards the narrow alley, admiring the stone buildings one last time. The aging structures were plagued with vines, their green limbs attaching to metal pipes and loose gutters. Rohania always reminded Spurious of the pictures he had seen of medieval Europe while studying art at the University of Tisaia, a year before they abolished the class. The area was designed to be a ghetto, housing as many people as possible. They were made almost completely of old stone and brick, constructed out of the rubble from the Biomass Wars.

A drop of water from a leaky rooftop plopped into a puddle in front of him. The splash reminded Spurious of how poorly constructed the beautiful buildings were. The aging stone and oblique structures illustrated the division between Lunia and Rohania - the privileged vs. the impoverished.

As he turned down another street, he realized how blind he had become. When had he stopped seeing the truth? He of all people should have known what the city had become, having grown up there. Within a decade the city had fallen into shambles, crumbling one building at a time, the citizens starving while the State workers and Tisaian politicians prospered in Lunia not a mile away. And it was then it struck him—the Biomass Revolution wasn't just about energy, it was about greed. This was something he chose to ignore in the past. And it wasn't the only thing he ignored. He had become so complacent he stopped questioning what lay beyond the gates of Tisaia. Paulo was right about everything.

He paused to catch his breath again, confusing thoughts racing through his mind. For a second, he realized how little he really knew of the rest of the world. The only thing he knew about the outside was derived from the images contained in his old textbooks, now nothing more than ash in some landfill. Most people in Tisaia didn't even think about the Wastelands; let alone what was beyond their border. Their world was Tisaia. And ever since history books were abolished, people had all but forgotten the past, the great Tisaian wall solidifying the small world defining their lives.

Spurious forgot his questions as the view of the barbed wire fence marking the border came into view. Relieved, he headed towards the idle storm drain he had used to enter earlier.

"Rohania is no place for a State worker," said a voice from the shadows in the alley. Spurious turned, his eyes scanning the darkness.

"Who's there?" he asked nervously, pulling his hands from his pockets and rolling them into fists. A few moments passed before Spurious entreated again. "I said, who's there?"

The alley remained still as Spurious waited for a face to emerge and take claim to the words. But silence followed the echo of his voice. Without further hesitation, Spurious rushed back into the alley, his fists raised to a fighting level.

"Over here," said the same voice again. Spurious turned, looking in all directions, trying to pinpoint the location the voice came from, but to no avail. Whoever was trying to get his attention did not want to be seen.

Another wave of panic gripped him. He knew it was imperative to escape back to the safety of Lunia, but something kept him from leaving. Perhaps it was the fear, or maybe the curiosity or a combination of both. Whatever it was he remained frozen.

"What do you want?" Spurious yelled, his eyes nervously darting across the shadows. In the distance he saw a street lamp flicker, struggling to turn on as night settled in. The light of Rohania was already dim at best, and the alleyway was just minutes away from being consumed by darkness.

He turned to head towards the storm drain. Within seconds his nervous hands reached for the cover of the storm drain he had hidden behind a large wooden crate. A bead of sweat crept down his face as he removed the box and pulled a small knife out of his breast pocket turning again to see if his stalker had emerged. But there was nothing but the constant sound of a leaky gutter and the intermittent glow of the light pole.

His hands shook uncontrollably as he tried to twist the screw out of the drain cover. Twice he dropped the knife as his fingers shook nervously. Anger overtook him as he tried the screw again.

Finally the screw popped out and he pulled the drain cover off; setting it down softly on the brick ground and shooting another fast glance back at the alley to make sure whoever was there wasn't sneaking up on him.

"You do not need to fear me, young Spurious," a voice said from the alley. Spurious froze before turning to face the man that had been following him for some time. He looked at him suspiciously, wondering how the old man knew his name.

"Let me begin by introducing myself. I'm Leo, brother of William Smith and son of Dave Smith."

The names immediately registered. They were old world names. Names his father had mentioned when he was a child, long after the Tisaian government assigned names to all citizens, in order to weed out immigrants.

Spurious raised a furrowed brow, curious as to why the stranger introduced himself by names from the past. "Those names mean nothing to me," he lied. "Why don't you get on with what you want and stop wasting my time?"

Leo paused. His features flexed, illustrating the deep lines of age engraved across his forehead. He rubbed his white beard, which appeared to be neatly groomed, unlike his coat and pants which were covered in dirt.

Spurious noticed the man's trembling hands and his twisted spine. For a second he almost felt empathy for the old man. His age and crooked back both indicated he had worked in the early Biomass factories, long before they were closed due to safety concerns. Most workers developed physical problems far worse than from the ones Leo appeared to be suffering. Yet he knew appearances could be deceiving and he could be suffering within his body as well.

"Spurious, when I saw you pass by a few hours ago, I knew I'd regret not talking with you. I also know as I stand here and speak with you that the threat of being caught runs higher and higher and yet I'm compelled to tell you a story — a story about the meaning behind the names I mentioned. You see, William, my younger brother, was your father's best friend. In fact, they were both TDU staffers in the beginning of the Biomass Revolution."

"Wait, TDU staffers? You have to be mistaken. You've confused my father with someone else. He was not part of the TDU. He was a factory worker."

"By day he was a factory worker. This is what you were told as a child, Spurious. Let me go on. Promise me you'll have an open mind."

Spurious frowned. "How do I know you aren't lying to me?"

"Just give me a chance, son."

Spurious stood at the edge of the drain, contemplating whether he should just climb into the tunnel and be done with the old man's nonsense, but once again curiosity kept him frozen in place. "Go on," he finally said, curiously.

Leo smiled and cautiously approached Spurious. "My father knew your father when he was a boy and young man. He helped train my brother and your father in peaceful ways to fight against the CRK. The building you visited today, the building you grew up in, was not just a flat for families. It was also an underground TDU stronghold, one of the first of its kind," Leo paused, waiting to see the reaction in Spurious' features.

Spurious, however, did not flinch. His defined jaw was tight and his dark brown eyes locked on this new stranger. He studied him, wondering if he should trust the old man.

"You look much like your father, but your curiosity to find the truth of what happened to your parents and your childhood home is what gave you away. You see, Spurious, I'm somewhat of the keeper of this side of Lunia. Everyone knows me, and I know everyone. I have kept myself alive by avoiding the CRK, thieves and stragglers, and now it has all been worth it, because I have met the man that will help free Tisaia from tyranny." Leo coughed, his face alive with excitement.

Perplexed, Spurious stared at the man, not sure what to say or do. The only thing he knew was he came to Rohania to find something about his parents and something about his past. He wasn't certain what it was, nor was he sure he would know if he found it. What he did know was the old man standing in front of him was the closest he had come to finding out anything about his parents for years.

"So..." Spurious paused, "so my parents were part of the TDU?"

"Spurious, your father was one of the founders of the TDU, and your mother was instrumental in bringing together women to oppose the first leaders of Tisaia. They kept these things from you to protect you from the fate they knew would eventually find them."

"Hold on, hold on, just one second," Spurious said, flailing his arms in the air. "You're telling me that my parents, who worked normal jobs, created the organization now recognized as the most significant terrorist threat to Tisaia? And if there is any truth behind this at all, then why am I, out of all people, still alive?"

"That is a good question. You're alive because the CRK never knew who you were. Your parents made plans for you before the TDU was conceived. In fact, they even had your birth records changed. To further protect you they registered you in a boarding school. They had an arrangement with Superintendent Angelo, who was one of the early members of the TDU. Luckily, the CRK never found out about you. After their deaths, Angelo had you transferred to the Tisaian Academy for Youth to further protect your identity."

Spurious kneeled, placing his head in his hands. The same warm rush of anxiety he felt just the other day passed through him as his knees hit the ground.

Leo stood at a distance, watching Spurious with a curious eye. He knew this information would be troubling to Spurious, but he did not know it would bring the young man to his knees.

"Are you okay?" Leo asked sympathetically.

Spurious kept his head in his hands but responded with a slow nod of his head.

"How do you know all of this?" Spurious asked.

"William told me most of what I know. I'm all that is left of my family now. And you're all that is left of yours. I tell you these things because when I saw you today I knew you had the right to know who you are and where you come from. You must be careful though, Spurious. If the CRK ever discover your true identity you'll never see beautiful Lunia ever again."

He paused, breaking into a coughing fit again before continuing. "I presume you'll soon be at a crossroads in your life. You'll question whether you should sympathize with the TDU or stay loyal to Tisaia. Whatever you choose is up to you. Your destiny is not written in stone. I can't tell you how or why, but you have the ability to shape the future of Tisaia."

Instantly Spurious brought his head out of the safety of his hands. He brushed a strand of brown hair from his eyes before he gazed back at Leo. And for a second he felt a tint of nostalgia, a connection founded by a history he had not known until this moment.

"What do you mean I'll have the opportunity to shape the future of Tisaia? Do you realize I'm just a simple State employee? I review maps. I go to work and I come home, that is it. I'm not part of the TDU. I don't have any special abilities, nor am I a soldier."

"Ah, but you do," Leo interrupted. "You have a connection with the past. The rebels are losing the battle for Tisaia's future. They need hope. And they need to know the son of the TDU's founders is still alive."

"I don't want to have anything to do with the TDU, I told you I am nothing more than a peon!" Spurious exclaimed.

Leo smiled. "You're much more, Spurious. This is why I tested you not ten minutes ago in the alley. I wanted to gauge your reaction. And react you did. Do you remember raising your fists? Do you remember rushing into the darkness? Deep down you have the same fears as your parents, but you also share their fighting spirit."

Spurious glanced down at the brick ground. Realizing what Leo was saying was true.

"You'll see, but for now you must get going. The future isn't set in stone. And you must take precautions, starting with returning to Lunia before anyone reports you missing."

Spurious nodded, turning for the storm drain. "Please don't tell anyone you saw me here Leo. I appreciate the information, I do, but I don't want to have anything to do with this. Goodbye!" Spurious yelled, climbing into the tunnel leading back to Lunia.

Leo stood in the darkness of the alleyway and watched Spurious as he crawled through the narrow storm drain. "Godspeed, my friend," he said, as Spurious disappeared from sight.

Time: 5:01 p.m. January 26, 2071
Location: Commons Building 21, Apt 44. Lunia, Tisaia

Two crows sat perched on the roof of Commons Building 21, home to Spurious and 50 other State workers. Their caws broke through the air like the sound of ice cracking on a frozen river. No one seemed to notice, except Spurious, who sat at his desk staring out his window at the two birds, the skeletons of shattered skyscrapers in the distance.

Demons. Two little black demons.

Behind him, the crackle of the fire in his stone fireplace drowned out the two crows, bringing him back to where he left off in his journal.

January 26th

It's hard to know where to begin. The past few days I have learned more about myself than I have in the past ten years. My parents, whom have been on my mind frequently as of late, were the founders of the TDU. So I was told by a man I met in Rohania. It's hard to know how he knew me, or if there is truth to the words he spoke, but I can't help but wonder if there is.

This information is not all that has changed my life. No, my life has been changing in many other ways as well. I have fallen for someone I know I shouldn't love. A woman named Lana that works in the same department. And if this isn't complicated enough, I have come to find her supervisor has fallen for her as well.

For as long as I can remember now, I have believed my parents were killed by a bomb in the beginning years of the Biomass Revolution, when the TDU first rose up against the young Tisaian state, and now all of this has changed.

If the CRK really did kill my parents, I'm not sure what I'll do. How can I continue to work for a State that killed my parents?

The predicament I find myself in now is one I'm not sure I'm prepared to face. As the years have gone by, my life has become one never-ending routine. And now, when something finally challenges me, I'm afraid I lack the courage to stand up for what I know to be true and just. If this burden wasn't enough, I now have to think of Lana. She is what I have grown to care about most. After only spending a short amount of time with her, she gives me a hope I have never felt in life.

Spurious rested his pen on the table and gazed out the window.

The two crows were gone, their white droppings the only evidence they had ever existed. In the distance he could see the eerily opaque images of skyscrapers, shredded and torn by the fiery blasts of the nuke that hit miles away. He never understood why the State didn't have them demolished; perhaps it was a reminder to the citizens of how lucky they were to have survived.

He groaned and walked over to one of the AI portals. He certainly didn't feel lucky.

"Anya, I want you to tap into the SGS mainframe and see if you can find any information about the first years of the Biomass Revolution."

The portal lit up and a blue hologram of Anya appeared in front of Spurious.

"Spurious, you know most of that information is classified; in fact, I doubt I'll be able to find anything at all."

"Just do your best," he replied, making his way over to his loft and plopping himself down on the soft bed.

"Sir, why are you interested in this information?"

Spurious rolled over and stared at her hologram. Her voice was feminine, but firm. He didn't want to make her suspicious; she had the power to ruin his life if she thought he wasn't patriotic.

"It's for one of the tunnel projects I'm working on, but don't worry about it," he lied.

A bead of sweat crawled down his forehead as he waited for her response.

"Very well. Is there anything else I can do for you this evening?"

Spurious shook his head and closed his eyes. He couldn't escape the scrutiny of the State or the laws and the Knights that enforced them. They were all tools the government used to keep him obedient. But he was sick of being a sheep—sick of being compliant.

As the lights dimmed and darkness carpeted the small room, Spurious decided it was time for a change.

CHAPTER 2: SCORPIONS

"All warfare is based on deception."
~Sun Tzu, *The Art Of War*

Time: 10:40 p.m. January 26, 2071
Location: The Wastelands

Night was Obi's favorite time in his day. It was, for the most part, the only time he had any peace, if you could call it that. During the day his unit moved about the outskirts of the great Tisaian walls, scavenging for weapons and food buried by the never ending dust and ash from the Biomass Wars. When he wasn't training or looking for his next meal, he was telling jokes and stories with his friends in his unit—Squad 19.

The number assigned to the small group of soldiers was nothing more than a few strands of string sewn carelessly into his uniform, but what they meant was a different story. The entire rebellion knew Squad 19 as a beacon of hope. They were the most respected unit in the entire Tisaian Democratic Union and even the CRK had grown to fear them.

It was an unusually clear night. The stars were bright and plentiful in the small opening at the top of the old windmill. Obi took great interest in examining them. When he was a child, his uncle brought him on a number of camping trips, pointing out different constellations and teaching him how to tell time by the position of the sun. A few years later he taught Obi the art of orientation, and he quickly became skilled with a compass and map—one of the main reasons he was the lead scout in Squad 19.

Obi shivered. It was now late winter and with the days getting longer and warmer he opted to leave his thermal gear at headquarters to cut down his load. Tonight the decision haunted him, the cold wind biting through his fatigues. It was only the crackling fire keeping him and his squad from freezing.

Obi sat dangerously close to the flames, warming his hands and wind burnt face. He checked his watch, realizing it was going on midnight. He should be asleep like the rest of his squad, who were already curled up in their sleeping bags.

A deep cough from one of his soldiers startled him. His eyes quickly darted from his watch to Nathar, a 24 year old former refugee from the east coast. He had fallen sick days ago and the crackling in his lungs was getting worse each day. Obi knew the young man needed medicine soon, before his cold turned into something worse.

The Wastelands was not the place to fall ill. He had seen men die from lesser things than a cold. It had a way of catching you by surprise, when you least expected it. But Nathar was no ordinary man. He was a survivor, like the rest of the squad.

Obi recalled the day he helped rescue Nathar from the mines. Nathar, like so many others, had snuck into Tisaia through an abandoned storm drain, only to be captured and placed in an immigrant camp. The conditions there nearly killed him, and if it wasn't for Obi and several other rebels, Nathar would surely have perished in the mines. It was at that point Obi offered him a chance to fight for immigrant rights and freedom, something Nathar couldn't turn down.

It was a dismal story and a common one. For a moment it reminded him of Sasa, another young immigrant he had rescued. The memory was too terrible—too painful to remember. She was still a teenager when Squad 15 brought her to him, but unlike any teenager Obi had ever met. She was mentally broken in the beginning, but she had a wild spirit and wanted so desperately to fight. Reluctantly he agreed to train her to shoot, in exchange for her loyalty. In the end she had died with her fingers gripped tightly around the .45 he had given her. She had sacrificed her life to save several members of Squad 19, taking two Tin Cans out in the process.

Obi felt nauseated. *If only I had been there—if only I had...*his thoughts trailed off. He couldn't go back there, not tonight. He had to keep his wits. His squad was in the Wastelands and falling prey to his demons would do nothing but get more innocent people killed.

His fingers found the cold silver of the necklace around his neck, the one she had given him the day of her death. It was the only thing that gave him solace—the only thing left of her.

He sucked in a lungful of air and continued to scan the room, his eyes falling on Alexir Jahn next. He was known to his friends and fellow squad mates as Ajax. The 30 year old soldier was given his second name by his companions after he single handedly killed two Tin Cans with nothing but a knife. Named after the Greek warrior from Homer's Iliad, Ajax had perhaps the most fitting nickname of anyone in his squad.

There was also Creo Saafi, lying in the middle of the pack. A Spaniard military refugee, he was considered the wisest of Squad 19. And while he did not have physical command of the group, he was often consulted by senior leadership about military strategy.

Squad 19 was made up of the best the TDU had to offer. If the rebellion had special forces, they were it.

Obi knew better than anyone that The Biomass Revolution would be won with flesh and bones, something the TDU lacked. The entire army consisted of around 100 soldiers, a mere fraction of the CRK forces. And while they could always replenish their ranks from immigrants and Rohanians looking for work, they weren't trained soldiers like the Knights. Most of the new recruits didn't make it past their first year.

Obi groaned, trying not to let the numbers affect his judgment.

He knew his life expectancy was cut in half the day he joined the rebellion, but he did so because he believed in the cause. Nothing would change that, not even if the TDU were outnumbered one hundred to one.

He looked back down at his watch. *Time to check the perimeter,* he thought, rising and walking to the entrance of the ancient stone windmill. He swiped his sniper rifle off the ground and glassed the darkness. The infrared scope allowed him to see any heat signatures approaching their camp, but tonight the small circular screen didn't pick up anything but several small rodents scavenging the barren dirt ground.

He placed the rifle back down, resting it against the thick stone. Next he checked the roof to ensure no smoke was escaping from the top of the windmill for anyone to see. Satisfied, he walked back to the entrance to examine the broken door hanging loosely off its hinges.

"Go to bed," Ajax grumbled.

His rough voice was almost soothing to Obi, comforting in the perilous world filled with danger at every turn. He watched Ajax turn over in his sleeping bag, his monstrous arms poking out from under the nylon blankets, revealing his chest plate of armor. The lightly bearded man rarely took the metal off; it was as much as part of him as the radiation scars on his arms.

Ajax scratched his receding blonde hair. "Creo already checked the place out, it's safe, boss."

"We're never truly safe," Obi shot back.

As lead scout it was his job to keep the squad out of harm's way. "I just wanted to make sure there isn't any smoke escaping from the roof."

The noise awoke Nathar as he stirred in his sleep. "Guys, go to bed. Goddamn, you're being loud," he moaned.

Obi walked back to his sleeping pad and took his .45 out of its holster, placing it under his small pillow. It was the same gun he had let Sasa borrow the night before she died.

He stretched out his fatigued body carefully on the rocky ground, caressing the silver of the necklace before folding his hands behind his head. He was so tired from traveling that he was dizzy, but he still couldn't sleep. He was too worried about the next few weeks of the campaign. More innocent people were going to die.

It was necessary to achieve their ultimate goals, but it was nonetheless disheartening to think of innocents being caught in the crossfire in a war that had already claimed so many lives—lives like Sasa's. His superiors made it quite clear he should take necessary steps to ensure innocent people were not killed in the next attack. But Obi knew from past experience that when bullets started flying he had little control over their final destination.

Obi opened his eyes again and glanced over at his men who were now all fast asleep. For some reason he scanned the youthful face of Nathar again. His thick brown hair was cropped short, and his eyes were crystal blue and kind—the type you couldn't help but trust. The combination of youthful features gave him the appearance of a teenager at first glance, which by TDU standards equated to a grown man, battle ready. It was the unfortunate fate of so many young people trapped in a never ending war. Nathar should have been in college or starting a career, but instead he was forced to fight.

I bet he misses his family.

All Obi knew was that Nathar's family had been killed in the first part of the Biomass Wars in the last offensive of the United States Army, just months before most of the country collapsed into ashes. Nathar sought refuge at a camp in New York City, before it was leveled by a tactical nuclear weapon.

Obi knew loss wasn't specific to Nathar. His entire squad had lost their families. They were all orphans now. Sasa had been too, like so many others, their innocence robbed from them at an early age. In an odd way Obi thought of them as his children, wanting more than anything to protect them and keep them safe. If it came down to it he would take a bullet for any one of them, but he couldn't save them all—he couldn't even save Sasa.

In his mind the only difference between his men and his biological son he chose to hide with a Rohanian family years ago was blood.

The thought of his estranged son filled his eyes with tears. It was a painful memory, recalling the look in his son's eyes when he was forced to say goodbye. It was a decision he lived with every day, but he sought comfort in the reality of the situation—giving up his son had saved him from the world of constant war. And growing up without a father wasn't as bad as not growing up at all.

Obi closed his tired eyes and massaged his temples in an attempt to relieve the pain of the past and his worries of the future. He thought once more of his duty to Tisaia and Squad 19 before he drifted off to sleep.

Time: 7:01 a.m. January 28, 2071
Location: The Wastelands

Obi's radio blared to life, the static crackling over the fierce wind.

"Obi, this is Jackson, standby for report. Over."

"Roger, Obi here. Standby to copy. Over."

"Reports of a convoy of Scorpions heading your way. Over."

"Copy that. Standby."

Obi crawled out onto the edge of the massive bluff overlooking an abandoned highway below. He covered his mouth with his bandana and glassed the valley, watching a trail of dust follow a few black specks in the distance. They were still about two clicks from the western wall surrounding the border of Tisaia.

He discarded his binoculars and pushed a button on his goggles, zooming in to get a better look. Sure enough a convoy of CRK Scorpions was racing towards their location.

The dune buggies were covered in gmetal, equipped with .50 cal machine guns, shocks for off-roading and massive Biomass fed engines. Their most infamous trait, however, wasn't their deadly equipment, it was the humming their engines made. Any reasonable TDU soldier knew when you heard that humming, you didn't stand your ground; you ran, or hid.

Scorpions were one of the most effective weapons the CRK had in its arsenal against the TDU, who primarily traveled by horseback, by foot, or in a vehicle if they were fortunate enough to steal one.

"Jackson, this is Obi. We have four CRK Scorpions heading our way, waiting for your orders. Over."

"Roger, Obi, sit tight, we're on our way with armor piercing rounds. Prepare to defend your location; we're still about three hours away, over."

Three hours? We aren't going to last 30 minutes against that type of firepower.

"Hurry the hell up, Jackson," Obi said, grabbing his rifle. He rose to his feet and stumbled over the broken ground.

"Nathar, you and Creo take up positions on the highest part of that rock formation you can find. Creo, you take my sniper rifle; I'm going to use our missile launcher," he said, pointing into the distance.

"Yes sir," they said simultaneously as they raced off towards a narrow path leading up to the rock formation. Obi watched them leave, his eyes following them as they turned their backs and began to climb up the steep trail.

The gray of morning consumed the landscape as a weak sun struggled to rise, the rays of crimson splitting the horizon in two. He turned, looking at Ajax, who still sat at the edge of the rock, peering out through his binoculars at the approaching vehicles.

"It's just you and me, Ajax. How many grenades are you carrying?"

Ajax turned his massive torso, gripping his black CRK assault rifle. It was his weapon of choice, and it came equipped with a double blade bayonet, a design the TDU gunsmith created at his request. Ajax was dressed completely in black fatigues outfitted for the severe cold weather they were experiencing in the Wastelands. If it weren't for his size he would look like one of the ninjas Obi remembered seeing in movies as a child.

"I have four, including the one I keep in my pack; what do you got in mind, boss?"

Obi thought for a moment, trying to contemplate the best way to approach the Scorpions. He remembered what he had learned in the CRK military academy before he dropped out and joined the rebellion.

The best defense is a good offense.

"Ajax, we're heading down to the road. Just follow me, and trust me." Without hesitation, Ajax fastened his assault rifle onto his back and they began their descent into the valley below.

Time: 7:59 a.m. January 28, 2071
Location: The Wastelands

Ajax and Obi lay waiting for the dust storm to pass. They sought refuge in the bed of a charred pickup truck, the paint now nothing more than a distant memory, a faint blue peeling off the weathered metal. Gray ash and dust drifted across the cracked blacktop. An army of limbless electrical poles lined the edge of the highway, a single remaining wire swaying violently in the fierce wind.

Obi pulled his mask tighter over his face, wiping a single bead of sweat off his nose. He wanted to ignore the death, the stark reality that the stumps of charred trees and the sun bleached bones jutting out of the scorched earth were not real. But they were. It was an image he had seen many times before and a reality he had accepted long ago.

"Men, I want radio silence from here on out," Obi whispered into his radio. "Nathar, you and Creo take out any foot soldiers from your position. Ajax and I'll take care of the Scorpions before they can call in reinforcements."

The dust storm shook the sides of the pickup truck, rattling it like a toy. Blasts of dust and rock bit Obi intermittently through the rusted out holes in the side of the metal truck, while the wind continued its tirade. The humming of the Scorpions in the distance sent a chill down his spine. The sound of their engines was deafening at close range, and even over the noise of the fierce wind, Obi could hear them buzzing through the Wastelands like a swarm of hornets.

Obi wasn't sure where they were going, or what their mission was, but he assumed they were scouts responding to intelligence they had received on TDU positions. His plan was to stop them before they could call in reinforcements.

His main concern wasn't the Scorpions racing towards his squad's position. It was the proximity of their location to the Tisaian walls. If the Scorpions had time to call in reinforcements, they could be there in minutes. And there was no way his squad could escape the Scorpions on foot. Not now. They were forced to fight, forced to stand their ground. It was the opposite strategy other TDU squads used in the past and exactly why Obi thought it would work.

Within minutes the dust storm passed and visibility returned to normal. Obi peeked over the bed of the pickup truck, watching the small black specs of the Scorpions growing in the distance.

"Time to move," he said, shaking Ajax's shoulder and jumping onto the blacktop, a cloud of recently deposited ash billowing into the air. Within seconds he was trotting through the maze of charred vehicles, Ajax following close behind, his weapon bobbing up and down on his back. As the humming got louder the pair broke into a sprint, grimacing when the intermittent wind stung their bare skin with sand, dirt and rocks. Obi raised his right hand and pointed to a slab of concrete bunker. "There!" he yelled. Ajax stopped, panting heavily, and squinting into his goggles to make out what appeared to be the basement of an old gas station.

As Obi neared the structure he saw it was about eight feet deep, a perfect foxhole for someone Ajax's size. It was also three feet above grade and would provide the perfect sniping point.

"Ajax, this is going to be your position. I'm going to take cover in…" Obi paused as he scanned his surroundings for the perfect spot. His eyes came to rest on a fully intact minivan not 100 yards away.

Out of all of these cars, the one to survive was a freaking minivan.

"Your grenades," Obi said, holding out his gloved hand.

Ajax reached into his side pockets and pulled out a handful of the explosives. For a second their eyes locked through their goggle lenses, and a look of uncertainty passed between both men. It wasn't fear, or nerves, just the feeling they might not see each other again. The feeling lingered momentarily before they nodded and parted ways to take up their positions. They were soldiers and were trained not to have emotions in combat situations, and the sharp buzz from the Scorpions was growing louder by the second.

Luck was on Obi's side today. The Scorpions were headed right for their location, blind to the danger ahead. By the time Obi detonated the first grenade the lead Scorpion was already in the air, the explosion lifting its front end off the dusty road and turning it into a spinning ball of flames. As the Scorpion smashed back onto the pavement, the collision caused the soldier manning the rocket launcher to fire prematurely into the blacktop, the explosion instantly enveloping the entire vehicle.

The other three Scorpions zipped away in different directions, one of them only narrowly missing the burning hull of the first destroyed Scorpion. Clouds of dark smoke erupted from the belly of the vehicle, now nothing more than a crater in the ground.

Obi peeked through one of the van windows, trying to keep track of the Scorpions as they raced away from the ambush. He pulled the mask down from his face and wiped the sweat from his scorched forehead. A piece of shrapnel from the first Scorpion had torn through the thin metal of the minivan door, narrowly missing his scalp and leaving a black streak of grease across his forehead. He wiped it clean and nodded to Ajax across the road, ready for the next phase.

Quickly, Obi opened the van door and took off in a sprint down the remnants of the old highway, his head down and tucked into his chest. Ajax followed closely behind, his rifle at the ready. They found the perfect refuge under the belly of an old semi-trailer on its side. The trailer looked like the skeleton of a large whale, with metal ribs poking out from the torn canvas.

He took a knee at the edge of the trailer where the twisted metal created a cage for them to set up position. The canvas clung to the metal columns like skin and provided the perfect camouflage.

"This gives us little protection if the Scorpions find us," Ajax whispered, taking a knee next to Obi.

"Don't worry, their heat sensors won't be able to pick us up in this storm. And besides, I'm not going to give them that opportunity."

"What do you have in mind?" Ajax asked, with a strained look of concern.

"I just need some bait," Obi said, surveying the stark landscape.

Time: 8:24 a.m. January 28, 2071
Location: The Wastelands

A mile away the three remaining Scorpions regrouped, their gunners anxious to start a search and destroy mission. Their engines humming, they sat paused in the dry gray ash.

In the middle of the unit Captain McNeill stood on the hood of his tan Scorpion. He was covered from neck to toe in gmetal, the polished silver armor glimmering naturally under the gray sky.

His men watched from the comfort and safety of their vehicles, wondering why he would risk making himself a target on the hood of the Scorpion. But the rookie Knights had not heard the stories of how Captain McNeill gained the respect and loyalty of his superiors. It certainly wasn't by hiding his face behind the armor of vehicles or the walls of bunkers. He rose to the top of his unit by fighting the rebels face to face for over two decades.

His skin was a canvas of scars, like a battle map; peppered with red streaks, each scar revealed a different story. It was his bravery, which appeared to some new recruits as foolishness, that earned him the rank of Captain from Commander Augustus personally. His wounds were a constant reminder of all the injuries suffered over his years of service; from his left cheekbone wrinkled and dark from radiation exposure during the Biomass Wars, to his prosthetic knees—they were all medals gained in the loyal service of a Royal Knight.

A blast of wind tore into his armor, whistling across the gmetal. He grimaced as his leg began to ache. The memory of the TDU ambush that had caused it slipped into his mind.

He could recall it vividly, almost able to taste the smoke from the bombs Squad 19 had planted in an apartment building. The trap had wiped out half of his squad.

Squad 19.

McNeill snarled. He had hunted the squad and Commander Obi for years, trailing their scent into the tunnels snaking deep beneath the cities and into the Wastelands.

Are they out there? he wondered, massaging the metal skin of his robotic arm and staring into the distance.

He shook the painful memories out of his mind and glassed the horizon for the rebels. His eyes read the landscape like a hawk searching for its prey, combing the dark gray ground, dry and peppered with ash. There was no sign of the people who once lived here, save for their charred vehicles and bones. The Wastelands were a graveyard, and disgusted him almost as much as the rebels.

As his eyes continued to scan the terrain he came across a rock structure jutting out of the ground like the spikes on the back of a prehistoric monster. Underneath the formation were the remains of an old highway. He could scarcely make out the shapes of ruined cars, but there was no mistaking it. He instantly knew it was where the rebels would be hiding. He knew because this was where he too would be hiding if he were them.

He jumped off the hood of the Scorpion; his assault rifle clanking on the back of his armor.

"Hand me your radio," he commanded, reaching into the vehicle's open window.

"Base this is Captain McNeill, over."

"Roger, base here, go ahead."

"We've been ambushed and suffered the loss of one Scorpion. I've identified a possible enemy location and request permission to engage, over."

The sound of static followed as McNeill waited for a response. The driver of the Scorpion shook noticeably, his armor-covered hands gripping the steering wheel as if he was clinging on for life.

"Captain, this is General Logsdon. What's your current location, over?"

"We're about 20 miles due west of the walls. The rebels are dug in close to a large rock formation. We do not know their exact location," McNeill paused for a second, more than enough for any veteran to notice a hint of reservation. Luckily none of the rookies seemed to notice it, or at least acknowledge it.

The static of the radio blurred to life. "Captain, do you need reinforcements? Over."

McNeill paused and stared at the rock formation in the distance. "No sir, I can handle this one. Over," he said firmly.

He had failed to eliminate Squad 19 many times before, almost losing his own life in the process. This time was going to be different—this time he had them cornered. He didn't need help to bring Obi's head to Commander Augustus.

"Roger. Keep us updated Captain. Over."

McNeill handed the radio back through the window to the

rookie Knight, who fumbled with the small device before placing it back into its charger.

"You better get with it," McNeill shouted before strolling confidently over to the passenger side door.

With over 20 years of experience, he had grown accustomed to routing out rebels and finding their leaders. Today, in his opinion, would be no different—today Obi's time as commander of Squad 19 was coming to an end.

Time: 8:26 a.m. January 28, 2071
Location: The Wastelands

Obi and Ajax knelt patiently under a sheet of torn canvas shaking violently in the wind. For a second Obi took his eyes off the terrain and looked over at the massive frame of Ajax beside him.

He recalled all the times the monstrous man saved his life in other battles, before the buzzing of the Scorpion engines tore his eyes back to the black top. He gripped his rocket launcher and tucked it under his shoulder, nodding at Ajax as he began to crawl under the metal planks of the trailer.

I'm only going to get one shot at this.

Obi knew the senior officer of the Scorpions' unit would use the cover of the dust to shield them during their counter attack. And while the conditions would likely confuse the drivers, the gunners had the advantage of a turret that rotated 360 degrees.

Obi froze as he saw the first Scorpion in the distance. Just as he predicted, the commander of the unit split the Scorpions up, something he should have done in the first place to protect them from possible ambushes. The commander probably didn't expect Obi's men to be so close to the wall, which would signal to the CRK that Squad 19 might be planning a larger attack. This was only a small concern; he didn't have time to think about that now. He just needed to find a way to stay alive and to keep his men alive.

The first Scorpion slowed and came to a complete stop, its engine humming as it sat idle near the rock formation.

Holy shit, he's using it as bait.

He brought the scope of his rocket launcher to his eye, lining the cross hairs up with the vehicle. Minutes crept by and Obi began to worry. He glanced down at his watch, knowing the CRK commander would have called in reinforcements by now. His only hope was that Jackson's units would show up before the reinforcements arrived. Either way Obi realized he was going to have to move to a different location in order to take out the commander of this unit.

Slowly he began to crawl out from the canvas canopy and signaled for Ajax to maintain at his position.

Obi pulled himself to his feet and took off in a sprint down the highway, his head tucked into his chest. He stopped twenty feet from Ajax's position and kneeled next to the front of an overturned pickup truck. Glancing around the front bumper, he checked for the location of the other Scorpions.

To the east he could make out the shape of a Scorpion patrolling the edge of the highway, the gunner bobbing up and down as the vehicle made its way over the rocky terrain. Obi rested his back against the charred metal of the pickup and then crept along the pavement to the back end, once again peering around the bumper to find the location of the other Scorpion.

A fierce blast of wind ravaged his face as he stuck his head around the corner. The wind was picking up again, with rocks and pieces of dirt sailing aimlessly about. Obi knew it was only a matter of time before he wasn't able to see five feet in front of him, and it was imperative he found the commander's Scorpion before it found his squad's location.

He crouched, waiting for the two Scorpions to make another pass before taking off in a sprint, hoping the swirling debris would disguise him.

Through the dust he could hardly see the outline of the third

Scorpion. If it weren't for the faint humming of its engine he would have run smack into the middle of it. He dove for cover behind the wreckage of another truck, his heart pounding in his chest.

Deep breath, deep breath.

Quickly he snuck a look around the corner of the truck's deflated rear tire. He crawled underneath the bumper and maneuvered the rocket launcher onto his shoulder, waiting for the crosshairs to lock onto its target. He gripped his weapon tightly.

Patience.

Obi lay in the ash, reciting a customary prayer for the soldiers he was about to kill. And then, without hesitation, he pulled the trigger, watching the fiery trail of the missile streak towards the idle Scorpion before exploding under its brush guard. The crimson wave of heat blasted the vehicle ten feet into the air before bringing it back to the dirt in a flaming ball of fire.

The second the missile exploded Obi was up and running, the fire singeing the hair on the back of his neck. The remaining two Scorpions were on him immediately, their mini-guns spitting hot lead into the pavement around him, sending chunks of asphalt into the air. He tossed his weapon to the ground and brought his hands to his face, shielding himself from the concrete shrapnel as he ran past a charred sedan. The bullets narrowly missed him as they blew holes the size of melons in the ruined torso of the car. Behind him the ping of the bullets rang out, the white streaks of lead zipping past his head. It was only a matter of time before one of them would tear into his exposed flesh.

It was at that moment, when Obi couldn't differentiate the howling wind from the bullets racing towards him, that the world slowed to a crawl. He watched as razor sharp bullets exploded out of Ajax's assault rifle. The muzzle erupted with flames as his friend fired blindly in the direction of the Scorpions—first at the one opposite his position, and then at the one heading towards him. But the bullets had little effect as the rounds bounced off the armor harmlessly on impact.

Obi closed his eyes. He had never felt so vulnerable, knowing at any second a .50 cal round could tear through his soft flesh. The *ping, ping, ping* of bullets exploded around him as he continued to run, holding his hands around his face as bullets whizzed past his goggles. He was now within 15 feet of Ajax's position, so close to safety and yet so far. He stole a quick glance behind him, to see the blue glow of the gunner's goggles as he slowly trained his mini-gun on him.

His legs were now carrying him faster than ever before. The muscles stretched, pulled and groaned as he leapt onto the hood of a car and then into the air, before coming down on the concrete floor of the bunker. He tucked his knees to help break his fall, landing with a thud. Obi coughed into his bandana as a thick cloud of ash rose into the air.

Ajax stopped firing and slouched down onto the bunker floor, scanning Obi from head to toe for injury.

"How did I just survive that?" Obi yelled, laughing as he frantically dusted himself off and scuffled across the floor next to Ajax.

"Holy shit, sir, that was awesome!" Ajax yelled, as he stood to fire off another clip.

Obi coughed again and massaged his inflamed right knee. "Don't waste your ammo, Ajax. We're going to need every round we can get," Obi said, bringing his wrist radio to his face.

"Creo, this is Obi. I took out another one of the Scorpions. Can you get a visual of the remaining two from your position, over?" At this point, Obi didn't care if the CRK heard their radio transmissions; they were cornered and needed help fast.

"Negative sir, the dust storm is too violent for us to get a visual, please advise, over."

Obi cursed under his breath, pulling his pistol from the holster attached to his right boot.

"We need to get the hell out of here," Ajax shouted over the gunfire.

"I know, god damn it, I know, but Creo and Nathar are too far away to get a shot. I think we're going to have to make a run for it."

Obi stood with his pistol at the ready. Ajax followed suit, jamming a new clip into his rifle with a click. They both peered over the edge of the bunker and were immediately forced back down as a barrage of bullets rained down on their position, sending chunks of concrete into the air.

"Creo, Ajax and I are going to try and make it back to the rock formation. Can you give us covering fire?" Obi asked, slumping back down next to Ajax.

"Negative. Visibility is zero," he said, an obvious quiver in his voice recognizable even over the static.

Obi paused, memories of past battles racing through his mind. Never had he been in a predicament like this: Cornered and outgunned. Sure, he was used to overwhelming odds, but a squad of Scorpions? No one in the TDU had lived against those odds.

Another barrage of bullets snapped him back to reality. He knew he needed his wits if they were going to survive. Reliving the past wasn't going to help.

"Ajax, on the count of ten, I want you to take off out of here. I'll lay down suppressing fire for you. Hopefully that will distract them enough for you to get out of range."

Ajax looked over at Obi. His face was covered with a black handkerchief and his eyes were hidden behind his goggles, but Obi could still see the emotional strain on Ajax's features.

"That's an order, Ajax. Go!" Obi shouted, firing off a round from his pistol into the air.

"Roger boss, you get back safe," he said, patting Obi hard on his shoulder.

"You got it, man, I'll be back with you guys as soon as you know it! Now go!" Obi yelled again, pulling the pin out of a grenade and cooking it in his hand. He stood up and looked for the outline of the nearest Scorpion through the dust before tossing the grenade like a baseball. As soon as the grenade left Obi's hand the wind took control of its destiny, sending it on a trajectory straight for the Scorpion closest to the highway.

He turned to watch Ajax strap his assault rifle to his back and shove himself against the wall of the concrete bunker, bracing for the impact of the grenade. Obi followed suit and put his hands over his ears. Before the gunner had time to react the grenade exploded in mid air, sending red metal raining down on the turret nest. The soldier was killed instantly as the red hot jagged pieces of shrapnel tore through his goggles and lodged in his skull.

Obi peeked over the concrete ledge again, squinting in time to see the dead gunner fall out of the turret and slump down the front of the Scorpion. A bright streak of red trailed his lifeless body. The blood looked almost surreal against the gray landscape, like an alien on a foreign world.

In the distance Obi could make out Ajax's vague outline through the dust. He was halfway to the rock formation, climbing up a steep path.

Obi took a deep breath in his bandana, relieved the dust storm disguised his friend's retreat. The remaining two Scorpions hadn't seen him leave the bunker, or were too busy painting Obi's position with bullets to care.

Obi kneeled back down on the floor of the bunker, pausing to think over his next move.

What the hell am I supposed to do now?

Another blast of dust swirled into the bunker, clouding his vision. Once the grime cleared from his goggles he scanned his belongings, looking for something, anything to keep him alive. He scrambled through his gear, tearing through his pack, but his hands came up empty.

Overhead the roar of mini-gun fire broke through the wind. Obi turned to shield his face as chunks of concrete rained down on him; then he saw it—Ajax's bag of grenades lying in a heap in the corner of the bunker. Why hadn't he thought of them before? The first grenade had been lucky, but with an entire bag of grenades he might not need luck.

He brought his radio back up to his mouth to radio a message to his squad. He pressed the speak button, but static crackled over the channel. He could hear faint voices over the channel, but could not send a message. His eyes shot down and fell upon the broken screen, cracked from his earlier fall. The panic crept through his veins.

"Shit!" He stomped and raised his pistol above the bunker wall, fired off a few random shots. The wall shook as another armada of bullets tore into its outer concrete shell. Obi shook from the blast and kneeled back on the ground.

Patience. Remember what you learned at the academy; the best defense is a good offense.

Obi took a deep breath and grabbed the bag of grenades. Standing up, he cocked his pistol and peered slightly over the edge of the concrete wall. The two Scorpions were less than 20 feet apart and were not firing, conserving their ammo for a solid target. "You cowards!" he yelled, standing and firing another couple of rounds in their direction before retreating back into the bunker.

The bag of grenades was his only chance. If he could land the bag in the middle of the Scorpions, he had a chance of getting out of there alive.

It's a long shot, but worth a try.

Obi had never been a man to contemplate his fate; he knew he might die on the battlefield and he accepted it for what it was. He was a soldier and had been his entire adult life. In situations where his demise seemed almost certain, he didn't waste time. He did what he was trained to do.

On the count of five, he thought, sucking in a chest full of dust as he tossed the grenades into the air and pulled himself out of the bunker high enough to get a decent shot.

"One."

"Two."

"Three."

A fiery blast erupted from the Scorpion's mini guns as he watched the bag land in the dirt directly in the middle of the two vehicles. He stopped counting and pulled the hard trigger of his pistol, watching the first bullet whizz past the bag and ping off the shell of the closest Scorpion harmlessly. Before he could fire another shot, a bullet ripped through his right shoulder, coming clean out the other side. A spurt of blood exploded out of his back, the bullet piercing the small bunker wall behind him.

He screamed in pain and fired another shot into the sky wildly, losing control of his pistol. Another bullet from the Scorpion's gun grazed his lower left thigh seconds later. Blood poured down his failing body as he began to fall backwards, down into the gray abyss of the bunker.

Time crawled to a stop as he fell. Above the world spun, ash and dust colliding, but inside him the terror of his impending doom mounted. It was a feeling he was accustomed to as a soldier. It was different every time, but this one was more powerful. The terror was deeper, gripping him with jagged claws.

He blinked to see the gray clouds splitting the sky, and then something that didn't belong, a flash of metal in the distance. It was another vehicle on the horizon.

Obi squinted to make out the shape and saw it wasn't one, but two vehicles, and then three. He first thought they were CRK reinforcements, but as his eyes focused on the small shapes in the distance he knew it was his own.

"You save any for us?" a voice said, crackling over the radio. Obi smiled, recognizing the hoarse voice of Jackson, seconds before a flash from an anti-tank missile raced through the air. He closed his eyes, the heat from the explosion searing his eyebrows, before he crashed onto the bunker floor and slipped into unconsciousness.

CHAPTER 3: AN OLD KNIGHT

"Politics is war without bloodshed while war is politics with bloodshed."
~Mao Tse Tung

Time: 6:36 a.m. January 29, 2071
Location: Governor's Private Chambers, Capitol Building. Lunia, Tisaia

A faint ray of orange crawled over the Eastern wall of Tisaia, spreading an unusual and gracious carpet of light over the city accustomed to vast shades of gray. At the center of the Capitol city the first rays of light reached the golden dome of the Capitol building, creating a radiant glare high in the morning sky. Inside, several of the Governor's staff members were already busy working and hardly noticed the rare light. Governor Felix Steppe was nowhere to be seen, however, and was likely still sleeping in his heavily guarded mansion.

In the Governor's private chamber, Chief of Staff Manx Sonii sat at the head of a marble table, reading over several pieces of legislation and savoring his morning tea. Sonii wanted to make sure he was prepared to brief the Governor later in the day. There were several controversial bills scheduled for debate in the one-chamber legislature.

He rustled through the stack of yellowed paper and pulled out Bill 12b, easily considered the most controversial. The bill, an extension of Bill 12a, was drafted by the Plebrocrats. Its main component was to outlaw Biomass from leaving Tisaia. With scientists creating a more efficient and plentiful version, there were those who argued it should be shared. The advocates for sharing Biomass believed there were other governments around the world that had survived the Biomass Wars, but none of these legislators could provide any evidence.

Sonii, like many other high ranking Tisaian officials, knew the rumors were true. He had spent days tucked away in his office, combing through the piles of briefs. Some contained information on pockets of civilization in South America, mostly in the coastal regions; Rio de Janerio, Lima and Buenos Aires. It was the brief on Iraq, however, that fascinated him the most.

Sonii was something of a history connoisseur. In his studies he came to know Iraq as the cradle of civilization. When he found out life had not only survived there, but was flourishing, he was amazed at the irony. The war torn country was one of the harshest environments known to man. Perhaps this was one reason humans survived there; it was engrained in their DNA, having survived war, famine and plague for a millennia. Whatever the reason, it gave him hope. Not the type easy to create either. It was deeper than that, more than just a dream. It was the type that drove an individual to madness. For him, it was a hope for Tisaia. That the TDU would be crushed and complete order restored.

Sonii was a very organized leader. He didn't like it when things became unmethodical. His life was like a puzzle; every piece had a place. When the pieces didn't fit, he found a solution. The TDU was the piece he just couldn't seem to find the solution for, but he knew in time there would be one. There was always a solution. He always made the pieces fit.

To Sonii, Tisaia was not an anomaly. There was a reason the State rose out of the ashes of the Biomass Wars intact and stronger than any other place in the world. He believed Tisaia was fated to be. It was a solution to rid the world of Democracy and Capitalism. And he would do anything to protect it, especially its secrets.

The briefs contained these secrets, and Sonii knew it was

imperative they remained in the right hands, for at the heart was the deepest secret of them all. It was one very few people knew.

Sonii could distinctly remember the first time he read the report. It was several years ago, but the mission name, Operation Fallout, was seared in his memory.

Not long after Tisaia was founded, the new government was desperate to know which other countries had survived. With the Biomass Wars fresh on their minds, Tisaian officials tasked the newly minted Council of Royal Knights with identifying any potential threats.

In time the Governor ordered the Knights on a secret mission. He hand-selected five Royal Knights and procured the only working plane in Tisaia. Engineers retrofitted it to run off Biomass and said the plane would be able to travel the world without stopping to refuel.

The engineers were right. In the first few weeks of the journey the Knights sent back startling images and reports of the cities on the coast of South America. From the sky the cities looked like total war zones, the infrastructure completely obliterated. Electricity was sporadic at best, but somehow people were alive, surviving in the grisly conditions.

As the Knights made their way to Europe the reports became bleaker. Not a single city remained from aerial view. Skeletons of skyscrapers and high rise office buildings were all that could be seen. No lights, no people, no sign of anything. The United Kingdom was nothing but a desert of ash.

Just when they thought conditions couldn't get any worse, they flew over Eastern Europe and Asia. There was nothing. Not a single city recorded. Not a sign of animal or human life. The trace of radiation from the air was so severe no human could have survived on the surface. It wasn't until they got to New Zealand and Australia that life appeared again. The radiation from the apocalypse, for the most part, had not affected these areas. Maybe it was the wind that blew most of it out to sea, or perhaps the jet stream. The Knights did not know exactly why these countries were spared, but New Zealand and Australia both had pockets of thriving life: green fields, livestock in the country, and electricity in the cities.

When the Knights finally returned to Tisaia, they met with leaders in a cloud of secrecy. It was then a committee was established, of mostly Plebrocrats and Royal Knights. The committee combed through the pictures and reports. Within days they sent their findings to the Governor, who filtered through the images in shock. The desolate landscape and charred cities of Europe and Asia were all he needed to see. His mind was made up. There would be no more recon missions. There would be no reaching out to help those outside the walls. Biomass would stay in Tisaia.

The Governor's immense fear influenced Bill 99. And soon the gates were closed. No refugees would be allowed in Tisaia and any recent immigrants were to be reported, put into camps and deported into the Wastelands. Anyone harboring an immigrant would be tried for crimes against the State.

No one, save for a few Royal Knights, the Governor and a handful of Plebrocrats who helped draft Bill 12a knew the truth of the recon mission from years ago. Over the years the Plebrocrats had become increasingly isolationist. They structured Bill 12b so the Biomass would forever stay in the control of Tisaia, who, they argued, "had won the right to reap the fruits of its labor."

Sonii knew Governor Felix would continue to side with the Plebrocrats, who made up 90 percent of the legislature. "Political parties" were words all but forgotten in Tisaia—the Plebrocrats had dominated the legislature for as long as he could remember. The other ten percent of the one-chamber elected representatives consisted of retired State employees or distinguished Knights who ran as independents. Rohania and the immigrants were not represented at all. Democracy was a word from the past, one forgotten by most. It was only a matter of time before the

Plebrocrats would control the entire legislature. It was part of Sonii's plan, a piece of the puzzle he had been constructing for years.

Sonii slid the bill back into the pile of legislation and watched the orange rays of sunlight peek through the rectangular glass windows. The warm glow was mesmerizing, a treasure in a normally gray bleak world. Every morning he found himself in the same seat, sipping out of the same tea glass, anxious to see if the sun would rise. He could still remember a time when the sun didn't hide behind the gray clouds and he would always welcome its bright warmth.

The clanking of armor from the adjacent hallway distracted his thoughts. He didn't need to turn around to see Leglo and Fonti, the Governor's two handpicked Royal Knights bodyguards as they entered the chamber.

Both Knights wore the traditional armor and were dressed with red capes, signifying their special rank as Protectorates. Sonii always felt at ease in their presence, as he knew they were two of the most well trained Knights in the entire State. They, like the other Protectorates, had sworn an oath to the Governor by committing to a life of seclusion. It was an oath broken only by death.

Sonii brought a hand to his aging forehead and massaged several wrinkles, while the two Knights guided Governor Felix into his chambers. He stood promptly to face the Governor. "Good morning, sir."

Governor Felix acknowledged him with a nod and sat down across from him at the monstrous marble table.

"You're in early this morning," Sonii said, trying to hide his surprise.

"Today is an important day for Tisaia," the Governor responded, running a finger through his thick mustache.

Governor Felix was a husky man; he wasn't overweight by any means and could probably even pass as one of his own bodyguards. His handlebar mustache was his most infamous feature, an attribute most of his staff would not dare copy. The combination of his mustache, size and booming voice made him a very intimidating leader.

Sonii continued to study the Governor's features as the large politician combed through the pile of bills in front of him. Governor Felix petted his thick mustache, something he always did before speaking. This frustrated Sonii, who was not a patient man. He didn't like to wait for the Governor's thoughts, especially when he could already guess what the man would say. Nonetheless he waited, knowing his place.

"Well, we've almost done it, Sonii."

"Sir?" Sonii asked, trying once again to hide his surprise.

The Governor looked up from Bill 12b, which he gripped in one of his massive paws.

"We're this close to passing this bill with a majority of the chamber!" The Governor said, pinching his fingers together.

"And if I can negotiate terms with the rest of the independents then perhaps we can get our unanimous vote after all," he finished, his grin hiding behind his carpet of a mustache.

Sonii crossed his legs and slouched back in his chair, taking a deep breath. He cocked his head and admired the sunrise still beaming in through the stained glass windows before responding.

"If we can get a unanimous vote in favor of this bill, then perhaps we can win over the general population that does not support it. How can citizens argue when the entire legislature votes in favor of this bill?"

Governor Felix stood and walked over to his wooden desk. "The point is..." the Governor paused at his loss of words.

"The point is, even if there are citizens that disagree with this bill, they won't for long. Commander Augustus has promised me the TDU will be crushed by the end of the year. With that victory, those supporting the TDU will lose all hope and be forced to accept defeat."

Sonii glanced over at Leglo and Fonti, who stood in the corner of the room, watching the Governor's every move. Their eyes were hidden behind their blue goggles, deep within their helmets. For a second they looked like statues, no more real than the ones in the courtyard outside the window. Reality washed back over him as Leglo reached down and massaged the electric blue tip of his sword. The Chief of Staff looked back at the Governor, who was staring out a bullet proof window overlooking the courtyard below.

"May I speak freely?" Sonii asked.

The Governor turned to face his highest ranking official. "You may."

Sonii cleared his voice and stood. "With respect sir, I think it would be in our best interest to request the Council of Royal Knights consider placing their finest soldiers in areas where there might be protests. Rohania would be a good start. As you know, in the past there have been several violent protests there, as well as outside the immigrant camps. The only way to deter citizens from thinking is by mere force, something Commander Augustus is very good at. And while I share your optimistic view that all of Tisaia's citizens will eventually agree with the legislature and our office, I think it's best we take appropriate measures," Sonii said, as he sat down, winded from his short speech.

The Governor massaged his mustache again.

"This is what I have been saying for some time as well. Just make sure it gets done, then."

Sonii nodded and rushed out of the room to a hallway leading to the staff offices. He would send a confidential memo via carrier to Commander Augustus immediately, informing him of the bill's progression through the legislature and the Governor's request for soldiers in Rohania. As the Chief of Staff made his way through the marble hallway, he felt a sense of victory. The pieces were coming together very well and soon the puzzle would be complete.

Time: 12:26 p.m. January 29, 2071

Location: Legislative Chambers, Capitol Building. Lunia, Tisaia

Sonii sat in a leather chair at the top of the legislative chamber, looking down on the chamber below. Next to him sat the most powerful man in all of Tisaia and probably the entire world, Governor Felix. Beneath them their Plebocrat puppets debated Bill 12b as the rest of the legislature sat silently at their desks. The discussion over the bill was nearing its second hour and not a single non-affiliated legislator had dared speak.

He couldn't help but smile as the debate continued. If none of the independents spoke up, the bill would come to a vote without any objection. But just when he looked down at his watch, one of the independents tapped his gavel to speak.

Sonii scowled when he saw it was Representative Eduro, a popular politician who had gained the respect of the Plebrocrats through the years. He was known for his distinguished career as a Royal Knight and for his willingness to caucus with the Plebrocrats.

Sonii watched Eduro, who was nearing the age of 70, limp over to the main podium with the assistance of his legislative aide. The representative slowly walked up the steps in the north end of the chambers, which overlooked the desks of more than a hundred other representatives. He grabbed the wooden podium and looked at his colleagues. Silence washed over the room.

The Chief of Staff moved uncomfortably in his chair to get a better look at Eduro, who stood directly below him. He thought of Eduro as a fossil, his face plagued with scars representing battles Sonii had only read about. The truth was the old man was more than just a fossil; he was a powerful voice, a voice of reason many other non-party members respected and listened to, a voice that even some of the more moderate Plebrocrats listened to.

Sonii sat back in his chair, careful not to alarm the Governor. Eduro was dangerous. Not only because he was popular with his colleagues, but because he was popular with the citizens of Tisaia. He would certainly have a monument resurrected in his memory after his death. All of these things made him a threat to the Governor's cause. It was people like Eduro who slowed progress in Tisaia.

"Representatives of Tisaia, we're called here today to vote on Bill 12b, and we're faced with a daunting question. Do we share our Biomass with governments who have survived the nuclear holocaust of the past century? Do we reach out to our fellow man, or do we keep our plentiful supply of Biomass for ourselves? We know from our past that energy does not always come in endless supply. However, times have changed.

"According to reports from some of the greatest scientific minds in all of Tisaia, we have found a way to engineer Biomass energy on a level that could sustain Tisaia for centuries. We can do this, I've been informed, efficiently and at a cost so low there should be no other option but to share this wealth with other governments."

Sonii groaned silently, realizing what was unfolding in front of his eyes. He did not dare look at the Governor who sat silently in the chair next to him.

The chamber ignited in protest as Eduro stepped back from the podium, a hint of a smile on his ancient face. His voice was strained and scratchy from years of battles behind the very podium where he now stood, but he still had some fight left in him. He approached it again, raising his hands to quiet the audience.

"Tisaian representatives, hear me now!" he yelled over the commotion.

"We now know of several other governments still intact and barely surviving."

Sonii flinched. *Was it possible Eduro knew of these other governments?*

He slouched in his chair as it all started to come together. Eduro was one of the Knights on the recon mission. He was breaking an oath he swore years ago. The Chief of Staff watched in horror, his surety and secrets crumbling in front of him.

"Some of these governments used to be our allies, others were our enemies, but now is a time to forget the past, to forget the killing, and to have a shared sense of humanity. Now is a time to share our energy with them so they may have the quality of life many of us have come to know."

Eduro paused to take a sip of water before continuing.

"For too long we've abandoned the principals on which Tisaia was founded—principals of freedom, justice and equality. We imprison our immigrants, starve our citizens in Rohania; and worst of all, we keep our resources stockpiled in bunkers beneath our cities. I ask you all now, what are we afraid of? Another war? Another holocaust? I can tell you humanity can't survive another war. Any just God would have already abandoned us. Now we must seek forgiveness, and share our energy, food and resources with others that need it now more than ever. It's our duty as Tisaians; it's our duty as men."

The room erupted into upheaval, some representatives standing, others jumping from their seats. Most of them were chanting "blasphemy," but there were a few that remained silent—a few that supported the old Royal Knight.

The chamber was divided. It was what Sonii feared the most. Now there would never be a unanimous vote on 12b. Eduro knew what he said would cause great turmoil in the chamber. In fact, it was one reason he hadn't discussed his short speech with his aides before giving it. He was old and wanted to die proud of his service. There wasn't any way he could support 12b. He had been diagnosed with terminal cancer only a month before and he knew he didn't have much time left. It was after his diagnosis he decided he could take whatever Governor Felix, Commander Augustus and any of their cohorts could throw at him. If he was going to die, then at least he was going to do it with honor.

Sonii looked down at Eduro as he limped away from the stage by himself. Even his aide was too terrified to help him back to his desk.

"I want Eduro's resignation on my desk by tomorrow," Governor Felix snorted, before disappearing into the bowels of the Capitol hallways.

Sonni listened to the echo of clanking armor from the Governor's two guards who raced after him. He sighed, reluctantly rising from his chair to follow the most powerful man in the world out of the chambers. "This is going to change things," he muttered.

CHAPTER 4: GUERRILLA WARFARE

"Guerrillas war is a kind of war waged by a few but dependent on the support of many."
~B.H. Liddell Hart

Time: 12:31 a.m. January 30, 2071
Location: Biomass Trolley Docking Station #4. Tisaia

Terminus sat at his post, overlooking the trolley station below. He took a bite of a cold turkey sandwich, chewing it slowly with his old and broken teeth. These days he had to be careful when eating, for he didn't have the money to get another one of his teeth fixed. His age had started to catch up with him, and his teeth were only one of the harsh realities he faced on a day to day basis.

The screech of a trolley screamed out in the night, bringing Terminus to his feet as he squinted to make out the train in the distance. The station Terminus worked had been in operation for ten years and was the largest trolley station in Tisaia. Its sole purpose was to carry Biomass across the country from the facilities to the cities, which powered their vehicles, and supplied their heat and energy needs.

As the massive oval light of the trolley burst over the horizon, Terminus put his sandwich on a handkerchief and raced down the stairs to the platform. Three other State workers joined him on the brick ledge of the trolley docking station. The red of their overalls blended in like camouflage under the red glow of the street lights lining the trolley platform. Terminus nodded at Decima, a maintenance worker he had worked with for years.

Terminus's radio blared to life as the trolley continued to close in on the station. "Biomass trolley 467, approaching dock station #10. Requesting permission to dock for repairs, over," the conductor said, over the static of the radio.

Terminus brought his black, wallet-sized radio up to his mouth, his overgrown mustache covering the small device. "Permission granted," he responded.

The mechanics waited at the edge of the tracks for the trolley to approach. They watched as the trolley began to slow, its electric brakes protesting, sending sparks shooting from the underbelly.

Decima stood by the edge of the tracks, his ears instantly picking up the whine of the trolley's engine. Over the years he had worked on hundreds of trains, and like the cries of a child, he became familiar with the sounds, knowing what each one meant. Tonight, however, the sound was different, unlike any he had ever heard.

The train docked at approximately 12:35 a.m., a cloud of smoke and steam rising from under the lid of the engine. Decima and Terminus immediately went to work, using the trolley's running boards to climb onto the side of the engine compartment and reach the hood. They waited momentarily for the scorching mist to subside before going to work.

"Decima, hand me a wrench and on the count of three, we'll open the hood."

Decima nodded as he slid a wrench across the metal hood of the trolley. Terminus grabbed it and placed it over a large screw securing the left side of the engine's lid. Decima mimicked this action, and they twisted their wrenches, freeing the lid from its restraint. The hood popped ajar and they worked together, lifting it to reveal the massive engine fed from a single pint of Biomass. *Hard to imagine this pint could power the trolley the entire 200 miles*, he thought, wiping the beads of sweat dripping off his wind burnt face. He placed his wrench back into the breast pocket of his red overalls and peered inside the bowels of the engine compartment. What they saw was something neither of them recognized – a tangled web of wires and plugs emerging from the overheated engine.

"What the hell," Terminus muttered.

"How did that happen?" Decima responded, perplexed. What the pair of maintenance workers didn't realize was the cords and wires were not part of the engine at all. The three years they spent at technical school had not prepared them for the mess of wires protruding from the engine compartment.

"I think we need to call this in to headquarters," Decima said, in a concerned voice.

"No, we can fix this, Decima, we just need to get in there and figure out what the hell happened. If we call this into headquarters they'll send us a brigade of Knights, and I really don't want to be interrogated tonight."

"It's your call, boss," Decima shrugged.

"Wait just one damn second, you two!" the trolley conductor cried from the side of the brick docking station. "That's my train, and I'm responsible for it. I don't know what you're looking at over there, but if there's a safety concern, then protocol is to contact the CRK."

Terminus turned to look at the old conductor. The man's face was pale and lined with age. A white mustache curled up towards his nose, looking as if it would tickle him and cause him to sneeze every time he spoke. The conductor spat a gob of brown chewing tobacco on the brick platform and waited for Terminus' response.

"Okay, you call it in then, but I'm not going to wait for the CRK to get here. We're going to try and fix this damn engine before we're interrogated by those damn Tin Cans," he said, smugly.

The conductor grunted. "Do what you have to do. I'll call it in from your post," he said, making his way up the ramp to the offices.

Terminus and Decima looked at one another. They both knew they had little chance of fixing the engine before a dozen Knights showed up with their shiny gmetal and a swarm of questions. Nonetheless they got to work pulling the loose wires from the engine, trying to determine where they were coming from.

After an hour of work the pair climbed off the running boards and back onto the sturdy brick docking station. They had cleared all but one wire out of the engine, and had found it attached to a small box under the Biomass cell. Neither of them had ever seen anything like it before. It was small, and if it weren't for the wires, tiny enough to be overlooked by an amateur mechanic. The black casing didn't appear to be an actual part of the engine. A dark red wire protruded from the center of it and ran up through the heart of the engine. Decima and Terminus stood by the side of the train, sipping from their canteens, and wondered if they really should wait for the CRK to arrive.

"I don't know about this, Decima, have you ever seen anything like it?"

"I was just about to ask you the same question."

"It's pretty apparent that someone put this thing here, and I'm not sure I want to cut that wire," Terminus said, sighing and taking another sip.

"Whatever it is, the wire is preventing the train from getting enough Biomass to run properly. So I suggest we cut the wire, remove the box, and get this train back on its way. This trolley has over five cars of Biomass, and it's due in Lunia in two hours. That's almost a week's supply," Decima explained. "Besides, we both know sabotaging a trolley is next to impossible. This is more than likely a new piece of technology the mechanics at a different post installed to help the train run more efficiently."

"And we didn't get the memo?" Terminus asked, frowning.

"They've stopped telling us when they add new parts to the trains. And with all the hype about new Biomass out there, it's possible some mechanic added this without sending us a note,"

Decima said, shrugging.

Terminus cocked his head to look back at the idle trolley. It was a truly magnificent machine. Its design, one he had studied at the Tisaian Engineering College, was developed by the same scientists who created the first batches of Biomass.

The trolley itself was over a thousand feet long and was made of a new lightweight metal, allowing it to literally glide over the tracks. It was so fast it could get anywhere in Tisaia within two hours. They rarely broke down, and when they did, it didn't take long to get them back on the tracks. It was a remarkably efficient machine.

Terminus groaned. The trolleys had become his life's work. Whenever something was wrong with one he felt it, like the metal was a part of him. In an odd sense, they were his giant pets. He was their caretaker, and fixing them so they could go back to work gave him great satisfaction.

"All right, Decima, let's cut it. We can explain later that the wires were preventing the engine from getting enough Biomass to run efficiently. The mechanics who installed the damn thing can fix it, for all I care; this shipment of Biomass has to get to Lunia."

Climbing back onto the running boards, Decima and Terminus stared back into the engine compartment. The tiny red wire peered back at them innocently.

Decima turned to look at his boss, who gave him the go ahead with a simple nod.

"Okay, you little son of a bitch. You're someone else's problem now," Decima said, under his breath, reaching in with his wire cutter.

The small wire snapped easily between the sharp blades. Instantly, a spark erupted from the black box. Neither of the mechanics had time to react as they were enveloped in flames.

From the road several miles away, a patrol of CRK soldiers watched in shock as a mushroom cloud rose into the sky above.

"Shit, shit!" the lead Knight screamed, fumbling for his

headset. "Headquarters! Come in. We have a situation. Over." Static sounded for a few short seconds before anyone responded on the other line.

"Headquarters here. It's almost 1:00 a.m.; what kind of situation do you guys have? Over," a tired operator muttered.

"I don't give a shit what time it is, get the Commanding Knight of District 1 on the line. We've lost a Biomass trolley. Over," the Knight coughed into his headset.

"Roger. I'm sorry, sir. Right away," the civilian responded, breaking proper radio procedure.

"Let's move out, men. Check the area for any survivors, but be ready for any TDU, this could be a trap we're walking into," the lead Knight ordered.

He watched his patrol head through the dead forest, the inferno in the distance glowing in the reflection of his blue goggles. He shook his head and followed his men. "Damn rebels."

Time: 7:41 a.m. January 30, 2071
Location: Trolley Station #14. Lunia, Tisaia

Paulo sat at Trolley Station #14, waiting for a passenger train to take him to work. He was already running late and didn't need another write up to further ruin his already dreary life. As he waited he pulled out his small blue screen tablet and read *The Lunia Post*. The tablet and subscription was just another one of the "perks" given to State workers. He would have preferred to read a paper copy of the Post, but the State had done away with all paper documents that weren't for official business years ago.

He thumbed through the news, or what the State deemed news. On the front page was a story about a skirmish with some stragglers outside the walls who tried to make their way into Lunia through old storm drains. There was another story about a new policy SGS had implemented, requiring all State employees to continue education in their respective work areas for at least 50 hours a year.

What's that going to help accomplish?

He sighed and put the tablet back into the bowels of his coat. The news was predictable, the same stories appearing in every edition with the occasional inspirational piece tied in. Paulo was no longer part of the State's targeted audience. He had slipped beyond, reading between the lines and becoming increasingly bitter every day.

The tunnel was dark, illuminated only by a few red lights. One flickered intermittently, reminding him of the red lights from the train stop in his hometown. Like a subliminal warning, the light blinked—the red radiance shedding an eerie glow on the other State workers lining up on the platform.

The trolley, which was already running five minutes late, was nowhere to be seen.

That's odd, this trolley is always on time.

Paulo quickly lost interest in the absent train and returned to people-watching. To his right sat a middle-aged businessman. The dark black suit and bright red sunglasses hugging the rims of his eyes gave him away. Paulo had seen his type before, but rarely at a trolley station. Most businessmen did not work for the State, but rather for companies developing new technologies that the State did not have the infrastructure or resources to develop. These businessmen mostly lived in the Commons Area with the other State workers, but some of them had built enough wealth to live outside the Commons and in gated communities.

Paulo chuckled under his breath. He remembered a time he was actually envious of these men and their fancy cars that broke the energy laws State workers were forced to follow. And why wouldn't they? It was all a game. The wealthy gave a share of their profits to the State by transferring funds to the Legislature and high level officials. In turn, they were not forced to follow the strict laws the State imposed on its workers and citizens. If a Knight stopped them, they would simply show their identification card and be allowed to proceed.

Businessmen rarely ventured out; many had been robbed or kidnapped in an upsurge of violence in the past few years. That's what really surprised Paulo about this one. He had seen them in trolley stations before, but usually with armed guards and an entourage of staff. This one, however, was traveling solo.

Paulo shrugged it off, glancing back down at his watch. The train was 11 minutes late, but there was nothing he could do about it. He pulled his tablet out again to pass the time and opened an article that actually interested him.

"New Biomass Production."

He scanned through it, reading that a new Biomass factory was producing enough Biomass in a month to fuel all of Tisaia for another 15 years.

The red flicker of the light snapped him back to reality, and he watched as the inconvenienced patrons began to get nervous, several of them shuffling back and forth on the platform. Paulo glanced over at the businessman again and noticed he was still staring at the train tracks, unmoved from his position. A wave of anxiety shot through Paulo's old body.

He stiffened and stood patiently, his eyes desperately scanning the tunnel before stopping on a sign that read, "Report Suspicious Activity to the CRK, Your Friends and Your Protectors."

Paulo grinned. *Yeah right, like I'd tell those Tin Cans if I saw anything suspicious.*

The train was now over 17 minutes late and Paulo began to make his way through the crowd. Unlike these other workers, he could not afford to be late to work. He was going to try and make it to the office on foot. It was only five blocks away, and with about 15 minutes to spare here, he could make it if he hustled. He knew the excuse of a late trolley would not be acceptable to his boss.

Paulo pushed his way through the crowded station, catching a glimpse of a fully armored CRK foot soldier standing at the bottom of the stairs leading to the street above. The soldier stood there frozen, like a statue; his rifle at his shoulders, resting perfectly on the skin of his gmetal armor. A shudder went down Paulo's back as he saw the soldier, but he didn't know why. For the most part contact with the CRK was an everyday occurrence, but today it frightened Paulo more than it normally would. The flickering red light, the late train, the out of place businessman, and now a soldier only reminded him he constantly lived in a state of fear.

The top step came into view just as he heard the whining of the trolley's engine. He turned in time to see the crowd move forward, the lump of people pushing their way closer to the tracks to ensure a seat on the trolley.

Just my luck.

He turned to head back down the stairs, his back slightly hunched over, clutching the hand rail of the stairway. As he took another step, a voice screamed out over the commotion. "He's got a gun!"

Paulo turned and scanned the crowd desperately, in time to see the businessman he had been sitting next to point a machine gun at the crowd. Deafening gun shots echoed off the concrete tunnel walls. Instinctively he dropped to the concrete, the stale taste of dust finding its way into his open mouth.

He watched as the trolley doors opened and several more men dressed like the businessman jumped out into the crowd, their machine guns raised. The CRK soldier opened fire immediately, the bullets tearing through two State workers who fell, thick pools of blood oozing out of their warm bodies.

"Oh my God," Paulo whispered, frozen in fear. It was really happening. This wasn't just a story in *The Lunia Post.* This was real.

Paulo gripped the railing tightly and watched the CRK soldier run towards the four terrorists. He fired haphazardly, his bullets cutting down innocent civilians in his path. The terrorists, who were most likely part of the TDU, fired back, their bullets ricocheting off the CRK soldier's armor with little effect.

The scene was straight out of a nightmare, one Paulo had seen so many times before in his dreams, and now he had a front row seat. He watched as the screaming civilians dove for cover. The terrorists were positioned behind the safety of stone pillars, firing desperately at the CRK soldier, who ducked behind a stone trash can, pieces of rock exploding from their incoming shots.

"Get down!" one of the terrorists screamed as he lobbed a grenade towards the CRK soldier. The small explosive rolled towards the trash can and came to a stop directly at the foot of the CRK soldier, who was too busy firing to notice it. Seconds later the device exploded, sending a cloud of orange flames and sparks through the air. The explosion rocked the tunnel and blew the CRK soldier in half, his torso landing several feet from a woman who lay screaming. The piercing noise of the explosion subsided as smoke began to fill the corridor.

Paulo sat stunned against the wall, a loud ringing echoing in his ears. He reached up and felt warm blood seeping from his face, but it did not faze him. His eyes remained glued to the scene, scanning the carnage. At least five civilians lay silently on the ground. Another 20 screamed in pain, clutching their bullet and shrapnel wounds. The rest of the civilians ran past Paulo as they tried to escape.

A man grabbed Paulo by the shoulders, his frightened eyes locking onto Paulo's. "Let's *go*, man, what are you doing?!" he screamed. He pulled on Paulo's tan sweater, but Paulo ignored him, his eyes darting back to the scene. The man let go of his sweater, and took off running with the rest of the survivors.

Below the four terrorists had gone back into the train and were kneeling around a small box. Paulo knew immediately it was a bomb, but the reality of the situation still had not fully hit him. In fact, in an odd way it fascinated him. He strained to hear what the terrorists were saying through his injured ears.

In the distance the whine of CRK sirens rang out, and the ground began to shake with the sound of armored vehicles approaching the tunnel.

"We don't have much time," one of the terrorists yelled. He took out a knife and cut the wire of the bomb he was attaching to the center of the trolley.

"Okay, it's armed!" He stood and patted his comrade on the shoulder. The other three terrorists rose as well. The one in the middle, the same one that Paulo had been sitting by earlier, brushed off his dusty black suit. He appeared to be limping.

"We do this and then make our escape. Nathar, you put the coordinates into the trolley's computer, so when it leaves here it goes straight to the CRK headquarters. When you're done, follow us down the tunnel. Ajax, you and Creo follow me back into the storm tunnels," the leader said.

Paulo sat watching the four men as they began to move in all different directions. The injured leader, the one Creo referred to as Obi slowly made his way off the train. The dark man grabbed his arm and helped him jump down onto the tracks. Then they disappeared from sight, Ajax close behind them.

Paulo continued to sit against the staircase; he gripped the railing so hard his knuckles turned white. Something compelled him to stay and watch. For years he heard about the TDU terrorists, and now he was watching the feared men conduct their work right in front of him. Part of his shock was from fear, but part of it was also from curiosity and mere fascination. In a way, he was almost rooting for the terrorists.

He scanned the bodies of his fellow State workers below and stopped on the torso of the CRK soldier. The truth was, he felt a sense of relief it wasn't him laying there in a pool of blood.

"Move, move, move!" screamed a dozen CRK soldiers. They ran past Paulo and into the carnage below. One of the soldiers stopped and glanced at Paulo. "Are you all right, sir?" he asked, a semi-concerned tone in his voice. Paulo simply nodded, and looked back down at the trolley as it began to move down the tunnel.

"Don't let that trolley leave!" the lead CRK soldier shouted. He opened fire on the metal skin of the trolley. Windows exploded as the bullets tore through the thin metal and fragile glass, but it was too late. Nathar had already plotted the train's course and put it on autopilot, and by now, he and his comrades were long gone down the dark tunnel. The soldiers continued to fire as the train slipped away from range.

Finally, shocked into motion, Paulo crawled up the stairway towards the light above. Step by step, he pulled himself higher, more faceless CRK soldiers and medical workers racing past him.

For Paulo, everything became silent. Thoughts of the carnage escaped his mind as he fixated on the bright white light of the street poles above. Nothing else seemed to matter to him. The TDU, Knights, and injured colleagues were now just an afterthought. All he cared about was reaching the light. It was captivating and beckoned him with its dazzling glow.

With a final push he reached the last step and crawled onto the stone ground above. He rolled on to his back, staring into the light, his chest heaving with every labored breathe.

Life is strange. So much death, and for what?

He laughed as his vision blurred and stars danced across his cloudy line of sight. The bright glare of the light became nothing but an illusion of swirling white. It was seconds later, just before an explosion from the tunnels swallowed him, that he answered his own question.

The death, misery, and suffering were all derived from the same thing; Biomass, and fossil fuels before it. As the inferno raced up the stairway, he cracked a smile. His eyes locked onto the Biomass-fed light pole before he was incinerated.

Time: 8:03 a.m. January 30, 2071
Location: Sector of Governmental Services. Lunia, Tisaia

Spurious was bored. He was sitting in his cubicle staring at Archie, when he felt the blast. It shook the entire building, and knocked his plastic clock off the wall. He immediately grabbed Archie's bowl, making sure it did not fall and break.

Spurious peeked out of his cubicle to examine the deafening roar, but all he could see were State workers running down the hall towards the receptionist desk, where a radio was transmitting something over the airwaves.

He quickly got up from his desk and followed his co-workers down the hall. He already knew something was terribly wrong. He thought about what Leo had told him a few days before, and deep down he knew his life had already changed. Part of this caused a great sense of excitement deep in his gut, but there was also the anxiety of change he always feared.

At the end of the hallway SGS workers cluttered around the receptionist's desk, listening to what sounded like the deep voice of Governor Felix.

"State employees and citizens of Tisaia. We're now at a cross roads between good and evil. This morning, at 1:30 a.m., terrorists affiliated with the TDU detonated a bomb in a trolley carrying a five week's supply of Biomass to Lunia. And at approximately 8:00 a.m. a second attack occurred as TDU terrorists boarded a passenger trolley and planted a second bomb. They had planned for the trolley to explode under the CRK headquarters building, but thanks to the bravery of our fine Knights, the bomb was detonated before it could reach its final target.

"It's with great sadness that I tell you we lost many good Knights and State workers today. But I assure all of you that you need not fear for your lives or for your safety. As of today, the CRK will engage in a campaign to eradicate the TDU from Tisaia and from the very dirt of this earth. Nothing will stop me from taking the lives of every last one of these terrorists."

Spurious could hear the anger in the words of the Governor. Confusion rushed over him as he thought about his dead colleagues, and then his family, who had been murdered by the

CRK. His heart fluttered heavily as he first thought of his mother and father, and then of Lana, the woman he had grown to love but could never have.

Nervous chatter exploded throughout the room as State workers began to discuss the Governor's announcement.

"All right, folks, let's get back to work. It does not seem like there's any immediate danger to us here in this building. If there is, I have been assured by CRK officials they will evacuate the building," Varius said.

It wasn't until lunch that news of the fatalities started trickling into the office. Spurious was attempting to work on a document when a pale Ing rushed into his cubicle, a look of despair streaked across his young face. Before Ing said, anything, Spurious knew something was terribly wrong.

"Paulo never made it to work today," Ing said, quietly.

A wave of panic washed over Spurious. "Let's go find him Ing."

Time: 12:15 a.m. January 31, 2071
Location: Trolley Station #14. Lunia, Tisaia

A crescent moon broke through the cloud of smoke covering Lunia like a blanket. It was shortly after midnight, and the CRK and SGS disaster teams were still digging through the rubble above Trolley Station #14.

The TDU had fallen short of their goal of destroying the CRK headquarters, but the damage to Tisaia's infrastructure was catastrophic.

Spurious and Ing watched the recovery effort from the middle of a massive crowd. Everyone was waiting to hear about their lost loved ones.

"How did it come to this?" Spurious asked, shielding his face from the heat of the raging fire. "It seemed like Paulo was beginning to come out of his depression, and now this. There is nothing left of him. Nothing left to bury."

"I shouldn't have been so hard on him lately," Ing finally replied.

"You couldn't have known this would happen."

Ing scowled. "It doesn't matter now. The TDU will pay for this."

Spurious thought again of Leo, and what the old man had told him only days before. Had his parents really been a part of the group that killed his friend and destroyed the lives of so many innocent civilians?

He watched the faceless Knights digging through the rubble. Were they the enemy, or were the rebels the ones he should blame?

A gust of scorching wind shook the confusing notions from his head and he stared back into the orange flames. "I hope you find peace, Paulo," Spurious said, patting Ing on his shoulder. They walked out of the crowd and began their trip back to the Commons area.

"I had to see it for myself," Spurious said.

"The TDU is going to pay for this," Ing responded.

Spurious stopped, resting his back on the cold metal of a light pole. He looked at his friend.

"Ing, there's a lot we do not know about this conflict. The CRK has murdered a lot of innocent civilians as well. And I..." Spurious paused to pick his words carefully. "Well, I just don't know what to think anymore," Spurious whispered, his gaze dropping to the cobblestone street.

"What are you saying, Spurious? The TDU just murdered our best friend, and you're questioning who is right in this situation?"

"I'm not questioning who is right," Spurious interrupted, his voice growing louder. "I'm questioning the point of all of this. The laws, the mechanical work, the power of the State, and why we don't share the Biomass with other States that still exist."

"You're questioning the very nature of Tisaia, then. That's treason, and you could be hung! You're lucky I'm your friend, Spurious. If I wasn't, you'd have some questions to answer," Ing finished calmly.

"You're right, I'm lucky you're my friend. Let's not speak of this any longer. Let's instead remember our friend Paulo. Tonight, we'll celebrate his life and forget the troubling times we live in."

Ing shot Spurious a defensive glance, and after a few moments of silence he nodded. "You're right, tonight we drink to Paulo," Ing said.

Time: 1:30 a.m. January 31, 2071
Location: The Ale House. Lunia, Tisaia

The Ale House was packed full of sweaty patrons, and the ale was flowing freely. Spurious figured most of the State employees knew the danger of the TDU attack was over, and most of them who weren't immediately affected by the bombing were drinking to celebrate life. Others were like Spurious and Ing, celebrating the life of lost loved ones.

That was the traditional Tisaian way, celebrating the life of those who died. There was so much death and this was the only way Tisaians knew how to grieve.

Spurious had always thought it ironic, considering how cheap the value of life could be at times.

"Things just don't feel the same," Spurious said, sipping his ale.

"I don't think they will be the same for a long time," Ing responded. "I wish I had treated Paulo better the last few times I had seen him. I was always arguing with him."

"He loved you like a son, Ing," Spurious said, reassuringly.

A tear crawled down Ing's face as he took another swig of ale. "It's going to take some time before things get back to normal."

"Yeah you're right about that. I never told you this, Ing, but my parents were killed in the beginning of the Biomass Revolution. I have never really gotten over it. One day I went to school, and when I came home, they just weren't there anymore. I was shipped off to another school shortly after. To this day, I still feel like a piece of me is gone, but after a while you get used to the loss, and the feeling you'll never be whole again."

Ing looked across the booth, his mouth quivering, but silent. Recognizing the anguish in his friend's features, Spurious reached across the table, patting Ing's hand.

"It's all right, life is difficult. We just have to look after each other now," Spurious said.

"You're the only friend I have now," Ing replied solemnly.

Spurious looked up to see his friend looking back at him. "Besides Lana, you're the only friend I have, too."

"Lana? What do you mean, you have Lana? She belongs to Varius. Spurious, you know that. What do you mean, she's all you have, other than me?"

Spurious slouched in his seat, realizing he had never told Ing about Lana. In fact, he had never told anyone about Lana. *What a perfect time to tell Ing about this,* Spurious thought, frustrated.

"Ing, I've been meaning to tell you. I really have. I just didn't ever know how to tell you that Lana and I have fallen for one another."

Ing gasped. "You've got to be kidding me, Spurious. First, you're questioning your loyalty to Tisaia, in *public.* And now you're in love with the assistant to our *supervisor?* What's gotten into you?"

Spurious brought his finger to his lips. "Calm down. Don't draw any attention to us. You know there could be an undercover CRK agent anywhere in here right now."

"Spurious. I just don't get it. You have the perfect life, a great job, a great flat. We have fun when we go out. You know you could find a wife through the regular process. Why do you have to put yourself in jeopardy?"

"The regular process? Ing, does that not seem a little odd to you? Do you really want the State telling you what you can eat, who you can marry and where you can travel? I mean, come on, when did you become so complacent? I don't want to go fill out an application at the Sector for Love and Compassion and roll the dice, hoping they find me someone I'm compatible with. Lana is perfect for me. And we've been able to keep it a secret this far. I don't want to go through the regular process with her. What if the State finds we're not compatible, and decides we shouldn't be together? Then what do I do? I love her!"

Ing rolled his eyes, and took a long swig of his ale. "I don't know what to tell you. I just know if Varius finds out, you're ruined. You'll lose your job, and he will probably push the Council's Office to prosecute you for crimes of passion."

"I have already thought of this, and to be honest, I don't care."

"Well, it seems like tonight you don't care about much at all, do you, Spurious?"

Spurious looked down at the table, using his sleeve to wipe it clean of ale. He thought again of what Leo told him only days before.

You have the ability to shape the future of Tisaia. Out of all people, how do I fight against a State that is so powerful, so ruthless? And through all of this, how do I keep Lana?

"Snap out of it, Spurious. I think we need to get out of here," Ing said, nodding to alert him to two Royal Knights in full armor walking towards them. Spurious looked quickly over his shoulder and watched the Knights push their way through the crowded bar.

Ing and Spurious remained still; their eyes aimed at the table, hoping to evade any unnecessary attention.

"Do you think they're really looking for us, Spurious?"

"Why the hell would they be looking for us, unless someone overheard us talking?"

"I really didn't think we were being loud," Ing shot back nervously.

"Well, what should we do?" Spurious asked.

"If they're here for us, they will catch us eventually. We better just stay put."

The two Royal Knights continued to push their way through the crowd, combing through patrons with their assault rifles. Their blue goggles glowed in the dark tavern, reminding Spurious of two large black owls descending on prey. With every beat of bass the Royal Knights moved closer to Spurious and Ing's table. He could feel his heart beating in his chest. *Thump. Thump. Thump.*

The bass pounded louder as the Knights approached their table. Out of the corner of his eye Spurious watched the ghostly blue radiating out of their goggles. He swallowed and felt his heart tighten in his chest. He was sure now they were coming for him. He didn't dare look up as the Knights moved closer.

Maybe he could outrun them, but what then? Where would he go? If they wanted him, they would find him. Ing was right. Spurious remained sitting and waited for the Knights to take him away. And just when they were almost on him, he saw them grab a straggly-looking man and drag him out of the tavern.

"No! I didn't do anything wrong!" he screamed.

"You're coming with us," one of the Knights said, picking the man up by the back of his shirt and tossing him through the open door and into the dark night.

Spurious took a deep breath of relief, his chest heaving in and out. "Holy shit, that was close. I think it's time to go home and get some rest," he said, his heart finally returning to a normal pace.

"Damn, I really thought they were coming for us." Ing said, his hand visibly shaking as he took another long swig of ale. He wiped the liquid off his mouth and stared across the table at his friend, a serious look painted on his semi-intoxicated face. "You better watch your back, especially with Lana. I don't know what I'd do if I lost you too, Spurious. Losing Paulo is enough. Please promise me you won't see her again."

Spurious took one last swig from his mug. "I'm sorry, Ing, All I can promise you is that I'll be careful."

Ing rolled his eyes, pushing his chair back under the table. "You know your secret is safe with me," he said, as he left to pay his tab.

Spurious watched his friend leave with a raised brow. "I sure hope so."

CHAPTER 5: SPARTANS

"Before you embark on a journey of revenge, dig two graves."
~Confucius

Time: 2:31 a.m. January 31, 2071
Location: Office of the Royal Knight Commander. Lunia,
Tisaia

It was two in the morning and the Commanding Royal Knight of Tisaia, Alexander Augustus, paced back and forth nervously in his quarters. His left hand grasped a half smoked cigar that bled a trail of smoke up into his nostrils. Two drops of sweat crept down the Knight's forehead, finding their way into a scar that left a deep ravine down his left cheek. At the age of 45, the Knight had his fair share of scars. It was one reason he had gained his rank so quickly. Historically the Commanding Royal Knights were picked for their distinguished military role in Tisaia. There were only two before him, both assassinated before their second year of service. Augustus had already served two terms and was entering his third. He had survived two assassination attempts and knew the next one was probably imminent.

Four of his staff members sat around the marble war table in the center of his office. He watched his most trusted confidante, Chief of Staff Simmon, discussing recent events with his subordinates.

The candle light flickered in the dark room, illuminating the murals painted across the ceiling. The scene depicted the ancient battle of Thermopylae in 480BC, where the small and vastly outnumbered Spartan armies of Greece prevented the Persian army from following the main Greek army in their retreat. The mural was created at the beginning of his first term. After long work days he was known to lock the monstrous oak doors to his office, pour a glass of whiskey and study the mural from the comfort of his plush leather chair.

"Sir, with respect, I think we have enough information to shut down the trolley stations indefinitely. It appears this was not an isolated attack and our intelligence sources indicate there may be other impending attacks. I think the rebels have the capability of launching another attack on this scale again, at any time," Staffer Marcus Mcaina argued.

Simmon did not respond. Instead his ocean blue eyes remained fixated on the holographic data streaming from a projector in the middle of the marble table. He studied the data, requesting the AI to move on after he had read one entry in its entirety. Behind him the Commander continued to pace back and forth in front of the fireplace that extended from the south wall of the room. As the sound of the minute hand on the grandfather clock clicked away, Simmon continued to read, analyzing the situation through every avenue he could think of. The uneasiness in the room faded away until the crack of a burning log in the fireplace brought Simmon to his feet.

"Commander, I'd like to issue my opinion," Simmon said, propping his sword against his chair out of respect. Augustus raised his brow, and moved his solid stone jaw in approval.

"Staffer Mcaina seems to think we should yield to the terrorist rebels. In fact, he would have you believe we should completely shut down our underground trolley stations. He claims this small group of radicals has the capability to launch similar attacks at any given time. And while our intelligence has given us adequate information to assume this to be true, I'd argue we meet this threat head on. Let us staff the trolley stations with more soldiers and launch an offensive into the heart of these rebels. We shall take this fight underground and crush this rebellion once and for all. The safety of Tisaia and her citizens depends on a victory, not to mention the financial well-being of our already fragile economy. If we shut down the trolley stations, our State workers will have to find new forms of transportation to work, which may place delays in all government departments," the Chief of Staff said.

Simmon was a man of few words. His motto was, *least said, easiest mended*, but there was never a time when he was afraid to voice his opinion. After analyzing the data, he came to what he thought was a reasonable solution and sold it to his commander. In fact, he was usually Augustus' voice of reason. It wasn't uncommon for Mcaina and Simmon to argue, but in situations with the TDU, Simmon's position had always allowed him to gain the upper hand.

For a few moments the entire room remained silent. The tick of the grandfather clock and occasional crack of the fire were the only source of noise in the uncomfortably quiet room. Every one of the staffers at the war table knew the stakes projected in front of them. If they did not act against the rebels, Tisaia's fate might not be much different from the rest of the world's.

As the hour hand of the grandfather clock struck midnight Augustus took one last drag of his cigar, savoring the smoke before he exhaled it into the air. He rose from his chair and placed both of his large and rough hands on the table.

"Gentlemen, I have made my final decision." He paused to watch his silent staffers. There was something about making his subordinates wait for his decision that was so gratifying.

"I have decided that we'll reopen and reverse Project 1200," he said, pausing to gauge their reaction.

Mcaina and Simmon immediately fidgeted in their chairs while another staffer reached for his tie, attempting to loosen it. Everyone around the table knew Project 1200 referenced the underground tunnels below Tisaia. They all remembered the horrors committed there by the Tisaian National Army before it was disbanded at the end of the war and replaced with the Council of Royal Knights. It was at the height of the Biomass Wars, when the survivors of the holocaust had gone underground to survive. There were entire cities of survivors underneath the surface of Tisaia, seeking refuge from the radiation poisoning above. And there wasn't enough food or shelter for all of them. So the young Tisaian government had simply closed off access to some of the tunnels, leaving the survivors on the other side to fend for themselves. Most of them starved to death, while others were said to have left to take their chances in the Wasteland. Reversing Project 1200 meant reopening the tombs of the past, something unthinkable until now.

"I'm authorizing this project to reopen under strict guidelines. The project shall be overseen primarily by the Special Forces group, the Dark Horses. They will be deployed as a hunter killer unit, sent out to explore the tunnels closed off for years. This is where we believe the TDU to be hiding. Only a handful of CRK officers will know about this project and it shall be conducted with the utmost secrecy. As for Simmon's recommendations, I have decided we shall divert half of the available reserve CRK forces to be posted in all public facilities. Furthermore, the trolley stations shall be staffed with our finest officers. Lastly, I'm going to recommend we increase our offensive against the rebels. I want their leader caught, and their headquarters discovered within two weeks. With the reopening of these tunnels that should be more than enough time, don't you think?" He turned his back to his staff to face the heat of the burning fire.

Simmon nodded in approval, savoring the small victory he had gained over Mcaina. The Dark Horses were the best Knights they had, but Simmon wasn't sure if even they had the stomach for what they would find. He could only imagine the horrors and utter terror those on the other side experienced when they were closed.

As the staffers filed quietly out his door, Augustus turned once again to view the mural of the Battle of Thermopylae. An uncharacteristic sense of fear washed over him as he thought of the battle that lay ahead. He always compared his men to the Spartans.

Their fierce loyalty, bravery, and skills as warriors defined the CRK, just like it had the Spartans. And for a second he questioned how history would remember his men. Would they compare them to the Spartans or the Persians? The thought disappeared quicker than the sparks crackling inside his fireplace. It was a shameful reflection to have, especially for the Commander of the CRK, and it only strengthened his resolve to crush the TDU.

He smiled, watching the fire consume the logs, knowing that history would remember him and his men as modern day Spartans after they destroyed the TDU.

Commander Augustus lay in his oversized bed, counting the small clouds of smoke trailing out of his burning cigarette. He looked to the empty pillow next to him, only to be reminded that his wife was no longer alive, the victim of a bullet meant for him. He rested his head back down on his pillow, thoughts of the past racing through his mind. Quickly, the memories brought back the familiar pain only cured by a heavy dose of whiskey.

The early morning hours were always the worst, as he began to mentally prepare himself for the day before him. In the years following the Biomass Wars, when the world went to shit, Augustus was just a young man. His father and brother were both in the United States Army before it crumbled with the rest of the government. Augustus and his family were a few of the fortunate survivors. They scratched out a living in the tunnels below what had once been the great city of Chicago, now nothing more than ruins in the distance.

He had risen to the top of the CRK through the fire and destitution many of his colleagues also faced. These hardships helped the survivors create a strong Tisaia, one he would do anything for. He would stop at nothing in his quest to rid Tisaia of the TDU terrorist threat. Politics meant little to him. The discussion of Bill 12b was nothing more than a side note on his desk. He never questioned Governor Felix's orders. It wasn't his job. His job was to protect Tisaia from her many enemies.

He blew another cloud of smoke into the air, forgetting his troubles. A clock in his sparsely furnished bedroom rang, indicating it was 6:00 am, and the day had officially begun. *Today everything is going to change,* he thought, smearing the butt of his cigarette on a glass ashtray beside his bed. The embers cooled and suffocated, dying in their glass grave.

Time: 8:46 a.m. January 31, 2071

Location: Council of Royal Knights Headquarters. Lunia, Tisaia

The auditorium was warm, so warm that the select group known as the Dark Horses had removed their helmets as they sat waiting for their new assignment. Many of them had heard the rumors already—Project 1200 was being reopened, but most of the Knights didn't believe it could be true. After all, a Knight was not selected and assigned to the Dark Horses by believing rumors or participating in gossip. The Dark Horses were the most honorable and skilled group of Knights in the CRK. They went through years of testing and training to get where they were, and not a single one of them dared jeopardize it in anyway. They knew the drill: sit and wait, listen to the orders, and execute them flawlessly. It was all just part of the job.

In the center of the room a blue hologram shot out of a small opening in the marble table, illuminating the CRK's main auditorium as the lights dimmed in the room. Supreme Royal Knight Morr stood at the side of the table, tapping his helmet, which he had removed to examine the blueprints.

"Listen up, men. We have intelligence indicating the rebels are hiding out somewhere on the western border of Lunia, shortly outside these walls," he said, pointing to several locations on the blueprints. "Jeriche, I need my glasses," Morr shouted impatiently. His assistant rose from the first row and quickly made his way to the center of the auditorium to hand Morr his glasses. "Thanks," he said, briefly acknowledging the short man's presence.

Jeriche walked back to his seat, waiting for Morr to give him another command. For the past four years he served with a staunch resolution, completing every task asked of him. He could only hope his commander would reward him for his unwavering loyalty someday.

Back at the table Morr slipped on his glasses and focused on the blueprints, the blue glow of the holograms illuminating his meticulously kept armor. He stood for several minutes, thumbing through the images, before bringing his fist down on the table in anger.

"Can someone explain why the hell we can't get a current map of these locations?" he screamed. The Knight scanned the dim room, but the Dark Horses stared back at their leader blankly.

"Well! Which one of you is responsible for these blueprints?" he demanded, anger growing in his voice.

Finally, after minutes of silence, an engineer assigned to the squad rose from his seat.

"Sir, with respect, the Sector of Governmental Services is supposed to be surveying all tunnels and storm drains below Tisaia. However, those tunnels aren't mapped because," the engineer paused and glanced nervously at his feet. "Those tunnels were part of Project 1200 and were closed off years ago," he finished nervously.

Morr paused to take his glasses off so his naked eyes could fall on his men with no impediments. He needed to gauge their reactions. It was a part of what made him one of the best: being able to read his soldiers, to see how far he could push them before they would break. It was a skill all great commanders in the history of warfare perfected. And it won wars.

"You know I'm not melodramatic, but men, you're some of

the finest damn soldiers in Tisaia. What I'm about to tell you, I don't do lightheartedly. Project 1200 is being reopened. This comes from the very top. We have two weeks to map these tunnels and flush out the TDU. Augustus believes they're hiding in these tunnels and Governor Felix has signed off on this plan."

The crowd of Knights stared back at him blankly. Not a single one of them flinched. The engineer was the only one squirming in his chair. Just when Morr was about to turn, satisfied his men were up for the challenge, a middle-aged Knight named Riya, who served as an adviser to Commander Augustus, stood. Most of his colleagues knew him for his quick thinking and his ability to negotiate.

"Permission to speak, Supreme Knight Morr," Riya asked.

"What possible input could you bring to this conversation, Knight Riya?"

Morr and Riya had a long past. They both joined the academy and served as cadets in the same class. They quickly became class rivals and it was Riya who obtained the highest rank a cadet could earn before becoming a Knight. Their history had since been a clouded one, where competition and rivalry fueled many of their policy moves.

Riya laughed arrogantly, showing no respect for his superior. "What could I possibly bring to this dialogue?" he asked, chuckling.

"The first thing I could do is tell you the tunnels that were closed off decades ago under Project 1200 are nowhere you want to send your best men. I know because I was there many years ago. The horrors in those tunnels are unspeakable. They would be the last place the TDU would be hiding." Riya said.

"Two weeks to map an area as large as this is an impossible task and will only result in more deaths of SGS employees and Knights. Being an advisor to the Governor, I could certainly ask him to reconsider," he finished.

Morr laughed. "Are you actually that ignorant, to believe the Governor would consider what you have to say on this matter?

Don't you think he would have asked you if he wanted your input?" he said, watching Riya's face turn red with embarrassment.

"Where along the lines did you forget what an order is? This plan is not open for negotiation, and has come from Commander Augustus' office and the Governor. This is the mission—this is your mission. And you will accept it." Morr paused and turned to look at Riya directly.

"You would be best to learn your place as a Knight, Riya. You aren't a politician. You're a soldier. The faster you learn that, the better or you'll face the consequences," Morr concluded, turning back to the hologram.

Riya sat back down in his chair silently, furious at the threat his superior had just thrown at him in front of his fellow Knights. And the fact Morr called him by his name without referring to his rank made him boil inside. One of the first things a Knight learned in the academy was the formal way of conversation. He didn't speak like a stiff robot because he enjoyed it; he did so because he was taught to.

If he was a younger man he would have struck Morr in the jaw, but he was old enough to know his place and what he could get away with. Even Riya knew when enough was enough, and today he had crossed a line he hadn't been fully prepared to cross.

Satisfied, Morr turned back to the rest of his men. "I presume the rest of you don't have any questions. Correct?" he asked, shuffling a few pieces of loose paper and raising a brow before proceeding, to avoid any further disruptions. "Okay then. Your team leaders will brief you in several hours. This mission is a green light. We're heading out, once we gear up and get briefed. That is all, men; you're dismissed. Good luck, and kill me some damn TDU."

"Dark Horses!" the men yelled in unison, standing and filtering out of the room.

Morr watched them leave, keeping an eye on Riya, who flashed him a quick glance. If it were up to him Riya would be pulled from the mission, but he was a Dark Horse and even Morr had to admit they needed him, especially with his experience in the tunnels. Morr put his glasses back on and watched the hologram slim and slip back into its small black home.

He gritted his teeth and thought back to what Riya said, about the horrors in the tunnels. The man was a lot of things, but he wasn't a liar. The tunnels contained unthinkable terrors, and it wasn't just the TDU hiding in the darkness. Deep down, Morr knew Riya was right; many of the Dark Horses would not be making it home from this mission.

Time: 12:30 p.m. January 31, 2071
Location: Council of Royal Knights Headquarters. Lunia, Tisaia

The Council of Royal Knight Headquarters was a monstrosity, reminding Riya of the medieval fortresses he saw in pictures as a child. It was in many ways a model castle; fortified and reinforced with concrete, rebar, and more concrete and rebar. It was, more than anything, a creation of intimidation, with its nine stories of gray concrete walls lined with cannons, machine guns, and rocket launchers. If there was any structure that confirmed the reality of the revolution, this building was it.

The outside of the headquarters was lined with three perimeters of barbed wire fences and stone walls bordered by buried land minds. The only way into the building was through a series of three checkpoints staffed by several Knights. Even the road was blocked off for three miles, to prevent any vehicles from entering the premises with bombs or other explosive devices. The headquarters were impregnable.

Riya quickly made his way through the white courtyard in front of the headquarters. He saluted a marble statue engraved with every fallen Knight's name. The monument was beautiful, with a waterfall running down the names and collecting in a pool below, where civilians and Knights would leave flower petals, notes, and other tributes. Saluting this monument was a tradition that Riya followed since the day he became a Knight.

Riya dropped his salute and continued through the courtyard, nodding at two Knights guarding the front door.

The powerful aroma of bleach immediately entered his nostrils as he walked through the front doors. Not even the air filtration system built into his helmet could remove the smell. It was simply too potent. He didn't mind, though; the glistening stone walls of the lobby were an acceptable trade off.

The interior of the building was not much different than the exterior. It wasn't built for its aesthetically pleasing features. The surface and walls of the lobby were almost completely bare; no art work, fountains or colorful flower designs would be seen here. A single portrait of Commander Augustus was the only item hanging above the oval stone receptionist's desk. The ceiling in the lobby extended nine stories high. At the top, the burning flame symbol of Tisaia was stenciled into the stone.

Riya hustled through the lobby, nodding at another two guards manning the front desk. He had been a Knight since Tisaia's conception, and served her loyally ever since. Well, for the most part, but even he had his limits. His main grievance was the immigration situation, which seemed to be getting progressively worse. There were just too many people who had survived the Biomass Wars living in the Wastelands. He had voiced his opinion carefully on this matter in the past, butting heads with Sonii, the Governor's Chief of Staff. This was more than likely the reason he was not consulted on the reopening of Project 1200.

Riya opened a door at the end of the lobby, slowly making his way down to the gymnasium. He had seen the stockpiles of food and Biomass, and he knew better than any politician there was plenty available to help the immigrants and those outside the walls. Sure, housing would be a problem, but the immigrant camps would be a perfect place to put refugees.

When Riya was first out of the academy, he was assigned to one of the early immigrant camps. It was there his empathy began, and the feelings had only grown over time.

He shook his head. Politics gave him a headache, and had since he was in the academy. At the bottom of the stairwell two more Knights stood guarding the double doors. As he approached they swung the doors open, the bright white glare of the ceiling lights blinding him momentarily.

The gymnasium was the only place large enough for all of the Knights assigned to Project 1200 to meet. At least that's what Commander Augustus and Supreme Knight Morr had decided. Neither of these men was present, having felt their expectations for the mission to be clear. They left the team leads in charge of handing out assignments to the Knights.

Riya removed his helmet and shuffled through the crowd of Knights, fidgeting with his sword so he didn't run into anyone. In the corner of the room he saw Lupa, one of his best friends and closest squad mates. Lupa was also middle aged, with far less hair. His face was lightly bearded and defined by a large nose that had been broken on several occasions. This resulted in much teasing, his fellow Knights claiming Lupa was an immigrant himself.

Riya nudged Lupa in his armored shoulder. "Where do you think they're going to send us?" he said, with a grin.

Lupa shrugged. "Wherever it's, it probably isn't going to be good. Honestly though, I'd rather get assigned to the tunnels. They've always fascinated me."

Riya laughed. "These tunnels are not the fascinating type, my friend. Whatever I tell you will not prepare you for what we see if we're assigned there."

"Knights, please line up by squad," Jeriche yelled over the crowd. "I'll keep this really short. As you already know, Commander Augustus has reopened Project 1200 to be led by the Dark Horses. Most of you will be assigned to the tunnels, while a few teams will be attached to Knight squads protecting the trolley stations. Expect to be deployed in phases during the next twenty-four hours. Your team leaders have your assignments," Jeriche concluded, heading towards the exit. Commotion broke out in the silent gymnasium as Knights searched for their teams.

Riya watched Albri, the commander of his unit, walk through the crowd. Within seconds Albri was standing in front of his men.

"We've been assigned to a tunnel area under the western wall of Tisaia's border. We move out in four hours, so I'd suggest you do a gear check, load up on ammo and catch an hour or so of sleep. Let's get moving guys," Albri said in his typical lighthearted voice.

He had hardly finished giving his orders before he was moving, leading the squad out of the gymnasium. As they made their way into the stairs leading to the surface, Lupa turned to Riya.

"Are the tunnels really that bad?" he asked, scratching his receding hairline.

"Have I ever lied to you?"

"That's what I was afraid you were going to say," Lupa replied.

CHAPTER 6: THE TUNNELS

"Those who dream by day are cognizant of many things which escape those who dream only by night."
~Edgar Allen Poe

Time: Unknown
Location: Unknown

Asoft rain peppered Spurious' leather coat, the drips of water forming small rivers on their paths down the black leather. Spurious wiped the rain off his forehead, brushing his hair out of his eyes. He rested his back against a stone bench beneath the feet of the stone statue of Koliam, the first Knight of Tisaia.

The rain didn't bother him; in fact, he liked the refreshing feeling of it as each drop touched his skin. He looked about the courtyard; admiring the statues of other Knights and the massive stone statue of Governor Lunia, the first Governor of Tisaia and the man after whom the capitol city had been named following his assassination.

The courtyard was truly a royal place, and to many, a holy place. It was only the second time Spurious had seen it. He could still remember the first time like it was yesterday. The memory of the tour guide leading his graduating class through the gardens many years ago remained engrained in his mind. Spurious could still feel the excitement pumping through his veins as he watched a squad of Royal Knights fire a volley of shots in awe. It was a tradition started by Governor Lunia in order to celebrate the

University of Tisaia's graduates. Each year, Spurious could hear the bark of the Knights' rifles from his office.

The rain began to pick up and collect in puddles on the stone courtyard. Lightning illuminated the oblique skeletons of the skyscrapers in the distance. Spurious ignored them, his eyes fixated on a man dressed in a white robe, slugging down the path of carefully cut stones towards him.

Something was not right. Spurious surveyed the rest of the courtyard. It was completely empty. There wasn't even a Royal Knight guarding the sacred place.

Another streak of yellow lightning lit up the garden of stone with a crack of thunder following close behind. The man was slowly creeping towards Spurious, undeterred by the brewing storm. He tried not to move, to remain completely silent, but the chilled night gave him away as his breath steamed into the gray sky.

The stranger continued slugging forward, his head tucked into his collarbones, staring intently at the stone pathway. In seconds, the man would be at his feet, but for some reason Spurious wasn't frightened by the man's presence. In an odd sense he was relieved. The empty courtyard was eerie and he still couldn't remember how he got there.

Spurious brought his fingers to his face, feeling his freezing skin. The night was so cold, clusters of ice were beginning to form on the stone statues. He knew he needed to go home, but he was frozen. His eyes were still fixated on the robed man who stopped in front of him, slowly pulling his face from his chin.

I'm asleep, Spurious finally realized, as another flash of lightning lit up the dark sky and illuminated the face of the old man.

"Paulo," Spurious gasped. "It can't be."

There was no mistaking it; his old friend stood staring at him, eyes wide and his face pale and gray like the sky.

"They're coming for you, Spurious," Paulo said.

"Who's coming for me, Paulo? Who?"

"You'll know soon," Paulo said, turning and walking back

down the same stone path.

"Paulo, wait! Who's coming for me?" Spurious yelled. It was too late, though; Paulo disappeared in the downpour. He looked again at the statue of Governor Lunia and darkness washed over him.

Time: 5:30 a.m. February 3, 2071
Location: Commons Building 21, Apt 14. Lunia, Tisaia

Spurious awoke in a sweat. "Anya, lights," he said urgently. An orange glow immediately washed over the room and Spurious sat up, clawing at his eyes in an attempt to clear the fog.

What the hell was that all about? Why would Paulo tell me that someone was coming for me?

The dream had to be related to his encounter with the Knights at The Ale House. *It's just my mind,* he thought, rubbing his eyes again. The cloud slowly began to clear and he pulled his blanket up to his neck, prompting Anya to change the temperature gauge. He listened to the Biomass-fed furnace flare to life in the utility closet. "Thanks," he said, laying his head back on his pillow. Anya was very observant, rarely overlooking any of his needs. She never slept, her mainframe only idling when he was asleep.

"Spurious, you don't appear well. Why don't you go back to sleep?" Anya suggested.

"I don't need to go back to sleep," he snapped.

"I'm sorry, sir, is there something I can do for you?"

"Yeah, actually, search the databases and see if you can find anything on the TDU members that attacked the trolley stations."

"Sir, this is classified information. I don't have access to it."

Spurious turned over in bed and stared at Anya's hologram. "I want to know who killed Paulo. Just see what you can find."

"Sir, your behavior is irrational. You have no logical reason to seek this information."

Spurious rolled his eyes. "Anya, you are a machine. You don't know what it is like to have friends. Paulo was a good man and I want to know who killed him. There isn't anything irrational about that."

Anya's hologram dimmed and disappeared before reappearing on a stand across from Spurious' bed.

"You are correct. I do not understand human emotion, but I know you have not been yourself and it is my job to take care of you."

"Then search the databases and help me find his killers."

"What do you hope to do with this information if I find it?" she asked.

Spurious paused. "Nothing," he lied. "I just want to know."

"Very well sir. I'll see what my resources uncover," she replied.

Spurious closed his eyes, fatigue washing over him. He wasn't sure if he could trust Anya, but she was the only connection he had to the State's archives.

Her blue hologram disappeared and darkness carpeted the room. Spurious yawned and rolled over. Part of him was afraid to return to sleep. He knew he was in a dark place. His past was haunting him both in sleep and during the day, and it was only a matter of time before it caught up to him.

Time: 11:30 p.m. February 3, 2071
Location: Lunia, Tisaia

By day Agrippa worked as an accountant in SGS Finances, by night he drove a Biomass-run automobile, one of the oldest heaps of trash he had ever seen. In fact, it was so old he could vaguely read the UPS lettering on the brown dashboard. Now the antique belonged to his boss and was property of Cyriaca United, a food transportation company.

Following State law, Cyriaca had registered for and received a permit to carry foods deemed healthy by the State. The majority of the foods he transported were grown in State-run greenhouses. There wasn't much money in this business, but his boss only used the company as a front.

During the day his other driver would deliver foods to State office buildings: cafeterias, markets, and food stands. By night Agrippa would pick up black market food and other fine perishable items and deliver these items to wealthy Tisaian citizens. The job was never dangerous, and the only threat he faced was the possibility of being caught by undercover CRK officers. That, however, was rare, and in the three years Cyriaca had been in business he had never been stopped. Besides, the State knew about operations like Cyriaca's and never intervened. The government needed his business as badly as he needed theirs.

The night began with a routine drop off just south of Lunia, at a gated community called Silver Terrace. It was on the outskirts of the city, where the wealthy built their mansions.

He looked down at the invoice, surprised to see the strict orders; the customers wanted their delivery dropped off outside a large oak tree on the edge of their property. The money would be waiting for Agrippa in their mailbox. It was a weird request, but not uncommon and Agrippa decided to think nothing of it.

He turned the key and the old truck coughed to life, the Biomass flowing through its veins. The beams from the truck's headlights tore through the darkness as he put it into gear and bellowed out of the garage.

"Holy shit!" he yelled. The truck fishtailed on the slick cobblestone streets. The tires spat chunks of freshly planted snow into the frothy air, shotgun-spraying the powder into parked cars. Agrippa grabbed the steering wheel tightly with his gloved hands, scanning the dark road ahead as he regained control of the vehicle. The small white flakes melted on his windshield as his truck crawled down the icy road.

In the distance he could make out the outline of several trees.

Even with the low visibility he could see they were young and still maturing, not the monstrous oak trees he was looking for. Silver Terrace was known for its forest of mature trees, some of the only ones that had survived the Biomass Wars.

He shifted the manual transmission into a higher gear, listening to the engine groan as the truck increased speed. The border of Lunia was only about a mile away. He knew the route by heart and had memorized each twist and bend in the road.

Within seconds, the white beams from his truck illuminated the black fence surrounding Silver Terrace. He took a deep breath, relieved to be off the main arterial road.

He eased his truck up to the edge of the gate and turned off the engine. He swung the brown door open, splintering the ice that had accumulated around the window into a thousand shards. A blast of frosty air took his breath away as he jumped into the snow below, prompting him to pull his stocking cap over his thinning hair. "Damn cold," he muttered aloud.

He braced himself for another gust of wind, but instead a voice rang out in the night. "Freeze, you piece of shit!"

Agrippa turned quickly and met the butt of a rifle with his chest. He fell coughing onto the snowy ground, not daring to look up at his attacker.

"Give me the fucking key," the voice ordered.

Agrippa quickly reached for the truck key deep in his pocket. He raised it into the air without looking up, terror racing through his veins. He knew the best thing to do was not look at his attacker, for if he could identify her, then he would surely be killed.

The attacker grabbed the keys. "Your truck is property of the TDU," she said, kicking Agrippa in the face.

"Stop, please, don't do this!" Agrippa screamed as a waterfall of blood poured from his nose onto the white blanket of snow, turning it a bright red.

"I'm sorry, man." the attacker said, turning to walk away.

Agrippa sucked in the cold air, his hands shaking nervously as they shielded his head. He listened as the crunch of footsteps became faint in the distance, but he still did not dare look up. For a minute he stayed put, kneeling in the wet snow, his toes beginning to freeze. And just when he thought he was safe, he heard the footsteps heading towards him again. He looked up to scream, but didn't get the chance.

A shot rang out in the cold night air, and Agrippa's dead body slumped into the white snow, a trail of blood seeping into the fresh powder. Another gust of wind hit his lifeless body as the attacker fired up the engine of her truck and drove off into the night.

"Why the hell did you have to kill him?" Ran shouted, punching Nordica in the arm.

"The guy could have freaking identified me, you ignorant piece of shit," Nordica roared back, swatting at him with her free hand while gripping the steering wheel.

"You didn't need to kill the guy, and you know it. You just wanted to try out your new gun."

"You're right, Ran; I just wanted to see his brains in the snow."

Ran shot Nordica a stern look, but then turned his attention back to the empty road. They were still several miles from their hidden storm drain location, and the truck was low on juice, the engine groaning like a sick child.

Nordica saw the worry in Ran's face and smiled. "Don't worry, little man. We're going to make it. And just think of the reception we're going to have." Nordica said, cocking her head to look at the cargo bay full of food.

Ran turned to gaze at the food, but quickly peered back at the dark road. Not even a semi trailer full of food would make him feel better. Whenever Nordica killed innocent civilians it made him sick. And tonight, his mind ached in anguish.

The TDU was no place for someone with a weak stomach. There was no room for hesitation when lives were on the line. It wasn't the lifestyle most children grew up fantasizing about.

Ran wasn't a natural soldier. A job as medical technician or aid worker would have fit him better, but as fate would have it he ended up fighting with the rebels. His reputation as a softy wasn't derived just from his empathetic nature either. It was his appearance that really gave him the most grief. He was only a little over five feet tall, so small he didn't fit into standard TDU fatigues. This resulted in a constant barrage of jokes by Nordica and others about his boyish appearance.

Nordica, on the other hand, had the frame of a soldier. She was just over six feet tall with a solid build rivaled only by Ajax. Her most identifying feature, however, was the dreadlocks that ran halfway down her back. The spent bullet shells she rolled into her locks were a bit much if you asked Ran, but he never dared mention them. Besides, on missions Nordica would take them out.

The truck barreled further away from Lunia, Ran watching as the faint lights of the State buildings disappeared in the rearview mirror. It was a lonely feeling, heading away from civilization, into the sprawl of shanty towns and rubble that had never been repaired after the Biomass Wars. The stretch of road between Lunia and Rohania was known by the TDU as the Pirate Highway due to all the robberies in the past. The Knights never patrolled the blacktop, and the State rarely sent work crews out to fix the potholes.

The truck's axles screamed in protest as they ran over a pot hole. Nordica swerved to the right to avoid another one, but over-corrected, causing the truck to slide on the icy surface. "Watch out!" Ran screamed as they fishtailed helplessly towards a concrete barrier.

Nordica slammed on the breaks and down shifted just in time to avoid it, the truck creeping to a stop. "Shit!" she screamed, pounding the steering wheel.

Ran slowly loosened his tight grip on the armrests, his eyes fixated on a collapsed building at the edge of the road. "That was close."

"Too close," Nordica replied, holding down the clutch while turning the key to start the engine again. The machine coughed and groaned in retaliation. "Come on!" Nordica yelled, her fist coming down on the steering wheel again.

After several tries, the engine blared back to life. Nordica backed the truck up and continued on down the blacktop, cautious not to exceed a safe speed. The two soldiers spent the rest of the journey in silence, staring ahead at the dark road.

Time: 1:30 a.m. February 4, 2071
Location: Tunnels. Tisaia

Nordica trained her headlamp on Ran, the light illuminating his distraught eyes. "God, you're such a sucker, man; that guy was no better than a Tin Can. For all we know, he works by day as one of those metal machines."

Ran kept silent, not wanting to relive the same conversation. He realized long ago he would never win an argument with Nordica. He could only hope the food would somehow make up for the man's death.

"We're almost there. Keep sharp," Nordica said, shooting a nervous look back at Ran.

"HQ should be a few tunnels ahead," Ran responded, pulling one of the bags loose from a rock it was caught on.

"Why wouldn't Obi send us any men to help us drag this food to HQ?" Ran asked.

"Now you are questioning Obi? I'm sure he had a good reason for not sending us help. Besides, you need the exercise. Maybe it will help you grow a bit," Nordica said, grinning.

"Very funny. One of these mornings, you're going to wake up bald, you know that?"

"Try it. Just try it. I'll make sure you end up more than bald."

A hint of a smile crawled across Ran's face as they continued in the darkness, but the foul scent of sewage quickly erased it from his mouth.

"There it is," Nordica said, dropping her sack of food and pointing at a small burning candle marking the HQs entrance. "Now be quiet. We don't want to get shot."

Ran dropped the sacks of food carefully on the ground and followed Nordica through the darkness towards the small candle. "Do you remember the password?" Ran asked nervously.

"Of course I remember the damn password," Nordica shouted.

"Shit, woman! Keep your voice low," Ran whispered.

Nordica nodded and approached the wall, reaching out and knocking on it four times before standing back, stepping on Ran's foot. The pain prompted the small soldier to scowl. "Watch it," Ran whispered in protest.

The odd pair stood there waiting patiently for a response. Moments later, the concrete wall creaked and opened. The sweet face of Juliana, a TDU staffer, poked out. "Evening, do you need some help with those bags?" she asked cheerfully, her smile extending from cheek to cheek.

"Hell yeah, beautiful, we could use some help," Nordica responded with a smirk. Juliana rolled her eyes before shooting a quick glance down the tunnels to ensure they hadn't been followed.

Inside, the headquarters was busy with movement. TDU staffers rushed about, some stopping to gawk at the sacks of food the trio were carrying. Others ignored them, their important tasks far outweighing their growling stomachs.

Nordica and Ran headed to the pantry, where Eddia, the main cook, was anxiously awaiting his new shipment of food. He was going to prepare a feast for everyone at HQ. Even the night shift staffers would have a plate waiting for them after their shifts were over.

They turned down a hallway leading to the cellar and were immediately greeted by the overweight cook. The thick man pinched his index finger and thumb together. "Ah, now, this is a something I can work with!" he shouted happily, his large belly jiggling over an aging belt that looked as if it could snap at any minute.

Ran tried to hold back a laugh, but a smile broke across his face as he dropped his sacks on the floor. No one knew where Eddia was from, but his broken English implied he was from somewhere in Eastern Europe. His passion, apparent by his round figure, was food. It was no secret he was the best fed in the TDU, more than likely due to sneaking bites of ingredients while he prepared meals. But it was a fair trade, and most of the men didn't mention it, happy to have decent meals when they were available.

Ran grimaced as the aroma of garlic entered his nostrils, resulting in a deep groan from the pit of his stomach. Hunger was a feeling he had grown accustomed to, much like the other soldiers in the TDU. In fact, most of the rebellion lacked proper nutrition, and some of the lower ranks were on the verge of starvation.

"We got your food, fatty. The biggest load yet," Nordica joked. Eddia glanced at her, frowning.

"I told you, don't call me that!" he yelled, quickly forgetting the insult as he rummaged through the contents of the bags. "You got fresh beef and lamb," he smiled, pulling out two slabs of meat. "And you got onions!" he yelled gleefully, juggling two of them.

Juliana giggled, she had always been entertained by Eddia. Nordica, however wasn't amused, and grunted as she turned to walk out of the pantry. "I'm going to get some shut eye," she said, her voice trailing off up the stairs.

"I suppose I should do the same," Ran said, following his comrade.

"Well," Juliana paused. "Welcome back, and don't forget about the staff meeting at 10 tonight. You two are expected to be there."

"We'll be there," Ran chirped, as he ran to catch up with Nordica.

Time: 5:30 p.m. February 5, 2071
Location: TDU HQ Sick Bay, Tunnels. Tisaia

Obi lay in a white bed, staring at the cold concrete walls around him, trying to shut the images of violence out of his mind. Every time he closed his eyes, he heard the screams of civilians in trolley station 14 and saw the horrified faces as he and his men descended upon the lone Royal Knight. No matter what he did he just couldn't manage to keep his eyes open. He was too exhausted. His last two missions had drained him, physically and emotionally.

Luck had once again been on his side, and for the moment he was beginning to believe he had a streak going. The small caliber bullet wound to his shoulder was the cleanest wound the TDU's doctor had ever seen. Miraculously there was no shrapnel, and the bullet had passed clean through. Once the injury healed he would have full range of motion.

He had survived the unthinkable, but the images of the innocent civilians who had not would be with him the rest of his life. His men had declared the assaults victories, even though the trolley exploded before it hit the CRK headquarters. Obi knew this was just hollow rhetoric, and in reality, the TDU was still losing the war. They would never be able to fight the CRK on an open battlefield; the TDU simply did not have the weapons or the manpower.

And it wasn't the only battle the TDU was losing. Their guerilla warfare tactics were constantly driving potential Tisaian sympathizers away from their cause.

He knew it would be difficult to win over the hearts and minds of the civilians in Tisaia, but even through the bloodshed and killing, many citizens had joined the ranks of the TDU. It was the platform, the principles of the TDU, which attracted a loyal following. Most people in Tisaia thought the State should share the Biomass and help other nations around the world. That was what rallied them to the TDU's cause.

A deep thirst distracted Obi from his reflections, and his eyes began to scan the dark room. They finally stopped on the table by his bed and fixated on a tall glass of water, just out of reach. He licked his dry lips and tried to swallow, but his throat was too parched.

Instead, he rubbed his eyes. The door to the room opened and his nurse entered, holding a tray of food and medicine. Obi had seen her around HQ before, but never actually spoken with her. She was close to his age, perhaps a few years older with graying hair and a striking set of brown eyes.

He almost cringed at the sight of her gaunt frame. She was more than likely suffering from malnutrition like many of the other women making up the ranks of the TDU. It was a bad sign, and he didn't recall her being so emaciated the last time he saw her, which meant food levels were dangerously low.

"Obi, you're not supposed to be up right now," she said, smiling.

"I can't sleep."

"Here," she said, holding out a small cup of pills and the glass of water, "this will help you sleep. Take them all and you should be able to rest within minutes."

"You read my mind," he said, returning her smile and snatching the glass of water from her hands. He gulped it down, before peering back at the cup of medicine. Pills made him nervous. He preferred to heal naturally.

"Well, go on," she said. Her brown eyes were persuasive, and besides, he decided he wasn't in any shape to argue. He gulped down the pills and collapsed back on his thin pillow.

Obi watched her walk over to the door and turn off the lights. "Yell for me if you need anything else," she said, before disappearing into the hallway.

Obi looked around the dark room again, dizziness beginning to set in. He closed his eyes, and surprisingly, the images he couldn't shake earlier were gone. Within minutes, he was asleep.

Time: 10:00 p.m. February 5, 2071
Location: TDU HQ, War Room. Lunia, Tisaia

"In the past 72 hours, Obi and his men have successfully taken out a squad of Scorpions and an entire trolley station within Lunia. I think we all should congratulate Squad 19 on this fine and much needed victory!" Commander Heri shouted. A crowd of TDU staffers were huddled in the small war room. A small wave of clapping quickly followed the words of the commander, but died down faster than it had started.

Obi winced as he sat. He knew morale amongst his comrades was low, but the response made it even clearer. The room was filled with veterans of a war that had been going on for over 10 years. The TDU was created after Tisaia had emerged from the aftermath of the Biomass Wars. Now, ten years later, some of the very same people who created the TDU sat in old broken chairs, listening to a new Commander talk of victory.

The bald commander continued, brushing his shiny scalp with one of his hands. "In the next few months, we'll continue to try and penetrate the CRK's headquarters. If we can destroy it, the Knights will be left in disarray. This will be the perfect opportunity for the Tisaian people to rise against the State," the Commander said, another wave of clapping following suit.

"We're at a crossroads now. The CRK will surely throw everything they have at us. Every Knight will be combing the land above our heads and the tunnels, searching for our headquarters. We must stand united in the face of the enemy. We must fight as if tomorrow is our last day on this earth," the Commander said, raising his hand above the wooden podium and bringing it down in a fist.

Obi looked over at Ran and Nordica, who shared a bench in the front of the room. Ran watched the commander speak, a sense of hope evident in his gaze. Obi had seen this before, especially in new recruits. In fact, he could remember the same hope he felt when he had joined the ranks of the TDU.

But that was a long time ago, under a different commander. Times were much different now, and Obi didn't share the same sense of loyalty to Commander Heri that he had to Commander Leona years ago. Heri was weak. Sure, he could inspire through hollow speeches, but he lacked the bravery Commander Leona had shown in battle after battle.

I can still remember fighting next to Leona in the Battle of Lunia, the fight which forced the TDU underground, he thought, watching Commander Heri continue to spit out meaningless words.

Leona had saved the lives of three TDU soldiers that day. Tragically, she was assassinated by a Knight who infiltrated HQ a few years later. She had been the one and only female leader in TDU ranks that consisted mostly of men.

Obi shook his head, trying to rid himself of memories that made him sick to his stomach. All he cared about now was his men and their missions, not Heri and his hollow promises.

He was done worrying about the commander's hopeless strategies that simply brought the TDU further from their goals. Instead, Obi focused on bringing his men home safe and finding a way to achieve the goal of a better life for those inside and outside of Tisaia. He had always told himself the world wasn't lost yet, and to this day he still believed it.

Commander Heri paused as his assistant Fukia stepped up to the podium and whispered something into his ear. Obi already knew it couldn't be good. Fukia would not interrupt a victory speech unless it was important.

Obi glanced over at his squad, who sat huddled around a wooden table. Creo looked back at him, obviously nervous.

"We have a situation," the Commander began. "Now everyone, please stay calm," he said, beads of sweat forming on his pale face. "We have intelligence reports that the CRK have scouts in our vicinity." The room exploded with chatter, as staffers and soldiers nervously began to fidget in their chairs.

"We have our own scouts monitoring for updates. If it comes down to an evacuation, you all know the drill and the rendezvous point. Your superiors will keep you updated. Until then I think it's best if everyone returns to their posts and prepares for the worst," the Commander said, as he quickly followed Fukia out of the room.

Obi waited behind and watched the area begin to clear. Through the crowd he could see his squad waiting for his orders. All it took was a simple nod, and the three followed the others out of the War Room. For a few moments Obi sat in silence, contemplating this new development, which he prayed was only a false report. Deep down, he knew it wasn't—deep down, he knew the Knights had found them again.

Time: 11:10 p.m. February 5, 2071.
Location: Tunnels, Tisaia

Riya clicked on his night vision, turning the nearly pitch black tunnel into a static green. Lupa, Albri and the other four members of the squad followed suit, their goggles coming to life. At a distance the squad almost looked paranormal, their blue goggles glowing like floating orbs in the darkness.

The tunnel came into focus as the team cautiously made their way down the narrow ledge of concrete. They were careful to avoid the standing water a foot below them, anxious not to draw unwanted attention.

Riya cringed as two rats scampered through his feet, prompting him to momentarily lose his footing. "I hate rats," he muttered, regaining his balance.

"Radio silence," Albri whispered into his mic, raising his right hand to signal the team to stop. After a moment of silence, he motioned his team forward with a short nod. Riya and Lupa continued on, hugging the bank of the tunnel's east side, while the rest of the squad took to the west bank.

Lupa grimaced as he stepped on an old can, the aluminum crumbling under the weight of his armored boot. Albri quickly shot him a glance, his blue goggles glowing in the darkness. They had entered what appeared to be an old camp. Several skeletons lay about the concrete walkway, dried up skin clinging to their bones.

Riya cautiously stepped over the empty cans of food and tattered blankets. The scene was one he recalled from his time in the tunnels straight out of the academy. And he knew it wouldn't be the last one his squad came across. They had entered the tunnels beyond the barrier, the tombs created as a result of Project 1200.

In all of his years combing the tunnels, Riya had only come across one live person. The man was in his seventies and claimed he was not part of the TDU; he had argued extensively he didn't even know who the TDU was, or what year it was, for that matter. Riya wasn't sure what happened to him, but he presumed he traded the darkness of the tunnels for some prison cell deep beneath Lunia.

Riya shook the memory out of his mind and continued on, watching Lupa, who cautiously made his way through the green darkness ahead. They came to another platform marking a break in the tunnels and Riya's heat signature sensor blared to life. His monitor was picking up a small red bleep of life. Albri saw it too, motioning again for the team to stop. He waited several seconds before firing off a quick hand gesture, commanding his squad forward. Lupa and Riya were the first to head out, hugging the concrete walls as they proceeded down the narrow platform.

Suddenly, another two signatures popped up on their displays. They both stopped immediately, using a blur of hand motions to signal contacts. Both Riya and Lupa stayed as close to the wall as possible as they waited for Albri to give them orders.

Silence washed over the tunnel as the squad waited in the darkness. For Riya, it was the stillness that killed him.

He took a deep breath, as Albri gave him and Lupa the green light to engage. Riya looked at his display before proceeding. The heat signals weren't moving. A knot tore into his stomach, his mind trying to tell him what he already knew. The contacts weren't rats. No, rats moved when they were scared. Rebels hid.

Riya nodded at Lupa as he followed him slowly onto the platform. *God, I hope this isn't an ambush,* he thought, raising his assault rifle and training it on the northern tunnel entrance. The sound of his clanking armor echoed in his helmet with every step. His armor was never as loud as he thought it was, and he knew his helmet amplified sounds while his ears further scrutinized his every move.

Riya watched Lupa jump gracefully from the tunnel ledge to the platform. He quickly followed suit, crashing on his armored knees, his rifle still trained on the heat signatures ahead. Within seconds he was back on his feet, making his way closer to the targets. Behind them Albri and company watched nervously.

Lupa stopped suddenly. It was deathly quiet, the tunnel almost completely void of noise, save for a small drip of water from a loose pipe somewhere above them.

Riya took a knee and brought his rifle to his goggles, glassing the tunnel with the crosshairs in his scope before peering back at Lupa. He was still crouched against the wall. His white outline reminded Riya of one of the statues lining the courtyards outside the State office buildings.

And then one of the red heat signatures moved. Without hesitation, both soldiers fired two shots at the mobile targets, the bullets penetrating the thick concrete walls of the tunnel and sending fragments of rock and concrete into the air. A trail of smoke bled out of their barrels as the Knights waited for a response, but once again, silence washed over them.

They dropped their rifles to their sides, signaling to the rest of the team to proceed. The heat signatures must have been rats.

The squad cautiously filtered out of the tunnel, jumping onto the platform one by one to join Riya and Lupa. Albri made his way through the soldiers and stopped in the middle of the concrete platform, taking a knee to examine his tablet.

"According to this map, we're standing on a platform that isn't supposed to exist. The only option is to head north. It will take us deeper into the tunnels," he said, calmly.

"I want Loi and Bria on point now. Ai, you, Riya, and Lupa watch our six."

The Knights nodded and headed for the north storm drain, but before Ai had time to jump off the platform, an explosion ripped through the ground, sending him flying through the air.

"Ambush!" Riya screamed, diving for cover.

An eruption of gunfire filled the dark tunnel, tails of fire spitting out of the Knights' assault rifles. Ahead, Riya could make out two men firing rifles from the north tunnel and another two from the south.

Riya kneeled, firing at the men in the north tunnel first, and turned to finish his clip at the attackers behind him.

In a matter of seconds the room was filled with chunks of rock and smoke as the Knights emptied their weapons into the darkness. The firing from the attackers grew silent.

"Cease fire," Albri said over the com.

Riya's armored chest heaved in and out as he pulled out his spent clip. He cocked his head to make sure Lupa was okay before turning back to the tunnel.

"Report," Albri whispered into his mic.

"Negative on heat signatures," Riya said, desperately trying to hide the fear in his voice.

"Riya, Lupa, check on contacts," Albri responded.

Within seconds the two were running towards the north tunnel while Albri and Loi went to check on the south tunnel. Bria headed towards the area he had last seen Ai.

Arriving at the end of the platform, Lupa and Riya looked down into the tunnel water below. The bodies of two men lay warped in the murky water, a trail of red liquid seeping from their cooling bodies.

"Two casualties," Riya said, over his com.

"Two here as well," Albri responded. "What's Ai's status?" A brief silence followed, and static crackled.

"He's gone; took a rocket right in the side. There isn't much left but twisted armor."

Albri grimaced, pausing before he brought his hand up to his com. "Roger. We'll get a crew down here to retrieve his body. In the meantime, we move on. We have to be close to their HQ. Bria, call in reinforcements and let Supreme Knight Morr know our location."

"Roger," Bria responded.

In seconds the team was moving, reloading their weapons and brushing dust off their armor. There was no time to mourn Ai, and everyone in the squad knew it. They were Dark Horses and had a job to do. Ai would get the proper funeral and respect he deserved when the mission was complete.

Riya led the smaller team into the north tunnel, firing two quick shots into the TDU member's skulls as he walked passed them, ensuring they were dead. He wasn't nervous about attracting any more attention with his rifle; the entire squad knew the TDU would more than likely be aware of their presence by now. The challenge was going to be infiltrating and destroying their HQ before they packed up and moved to another location.

Somewhere in Riya's gut, he felt lucky. Part of it was probably due to the fact he hadn't ended up mangled like Ai, but it wasn't just that. He couldn't deny the tingle of excitement racing through his body. It could have been adrenaline, or it could have been the scent of the elusive TDU. Whatever it was, he was just glad the knot began to loosen as he made his way through the darkness. If Albri was right, then they were close to the TDU's headquarters. Whatever danger lurked in the darkness he was prepared to face it. He wasn't just a Knight; he was a Dark Horse.

CHAPTER 7: A NOTE FROM THE PAST

"Learn from yesterday, love for today, hope for tomorrow. The important thing is not to stop questioning."
~Albert Einstein

Time: 5:00 p.m. February 9, 2071.
Location: Lunia, Tisaia

Aweak sun emerged out of the dreary clouds, attempting to shine down on the cobblestone streets of Lunia below. Spurious admired the melting snow, watching a river of water empty into a storm drain below before looking back at Lana.

"God you're beautiful," Spurious said, gazing into her eyes. Lana shot a shy smile back at him, a tint of blush apparent on her cheeks.

"Thanks. You always make me feel pretty. I've never been with anyone that has been able to do that," she replied.

The two had been seeing each other off and on for weeks now, an hour here and an hour there. For Spurious it helped keep his mind off the death of Paulo, and his conversation with Leo, who he was hoping to avoid. Today Spurious had a special plan. He was taking Lana to his old flat.

"You know, one thing I don't know about you is where you grew up," Spurious began as he guided her by hand through the crowd.

"That's because I don't think I've told you."

"In fact, you haven't told me where your family is from at all, or where they are now," Spurious continued.

Lana stopped and dropped his hand, kicking a rock across the street.

"There are a lot of things I haven't told you because I want to protect you. So far, I have felt comfortable telling you most everything, but there are some things that should just be left unsaid. Look around you, you know where we live."

How stupid, she is an immigrant.

"Don't worry, Lana; you don't have to tell me anything about your family. I haven't told you anything about my family either, but today I'm taking you somewhere very special—I'm taking you to the place I grew up."

Lana turned away. "You grew up in Rohania?" she asked, studying the cracked walls of stone buildings and the citizens who littered the dirty streets. The scene brought back a wave of memories of her own childhood - a childhood she tried to forget. Oblivious to their conversation, the crowd of Rohanian residents continued about their daily routines. Spurious stole a glance at Lana once again. Her olive skin looked dark, even in the dull gray afternoon.

"Shall we go?" he asked. Lana smiled, taking his hand.

"Thank you for taking me here today. I'm excited to learn more about you," she said, softly.

"Trust me; it's worth the journey and the risk."

"There isn't a risk, is there?" Lana asked, biting her lip.

"Does that excite you?"

Lana smiled, revealing her perfectly aligned teeth. "You excite me, Spurious," she said, grabbing his arm and following him through a dense gathering of patrons waiting outside a food stand.

Spurious laughed and continued to pull her along. For some reason he was only slightly nervous. He wasn't quite sure why he wanted to bring Lana to his old flat, but something inspired him. Perhaps it was losing Paulo, or perhaps he simply wanted to share a part of his life with Lana. He had looked for a way to tell Lana his parents helped create the TDU, but was terrified she would not understand. And deep down, he knew he wasn't ready to share this piece of his past with her. The day wore on, and before he knew it, the white stone marking his old building was in front of them.

"This is it," he whispered.

"Where are the windows and the doors?" she asked.

"I'll tell you in a few minutes, come with me," he said, extending his hand to her again.

They darted across the busy street, Spurious pulling Lana towards the narrow alleyway. They entered hesitantly, avoiding heaps of trash and rotting wood. He scanned the street for anyone who might be following them before disappearing into the alley.

The alley was illuminated only by a sliver of sun that began to fade as a cloud passed overhead. Spurious scanned the shadows for the gargoyles that marked the entrance to the ancient building.

"There," he said, under his breath, leading Lana carefully through the narrow passageway. A pair of gargoyle heads emerged out of the shadows. Spurious anxiously dropped her hand and reached for the wooden door.

"Stay where you are. It could be dangerous," he whispered to Lana.

Spurious pushed on the massive frame of the door, but it wouldn't budge. There was something blocking it from within the building.

"Damn," he said, shoving his body against the frame of the door and pushing with all of his strength. The door moved slightly, but not more than a crack. Spurious stopped, wiping beads of sweat off his forehead.

"Be careful, Spurious. There might be nails."

He walked down the alleyway, jumping over piles of wood, looking for something that could pry the door open. As he searched, a ray of sun finally broke through a cloud pattern and illuminated an object under a pile of trash. Spurious bent down, picking up a rusted piece of metal piping.

"This should work," he whispered, inserting the pipe into the small crack. He pried the door back, creating a gap wide enough for them to slip in.

"Let's go," Spurious said, once again taking her hand and cautiously pulling her through the dark gap.

"It's going to be dark in here," Lana speculated, entering the dark building.

"That's okay. I figured as much, so I brought a candle and some matches."

The two stopped and Spurious reached into his knapsack, pulling out a large white candle and a small book of matches.

"Here, light this," he said, handing her the candle.

The tiny flame quickly grew into an impressive orange blaze, illuminating the interior of the building. The inside was just as he remembered it; the walls lined with solid oak, not the cheap stuff that rotted after a solid rain. The first floor hallway was filled with broken lamp shades and pictures hanging loose from their hinges on the walls. On the floor were yellowed newspapers in front of the doors of residents now lost to the past.

A sense of nostalgia washed over Spurious, who stood staring down the ghostly hallway, his face turning pale.

"Are you all right?" Lana asked, noticing his quick change of demeanor.

Spurious shook his head. "I'm fine, I just haven't been here for a long time and it brings back memories. Sorry, I didn't realize it was going to have this effect on me."

Lana squeezed his hand. "Are you sure you want to do this?"

He smiled. "It's okay, really. I want to do this. I need to do this."

The flicker of the candle illuminated the hallway, sending orange light dancing across the walls of the building. At the end of the hall a broken door leading to the stairs hung loosely off its hinges.

"Careful," Spurious warned as they made their way through the open door. He stopped to examine the condition of the steps under the weak light. He didn't want to end up falling through the stairway or breaking his leg on a step.

The stairway looked safe enough, and Spurious held the candle up farther, cautiously climbing the steps, guided by the orange glow. The first step moaned under the weight of his foot, but held. "I think it's safe. Stay close."

Lana nodded and followed Spurious up the flight of stairs. By the time they had made their way to the third floor, his nervousness had mostly subsided.

"We're almost there. Just one more flight of stairs and we'll be there."

"Do you think there will be anything left in your old flat?"

"We're going to find out in a few seconds. Here, hold this," Spurious said, handing the candle down to Lana, who stood a few stairs below.

He reached for the hallway door's handle, twisting it with ease. Spurious swung the door open, swallowing a mouthful of musky air and breaking into a deep cough.

"Are you sure you're okay?"

Spurious stopped in front of the hallway trying to regain his breath and make out the numbers on the doors simultaneously. "Yeah, I'm fine," he finally replied.

"Which one did you live in?" Lana asked, grabbing Spurious by his forearm softly.

"I'll show you, follow me."

The hallway was pitch black, with only the glow of the candle to guide them. The windows at both ends of the hallway had been boarded up and appeared to be spray painted black to prevent any light from coming in. Spurious examined the flat numbers door by door, each time raising his candle to the small black numbers. Some of the numbers had fallen off or were cracked, but Spurious knew he would recognize his old door when he saw it.

Halfway down the hall Spurious stopped, handing the candle back to Lana. *Is this it?* he wondered, rubbing the exterior of the wooden door with his hand.

"I'm home again, Lana!" Spurious exclaimed, nearly bumping the candle out of her hand with excitement. He reached for the handle, opening the door and revealing a dark and musty old room.

"Not exactly the way I remember it," he said, taking a deep breath and entering the flat, with Lana close behind. The floor boards creaked loudly, prompting them both to jump in surprise. The aged wood was smudged with water stains, and thick cobwebs clung to the ceiling like white veins. Spurious continued to scan the room with his candle, but he knew there would probably be no trace of his former life. He kicked a pile of old newspapers and fliers that must have been left behind, nothing that would reveal anything about his parents.

"Well this is it," he said, relieved in a way.

"What do you think happened to all of your old furniture?" she asked.

Spurious shrugged. "Repossessed by the CRK, stolen by stragglers. Who knows?"

The flat was simple, consisting of a living room and kitchen with two small bedrooms and a single bathroom branching off on the west side. Curiously he walked to his old bedroom first, excited to explore his old room.

He stepped over the door lying like a skeleton on the floor. Spurious craned his neck cautiously into the darkness, holding his candle high so the orange glow lit up the walls of the room with warm light.

In the east corner a small mattress lay on the ground. It was torn in the middle, guts of cotton pouring out like a nasty flesh wound. Mold had also found its way into the room and badly stained the mattress.

The west corner revealed a small wooden chest that was harnessed to the wall. He immediately recognized it and rushed over to an ancient box.

"This is where my parents used to keep all of their personal items. They must have thought they were safer in my room, because no one would have looked for them in here."

Lana walked over to Spurious, putting her hand on his shoulder as he leaned down and opened the chest. It was empty, except for a cloud of dust that rose into the air, prompting Spurious and Lana both to cough.

He reached inside the box and felt around. Somewhere in the bottom was a secret compartment where he had seen his mother put coins, keys and other special items. His hand combed the smooth wooden bottom of the crate frantically until he found a small crack. Pulling out his pocket knife, he inserted the blade into the sliver and lifted up a small hatch, revealing a secret compartment.

"Wow, what's that?" Lana asked, startled.

Reaching inside, Spurious felt around. His fingers came to rest on a small object. He froze, looking up at Lana.

"Well, what is it?" she asked.

Spurious slowly pulled out a small piece of paper, yellowed with age.

"What's it say?" she entreated.

Spurious moved to the small bed, placing the candle on the ground. Lana hurried after him and sat cross-legged on the soft mattress. Through the warm glow of the candle light, Spurious read the note aloud.

"December 13, 2050

The Biomass Wars have ended life as I knew it. The countries I loved as a child have all but disappeared. All I can do now is pray for the souls of those caught up in the bloodshed and chaos that knows no boundaries.

My hope is that our son, Spurious, will grow up in a better world. Now that scientists in Tisaia have created a new form of Biomass, it may be possible.

Yet I know our new government is fragile. There has been talk of legislation that will ban all immigrants from our country.

If that isn't frightening enough, Governor Lunia has replaced the Tisaian National Army with a Council of Royal Knights to protect the citizens of Tisaia. But, I wonder, from what? Our walls protect us from the outside, and it has been years since any stragglers have tried to attack us. Why then do we need a massive military force to police our streets and walls? There is no one left to fight against."

Spurious paused to check on Lana who sat quietly, her eyes locked on the note.

"Go on," she said.

"April 1ˢᵗ, 2051

Late last night the legislature passed Bill 99, which deems any immigrant entering Tisaia in the past 10 years as a criminal facing immediate detention and deportation. A group called the Justice Committee has been formed to help track down all of these men, women, and children who will be put into camps until they can officially be deported outside the Tisaian walls.

Many of us, my husband included, have been talking about forming an underground movement to fight against this legislation. Right now we're still in the tentative planning stages, but I know in my heart that something must be done to stop the State from doing this.

As I look at Spurious, I realize that my own life is worth sacrificing if it means his life will be better.

I have to go now; I hope to write again soon. Tonight we're holding a secret meeting, and we're going to call ourselves the Tisaian Democratic Union."

Spurious folded the paper and placed it in his pocket.

"Leo was right."

The words rolled off his tongue and echoed in his mind, repeating over and over.

My parents were the founders of the TDU.

Lana's touch finally brought him back to reality. For a few moments she sat by his side, waiting for him to speak, but when he turned to face her the words would not form. He was lost in the brilliance of her brown eyes—captivated by her exotic beauty.

Finally Lana squeezed his hand. "Spurious, your parents created the TDU!" she exclaimed.

"I know," he said pausing. "I have been told this before."

"Oh," Lana said quickly.

Spurious caught her gaze again. For a moment he studied her seemingly perfect features; her small nose, gleaming brown eyes, perky lips and full eyebrows. She was the most beautiful woman he had ever laid eyes on, something worth protecting and dying for.

"The Council never knew who I was. My parents made sure of it, and far as I know only you and an old man from Rohania knows the truth." Spurious paused, afraid what he was about to say would offend her. "Don't act like you don't have your secrets too, Lana. We all have our secrets, but I want you to know I'm here for you, no matter what your past holds."

Lana scooted over closer to Spurious. "I guess we both have our secrets then, don't we?"

"We do indeed. The only thing is, I don't know about many of yours."

Lana leaned over to kiss him, her eyes syncing with his. "Well that is something we'll have to remedy, isn't it?" she said, her lips meeting his.

The two rested on the bed for another hour, listening to the soft drizzle of rain on the boards outside the window. Spurious massaged Lana's right arm as she lay with her head on his chest, listening to his heartbeat.

"I can't believe my parents were part of the TDU. I just can't believe it," Spurious whispered.

"You probably wouldn't believe me if I told you that I'm an immigrant."

Spurious slowly sat up as Lana pulled away to gauge his

reaction. "Honestly, I'd be lying if I told you I didn't already suspect that, Lana."

She smiled and rested her head back on his lap. "How did you know?"

"A hunch," he said, running his fingers through her hair.

"Well, now you know all of my secrets. It's a good thing I trust you."

"And I suppose it's good I trust you too," he said, settling back down onto the aged mattress, his heart slowing back down to a normal beat.

"You know, for the longest time I'd never have imagined myself here, with you. And now that we're here, I don't want to be anywhere else," he said.

Lana tilted her head so she could kiss his hand. "I want nothing else than to be here with you, but I have to be honest. What if someone finds out? What if the Knights find us? You'd be lying if you told me you weren't worried about the same thing."

Spurious sighed and looked up at the orange radiance of candle light dancing across the ceiling.

"All I want to think about is the here, the now, with you. If we get caught then at least I can say a part of my life was worth living. Besides, my parents risked everything for me. I'm not going to throw it away anymore. I've been wasting my life for too long!" Spurious exclaimed.

He glanced down at his watch. "It's getting late, Lana, we better go. Unless you have some weird fantasy about being interrogated by your AI--I know I don't. She can be pretty mean."

Lana laughed. "You're probably right. I'd like to stay out of prison for a little longer."

The two got up and headed out of the room, turning to take one last glance at the place he had once called home. *This can be our place,* he thought, closing the door and heading into the darkness.

Time: 7:01 p.m. February 10, 2071.
Location: Commons Building #21, Apt 44. Lunia, Tisaia

Spurious sat at the edge of his windowsill, peering at the surrounding buildings. The snow in Tisaia had all but melted, once again revealing the copper and gold dome roofs of the Commons buildings and State offices. With the snow gone, Lunia began to bloom back into the architectural wonder it really was.

He watched State workers walk across the courtyard and thought briefly of Paulo, who would never walk across the terrace again. For a second he remembered his old friend's gleaming smile and wisdom. Things just weren't the same without him. A tear crept down the side of his cheek. He wiped it away and pulled out his journal.

Feb 10th, 2071

I have been seeing Lana for a little over a few weeks now, and I must confess my love grows stronger for her with every passing day. The time has allowed me to realize how fragile both life and love can be. I have known for only a short time that my parents were killed by the CRK, but now one of my best friends has been killed by the TDU. My heart is torn as I have tried desperately to find where my loyalties should lie.

Lana is all that is good in my life now. Ing and I have grown apart, and without Paulo, our friendship has began to dwindle.

The future is so uncertain now, but as I think about the future I'm reminded of a quote I once read. "Dreams come true. Without that possibility, nature would not incite us to have them."

This couldn't be any more relevant as I find myself dreaming of a day I can live with Lana in a free State. My fear is that before long, I'm going to be forced to pick a side.

Spurious closed his journal and another tear dropped from his chin, landing silently on the black leather cover of the book.

Time: 1:00 p.m. February 12, 2071.
Location: Sector of Governmental Services. Lunia, Tisaia

Spurious sat at his desk, staring into Archie's bowl. He tapped on the thick glass, causing Archie to dart towards a small shipwreck replica.

"Sorry little guy," he said, scooting his chair back towards his computer. Today his mind was completely locked. He was unable to focus on anything but Lana, who had finally come back to work. He found it hard to believe she sat less than one hundred feet away and no one knew about them.

A blank blue screen stared back at Spurious as his mind continued to replay the night he had shared with Lana a few days ago.

"Do you have that report?" a voice said, from the doorway of his cubicle. Spurious turned to see Varius standing at the edge of his workstation staring at him through his thick glasses.

"It's just about done. I'm downloading some files that Mica in engineering sent me this morning," he responded calmly.

Spurious stared at Varius, who simply nodded at his response. Never had Spurious once heard the man tell him or any other employee that they were doing their job well.

"I'll check back in a few hours. The CRK wants this document as soon as possible. We're counting on you," Varius said.

Spurious groaned and looked back at his blank blue screen. The truth was he hadn't even begun the project, and the only thing he knew about it was it was classified.

At least this might be interesting, he thought, reaching for the sealed document.

February 11, 2071
Attn: Varius Lupita
Sector of Governmental Service
Architectural and Engineering Affairs

The following project is classified and thus shall only be viewed by a supervisor or a designated employee who has access to drawings/blueprints and specifications of the underground tunnel system under Tisaia.

Project 1200 is being reversed and the Council is looking for any drawings/blueprints from the archives that would map the area outside Project 1200. SGS engineer Edil Leon had previously been in charge of this mission, but has recently been assigned to another role. We're asking for all of his documents to be sent to the Council immediately.

We look to receive these documents in a timely manner.

In Honor,
Supreme Knight Felix Morr

"Holy shit," Spurious said, aloud, dropping the letter onto his desk. He had known Edil personally, and had been told he passed away from cancer.

The lies run deeper and deeper every day.

It took Spurious a few moments to regain his focus before he was able to start searching for Edil's files. Minutes later he had successfully uploaded all of the old files onto his blue screen. He thumbed through the blueprints of the tunnels from Project 1200 slowly, memorizing their twists and turns.

The sound of footsteps distracted him, and he instantly minimized the blue screen with the swipe of his index finger. He cocked his head to make sure no one was watching him before enlarging the blueprints again.

He combed through the drawings before he came across one titled, "Project 1200." The images showed a subterranean web of tunnels buried deep beneath the surface of the city. There had to be hundreds of them.

Some of the tunnels appeared to have been created as storm drains; others were sewer pipes long abandoned, while others were facilities built to protect citizens from the sun years ago. The maze was confusing, even from his viewpoint; he could only imagine what the CRK was dealing with, combing each and every one of them for the TDU headquarters.

Spurious picked up the tiny disc, inserting it into his hard drive with a click. He downloaded the data and before Varius returned to check on him, he had resealed and inserted the package into a tube to be sent by carrier back to the CRK HQ.

The metallic click from a small clock reminded him he had almost worked through his lunch break. He was so immersed in the tunnel blueprints he had forgotten about his favorite time of day. Quickly he turned off his blue screen and headed for the cafeteria, hoping to avoid eye contact with Lana.

Simple things like this never really seemed to work properly for him. He could reassure himself he had the ability to control his behavior, but it never turned out that way. As her cubicle approached, he stole a quick glance inside, his eyes connecting with hers. It was no longer than a heartbeat, but more than adequate for Varius to get a scent of something astray. There was no denying the passion in Spurious' eyes. It would have been apparent to anyone as watchful as Varius.

His heart pounded deep in his chest.

Why do I do that to myself?

It was no use. He failed and although he was quite sure no one noticed, his lack of self control bothered him. If there wasn't so much on the line he wouldn't have cared so much, but this was his life. He could end up in jail, or worse, dead, if the Knights ever found out about his past or Lana.

A growl from the pit of Spurious' stomach reminded him what time it was. At the end of the hall he could see the colossal white-walled cafeteria. The smell of cabbage and porridge filled his nostrils as he entered the mostly vacant room. He headed for the counter, opting for a bowl of warm soup instead of the usual.

The scent of the broth made his stomach growl deeper as he made his way down an aisle full of round tables, avoiding eye contact with other employees.

In the corner of the room he saw Ing sitting by himself. Spurious approached his friend cautiously. He knew he couldn't speak to him about Lana or the TDU again. It was a dreadful feeling, knowing he couldn't completely trust his friend anymore. Times had changed and their friendship had drifted. Yet Spurious knew they would always be friends, no matter what difficulties got in their way.

"Hey, Ing. What ya got there?" Spurious asked, pulling up a chair next to him.

Ing looked over, his blue eyes scanning his friend's face as if he was an imposter. His eyes glared with contempt, something Spurious had never seen in his friend before.

"What's wrong? Why are you looking at me like that?"

Ing looked back down at his sandwich and tossed it aside. "You sure have a short memory. Do you not recall our conversation the other night?"

"Yes, I do, but I don't think this is the proper time or place to relive it," Spurious snapped back.

"Ing, I confided in you, I hope you aren't thinking what I think you're thinking."

"Don't worry, Spurious, you have everything you want now; you don't need to worry about me."

"What do you mean? You're still my best friend..." Spurious paused, "it's just that things are complicated right now."

"Where have you been the past few weekends? Every time I knock on your door, I get Anya's artificial voice. She tells me you're doing a special project at work."

Spurious shrugged, realizing they were going to have this conversation whether he liked it or not.

"Well, that is partly true. I have been assigned to work on a classified project and it's required some overtime," he lied, keeping his eyes fixed on the smooth white surface of the table below.

Ing nodded. "Well, when you actually want to get together again, let me know. By the way, I have an appointment set up with the State to explore finding me a suitable wife," Ing said, studying his friend's face for a reaction.

Spurious couldn't help but smile. "Well, good, maybe they will find someone you're really compatible with."

"You should think about doing the same thing," Ing replied.

Spurious paused to take a sip of his steaming soup. "I'd rather not. I don't want the State deciding who I end up with."

"The program works, Spurious. Do you remember Anita and Furio from accounting? Their marriage was arranged by the State. Timea and Maria from fleet too."

"Good for them. I'm sure they're really happy."

Ing frowned. "So your mind is made up, then. You're going to pursue your other avenue?"

Spurious shot him a quick glance and dropped his spoon in his bowl. He had lost his appetite and decided he would use what little time he had left to go for a walk through the courtyards. He patted Ing on the back and left his distressed friend with a few words of advice. "Don't pick the first one they match you with." Ing laughed nervously and took another bite of his sandwich.

Outside, the courtyard was filled with commotion. At the edge of the stone rotunda, Spurious could see several fully armored Knights, their swords clashing loudly against their thick armor with every move.

Spurious could see a large CRK tank called a Fox Hound, one whose function had changed over the years. During the Biomass Wars the Fox Hound was used against enemy forces to destroy bunkers and reinforced enemy locations with its uranium tipped shells. Now the Fox Hound was used for demolition purposes, and at times was used outside the walls to cave in tunnels thought to be used for illegal immigrants.

The Fox Hound had seen better days. It had been commissioned in the early 21st century. This one had two large dents in its armored plating, more than likely a result of rocket-propelled grenades.

On the top of the tan tank, a Knight dressed in military fatigues manned a megaphone and was addressing a growing crowd of State employees from SGS and the other agencies in the vicinity.

"Citizens of Tisaia! Employees who have given your lives to the betterment of human kind! Today, the Council of Royal Knights and The Governor address you with news we have all been waiting for. Today we tell you the TDU Headquarters have been found, and missions are currently underway to eradicate any surviving TDU members from Tisaia, and from the very dirt of this earth."

The soldier continued repeating the exact same lines, each time receiving a round of applause from the citizens and employees crowding around the archaic tank.

Spurious shuddered. Thoughts of tyranny raced through his mind as the reality of his situation finally made sense to him. For his adult years he complained about the routine nature of his life. He always knew something about his life wasn't right.
And now he knew why. It was at that moment, when the future of the TDU was uncertain, that he finally understood.

Spurious walked away from the growing crowd, disguising his anger with a smile. He shoved his way through his co-workers, beaming with excitement. He finally knew he had a purpose. The only thing to figure out now was what he was going to do to change the future. He could be a part of this change, just like his parents.

He left the courtyard thinking again of what Leo told him just weeks ago. "You have the ability to shape Tisaia's future."

Finally understanding what that meant, Spurious tucked his head into the safety of his collar and headed back to work, avoiding the growing wind.

Another storm is coming.

CHAPTER 8: A DARING ESCAPE

"Desperation is the raw material of drastic change. Only those who can leave behind everything they have ever believed in can hope to escape."
~William S. Burroughs

Time: 2:22 p.m. February 14, 2071.
Location: Tunnels. Tisaia

What had been the TDU's stronghold was now nothing more than a smoking wreck of tangled metal, wires and concrete. A thick layer of smoke trailed through the corridors, mixing with the stench of burned flesh and death. The underground beacon of hope was now a grave of ruined hallways. The mangled bodies of TDU staffers and soldiers lay scattered in the smoldering wreckage, some of them still whimpering and crying out in pain.

It was early afternoon and the clean-up process was well underway. A small army of Royal Knights was combing through documents in the war room, while another team worked on confiscating weapons and defusing booby traps in the armory. In the pantry a pair of Knights moved the broken body of Eddia, whose hand still clung tightly around a kitchen knife, his eyes wide with fear.

The sound of sporadic gunfire broke out in the smoky tunnels as Knights uncovered TDU soldiers who managed to escape the initial onslaught.

Obi and his team had been lucky, escaping through a hidden tunnel used to transport patients to Lunia. To cover their tracks he had ordered his men into a sanitary sewer, where a foot of raw sewage ensured their escape. The Knights would never look for them there.

Commander Heri, however, hadn't been so lucky. He had attempted his escape from within the control room, ordering soldiers to the northern tunnels. The Dark Horses were waiting for him in the darkness, their swords drawn and blue goggles glowing through the smoke.

Obi shuddered, recalling the image of the commander being hacked down by the swords, his blood peppering the concrete walls as he cried out in pain. But it wasn't the way he met his fate that bothered Obi. It was the surprise in the man's eyes. As if he never imagined the Knights would find him.

The bastard was too arrogant to see the damn Tin Cans coming, Obi thought, crawling on his belly through the wretched sewer water. He looked back and saw his squad members battling through the mucky brown sewage behind him, relieved they had all made it out.

Time: 2:42 p.m. February 14, 2071.
Location: TDU HQ War Room, Tunnels. Tisaia.

Commanding Knight Augustus arrived with an entourage of his most trusted Knights, their swords still tipped with the fresh red stain of blood. They stood around what was left of a conference table, snapped in half by a block of concrete.

"Where is Commander Heri?" Augustus shouted. "I want his body brought to me immediately."

The eerie sound of a body being dragged across the concrete filled the room. Augustus turned to watch two Knights pull the limp body of Heri into the office, dumping him at his feet. *So this is my adversary*, Augustus thought, staring at the corpse at his feet.

"We've broken them," Augustus muttered under his breath. He wanted to smile, to laugh even. He had waited for this day for so long and now it was finally here, he was amused.

"This is the man who evaded us for so long?" Augustus asked, laughing. "Take this scum away," he ordered. He watched the cold body of Heri being dragged out of the office.

"Supreme Knight Morr," Augustus said, taking a puff out of a nearly spent cigar. "Can you give me a status? I want to know exactly how many of the terrorists escaped."

"Sir, as far as I know, none of the terrorists have escaped."

The sporadic popping of gunfire in the distance interrupted them, prompting Augustus to shoot Morr an irritated look.

"Do you hear that, Morr?" Augustus asked arrogantly, putting one of his arms around Morr's shoulders.

"That is the sound of gunfire. And unless our men are shooting at rats, I'm assuming there are still some terrorists out there. So I'd suggest you get your men in order and eradicate every living thing that moves!" Augustus screamed, pushing Morr through the office doorway.

"Yes. Yes sir," Morr yelled. He rushed back down the hall towards his men.

Augustus sat in an ancient wooden chair, careful not to scuff his recently buffed armor on the protruding splinters. He propped his legs up on the broken table and stared up at the ceiling, blowing another trail of smoke into the air. An odd sense of disappointment overwhelmed him. He had waited for this day for so long, but now that it was finally here something didn't feel right—something was wrong.

Another shot rang out, echoing off the concrete walls. Augustus took one last drag of his cigar before standing up. It wasn't time to put his feet up yet, there were still TDU to kill.

Time: 3:00 p.m. February 14, 2071.
Location: Tunnels, Tisaia

Obi could see a slight sliver of light in the tunnel far ahead. He took a deep breath, forgetting momentarily of the filth he was crawling through. That mistake cost him his last meal. The stench crawled up his nostrils, prompting him to dry heave into the muck beneath him.

"Are you all right up there?" Creo asked, a hint of concern in his deep voice.

Obi nodded and continued on. "It looks like we're almost there," he said.

"We need to keep moving."

"Where are we headed?" Ajax shouted from behind.

"We need to find a safe house in the city, and regroup with the rest of the survivors at the checkpoint in a few days."

Ajax nodded in approval with the rest of the team, who at the moment were just happy to be alive. The small squad knew the dream of the TDU was still alive, but today they had suffered significant losses. Obi knew it would be hard to replace many of his friends, but there would always be a pool of citizens they could recruit from. As long as the State continued its oppressive policies the TDU would exist. The main obstacles would be finding the weapons and a secure location to rebuild their headquarters.

The team continued to crawl through the narrow tunnel swiftly, the stench of waste infiltrating their nostrils. A faint light was growing and as they got closer they pressed on, anxious to get out of the sewage.

They crawled faster, their weapons scraping against the concrete sides of the tunnel, but quickly they realized the light was nothing more than an anomaly- an energy efficient light bulb managing to survive years of life underground, still yielding a small but bright glow. It had more than likely been changed by some straggler or refugee who had used the tunnel as a shelter long ago.

Two hours later they emerged from the tunnel. Their armor and skin were stained with brown filth and sweat. Nathar dropped to his knees, dry-heaving until nothing but a milky fluid came out.

Creo patted the young man on his back while the rest of the team scraped the waste off their uniforms in the cold winter night.

Obi took a step towards the ledge and glassed the landscape with his binoculars. He could vaguely make out the shape of a storm drain jetting out over a small body of water below, most likely an old sewage treatment plant. He knew they were somewhere outside Rohania, but he wasn't sure exactly where.

He squinted and glassed the horizon again, the skeletons of high rises and office buildings staring back at him. Judging by the broken shapes of the buildings, he assumed they were close to the Boondocks. It was the one place where the majority of buildings were from the old world, artifacts rising into the sky as a reminder of a war not so distant. It was also not the place he wanted to be at the moment. The Boondocks were controlled by gangs; a number of them squatted in the old buildings.

"Here we go," Obi said, turning. "When I give the green light I'm going to remove this gate and we're all jumping into the pool of water below us. I don't care if you don't want to, you're doing it," he said, glaring at Nathar, who was terrified of water.

Nathar scowled, still recovering from throwing up his guts moments earlier. Obi turned his attention to the gate, kicking it twice with his steel toed boots, but the gate was secured tightly to the concrete wall and didn't budge.

"Let me try, boss," Ajax said, maneuvering behind Obi. He let out a grunt and kicked the center of the gate, sending it flying off its hinges and into the water below. A large splash broke the silence of the night, as two large birds took off flying from where they were nesting.

"Nice work. Now, hold my rifle," Obi said, as he jumped into the cold water below without hesitation. His men followed closely behind, taking turns so their weapons didn't get wet.

Silence flooded over the junk yard as Obi sat shaking in the frozen dirt, his eyes scanning his surroundings for potential danger. Within seconds, his three comrades were next to him. Nathar spit a mouthful of water onto the ground. Ajax laughed and swatted him on the back, but Obi shot them a stern look to quiet down. They sat for a few moments before Obi took off limping across the gravel. His two wounds burned from what he knew was the beginning of an infection.

He crashed against the rusted metal of the building, the fragile wall vibrating from the impact. Obi could only imagine what the roof looked like, hoping it even had one. They needed a place to get dry and clean.

He made two hand signals from the edge of the building and Creo and Nathar took off running, Ajax staying behind to offer covering fire.

The front door had been kicked in long ago and lay resting on the concrete ground. The glass cracked under Obi's boots as he surveyed the guts of the building.

Nathar and Creo stood on the outside of the entryway, waiting for their commander's order to enter and secure the building.

Obi hesitated. He wasn't afraid of Knights, but he was nervous that there might be stragglers that could give away their position. He waited a few minutes for Ajax to catch up with them before signaling Nathar and Creo to enter the building.

He clicked on his night vision and continued to scan the junkyard from the outside of the building, making a mental map of the landscape. Two water silos towered above them in the distance, gaping holes visible in their sides. They hadn't held water in their guts for years. The north side was filled with old construction equipment: forklifts, cranes, bull dozers, all machines designed to run off gasoline and now nothing more than useless artifacts from the past.

A large moon illuminated the junkyard below, keeping Obi on edge. Any straggler could be lurking around in the shadows, but silence crept across the landscape. Satisfied, Obi clicked off his night vision and slipped into the darkness of the building.

Time: 11:12 p.m. February 14, 2071.
Location: TDU Headquarters Pantry, Tunnels. Tisaia

Nordica and Ran took turns peeking through a small opening in the fortress of stone where they were hiding. They watched helplessly as Knights gunned down their comrades, who lay dying. With each shot Ran shuddered, holding his ears and fighting back the tears swelling in his eyes.

"Keep quiet," Nordica whispered, smacking Ran with her dreadlocks by accident. "We can't help them now."

"We have to do something."

"We don't have to do anything, because there isn't anything we can do," Nordica responded. "But go ahead and be my guest. See how many Knights you can kill before you end up just like them," she said, pointing towards the carnage beyond the safety of the pantry's walls.

Ran looked down at Juliana and Tsui, who shook their heads at him, agreeing with Nordica. Defeated, Ran sat back on the stone floor stroking his pistol slowly, tears running down his face. Juliana crawled over to him and put her arms around him, embracing him in a hug. "It's going to be ok," she whispered in his ear.

———

"Do we have a body count?" Morr asked.

"Riya confirmed we have fifty bodies," Albri responded.

Morr nodded in approval. "That's about what we anticipated, but fifty strong and able to produce so much chaos? Damn, they were resilient little bastards," he shouted over the commotion.

A clatter of armor echoed down the hall, bringing Morr and Albri to attention. Augustus and his entourage had been surveying the headquarters and were now headed towards the war room.

Morr stood nervously. He knew even with a tentative body count there was no way of providing an accurate estimate of those that managed to escape. His men had made every attempt to salvage documents containing names of TDU members, but most were burned or destroyed before the Knights had a chance to recover them. There was simply no way to know how many escaped.

Albri watched as Augustus approached. The Commander's armor was bone white, reflecting the highest rank a Knight could obtain. He did not wear a helmet or the standard blue goggles other Knights wore. Instead he carried a massive sword and a small machine gun strapped to his right hip. Sometimes Albri thought Augustus cared more about his appearance than his men. Riya came to know Augustus all too well through the years; his vain habits and arrogant behavior rivaled that of Morr's. It was the vanity that threw Riya off the most.

Today Augustus put his appearance before safety by entering the complex without a helmet.

Riya shook his head and prepared himself for any questions Augustus might ask.

"I assume you have an update for me," Augustus said.

"Yes sir, we have a body count of 50 and counting. And I have reports that all skirmishes with the terrorists are over, bodies are being retrieved and counted."

"Well done Morr, I'm happy to say you have done your job well today," Augustus replied, offering Morr his armored hand.

Morr took it quickly and bowed.

Augustus turned to his entourage of Knights. "That is all, men. There is nothing left to do here; the Governor will be anxious for an update."

Knights on clean-up duty watched as their commander left them in the smoke infested room. Riya turned, his eyes falling upon the lifeless body of a nurse who lay in a puddle of her own blood. She stared up at him with piercing brown eyes, still reeling in terror. Quickly he bent down to close her eyelids before any other Knights saw him. In his years of service he had seen a lot of bloodshed, but this was the worst massacre. And his intuition told him this wasn't going to be the last of the TDU.

CHAPTER 9: THE DISAPPEARANCE

"To fear love is to fear life, and those who fear life are already three parts dead."
~Bertrand Russell

Time: 9:11 a.m. February 17, 2071.
Location: SGS Headquarters. Lunia, Tisaia

Spurious leaned back in his chair, the wooden legs groaning in restraint. In one hand he held his morning coffee, and in the other his tablet. He sat there staring at the headline featured on the *Lunia Post*, unable to read any further.

Was it true? Had the TDU been eradicated? Curiosity drew his eyes to the headlines again. He had to know.

TDU Crushed, Headquarters Destroyed and Terrorists Slaughtered

He put the tablet down on his desk in disbelief and took a small sip of his cold coffee.

If this was in fact true, then what Leo told him wasn't. Without the TDU how could he have any hope of making a difference? It was impossible. Leo had lied.

Nothing but a senile old man.

Something inside of him hoped he was wrong. For weeks he had found himself torn in the conflict, especially after Paulo's death, but could the TDU really be completely destroyed?

The morning slowly ticked by, and Spurious counted the

seconds as his wall clock coughed them out. It was mid-morning, and Spurious still hadn't been able to bring himself to do any real work. He had always been good at putting on the facade of doing something that at least looked like work, but today he was failing at even this menial task—today his mind was interfering.

He craned his neck and looked back at the glowing blue screen, pulling up an article he had saved describing the gruesome details of the attack on the TDU headquarters. Commander Augustus and Supreme Knight Morr were being hailed as saviors of Tisaia and a special ceremony was being planned to mark their accomplishments, an event he would not be attending.

Spurious took in a deep breath and got up from his chair, deciding a walk might make him feel better. He headed into the hallway trying not to focus on Lana's cubicle. The last thing he needed right now was to draw attention to their affair.

The tan structure of her office appeared around the corner. He pressed on, and as he was just about to pass the entry to her work station, Lana walked out into the narrow hall, ramming directly into him.

The two fell in a tangled mess on the ground. Varius and two other employees immediately popped their heads out of their cubicles to see the cause of the commotion.

"My apologies," Spurious said.

"No, no, it was my fault, I wasn't looking where I was going," she responded.

Spurious rose from the ground. "You're all right, then?" he asked, lending her his hand.

"Yeah, are you?" she responded, brushing off her black dress.

Spurious nodded, shooting a nervous glance over to Varius, who watched quizzically.

"I better be on my way," Spurious said, looking at Lana one last time. She nodded and walked back into her cubicle.

Spurious turned and continued down the hall, his pace much faster than normal. He could feel the acid turning in his empty stomach. He was no longer paranoid Varius would find out about him and Lana. Unless Varius was a fool, he already knew.

Time: 6:45 a.m. February 18, 2071.
Location: Commons Building, Lunia, Tisaia

Spurious awoke to crackling from his archaic metal radio, another artifact from the old world he bought at his favorite thrift store, *The Magician*.

"Good morning Tisaian workers. It's windy outside today with a hint of radiation," the announcer said. "Today you can expect temperatures ranging from a low of 30 degrees and a high of 55 degrees. The wind will be at 15 mph out of the east. Climatologists estimate a small presence of radioactive particles in the Rohania area. RRAD vehicles have already been deployed to mitigate this threat."

He rolled over and rubbed the sleep out of his eyes. Morning was always a difficult time. Even when the blare of the alarm pounded in his ears, shaking sleep was difficult, especially when he only had his cubicle to look forward to. The dark mornings of winter weren't exactly helping either.

To make things worse, the sky had become considerably grayer and the clouds more dense. State climatologists attributed it to lingering radiation in the atmosphere. That's where the RRAD vehicles came in. Short for Radiation Removal Atmospheric Device, the machines were designed specifically to safely remove radiation from the air, water and soil in Tisaia. After the nuclear fallout settled from the Biomass Wars, there was a consistent level of smog, dust and smoke lining the atmosphere. For years the sun was blocked, killing any crops that had survived and lowering temperatures worldwide. RRAD was the miracle that not only cleaned the radiation poison from Tisaia's soil but also the sky above. Without RRAD Biomass would never have been possible.

Spurious pulled the curtain back from his window, revealing the dark courtyard below. Somewhere in the distance he could see a hint of light. It wasn't clear whether it was artificial or solar, but as it infiltrated his apartment he could tell it wasn't going to be enough to get ready for the day. He let the curtain go and headed for the bathroom.

"Lights, Anya."

An immediate orange glow illuminated his apartment. He slugged across the small space and entered the rain room where he sat and huddled on the marble ground, soaking in the warm water and breathing in the steam. He ran his fingers through his wet hair and rubbed the soap out of his burning eyes.

His mind filtered over the previous day's events—his muscles were tense and his head pounded from the lack of sleep. He pulled his knees up to his stomach and dug his head into his chest, letting the warm water wash over him.

"Anya, did I miss any news yesterday?" he shouted over the noise of the shower.

"Yes, let me retrieve the data," she responded. Spurious cracked a half smile. He had half expected her to respond by saying the CRK had contacted her, but instead she started rambling off information he had already read in the *Lunia Post*.

Satisfied, he pulled himself from the warmth of the shower, dried off and headed to his closet. He yawned, desperately wishing he could go back to bed. Sleep seemed more and more like the perfect remedy to clear his mind, but he had no choice but to go back to work.

As he slipped into his coat he remembered he did have an incentive to get his day started after all. Tonight he was going back to Rohania—tonight he was going to tell Lana he loved her.

Time: 10:02 p.m. February 18, 2071.
Location: Commons Building 21, Apt #44. Lunia, Tisaia

A holographic image of Anya appeared on the stand next to the front door. "Where are you heading this late, sir?" she asked, her hands on her hips.

Spurious' heart stopped in his chest. He swallowed and pulled a black hooded sweatshirt over his head. "I'm heading back to work to finish up mapping the tunnels under a section of Rohania," he said quickly.

"Sir, my system sensors show your eyes are dilated. This indicates you are not being truthful," she said without hesitation.

He paused, thinking desperately for a new excuse. "Anya, you know I haven't been sleeping much lately. I'm just tired, and I really don't want to go back to work."

Silence filled the room before Anya responded. "My memory shows you have been averaging approximately five hours of sleep per night. This is far less than your normal amount and not enough for you to function properly."

"Trust me Anya, I know."

"Very well sir. You can get caught up on sleep tomorrow night. I expect you will be home promptly after work."

"Yes, promptly," he responded, closing his flat door behind him, swiftly locking it with one twist of his metal key.

He paused in the hallway, letting his heart rate return to normal. His luck was running out. It was only a matter of time before Anya found out the truth.

Spurious sucked in a deep breath and went over his routine. It was pretty simple after he left the apartment. He always checked the hallway through his peephole to make sure no one was coming, and after making his way through the commons, he would head to Trolley Station #15. The train would take him straight to the last stop on the border of Lunia and Rohania. From there, he would take the same storm drain and sneak through the streets until he arrived at his old flat.

Tonight the station was unusually busy. Several patrons were waiting for the train that wasn't due for ten minutes. Spurious was surprised that the fear of another attack hadn't deterred employees and citizens from riding the trolleys. But then again, it hadn't deterred him either.

He plopped down on a bench far from the view of several Knights patrolling the station and scanned the other passengers to make sure he didn't know anyone.

Satisfied no one was eyeing him suspiciously, he surveyed the rest of the station, admiring the large rectangular lights that warmed the otherwise cold and dark platform. According to a report he had picked up, it took more Biomass to light the trolley stations in a given day than it did to light the entire SGS building in a year.

Spurious sat listening to the crackling of bugs being zapped by the hot lights as he waited for the train to arrive, clenching his teeth each time a bug met a fiery fate. Most people around him didn't seem to notice.

A bright beam ripped through the darkness, the shriek of the brakes pulling Spurious from his trance. The doors creaked slowly and opened, several patrons descending from the train. He glanced at the two Knights, who continued to patrol the station before he boarded, reassured he had not drawn their attention.

The doors closed and the engine sparked back to life, moaning as it gained energy. Spurious continued to watch the Knights through the window. The blue glow of their goggles grew faint as the train raced away from the station. He continued to watch nervously even after they disappeared from view. There was something about their robotic appearance that terrified him.

He finally turned and watched the darkness consume the tunnel, his hands folded tightly in his lap to prevent them from shaking. Two of the passengers who had sat next to him had gotten up and moved, while two others across the aisle continued to read their tablets.

Spurious got up from his seat and walked down the aisle, bracing himself on the seats in front of him. He wanted to get away from these people. The only person he wanted to see was Lana.

The train finally slowed and crawled to a stop and he anxiously jumped out of the car and headed for the stairs.

———

The cobblestone streets of the East Square in Rohania were empty, save for a homeless man sleeping on a cold park bench. Spurious clung to the shadows, guided only by the sporadic light of street poles that were still in working order.

It was going on one month since he first started seeing Lana, but he knew their affair couldn't go on forever. So far they hadn't attracted the attention of anyone besides Ing and potentially Anya. He had been overly cautious, but knew it was only a matter of time before they were caught. The truth sent a chill down his spine. He couldn't lie to himself anymore. He knew his time with Lana was limited.

The bright moon paved a trail of white light through the dark streets of Rohania. The streets continued to be mostly bare, save for a few drunken citizens stumbling home. Spurious was pretty much alone on this eve, which was the way he liked it. The less people to worry about, the faster he could make his way safely to his destination.

Before he knew it he was only a block away. He ducked into the back alleyway that lined the brick skin of the abandoned structure.

The door to his old apartment building was closed. He slid in checking his watch. It was just before midnight and he was a few minutes early.

He entered the apartment cautiously, lighting a match to shed light on the old room. Quickly he made his way to his old bedroom and lit several candles he had left on the floor. Making his way to the mattress, he organized the pillows and blankets they had bought from a vendor several weeks back. He wanted to make sure it was suitable for Lana when she arrived. His wrist watch chirped as the small hand hit midnight. *Where is she*, he wondered, starting to worry. After 20 minutes his concern grew.

An hour later Spurious began to doze off on the old, but comfortable, mattress. He awoke in a daze shortly after, realizing Lana was still not there.

Something must have gone wrong. I should have come with her.

Images of Lana being taken by the Knights or worse, raped by Varius, began to play out in his anxious mind. A knot formed in his stomach and a wave of nausea passed over him. The world began to spin; reminding him of all the times he had laid in his bed in the orphanage, wondering why he would never see his parents again.

"Damn it!" he yelled, kicking one of the candles across the room. He watched the wax spread across the wooden floor, contemplating his next move. It was late, but he knew he had to look for her. He couldn't sit and wait any longer. If she was out there he was going to find her. He blew out the remaining candles, leaving the mess and racing out the door.

———

A loud grumble from a vehicle vibrated through the cobblestone streets. Spurious immediately recognized the sound. As he rounded a corner he could see the outline of a massive RRAD truck. The blue glow from the unmanned cockpit appeared ghostly in the darkness. It was the same blue the Knight's goggles emitted. For a second he forgot about Lana and watched the machine slowly creep down the road on massive caterpillar tracks. Chemicals shot out of the two rotary fans attached to the roof of the truck, filtering radiation out of the air. Another pair of fans swept the streets below the tracks, cleaning the poison from the ground and healing the earth one street at a time.

Spurious pulled himself from the sight of the extraordinary machinery and continued down an alleyway, combing the darkness for any sign of Lana. He peeked inside pubs, and eateries, but to no avail. For hours he followed the glow from the street lights before they flickered and turned off, indicating morning was rapidly approaching. His heart sank as he headed back to Lunia.

She must have been caught. There wasn't any other explanation. Spurious wasn't sure which was worse; Lana changing her mind about him or the Justice Knights arresting him and taking him to prison. Either way, his life would be over, but at least he would have something to live for if the situation was the latter of the two. Deep down, somewhere beneath the misery boiling inside his guts, he knew he would see Lana again. He had to believe it, and repeated it over and over in his mind as he made his way back to Lunia.

His eyes finally spotted the copper roofs of the Commons building, and he slipped into his building without being noticed.

The sound of Anya's familiar voice greeted him as he entered his apartment. "Did you complete your project sir? Would you like me to prepare the rain room?"

Spurious was too fatigued to decipher her words. Was she toying with him? Did she know? There was no way to tell. She didn't have human emotions—she didn't frown, sigh or sweat. Her tone never deviated.

Spurious took in a deep breath and trudged through his apartment, leaving his muddy shoes on the rug before flopping down on his mattress. "Yes, the project is now complete. Don't bother. I think I'd rather go straight to bed."

But sleep didn't come. Spurious couldn't stop thinking of Lana, and his eyes wouldn't obey. Every time he closed them images of her emerged. The terror deep in his gut began to increase as the horrid images continued. He had lost her, just like he lost his parents.

CHAPTER 10: THE SILO

"Only our individual faith in freedom can keep us free. "
~Dwight D. Eisenhower

Time: 6:00 a.m. February 21, 2071.
Location: Junkyard. Rohania, Tisaia

Lightning tore through a thick layer of smog lingering above Rohania. A series of thunder claps shook the roof of Squad 19's shelter. They watched as the brilliant flashes of electricity ripped through the clouds, a mirage of colors flowing like waves across the poisoned skyline.

Obi should have remained inside with his men but he wanted to watch the lighting in solitude while he contemplated their next move. He wasn't sure if anyone else had survived the attack. And there was no way to know if any survivors would actually head to the pre-arranged rendezvous point, assuming the CRK didn't already know about it.

Another flash of electricity slashed across the sky, the yellow glow so intense it remained frozen in Obi's vision for several moments. The glare slowly faded and disappeared as he walked back inside.

The soldiers sat huddled around a small fire, warming their hands in silence. Obi was worried. And he didn't like to worry, but he had never seen his squad so distraught. He knew how important morale was in a military unit, especially after a battle.

"Listen up," Obi said, limping over to them. "I'm going to leave this one up to you. We got out safe, and we're all together now. I figure we have three options ahead of us."

The soldiers stared up at their commander, ready to fulfill any request he would ask of them.

"Option one is head to the rendezvous position now. I'm sure you're all aware this could be a trap and the CRK could be waiting for us."

Ajax's lips quivered as if he wanted to respond, but he remained silent.

"Option two is head to Rohania and find a safe house, recruit some new TDU members, and meet up at the rendezvous point. If the Knights are waiting for us, we would have a fighting chance with more men. And that brings me to option three." Obi paused again. "You have all fought valiantly with me for years now. And I won't be ashamed or judge any of you if you want out. This is your pass out of the TDU. If you want to disappear into Rohania, you won't be considered a deserter."

None of his men said a word until he had finished. Creo was the first to rise, resting his rifle against a chair.

"There's really just one option. I joined the TDU because I believed we could restore equality in Tisaia. I believed immigrants have a right to the same benefits as those born within the Tisaian walls. Even more importantly, I joined the TDU because I believe Biomass is a human right and should be shared with other countries. I don't want to give up now. I'm still willing to give my life for this cause." Creo sat back down, tears swelling in his eyes.

"We lost so many brothers and sisters, and killed so many innocents over the years, but we must continue to fight. We must head to the checkpoint and pray there are others waiting for us. If they are not, and instead the CRK is waiting with their guns, then at least we'll all die honorable deaths," he said, grabbing his rifle and raising it into the air.

Ajax put an arm around Creo's shoulder. "He is right; we don't have any other choice. Life in Rohania is a worst fate to me than dying in battle. I'd rather take my chances at the rendezvous point than give up now."

"And you Nathar, what do you think?" Obi asked.

"You know I'm in this to the end, brother," he said, laughing.

Obi smiled. "Then I believe we have some work to do." He coughed and sat down on an old folding chair.

"Here is what I have in mind. I have a contact in Rohania. He knows TDU sympathizers in Lunia, many of which work for the State. Ajax and I will meet with him and see if he can put us in contact with someone who has access to the tunnels leading to the CRK headquarters. This was always my plan, but Commander Heri never bought it. He said it was too risky. Maybe he was right, but we don't have any other choice now."

"What about us?" Nathar asked.

"I want you and Creo to travel to the Boondocks and recruit several more TDU members. We'll meet back here in 48 hours before heading to the rendezvous point. Any questions?"

The three soldiers shook their heads simultaneously.

"Let's move out. Be careful, men," Obi said, grabbing his rifle and following Ajax out into the muddy junkyard. He froze as a crack of lightning broke through the silence of the night like a gunshot, and he was reminded of the fragility of their cause. Squad 19 fighting against an entire army wasn't the type of odds Obi would ever gamble on, but his squad hadn't survived this long just by getting lucky.

Obi jogged to catch up to Ajax, cracking a smirk. If anyone could take down the CRK, it was Squad 19.

Time: 11:00 p.m. February 21, 2071.

Location: TDU Headquarters Pantry, Tunnels. Tisaia

The view from the hideaway was much clearer than days before, when a smoky haze still lingered in the ruined headquarters. Ran crouched in the corner of the small room, his eyes glued to the small hole he had used to watch the slaughter. The Knights appeared to be gone, but the destruction and stench of death remained.

Ran turned away from the hole and crawled back over to Nordica, who was sleeping. He grabbed a piece of stale bread out of his knapsack and stuffed it down his dry gullet, chewing as fast as possible to get the disgusting nourishment down.

"When can we get out of here?" Juliana asked, her back against the concrete wall.

"Technically, Nordica is in charge now," Tsui whispered.

The three soldiers looked down at Nordica as she slept, her chest heaving slowly up and down. They all knew her as one of the most barbaric soldiers in the TDU. She killed for fun. Some of the soldiers dealt in credits and cash, but Nordica dealt in calibers. Her currency wasn't in paper notes or credits, it was in lead. Some of the other soldiers dreamt of a time where they could have a savings account again, a time they could rent an apartment and go to the grocery store. Nordica did not.

Ran often wondered what would happen if the TDU won the revolution. Would Nordica be able to assimilate into society? Sometimes it seemed Nordica liked the life of a rebel too much and didn't want to win the war, kind of like a prisoner who had been behind bars for so long they were terrified of rejoining society.

Nordica stirred and woke.

"What the hell are you guys looking at?" she asked, rubbing the sleep from her eyes.

Tsui brought a finger to his lips. "We're deliberating. What are your orders?" he asked bluntly.

Nordica sat up and brushed a few dreadlocks out of her face. "If Ran is convinced the Knights are gone, then we head to the rendezvous point."

Juliana and Ran nodded in agreement, but Tsui remained silent until Nordica was finished.

"How do we even know there will be a checkpoint?" he asked.

"Because there will be one, and you're an asshole for asking that," she grumbled.

Ran and Juliana looked at one another, their eyes gleaming with fear. They both shared Tsui's concerns, but were too afraid to voice the obvious.

Nordica stood up, pulling her locks back into a tail. "When is the last time you heard any movement, Ran?"

"It's been 12 hours since I saw the last guard. And the cleanup crews left around 24 hours ago. It looks clear to me."

"We need to get to the rendezvous point. Let's find some weapons, grab some supplies and get moving," she said, ordering the three TDU soldiers out of the room.

With the help of Ran and Tsui, Nordica was able to move the massive pantry shelves. Together the four soldiers entered the pantry, where the stale air reeked of rotting food and death.

"See if you guys can salvage anything," Ran said, as he followed Nordica up the stairs and back into the complex. They were headed for the armory, knowing the chances the CRK overlooked anything or left any weapons behind were remote. Nonetheless it was worth a try, and any weapon was better than the two small pistols Ran and Nordica held at ready.

The two walked cautiously down the hall, covering each other with their weapons through each pass. The challenge was to avoid stepping on fallen glass or tripping on anything that might alert anyone to their presence.

As they covered more ground inside the complex, Ran recalled one of the many times he and Nordica robbed food trucks in Rohania. It had been years ago, but this specific time was still fresh inside his mind.

The driver radioed in for help and moments later a single Knight responded, assault rifle blazing as soon as he spotted the two TDU thieves. Ran and Nordica had been armed only with their pistols.

Ran immediately dove for cover behind a couple of trash cans, while Nordica stood her ground and fired her 9mm at the Knight, the rounds bouncing off his armor harmlessly.

What happened next was something Ran would never forget. One of Nordica's rounds hit the Knight's right goggle, the blue glass exploding in a spray of blood, glass and metal. The Knight's lifeless body slumped to the ground.

Her heroism gave them just enough time to escape back to the tunnel, along with two sacks of food and a pack full of grenades that Ran took off the dead Knight. It wasn't the first time she had saved his life, and he knew it probably wouldn't be the last.

"You need to keep up," Nordica whispered from behind a concrete pillar a few feet ahead.

"Sorry," Ran whispered back, his attention returning to his task.

He squinted, vaguely making out the entrance to the armory. Several downed electrical wires shot out sporadic bursts of electricity, faintly lighting the hallway. There was still no sign of the CRK.

The two soldiers simultaneously ran into the smoking ruins of the armory, their guns drawn. Their eyes fell on a smoldering heap of twisted weapons.

"Damn, that must've been what we heard." Nordica said, kicking a ruined rifle across the concrete floor.

"The CRK decided to destroy the weapons instead of hauling them out of the tunnels," Ran replied, gazing upon the smoldering concrete room, pieces of rifles and burnt shell cases littered across the ground.

"Come on, let's see if we can salvage anything," Nordica said.

Ran ducked under the loose electrical wires and began combing the room for anything they could use. He watched Nordica pick up pieces of a table and door, quietly tossing them to the side. Digging through a pile of concrete, Nordica found a charred shotgun. She quickly examined it and, satisfied she tossed the strap over her shoulder and continued with the search.

In the east corner of the room Ran uncovered a submachine gun, burned severely but appearing to still be intact. He peered down the sights and released the safety.

"I think I found something worth saving," he shouted over his shoulder.

"Me too," Nordica responded. She pulled another shotgun from the blackened pile of weapons below her.

By the time their search was over they had salvaged three shotguns and four cartons of ammunition. They also found three 9mms and two assault rifles, in addition to the small machine gun Ran tucked away in the back of his belt.

Balancing all of her newly found weapons in her arms, Nordica followed Ran towards the exit of the room. "Let's head back to pantry and see what Juliana and Tsui were able to recover," Nordica ordered.

A small glimmer of hope crept into Ran's thoughts as they made their way back. He knew how many times he "hoped" in the past, only to be disappointed. Most of his comrades and friends were dead. He wondered if Squad 19 was still out there. They were the most important unit in the TDU. Without them, the TDU would surely be lost.

Time: 2:05 a.m. February 22, 2071.
Location: Tunnels, Tisaia

Nordica sat perched on the concrete surface of a tunnel platform. The night vision goggles she took off a dead TDU member emitted a warm orange glow into the darkness. They were heading south through a tunnel once used to transport supplies to and from Rohania.

"We better get going," Juliana said, throwing her backpack around her shoulders and grabbing her rifle. "We have a lot of ground to cover and we don't know if there are still Knights patrolling these tunnels."

Nordica chuckled. "I think the CRK did a hit and run, and thought we were all dead. I'm guessing they're back in Lunia, celebrating with ale and prostitutes."

Ran laughed nervously. He hoped what Nordica said was true, but at every corner they rounded he expected to see a squad of Knights, waiting to cut them down.

So far, Ran knew they had been lucky, but there was the remote possibility the Knights weren't heading back to Lunia victorious, and that they were waiting in the shadows.

Victory was a sobering thought, one he secretly wished he could feel someday, but he knew the chances were unlikely, especially now, when hope seemed all but lost.

Nordica led the small group of survivors through the tunnels for hours, stopping only to piss and eat a few bites of food. They were exhausted but pressed on, knowing they were already days late to the rendezvous.

"Are we almost there?" Ran asked.

Nordica looked back at him, bringing her finger to her lips and signaling for Ran to climb up onto the concrete banks of the tunnel. Ran nodded in confirmation, climbing out of the murky water. Nordica was right; the water made too much noise, and Ran needed to focus on his surroundings. They were still not free of danger.

The tunnels were getting narrower, which indicated they were almost to the edge of Lunia. Once they were outside the walls they would climb above ground into the Wastelands, making the rest of the journey considerably more dangerous. The missile silo was almost 30 miles outside the Tisaian walls. This presented a problem in and of itself. If they did evade the Knights they would still be faced with other potential threats in the Wastelands: wild animals, stragglers, land mines and bands of raiders.

Ran had never seen a raider, but had heard plenty of stories to know they could be just as lethal as Knights. The raiders fought like animals, tearing their enemies to pieces and wearing their bones as trophies. The notion made him shudder. He would almost prefer to face a Knight over one of the barbaric raiders.

Nordica, on the other hand, would never forget her run in with raiders. It was years ago, on a scavenging mission. She was headed towards an abandoned building said to house a cache of 21ˢᵗ century weapons when she heard them.

At first she thought it was an earthquake as the ground began to rumble. But as a cloud of dust emerged in the distance, she realized it was no earthquake. It wasn't long before she could see an armada of riders, their skin tattooed and scarred. They were led by a man riding a dark stallion, his bald head and pierced ears gleaming under the weak sun.

As they rode closer Nordica could see something on the man's shoulders. The dust made it difficult for Nordica's goggles to function properly, so she removed them and took out a pair of binoculars. It was then she could clearly see the skulls mounted on the man's shoulders. These weren't just any skulls either; they were human.

Since that day Nordica avoided the raiders of the Wastelands at all costs. She was known for fearing no one, but even Ran knew Nordica feared these barbaric men.

Ran set his rifle down and looked upward. He could see a small ray of light peeking through a manhole far above. "Guys, I think I found our way out."

Nordica crowded him, gently pushing him away. "That must be it!" she shouted, neglecting her own orders to keep quiet.

"Careful everyone," Juliana said, emerging from behind. "We don't know what or who is out there right now. Someone should climb up and have a look before we all charge up."

"She's right," Ran said. "I'll do it," he volunteered, approaching the ladder. He looked back at Nordica, who gave him a nod of approval.

"I'll be right back," he said, turning, strapping his shotgun across his back and grabbing the rusted steps of the ladder. Rays of light struck his eyes as he climbed, blinding him momentarily. Having lived in the tunnels for so long meant that his eyes took a few moments to adjust to natural light, especially from the sun.

"What's going on up there?" Nordica shouted from below, her voice echoing through the silent tunnel.

"I just couldn't see, don't worry, everything's fine," Ran yelled back as he began to climb again.

The small holes in the drain cover revealed they were in the Wastelands. The viewpoint was not good at all, though, so he pushed the drain cover up a few inches and surveyed the grayness.

To the east were the steel walls of Tisaia, towering above the Wastelands like a fruit tree over the desert. To the west was death—the skeletons of trees and remnants of what was once beautiful green farm fields. Ran had seen pictures of what the area used to look like. It was now unrecognizable. Satisfied that there wasn't any threat, he descended the ladder to rejoin his team.

"It looks clear to me."

Nordica grabbed her shotgun and pulled a shell from her bag. "Although I'd prefer to do this under the cover of darkness, I think we need to move immediately," she said, turning to Tsui. "What do you think? It's possible they could have guards on the walls within range to spot us."

Tsui nodded his head in agreement. "I think we need to get moving too. We can't wait another 24 hours. If there are guards up there, they would spot us at night with their goggles anyways."

Nordica put the shell into her shotgun and pumped it. "Let's move, guys, the survivors aren't going to wait for us much longer," she said, heading towards the ladder.

The storm drain was slightly less than a mile from an old highway, another token of good luck, with plenty of old vehicles to use for cover. Nordica led the four TDU soldiers through the maze of broken-down cars. The wind beat down on them without mercy, burning any uncovered skin. Ran looked down at his bare arms and noticed there were blisters forming. He tried to roll his sleeves down, but they wouldn't go much further than his elbow.

"We need to find cover!" he shouted.

Nordica knelt in front of an old truck, glancing at her watch.

"Gather round. Let's take five. Tsui, you keep watch on our six."

Juliana stopped and reached inside her bag, retrieving a small white bottle.

"Here, use some of this on your arms. They look like they're starting to burn," she said, handing him the bottle.

"Thanks," Ran responded, taking a knee next to Nordica.

"The way I figure it, we have about five miles left before we reach the silo," Nordica said, in between drinks from her canteen. She coughed and wiped the excess water from her lips.

The group sat, eating what bits of food they had brought with them, listening to the howling wind. For a few moments Ran felt as if everything was going to be fine. He forgot the massacre from a week earlier and watched a pair of clouds crash into one another, further blocking out the weak sun.

Ran felt an itch, and clawed at his face to feel another sore forming on his forehead. He took a moment to rub some of the lotion Juliana gave him on the spot. The wind wasn't the only enemy in the Wastelands. There were also radiation pockets that could burn you as fast as the wind could. It was possible they had passed through one already and the sores on his body were radiation poisoning.

"Let's move out," Nordica commanded.

Ran forget the sores and put the bottle of lotion into his pack. In the distance he could see the remnants of a dead forest, the dark trees lining the horizon like foot soldiers ready for battle. The trees would not offer much more protection from the wind, but it was better than being out in the open. He strapped his rifle to his back again and took off after the others.

It only took an hour to reach the edge of the dead forest. Ran and Nordica hugged the tree line, or what was left of it. Every once in a while they would come across a tree that appeared to have a green leaf, but every time Ran went to touch it, the leaf would crumble into ash in the palm of his glove. There wasn't much that could survive in the Wastelands.

Ran liked survival stories. He enjoyed finding anomalies in an otherwise lifeless world. There had been a time he came across a plant living in a small pocket of life just outside the Tisaian walls. He was scavenging for supplies when he found it. It survived against all odds, living through season after season of harsh conditions.

"Keep focused, Ran. We could be walking into a trap," Tsui whispered.

Ran nodded and continued on, his rifle drawn, waiting to blast anything that moved. He saw the tree line ended just yards away from the old building. The structure was surrounded by an ancient metal fence, topped with a layer of barbed wire. At the front gate an old sign swayed back and forth in the wind, creaking and groaning with every twist. Ran read the sign aloud as he made his way closer. "Government Property; Trespassers Will Be Subject to Arrest and Prosecution."

"Arrest us," Nordica said, passing through the open gate with her rifle drawn.

"This must not have been much of a military base in its day," Ran muttered from a few yards behind.

"It wasn't really a base," Nordica replied quickly. "In fact, there's only one building here."

Ran found cover behind a large dead oak tree and pulled out his binoculars to get a better look.

He scanned the building first; stopping on a large antenna that rested obliquely on the roof, pointing towards the gray skyline. Then he glassed the compound, finally stopping on a pair of metal doors in the middle of the lot.

"Doesn't look like anyone's home," Tsui whispered from his six, startling him.

"What do you make of this?" Ran asked, handing the binoculars to Tsui.

"Looks like that's the silo we're searching for. Hasn't been used in years, from the look of it."

Ran stole another glance around the trunk of the tree, scanning the area to see if he missed anything.

"I think you're right. If there are any survivors they're already in the building, which seems unlikely, considering we haven't seen any scouts at all."

Satisfied the base was empty, Ran took off running and dove behind a concrete block where Nordica had taken up position.

"I'll go first, you cover me," she said, already in flight before Ran could raise his weapon.

Ran kept his rifle trained on the building as Nordica sprinted towards another fence, which was swinging awkwardly back and forth in the wind. Nearing the building, she crouched and rested her back against the concrete wall before motioning for the rest of the soldiers to follow.

As Ran sprinted towards the structure a wave of trepidation overtook him, one he felt only when he was sure something was going to go wrong. He had felt something like it the day the CRK attacked the headquarters.

"Halt, you sons of bitches! Get on the ground now!" a voice screamed from the roof.

Nordica jumped back from the wall, her gun raised, while Ran stopped dead in his tracks and pointed his rifle towards the roof.

Where are they, where are they? Ran thought, desperately trying to get a target, his cross hair scanning the roof of the building frantically.

"Drop your freaking weapons before I put one between your eyes!" the voice screamed again.

Ran continued to scan the roof top with his rifle, watching

Nordica crouch-walk towards the front door of the building. If this had been a trap and there were Knights waiting, then they would already be dead. Whoever was on the roof was not part of the CRK.

"We're looking for our squad." Ran shouted back. "We aren't here to harm you."

"Like hell you're not; you're on my property!" the voice shouted again.

"We're here to meet with the rest of the TDU!" Ran shot back quickly.

"I don't know of any TDU!" the man screamed again. "You have ten seconds to tell me what you're doing on my property before I start shooting. And five seconds are already gone!"

Ran looked back at Nordica, his rifle shaking, unsure what to do.

"We're part of the TDU!" Ran repeated. "You must know of the TDU?" Ran asked, as he began to realize they may have stumbled upon a lonely straggler.

"Like hell I do!" he shouted back.

"Listen, I'm going to put my rifle down, and so will my friends, and we can talk this out. I promise we aren't here to harm you or steal from you. We were supposed to…" Ran paused, deciding it wouldn't be safe to tell the entire truth.

"We're just looking for a place to rest and then we'll be on our way."

Ran caught Nordica staring at him and shaking her head.

Silence crept across the compound. Ran knew if Nordica had the chance, she would take the straggler out. With all the killing in the past week, Ran didn't want to see anyone else die.

"Can we rest here for the night? We have some food and supplies we can trade with you."

Ran stood completely still, his arms burning from holding his rifle pointed at the roof top. "See, I'm dropping my weapon. And my friends will too," he said, as he slowly knelt and placed his rifle at his feet. He turned and motioned Tsui to as well.

Ran waited, his eyes darting back from Nordica to the roof. *Well, this is it,* he thought silently, desperately wishing he could tell his arrogant friend how much he actually cared about her.

"Stay where you are. I'm coming out," the voice shouted back again.

Ran took a deep breath and motioned Nordica over to him.

"What the hell are you doing?" Nordica asked.

"I think we've stumbled across a straggler, not a trap set by the Tin Cans. If they were here, we would already be dead."

"Where are the others, then?" Nordica snarled back.

Ran frowned. "I think we're it."

For a split second, Ran caught a glimpse of sadness in Nordica's demeanor. It was a rare moment and was interrupted as the front door to the building swung open.

The two soldiers turned to watch an older man walk out into the wind, shielding his eyes from the dust and ash. He wore a tattered old flannel shirt tucked into a pair of denim jeans. It was something neither of them had seen in years. He gripped a shotgun in his right hand, with the barrel pointing at the ground. His face was thinly bearded, with specks of white hair clinging to his wind burnt cheeks. He wore a green cap with an image of a yellow tractor.

"I'm sorry; I don't get many visitors out here. In fact, I haven't gotten any in about a year now."

Nordica and Ran looked at one another, realizing what they had feared was true. They were all that was left of the TDU.

The man propped his shotgun against the concrete wall of the building. "I'm the only one here," he responded. "Looks like you three will be the first visitors to join me for a meal, in..." the man paused. "Well, in about four years. Since my wife died," he said, looking down at the dirt.

"Four visitors," Juliana yelled, approaching the building with her hands in the air. Nordica and Ran turned, while the man picked up his shotgun again.

"It's okay, sir, she's with us," Nordica said calmly.

The man lowered his weapon and approached his new guests, offering his hand to Nordica, who was closest.

"The name's John," he said, shaking each of their hands one by one.

"Like I said, it's been a few years since I saw anyone out here. In fact, the last person I saw I had to shoot because he tried to steal my stash of food. Y'all aren't going to try and steal my food, are you?" he asked, raising his brow suspiciously.

Juliana looked at the man. "No sir, we're not here to steal your food."

The man chuckled, dropping his expression. "I'm just messing with you."

The four TDU soldiers looked at one another quizzically. They weren't sure whether to laugh or turn and run.

"Yeah I used to get that reaction a lot. I changed my name to my grandfather's once I moved out here. I haven't known anyone named John for a long time, so I thought it would be a good change."

Ran laughed. "I knew a John a long time ago. He was deported because the Justice Committee thought he was an immigrant."

"Well, I suppose I should invite you in for dinner," John said, motioning his guests towards the door.

The four soldiers followed him cautiously into the building. The inside was a single dwelling with two beds against the north wall, a kitchen table against the east wall, and a couch in the center of the room. There was also a bathroom and supply pantry, both in horrid shape, but nonetheless appearing to be in working order.

Nordica followed the others into the house, resting her bag on the worn carpet. In the corner of the room she saw a door slightly ajar, hidden by darkness. She assumed it was one of two entrances to the silo, but decided to find out more information later, after John had gained their trust.

———

Dinner was a large plate of spaghetti and canned spam rolled up into meatballs. A bright candle burned in the middle of the wooden table, illuminating the home cooked meal in front of them.

"I raided the best of my supplies to make this meal. I hope y'all like it," John said with a grin. He didn't hesitate before attacking his food with a fork, shoveling it into his mouth.

Juliana smiled in pleasure after her first bite. "Wow. You're almost as good as cook as the one we used to have at our headquarters."

"I don't know about that, but these meatballs are better than I've had in a long time," Nordica chimed in.

"Yeah, I think you're right," Ran said, plopping another meatball into his mouth.

"Thanks. It's been..." John paused and looked down at his plate. "It's been awhile since I cooked for anyone. So I was worried how this meal would turn out." He shook his head, changing the subject. "So I don't mean to pry into your business, but what happened to your headquarters?" John asked, raising an eyebrow.

Ran looked up from his meatball before plopping it in to his mouth. He figured if John invited them in for dinner he wouldn't be that upset when he found out his home was a rendezvous point for a rebel group in the middle of a war.

"It was discovered and destroyed. We barely escaped," Ran replied. "I'm sure you're aware of the wall surrounding Tisaia not twenty miles from here."

John nodded.

"We're in the middle of a war with the State, and last week the Council of Royal Knights destroyed our headquarters and killed most of our friends."

John dropped his fork onto his plate and brought a handkerchief to his mouth, wiping spaghetti sauce from his white beard.

"You all are fighting the CRK?"

"Yeah, so you have heard of it?" Nordica asked.

"Of course I have, I moved out here to escape Tisaia fifteen years ago when things started to change radically."

"Holy shit, we got lucky meeting you. We were ordered to rendezvous at the Silo," Ran added.

John wiped his lips once again with the handkerchief.

"Silo?" he asked.

"Tsui, why don't you fill John in on what we're talking about?"

Tsui nodded, placing his fork and spoon down softly on the table. The massive Asian man scooted his chair back from the table so he could cross his legs.

"Our intelligence said that in the year 1965, the United States Army built a nuclear missile silo under this building. The silo was decommissioned in the early 1990s, when the Cold War with the Soviet Union ended. The United States put the silo up for sale to private citizens, but it never sold, and according to our records, it has remained idle ever since."

"One of our recon teams came across this location a few years back," Nordica said.

"This place was idle. Idle until I got here," John said, laughing. "Hell, I had no idea there was a silo under here. Which brings me to my next question, where is the damn entrance?"

"You mean there isn't an entrance in this building?" Ran asked politely.

"If there was an entrance don't you think I'd know about it?" John shot back, somewhat annoyed with Ran's question.

"I suppose you're right. I'm sorry," Ran replied.

"After you're all done, I suggest we get some shuteye. In the morning we can start combing the area for some sort of an entrance," John said, sipping ale from an old wooden glass.

Time: 7:08 p.m. February 22, 2071.
Location: Rira's Pub. Rohania, Tisaia.

The most successful establishments in Rohania were bars. Most Rohanians made very little money, scraping together a living by bartering and selling what they could. At night the pubs collected most of the credits earned by these hardworking people during the day.

Nathar and Creo sat in a dimly lit booth in the back of Rira's Pub. It was an irritatingly loud joint, and made up for the solitude the two soldiers had grown accustomed to the past couple days.

Picking the pub was an easy decision. Not only was the owner a long time sympathizer of the TDU, he also had several exits in the back.

The two sat comfortably in their newly purchased pea coats hoping they would blend in with the crowd, watching patrons come and go; some drunk were, others were nearing the point.

Rira was a small man in his late 50's with a booming voice. Those that knew him never double crossed him. He was one of the most honest black market dealers in Rohania, honest as black market dealers came. And he expected his clients to show him the same courtesy. When they skipped a payment or failed to hold up their side of a bargain, he would send his henchman, Lupai, after them.

When Lupai wasn't breaking people's kneecaps for Rira, he was selling small arms to anyone with the credits to buy them. The TDU had used him for years and he had shown fierce loyalty to Obi, which is why Creo trusted him.

Tonight Creo wasn't going to be discussing weapons—tonight his mission was to procure soldiers. And something inside him told him Lupai was the right man for the job.

A thick layer of smoke hovered over the bar, prompting a deep cough from Nathar. He pretended not to care, but Creo knew the man better. It wasn't often the young soldier voiced his opinion, but one of the things he hated most were watering holes just like Rira's and the filth that patronized them.

Creo understood. His friend had asthma and smoke inflamed

his lungs and he was still recovering from a bad cold he had developed.

The Spaniard did not, however, share Nathar's hatred of bars. He was used to the people and enjoyed the potent, thick smell of cigarette smoke. He grew up in places just like Rira's, and felt a strange sense of nostalgia while waiting for the arms dealer.

It was a half-hour before Lupai entered the building, with two equally large men who appeared to be bodyguards. Their eyes gave them away, darting from booth to booth, scanning the shadows for danger.

At first glance Lupai looked like any other Rohanian resident. His facial hair was thick and his mop of dark brown hair hung down to his shoulders. He wore a thick pea coat and pair of worn trousers. What set him aside from the average citizen wasn't his appearance, it was his wit and charm.

Most Rohanians never received a diploma, and those who didn't drop out of school to work by the age of 14 didn't receive much of an education. The schools were old and, like everything else in Rohania, in severe need of routine and major maintenance. They were understaffed and most of the curriculum was developed by the teachers. If a teacher wanted to spend the day talking about the last time they got drunk, there was nothing to stop them.

Creo recalled hearing that Lupai received a formal education in Lunia. His wit, combined with his rough appearance, allowed him to evade the Knights, who had hunted him for years.

Creo and Nathar scooted over in their booth, making room for Lupai and his bodyguards. They approached slyly, eyeing the two TDU soldiers through their sunglasses.

Lupai brushed his long brown hair out of his face and sat down across from Creo and Nathar, cracking a grin full of pearly white teeth. He nodded at his two guards and they disappeared into the dark smoke of the pub, hiding in the corners and waiting to be beckoned again.

"So, I hear you two have had a tough week," he said, smirking and pulling a half-spent pack of cigarettes from the bowels of his trench coat. "The Tin Cans finally caught up to you?"

"It was only a matter of time," Creo responded.

Lupai paused, scratching a match against the wood table and lighting his cigarette. He took a deep drag and exhaled the smoke into the air, watching it disappear in the cloud above their booth.

He laid the burning cigarette down on the table and folded his hands. A look of seriousness washed over his face, his smile disappearing in the dim light.

"You have my sympathies, but this is a dangerous time. So let's get to the details quickly, shall we? How about you two tell me what you need and I'll tell you what I can provide."

"We need new recruits, at least half a dozen of them, and..." Creo said, hesitating.

"And we need some explosives," Nathar piped in.

The brightness in Lupai's eyes seemed to grow with every pass of the loosely dangling light above their booth.

"We need double the explosives we bought from you last time," Nathar continued.

"Ah." Lupai said, sitting back in the booth and folding his arms, his eyes studying the two soldiers across from him.

He took a deep breath and leaned back towards the table. "Your request comes at a bad time," he whispered, turning to see if anyone was listening.

"Fear runs rampant in Rohania right now. Those who have sympathized with your cause in the past have lost hope. The CRK has been advertising the attack last week everywhere. They say the TDU is gone, eradicated..." he paused again.

"I don't know if I can come through with this many men. And the explosives, I can't sell them to you if I don't know what they're going to be used for," he finished.

Creo got up from his seat, Nathar quickly following him. "You know we can't tell you what they're for, which is why Obi trusted you in the past. If you can't meet this request, then we'll find someone else," Creo said.

"Times have changed, gentlemen. That stunt you all pulled in the trolley station a couple of weeks ago. It killed a lot of innocent people. I don't like it when my weapons kill innocent people, but I'm sure we can work something out," he said, revealing his pearly white teeth again and motioning the two soldiers back into their seats.

"I suppose my policy can be bypassed, if, say, you assure me collateral damage will be kept at a minimum and…" Lupai paused again, his grin getting wider. "If the price is right. Do you get my drift?"

Creo and Nathar nodded in agreement, settling back into the booth.

Lupai smiled again. "I can spare four men right now. That is it. I'm sorry, but until the TDU reemerges with another attack to give this area hope, men will be in short supply."

"Four will work," Creo said reluctantly.

Lupia offered his hand across the table. "We have a deal then. Your men and supplies will be waiting for you at this address," he said, handing Creo a small slip of paper.

"If you need anything else, you know where to find me," he said, scooting out of the booth and disappearing back into the crowd.

Nathar and Creo both took another swig of their ale. "Let's get back to the junkyard. This freaking place gives me the creeps," Nathar said.

Creo caught one last glimpse of Lupai before he followed Nathar out the closest exit. *This guy better be as good as Obi says he is,* he thought, heading into the dark bowels of the alleyway.

Time: 7:35 p.m. February 23, 2071.
Location: Immigrant Camp #4. Rohania, Tisaia

Mulia jumped off the back of an old pickup before the guard riding in the bed could push him onto the dirt street below. A squad of Knights marched by him, their armor clanking noisily. It was a sound he had learned to accept, one as common as the morning alarm.

He paused to glance up at the familiar sight of immigrant camp #4. It was dusk, and the search lights on the guard towers rising far above him were already brighter than the moon hovering above them. There was never a moment of true darkness in the camp. Never a reprieve for the exhausted immigrants, rounded up like livestock and forced to live in tents, before being deported back into the Wastelands.

The camp was surrounded by monstrous electric fences and backed up to the great walls. There was no escaping. Anyone that tried ended up dead.

The only way into camp was a 20 foot tall metal gate. It screeched open three times a day. Once in the morning for immigrants lucky enough to have a job; again at three in the afternoon, for any newly rounded up immigrants, and then at dusk, when the immigrants returned from their jobs.

Mulia ran his hand through his greasy, thinning hair, waiting for the gate to open. He watched a pair of Knights striding in unison towards him like a robotic centipede, their armor clanking as they walked.

"Move it," said one of the Knights.

Mulia jumped out of the way, dropping his hands to his sides and his gaze to the ground. Eye contact with the guards wasn't forbidden, but for the past four years in captivity Mulia had never looked a Knight in the eye. He knew his role and accepted it. It was this mentality that helped him form a mutual relationship of convenience with nearly every guard in the camp. He did this by showing them respect and following their every command. It wasn't that he lacked a conscience or respect for himself, he simply wanted to survive. And so far he had done exactly that.

There were also the memories from his past that played a

distinct role in his survival. He vaguely remembered his childhood, but his journey to Tisaia was burned into his memory like a tattoo. From the time the raiders pillaged the shanty town he grew up in, to the subsequent trip his father financed to smuggle his family into Tisaia, these memories were as much as part of him as the scars on his back.

Mulia knew what life was like outside the walls, and he would do anything to keep from going back out there. He would rather kiss the boots of the Knight who gave him the scars on his back than be thrown back into the hell and misery of the Wastelands.

He looked back down at his feet and saw the radiation scars lining both of his legs. Every day he remembered how he got them and the cave he and his parents took refuge in when the trip to the storm drains went astray. His family hadn't made it more than 20 miles before the same group of raiders caught up with them and cornered them in a cave. Their guide took off the moment he saw the raiders, but his family was not so lucky.

It took only a few days for the symptoms of radiation poisoning to manifest. His mom and sister didn't live much longer than that. He would never forget watching his sister, the life slowly draining from her, a combination of terror and confusion burning in her eyes. Nor would he forget the sores and boils over his Mother's arms and head where her hair had fallen out. And worst of all was his last image of his father, firing his shotgun harmlessly at the Raiders while their bullets tore through his soft flesh.

Ironically, it was the guide that saved Mulia after the pirates had taken what they wanted and left him for dead. The skinny, toothless man dressed in raggedy tan military fatigues carried him all the way to the great Tisaian walls without saying a word. He turned Mulia over to a sympathetic family living in Rohania. They tried to help him, but his wounds were too severe so they took him to a hospital where he spent a month healing. He never found out why the guide returned for him. Was it a sense of regret from abandoning his family, or something else? He would never know.

"Get moving," another guard said, nudging his rifle into Mulia's ribcage. He moaned in pain but continued forward, cringing at the sound of the two ton gate slowly creaking open. It was a sound he heard every day, multiple times a day, and one his ears still rebelled against.

"Let's go," the guard said again, his voice muffled by the breathing apparatus inside his helmet.

Mulia hustled towards the customs station. He was a gunsmith, having been taught the trade by his father in the trading town years ago. It was there he learned how to build guns, change out parts, and fix pretty much any gun that came his way. This made him invaluable to the guards, who constantly needed their weapons serviced. It also meant he was strip searched at the end of every working day to make sure he wasn't stealing any parts. In the past four years, Mulia had made certain every part he did steal for his TDU contacts was never detected.

A sharp pain shot down his leg while he ran, reminding him of the secret place he kept bullets and parts squirreled away for the TDU. He stopped for a second to massage his thigh, where a loose piece of skin covered a hollowed out piece of flesh, just large enough for a round of ammunition or a part to a gun. The wound was a result of the radiation poisoning. It was one of many places where the amateur TDU doctor opted to remove flesh rather than let it heal properly when he was first brought to Tisaia. At first the pain was excruciating, but over the years of hiding weapon parts he grew mostly numb to the pain.

After his strip search he was free to head back to his corridors where his tent mate, Kalah, would be preparing dinner from their rationed food.

The camp was set up in three rows of tents with 30 in each row. The middle row was reserved for families, while the outside rows were used by single occupants. With four guard towers rising far above the camp, it was designed so the CRK would have full range of view at all times.

Most of the guards were Knight Cadets and were training for service, but some were veteran Knights who transferred to the camp for a variety of reasons. The most infamous veteran was Royal Knight Nemir. His hatred for immigrants dated back to when his brother was killed in an uprising at the camp years ago.

Mulia made it to his tent just as the street lights glowed to life.

"Just in time for dinner, my friend," Kalah said, without looking up from a pot he was stirring. Mulia nodded and sat down on his cot, slowly slipping out of his work boots. He leaned back and watched the old man stir the stew slowly, checking the density with every other stir.

Kalah was a master cook. It was the only thing keeping him from being deported to the Wastelands. The Knights grew so fond of his cooking, they continued to delay his paperwork so he could stay in the camp's main kitchen.

"I heard Nemir beat another young man today."

Mulia shrugged. "Someday he will get what he is owed."

"That day may be approaching quicker than we thought," Kalah said, a sly grin streaking across his old dark weather-beaten skin.

Mulia sat up, his interest sparked. "What do you mean? I thought we lost contact with the TDU after their headquarters was destroyed."

"Ah, but we both know the TDU had other locations. The Tin Cans can never kill them all. New freedom fighters will replace the fallen. History proves the just are always victorious in the long run."

Mulia shrugged again. He wasn't in the mood to argue tonight.

"There is something else you may be interested in," Kalah said, picking up on Mulia's solemn demeanor.

"The Samoan is fighting Royal Knight Tinus at the Golden Dome tomorrow night. Many of the immigrants believe he can win."

Mulia finished taking off his work boots and caught his friend's excited gaze.

"Don't get your hopes up. Tinus has never lost a battle in the arena and I don't expect he will tomorrow. Besides, you know the fights are rigged."

Kalah frowned and looked back down at his stew. As a young man he had driven a cab in New York. He survived the nuclear blast in Manhattan and escaped to a refugee camp set up on the east coast before Tisaia was ever formed. He immigrated to Tisaia a decade ago when the refugee camp finally collapsed from disease and famine. He had seen so much in his years, but he wasn't sure if he would ever see an immigrant win their freedom in the Golden Dome.

Kalah took the pot of stew off the fire and placed it on a pad atop a crate between their two cots. He scooped a steaming spoonful of the dish into two small bowls, sprinkling a pinch of salt into the bowl before handing it to Mulia.

"Hope you like," he said, with another grin, revealing the last three teeth in his mouth.

"Thank you. I have something for you too."

Slowly Mulia pulled up his pant leg and peeled back the three inches of dead skin on his thigh. He reached into the opening and pulled out an inch long piece of metal.

"Is that what I think it is?" Kalah asked, beaming.

"It is. This should complete the sniper rifle I have been working on for over a year. When the riots start, we shall be ready," Mulia said, his voice at a hoarse whisper.

He picked up his bowl and began to shovel the hot stew into his mouth, stopping momentarily to cool it with his breath. Kalah quickly followed suit, and the two men ate the rest of their dinner in silence. When they were finished, Kalah rinsed the bowls with a small bit of left over water and placed the bowls neatly on top of the crate.

Normally Kalah would tell a story before bed, or the two would read, but tonight he was exhausted. Mulia blew the flame out in the lantern hanging from the wood rafters of their tent and lay back down in his cot, pulling the covers up to his chin.

"Goodnight, Kalah," he said, closing his eyes. He listened to the sounds of the camp in the distance, the chatter of voices and the smell of fires cooking exotic dishes he had never heard of before. He felt oddly at home for the first time in a very long time. The sensation lasted only a few moments and was interrupted by the memory of the pirates, the Knights, and the world he lived in. He would never have a home. Not until the Knights were gone and the TDU restored peace and human rights to the last great city on Earth.

"Goodnight, Mulia," Kalah replied, blowing out the candle on the wooden crate. "Soon we shall be free, my friend."

CHAPTER 11: MODERN GLADIATORS

"Victory is always possible for the person who refuses to stop fighting."
~Napoleon Hill

Time: 8:14 p.m. February 24, 2071
Location: The Golden Dome. Lunia, Tisaia

It was no secret that violence from the Biomass Wars spilled over into everyday life. Those who survived the radioactive holocaust became accustomed to it. In fact, many of them yearned for it. State workers flocked to the arena every week to watch the Royal Knights fight refugees and criminals trying to win their freedom.

Tonight was no different. The Golden Dome was packed full of State workers waiting to watch blood spill. Even the workers who normally skipped the gladiator fights came from all areas of Tisaia to watch Royal Knight Tinus fight his final match.

Alexria and her husband Roni were two newcomers. They had heard word of an immigrant known as the Samoan, who was one fight from winning his freedom—a freedom no other refugee had been able to win. The couple was curious. Did he actually have a shot at winning his? After the fall of the TDU headquarters, many sympathizers believed he was the revolution's last hope.

And they weren't the only ones. The crowd was packed with immigrant supporters and TDU sympathizers. Many of them believed immigrants deserved the same rights as any other Tisaian citizen.

They settled into their uncomfortable stadium seats, shuffling to get a better view of the ring below. The crowd grew excited, eager for blood, but Roni and Alexria remained silent. They watched nervously, hand in hand, as the monstrous clock struck nine.

At the bottom of the arena a man dressed in a black suit slowly made his way across the concrete floor of the arena towards the hexagon cage. Everyone around them stood and clapped until the man stopped at the edge of the arena and held up his hand.

The crowd grew silent and, one by one, the large orb-shaped lights hanging from the ceiling clicked off, and the stadium became consumed by darkness. Silence swept across the full arena. Not even a muffled cough could be heard.

A brilliant spot light tore through the arena and illuminated the hexagon cage where the announcer erupted into speech.

"Ladies and gentlemen of Tisaia! Men and women of the last great city in the world! Tonight we have a delightful show planned for you all. Tonight you shall witness the best the State has to offer and the worst the outside world has to offer! For tonight, Royal Knight Tinus will fight the refugee you have come to know as the Samoan. Tonight they fight to the death." The crowd erupted with excitement and the announcer paused, once again holding up his hand to silence them.

"Honor versus dishonor. Strength versus frailty. Loyalty versus non-allegiance. Royal Knight Tinus will strike down that which seeks to challenge the Tisaian creed of Honor, Strength and Loyalty."

The crowd erupted into screams and applause again, prompting the couple to shift nervously in their seats. Alexria shot Roni a frightened glance who watched the crowd in silence.

The thirst for blood was ripe in the air. The arena was alive with it, but mixed in was also the taste of fear. They both felt it within their bones. It was something indescribable, a product of war and destruction—something they had lived with most of their lives. They also knew that along with blood came the loss of life, and even in the violence- plagued society of Tisaia death was still death. It was unnatural to most and easy for others.

The announcer raised his arms towards the ceiling, fueling the crowd's blood lust. Alexria fidgeted nervously in her chair, grabbing her husband's hand again.

Overhead another spotlight clicked on, illuminating the gate at the south side of the arena. Slowly it creaked open and the crowd grew silent.

Alexria took a deep breath, the anticipation of the fight growing inside her. It wasn't excitement, or fear; but a combination of both, a sentiment she wasn't accustomed to feeling. She gripped Roni's hand tighter, biting her bottom lip.

For several minutes the crowd stood waiting. Their anticipation quickly turned into impatience, several members of the crowd breaking the quiet with drunken screams.

Finally, the smiling announcer held up his hands yelling, "State workers, let's give a round of applause to Royal Knight Tinus!"

The crowd immediately erupted in screams and chants as Royal Knight Tinus came riding out on a black stallion. The spotlight revealed perfection: polished armor from head to toe, a helmet bearing the feathers of the hawk, a chest plate draped with medals, and a sword attached to his side that had struck down countless enemies.

Alexria took another deep breath. She didn't know what to think. On the one hand he was a hero, having protected the Tisaian walls from raiders and scavengers. On the other he was the symbol of the State; a living, breathing symbol of oppression and death.

She watched him circle the arena. With every pass he raised his sword into the air and screamed before finally stopping at the center of the arena and dismounting his horse.

Two immigrant slaves waited for him at the cage door. He nodded and they opened the metal gate, closing it behind him and locking him in. This was done more as a formality, but there were cases in past games where the Knights' opponents tried to climb the metal fence and escape the cage.

The crowd began to settle down while they anxiously awaited the Samoan's return to the arena. The announcer's aim was always to keep the crowd on its toes, to drag the show on. Traditionally, Knights' opponents had little chance of surviving for more than a few minutes.

The metallic click of another spotlight turned the crowd's attention to the gate on the north side of the arena. This time there was no waiting, just the Samoan running out of the rising gate.

He was quite a sight with axe in hand, screaming, barefoot and naked except for a small tan cloth covering his genitals. His naturally tan body was peppered with tribal tattoos that snaked up his legs to his neck. The man was built like a wild animal, his chest muscles bulging and his biceps balls of strength. Even his short legs were swelling with muscle. He knew what was at stake. If he beat Royal Knight Tinus, he would be a free man and would be the first to have ever done so.

The crowd knew the stakes as well, and while many stood and cheered for the Samoan, most of them sat and watched in disgust.

Alexria and Roni sat quietly, watching the games unfold. They had come out of curiosity and were smart enough to not show any biased support for the Samoan, even though deep down they both secretly hoped he would win the battle. The couple watched the two arena slaves open the opposite gate, allowing the Samoan to enter.

The announcer stepped in between the two warriors to explain the rules, raising the microphone to his mouth. "Royal Knight Tinus and…" he paused to look over at the Samoan but purposely refused to acknowledge him with anything but a quick glance.

"I'm now to instruct you on any rules you must abide by during this historic battle. And, I'm happy to say, there are no rules!" he said, flailing his arms in the air with a laugh. Once again the crowd roared with excitement, their blood lust quickly growing.

"Once I leave the arena the battle will begin. Until then go to your corners," he commanded.

Slowly the Samoan made his way to the middle of the hexagon with his axe raised in both hands. Tinus carefully maneuvered himself to the outside of the hexagon, creeping along the metal fence and drawing his sword from its sheath. He appeared calm, almost stoic, staring through his metal visor at the Samoan. The warrior stared back, his face bright read, his chest heaving in and out.

The crowd watched in silence as the two men carefully navigated their way through the hexagon, trying to find the proper footing for their first strike. Tinus had always waited for his opponent to make the first move. Patience was his game, and it appeared he was going to follow this strategy. He knew it wouldn't take long for the anger building inside of the Samoan to overtake him. For what seemed like hours the warriors stared at each other, the crowd waiting for the first strike.

Before the crowd could react, the Samoan screamed with rage and raced toward Tinus with his axe. He swung, but missed. Tinus skipped to the side and lashed out with his sword. He narrowly missed the Samoan's head; the warrior moved with surprising speed, ducking and going down on one knee. He rose, recovering rapidly and swinging his axe at Tinus' armored feet. The blade connected, knocking the armored Knight to the ground.

The crowd erupted into pandemonium. In a blur the Samoan rushed the disabled Knight and brought his axe down swiftly. The blade grazed the side of Tinus' helmet, sending sparks exploding in all directions. The sharp edge of the axe peeled back the metal skin of the helmet, temporarily blinding the Knight.

Tinus screamed and kicked the Samoan in the chest, his feet planting firmly into the immigrant's rib cage and sending him flying back into the cage.

The Knight jumped to his feet without hesitation, grabbing his sword and discarding his now useless helmet. He threw it with his free hand at the recovering Samoan and struck him in the face with the rough edge of the sharp helmet. The crowd erupted again, roaring with satisfaction.

"Should I kill him now? Or make him suffer?" Tinus yelled, turning to face the crowd.

"Make him suffer, make him suffer, make him suffer!" the crowd chanted.

Tinus peeled off his chest armor and dropped it to the floor, revealing his own bulging muscles and a scar that ran down the length of his back.

Behind him the dazed Samoan rose to his feet. He raised a hand to the gash on his face and spat out a broken tooth. The gaping wound dripped, adding to the puddle of red on the floor, and his vision swam. It was the first major injury he had sustained in the ring, and it shocked him into motion. He yelled something in a foreign tongue and rushed forward, his face streaked with blood like war paint on his skin.

The immigrant was dangerously skilled with the axe, and although he appeared careless, the power behind his strike was what his opponents feared the most. He had decapitated several of his victims with one swift swing in countless previous matches. But his next swing went wide, allowing Tinus to swing with his own blade. The sword clipped the Samoan's back and sent blood spraying into the air. He grunted in pain but recovered quickly, turning and swinging his axe with all of his strength.

Tinus moved hastily and much faster now without his armor. He spun around in time to meet his opponent's axe with his own blade. The metal connected perfectly, sending sparks into the air. For a split second the two warriors stood, their legs firmly planted on the ground, neither yielding ground to the other. Their eyes locked, revealing a combination of pain, fear and anger.

It was at that moment both men knew neither of them was immune to fear. They both felt it. And they both knew the obvious. The fight would be to the death. Both had killed many men, but this battle was different. This battle was to determine whether the Council of Royal Knights would remain undefeated in the arena against the best the immigrants had to offer. Tinus was a man of honor, a man who had spent his entire life defending his country. His scars, his medals, they were parts of him now, telling the story of his career as a Knight.

Tinus, trusting his instincts, pulled his blade out of the stalemate and slid back to the chain fence to regain his footing. He planted his right foot back into the floor and gripped his sword with his left hand.

The Samoan remained in the middle of the arena, snorting and beating his chest with his free hand to tempt the Knight back into the battle. But Tinus was too smart to fall for his mind games. He was used to being taunted, and each time he waited patiently for his opponent to lash out with a careless blow.

The Samoan grew angry and taunted Tinus more, waving at the Knight and motioning him back into the middle of the arena. "What? What waiting for?" he yelled.

Tinus stood, his stance unchanged, gripping his sword with both hands now. He expected that it would be only seconds before the refugee charged him, but both warriors stood their ground. The crowd began to grow impatient. They had come to watch a battle that had been advertised for months as the, *"The Fight of the Century."*

There wasn't supposed to be a stalemate. There would be no truce. The crowd wanted blood. And they didn't care from whom, as long as it was plentiful.

The crowd's boos aggravated the Samoan. He wiped the blood off his chin and switched hands with his axe. Seconds turned into minutes, and the Samoan's patience began to lapse sending him into a fit of rage. He rushed Tinus once again, swinging his axe horizontally, aiming for the Knight's torso. Tinus simply took a step back, narrowly avoiding the axe. He took in a short breath and struck his sword at the Samoan, slicing a big chunk of flesh out of his leathery back.

The Samoan screamed in pain, sprinting back to his corner, holding his fresh wound with one hand and gripping his axe in the other. The weapon was heavier now, his muscles weaker, his breathing deeper. He was in trouble and he knew it, but it wasn't his first brush with death, and victory was still in sight. His freedom could still be turned into a reality.

He regained his composure and rushed Tinus again, swinging his axe with a speed that no ordinary man would have been able to match. Once again the Knight danced around the blade and swiftly stabbed the Samoan in his back, opening another deep wound.

Rage. It was painted on the Samoan's face. The crowd grew silent, watching Tinus cut the man over and over. Blood flowed from the Samoan's open wounds, staining the floor a bright red. The weaker spectators turned away.

Alexria sat gripping Roni's hand tightly, but she did not turn away. "How much longer can this go on?" she whispered.

"I'm afraid not much longer; he will bleed out if his wounds aren't dressed," Roni replied, his eyes fixed on the warriors below.

What had been promised to be the fight of the century was turning out to be one of the worst slaughters in the history of the arena.

On his fifth attempt the Samoan fell to the ground, his wounds too severe to go on. He lay in a puddle of his own blood, looking up at the great round lights of the arena, watching his chance at freedom slip away.

Tinus approached the fallen warrior, his sword gripped tightly in both hands. The Knight would not be taken off guard. He approached with caution, knowing the savage was like a wounded dog and could still have bite left in him.

"This is it," Roni whispered to his wife, squeezing her hand tighter.

The Knight stood over the Samoan, raising his sword to finish the man. His hands raised the sword directly above the Samoan's neck. The crowd was completely silent. No screams of bloodlust, no requests to punish the warrior any more. And as the Samoan looked up into the eyes of Tinus, something unexpected happened, something never done in the history of the arena.

Alexria stood up, dropping her husband's hand. She cupped her hands and yelled at the top of her lungs. "Mercy! Show him mercy, Royal Knight Tinus!" The words traveled through the packed arena rapidly. State employees stirred, many trying to see the woman who made such an odd request. Even Tinus, who usually remained completely focused on the fight, looked into the dark crowd for a few seconds before peering back down at the savage, who was slipping in and out of consciousness. His hands did not tremble, and he prepared to strike the final blow with his sword.

"Mercy!" Alexria yelled again. This time, Roni grabbed at her hand and hushed her, "What are you doing? Sit back down!" he pleaded.

But Alexria would not be deterred. She repeated her request. "Mercy, Royal Knight Tinus, show him mercy," she yelled. And then another State employee, a man who Roni and Alexria did not recognize, stood up and yelled the same request. One after another, the crowd began to stand, pleading for the Samoan's life. They had watched the Samoan fight bravely for his freedom, and many of them had watched him fight many times before. He deserved his freedom, and they would not stand to watch him be executed. Not like this.

As the crowd began to protest, louder and louder, Tinus stood back, his sword dropping to his side. His chest heaved up and down, baring the scars he had suffered in so many fights before. He looked down at the savage, who had slipped into unconsciousness. He had no idea why the crowd was trying to save him. *What a pity*, Tinus thought, waiting for the announcer to calm the crowd.

Within seconds, a dozen Knights came rushing into the arena. They were dressed in full regalia, their armor shining brightly under the intense spotlights.

"Mercy! Mercy! Mercy!" the crowd chanted. Some began to throw items at the cage as they grew more enthralled with saving the Samoan's life.

The announcer, who hadn't appeared since the beginning of the fight, stepped back onto his platform outside the hexagon cage. He raised the microphone to his mouth. "Citizens! Calm yourselves. There is no mercy in the arena. You do not come here to see mercy. You come here to see blood. And now it's time for Royal Knight Tinus to finish the savage. Kill him, Tinus!" the announcer yelled.

The crowd erupted into pandemonium and began to throw whatever items they could find at the announcer. They grew louder as they ran the man off the stage, prompting more Knights to rush into the arena, assault rifles drawn.

The crowd finally quieted, watching cautiously from their seats. They knew the Council of Royal Knights would not hesitate to kill civilians, even State employees. They should have known mercy was not an option. With the crowd nearly silent, Tinus raised his sword again.

"There is honor in this death," he muttered under his breath, bringing the sword down on the Samoan. The last hope for the immigrant cause ended with the blade parting the warriors head from his body, sending a fresh red splatter onto the ground. A tear crawled down Alexria's cheek, but she did not turn away. She watched, her heart throbbing with anger as Tinus dropped his sword and shook his head at the crowd.

It was over. The TDU was finished, and so was the Samoan. The State had further secured its iron grip. She knew no immigrant would ever gain their freedom as long as the Knights remained the gatekeepers.

CHAPTER 12: THE BETRAYAL

"To the betrayers, liars and the thieves; your fate will be waiting in the dark of night, burrowing like a snake. And it will come for you when you least expect it. It always comes when you least expect it."
~NSS

Time: 11:09 p.m. February 22, 2071.
Location: Abandoned Apartment Building. Rohania, Tisaia

Lana rushed inside the apartment and hugged Spurious forcefully, knocking the wind out of him.

"Lana!" he huffed. "Are you all right?"

"It was so awful, Spurious. I wanted to tell you at work, but I just couldn't. Varius was watching me all day."

"Calm down," he said, brushing her frizzled hair back around her ears.

"I was so afraid I lost you," he whispered into her ear.

"It was Varius. He came to my flat and forced his way in."

Spurious took a step back and caught Lana's gaze for the first time in days.

"Did he hurt you?" he asked scanning her body for bruises.

Lana shook her head and buried it back in his chest. "He said he wanted to talk, but quickly it turned into more. He touched my leg and told me he had something for me," she said, holding out a small bracelet.

Spurious stiffened, his face turning bright red. "I'm going to freaking kill him." he said venomously.

"No, Spurious, I think he is beginning to suspect something. I can't hold him at bay much longer."

"It's going to be all right. I have a plan to end all of this," he replied.

Lana looked out from behind her curtain of hair, her eyes searching his with curiosity. "What do you mean?" she asked.

Spurious rubbed his eyes. "I'll tell you in the morning. The past couple days have been a whirlwind and I need to get some rest," he said, hugging her before crashing onto the mattress.

———

Spurious gazed at Lana's sleeping body, watching her eyelids flutter as she slept. He reached over to her, touching her face softly so he wouldn't wake her. He closed his eyes and tried not to imagine what Lana had encountered the other night, but his thoughts quickly betrayed him, slipping into his mind against his will.

Spurious sat up and rested his back against the wood wall, running his hand through her thick hair. Touching her calmed him, putting him at ease. He sat and watched the shadows from the dying candle flame dance across the ceiling.

An hour of silence passed, reminding him of the countless nights he had laid awake as a child in the same room, wondering why his parents were not home. Now he knew. They were attending secret TDU meetings.

He looked back down at Lana, trying to forget his past for the night and ran his fingers through her hair again, waking her by accident. She let out a soft moan, her eyelids fluttering and her eyes struggling to open. A half smile rushed across his face. "Well hello, beautiful," he whispered.

"Hi," she said, her own smile interrupted by a small yawn. "Are you going to stay awake for a while and talk with me?"

Lana sat up, pulling her long hair back and tying it into a ponytail with a small wrist band. "I don't want to wait until the morning Spurious, I want to know what you are thinking now!" she said, poking him in the stomach.

"Hey," he laughed playfully before his smile faded and a serious tone washed across his face.

"No more talking," he said, placing her hands in his and leaning in to kiss her. Her lips met his, the warmth sending a chill down his back. They kissed deeper and he pulled her on top of him, his hand finding its way down her thigh and working its way up. He could feel the blood moving inside of him as his heart beat faster. Her shirt came off easily and he stared at her beautiful skin, leaning in to kiss her neck softly, slowly making his way back to her lips.

"You have gotten good at this," she laughed.

Spurious smiled. "I've had a good teacher."

"You know that isn't true." Lana said, blushing.

He climbed on top of her, looking into her eyes.

"I love you, Lana. And I'm going to make sure nothing happens to us."

"I love you too. Now come close to me," she whispered, pulling him onto her.

A small poof from the suffocating candle sent a trail of smoke into the air. Darkness washed over them, sending another chill down his spine. But it wasn't a chill of passion—it was a chill of fear. The same feeling he had before he lost his parents.

Spurious ignored it and leaned back in to kiss Lana deeply. She would not suffer the same fate as his parents. He would not let that happen.

Time: 10:02 a.m. February 23, 2071.
Location: Market Area. Rohania, Tisaia

Leo sat perched against an old light pole, staring into the crowded market. People watching was his job now; he gave up on making a living as a black market smuggler and instead survived off the charity he could manage to squeeze out of people. He was too old for a life of crime. Besides, his age and ragged appearance provided him a unique advantage over the other beggars.

He watched the crowded market, narrowing down his options and paying close attention to a tomato stand attracting several customers. The vendor had arrived minutes before with a fresh harvest, some dirt still present on the skin of the tomatoes.

Leo licked his lips. He hadn't eaten for a day now, his last meal being a half-loaf of bread an old friend gave him the night before.

Rohania was full of people just like him, waiting for a handout. There was normally a beggar on every corner. In fact, many of the panhandlers worked the same corner every day. People got to know them and most would avoid them. His strategy was different. He had brains; sometimes he waited an hour in a crowded market before approaching a customer or vendor with a sob story. It worked *almost* every time.

After much deliberation, he selected a young man who was in the process of purchasing two bags of tomatoes. He didn't recognize this man and was quite positive they had never met. This was step one. Find someone he didn't know, someone who had never given him food before. Next, he would approach them when their hands were full and they were preoccupied. Finally, he would quickly spout out a story explaining why he was in desperate need of a meal. There were countless stories he had used in the past. His favorite was the CRK narrative; it was something all Rohanians could relate to.

"Sir, do you have a moment?" Leo asked, approaching the man from behind.

The customer turned slightly. "What is it?" the man asked, his gaze falling on Leo's tattered clothing.

"Sir, the Tin Cans, they took everything. My last credits, my food, everything. I have nothing left. Can you please spare a few tomatoes?"

The man stiffened. He scratched his small nose uncomfortably. "Why did they do that?" he asked curiously.

Leo paused. No one ever asked why. "They... uh... they

thought I was a TDU sympathizer. And when they found out I wasn't one they kept all my belongings anyways," Leo said, stuttering.

The man raised a brow. "Are you a TDU sympathizer?"

"I'm hungry, sir. That is all. Can you please spare a tomato or two?"

The man looked over Leo's shoulders into the crowd, clearly growing annoyed.

"I need to get going."

"Just one tomato, sir, please?" Leo pleaded.

The man let out a huff. "Fine, if you get out of my way you can have a tomato," he said, grabbing the two bags from the vendor and placing them on the ground. He scanned the produce and grabbed the smallest tomato off the top.

Leo took it graciously. "Thank you sir, thank you," he said, backing away and disappearing into the crowd with a grin on his face. The ripe tomato exploded as he bit into it, the juices racing down his chin. He brought his hand to his chin, wiping away the excess juice and licking his fingers clean. In the distance he could see an empty park bench, the perfect place to find his next customer.

It was almost noon and the crowd was thicker, common for the lunch hour. People were searching for a quick bite to eat between shifts and looking for a bargain. It was the perfect time to get his next meal.

The cold metal of the park bench sent a chill up his damaged back. His ragged coat was full of holes. It was on his 'to replace' list, but a warm coat was hard to come by in Rohania, and he didn't expect to get his hands on a decent one this winter.

He bit into the tomato again, scanning the crowd for another unsuspecting shopper. In the center of the market there was a bronze statue of a middle-aged man, sitting on a chair and reading a book to a young boy on his lap. Leo didn't need to see the worn engraving at the bottom to know it read *Lincoln and Tad*. It was an artifact from the old world, a surviving clue from before the Biomass Wars, when education was an investment and books were valued.

Leo could only vaguely remember his own childhood now. It was so long ago, before the oil wells dried up and the nuclear tipped rockets sailed across the oceans, a time when men marveled in their creations and resources were plentiful for all. But it was simply not to be. Men had become experts at building, producing and manufacturing, but sadly, they were better at destroying these creations.

In the distance he watched a pair of leaves chase each other in a fickle wind. He watched them sail back and forth around the statue. They came to rest on the boot of a hefty man, who paid no attention to the insignificant leaves. He appeared to be in an argument with another man, flailing his hands in the air as they talked.

Leo crept forward, his eyes trained on these two strangers; his curiosity was building like a cat fixating upon its prey. He shoved the remaining bit of tomato in his mouth and stood up to get a better look. Something was different about them—something told him he had seen them before.

They were both dressed in aged thermal jackets, very uncommon for a Rohanian but not incredibly rare. It wasn't the jackets or their thick scarves, which could be used as dust masks in the Wastelands, that gave them away. It wasn't even the impression of their pistols inconspicuously hidden in their cargo pants either. It was their boots. Leo never mistook the boots of a TDU soldier. They all wore the same type; black, steel toed, and stained by the dust of the tunnels where the TDU operated.

Leo smiled. In another life he must have been a police officer, he told himself. His detective skills were unrivaled. He chuckled and shook his head in amusement at the two foolish soldiers. Not a week after the attack and they show up in Rohania and they didn't think to change their boots? No wonder they were losing the war.

Leo recalled what he had read in the *Lunia Post*. He snagged one of the free copies the State distributed the day after the TDU's headquarters were reportedly destroyed. He knew better to believe anything in the Post though. It was controlled by the State and their attempt at convincing Rohanians the TDU was gone had failed yet again. It wasn't the first time they had tried. The State had issued the same propaganda in the past, the headlines reading, "TDU Destroyed."

Leo cautiously made his way through the dense crowd, chuckling to himself. The fact that the State believed free papers would spread their rhetoric, considering the literacy rate in Rohania wasn't even 50 percent, was laughable.

"Ah, I remember now, Commander Obi and his loyal comrade Ajax," Leo muttered under his breath, making his way towards the two soldiers.

He had met the soldiers a few years back when he still worked in the smuggling business. If they were still alive, then there was still hope for the TDU.

"Get out of my way!" yelled a muffled voice Leo knew could only be from the breathing apparatus of a Knight. He turned and saw three Knights racing through the crowd, their assault rifles drawn.

"Move, move, move!" another one of the faceless Knights yelled.

Panic rushed through Leo as he followed the screaming crowd towards any exit from the market, pushing a young girl out of his way.

"Hey!" her mother yelled out in defense.

"Sorry," was all Leo could muster, before he disappeared back into the crowd.

He turned quickly to look for the Knights. He was gaining ground on them, but he had lost track of Obi and Ajax. If the two were caught the TDU really would be in danger of falling apart. Both soldiers were well known in Rohania, and were heroes in a war which had so far been very one sided. "Shit, where are they?" he cursed under his breath.

Leo pushed forward, his old legs protesting and groaning with every move as he clawed through the patrons. Finally he made his way into an alleyway, the brick buildings passing by in a blur. To his left was Sacred Heart, an abandoned church from the early 21st century. He knew its passages well and slept there many restless nights. To his right was an entrance to the Boondocks, a street the Knights would normally avoid.

I need to make sure they escape, he thought, running past the church and market in hope of catching sight of Obi and Ajax.

He rounded another street corner just as a thick arm reached out and grabbed him by his collar, yanking him clear off his feet and slamming him into the brick wall of a building.

"What the hell do you think you're doing, old man?" his attacker yelled.

Dazed, Leo's vision slowly came back into focus. The blurriness finally subsided and his eyes fell upon the scruffy chin of Ajax.

A smile instantly raced across Leo's face.

"I was coming to talk to you!" he exclaimed.

Ajax pounded one of his fists into the brick wall. "You could have led those Tin Cans right to us!" he said.

"I'm sorry, but I can help you. I know things." Leo pleaded.

Obi stepped towards the old man, pushing Ajax out of the way. "What could you possibly know that could help us?"

A sense of hope glimmered in Leo's eyes. "I know of someone you two would be very interested in. A man named Spurious who works in the Sector of Government Services. His parents..." Leo paused, his eyes darting back and forth from Ajax to Obi. "His parents were the founders of the TDU!" Leo exclaimed.

Obi shot Ajax a quick glance. "What do you know of this man?" he asked.

"I came across him a few weeks back. He travels to Rohania

every couple days to meet with his lover."

Ajax cut him off. "How do you know these things?"

"I know everything in Rohania and everyone." Leo said, grinning.

Ajax slammed Leo back into the wall. "I don't trust him, boss."

"We don't have a choice. This Spurious sounds just like the person we're looking for. If he does work for SGS, he probably knows the tunnel system, and he could help us get access."

Ajax frowned. "I don't like this. He's nothing more than a crazy old man," Ajax said venomously.

"We have to trust him for now," Obi responded.

Ajax nodded and let Leo back down, patting the dust off his shoulders.

"Lead the way, old man." Obi said, following Leo down the dark alleyway.

Time: 12:05 p.m. February 23, 2071.

Location: Sector of Governmental Services. Lunia, Tisaia

A powerful rain beat the metal roof of the SGS building. Spurious typed busily on his blue screen. The steady downpour sounded like dancing feet, reminding him of Paulo and his love for salsa.

He frowned and pulled up a new screen of tunnel blueprints, desperately trying to put Lana and Paulo out of his mind. It was of no use; his thoughts would betray him no matter how hard he tried.

He turned to look at Archie and began to consider his options with Lana. There were only two. They could escape to Rohania and try to survive with the help of strangers until they were able to procure secure jobs, or they could leave Tisaia and take their chances in the Wastelands.

Spurious recalled a confidential document he came across years ago. It was a map of several tunnel systems in underground Lunia. There was a sporadic red 'X' marked in multiple locations, indicating what he thought were potential TDU hideouts. After digging a bit deeper, Spurious found they weren't TDU related at all. They were locations State employees were caught trying to escape Tisaia and into the Wastelands. He remembered the shock when the dozens of red splotches finally made sense. There were others out there just like him, longing to escape the monotony of their lives and the State controlling them. Every dot represented someone willing to risk everything to escape.

Archie swam to the top of his bowl, his tiny lips pecking at the fragments of food at the surface. Spurious watched him, wondering if he too felt trapped in his small world. He thought back to his options, neither seeming very realistic.

Leaving Tisaia, even with his knowledge of the tunnel systems, would probably result in another red dot on the map. Except this time, there would be two—one for him and one for Lana, something he wouldn't let happen.

Rohania, on the other hand seemed more plausible, especially if he could make some contacts there ahead of time.

His stomach growled, reminding him he had skipped lunch.

Maybe I'll go for a short walk, he thought, turning off his blue screen and heading for the stairs. The stifling concrete staircase was filled with the scent of bleach, recently cleaned by a crew of service workers. As he descended the last few floors and headed for the lobby exit, a voice rang out over the silence. "Hi, Spurious!"

He turned to see Cleoa working from behind the same oval receptionist desk where she had been the day he started at SGS. The only difference was a few more grays in her curtain of hair. Her smile always reminded him of those first few days when he walked through the sea of endless cubicles, meeting rooms, and the cafeteria, all reeking of bleach. It was that first day he realized the building felt like a prison, one in which he would spend the rest of his life.

Spurious waved at Cleoa quickly, eager to escape the building. He pushed the lobby doors open and stepped outside, taking in a long breath of air. Slowly the scent of bleach faded only to be replaced with the fresh aroma of rain. He opened his eyes to see a curtain of sleet falling to the ground. The climatologists were wrong again, forecasting a mostly clear afternoon.

Spurious sighed, heading back into the building with his head tucked in his collar. He passed several other workers on his way to the stairs and entered the hallway, catching a glimpse of Lana out of the corner of his eye. Quickly, he hid behind one of the thick concrete pillars lining the hallway. He glanced around the edge; inconspicuously as possible, his face rubbing against the cool rough surface of the concrete.

Half way down the hall he could see Lana, her head pointed at the ground as Varius yelled at her. Other employees hurried past, ignoring them.

Spurious pulled himself away from the view, resting his back against the pillar, his chest heaving in and out as he tried to catch his breath before heading back to his desk.

This is just too much. I can't take it anymore. I want to kill him, he thought, slipping back into his cubicle. Tonight he would settle everything with Lana—tonight he would meet her at his old apartment and tell her they were leaving Lunia.

Time: 7:05 p.m. February 23, 2071.
Location: Commons Building 21, Apt #44. Lunia, Tisaia

Spurious sat at his wooden desk, nestled next to his lofted bed. On the cherry wood surface sat a blank piece of aging paper, waiting for his pen. For an hour Spurious sat, his right hand supporting his worried head. But the words wouldn't come. He simply sat staring blankly at the yellow paper.

Through the single window in his flat he watched the weak sun disappear on the horizon, darkness slowly swallowing Tisaia. Finally his thoughts met paper with a swift stroke of his pen.

Feb 23, 2071

Dear Ing:

Every morning I walk past the same ancient tree whose home is in the middle of the courtyard outside my building. Its branches protrude like vines up towards the sky and brush the nearby buildings. Not a day goes by I don't stop to admire this tree, which is dying on one side and healthy and strong on the other. And lately I feel as if I have a connection to this tree, one that symbolizes my own struggles.

It's not a secret that times are changing in Lunia, nor is it a secret that things have changed drastically everywhere.

Before Paulo died, he said he feared a State that limited liberties and rights. His fear was Tisaia would eventually become this State, and it would rule by fueling so much fear in its citizens they would blindly follow every law and rule the legislature could pass.

I honestly never believed this would happen. For years I have been brainwashed and manipulated by the Lunia Post, the Sector of Education, the Council of Royal Knights, and every other State-run agency that nourishes the general population with false hope. Their words are empty lies in a bottomless pit full of so many before them, with the sole purpose of keeping employees working like robots.

In many ways, Tisaia has become like a worker bee colony. We work and die for the betterment of a single idea — but the idea has turned to greed. And now it's time to leave. I can't tell you where, but as a friend, you deserve to know why.

Tonight I'll meet Lana in Rohania one last time as I leave Tisaia forever.

I'm sorry.

Your friend always,
Spurious

His pen dropped softly onto the worn surface of the wooden desk, rolling down its surface towards the edge. For what seemed like hours he stared at the note, wondering if it was the right thing to do. He knew if he risked telling Ing in person there was the chance he would be caught. It was a risk he couldn't take.

He shut off his desk lamp and headed for his closet. There was packing to do, and he wasn't packing just for himself.

Time: 9:05 p.m. February 23, 2071.
Location: Tunnels. Rohania, Tisaia

Spurious crawled on his belly through the storm drain he used to enter Rohania. In the distance he heard the humming of a Scorpion on a road somewhere above. He froze, pressing his ear against the vibrating concrete wall to listen. There was no way to determine how many Scorpions there were; the tunnel muffled the sound making it impossible to determine their location. For a minute he lay petrified on the cold floor, waiting until the Scorpion patrol passed.

Silence washed over the tunnel, leaving only the sound of a slight wind in the distance. He grabbed his pack and started crawling again, knowing it was too late to head back. Anya would ask questions, and he knew his luck was almost gone, having evaded detection for so long.

The heavy pack made it difficult to crawl. It was filled with items he knew they would need to survive until they found a safe house in Rohania or attempted to cross the Wastelands. It was best they left without warning, and it was even better Lana didn't know they were leaving until the last minute. He knew they would need more than food, water, and anti-radiation tablets to survive; they would need luck, lots of it.

After a few minutes of struggling through the narrow storm drain, Spurious climbed out in to Rohania. He darted down the narrow alley where he'd first met Leo, and made his way down the dark city streets, clinging to the shadows on his way to his old flat.

The slick streets were mostly empty, save for the random drunk stumbling about. It was eerily quiet. Nothing but the whipping wind and the drip of a clogged roof drain. Spurious stopped in the alleyway connecting to his building, looking at the sparse shapes jetting out of the darkness – the crumbling brick of the hastily constructed buildings, the filthy storm drains clogged with trash. It wasn't the type of place he wanted to live the rest of his life, but he had no choice. If he wanted to be with Lana he would live anywhere, through anything.

Inside the building, Spurious lit a candle and climbed the creaky stairs to the third floor where he hoped Lana was already waiting for him.

Spurious looked down at his watch. Lana should be here, he thought, twisting the knob to his old flat.

The warm glow of orange candle light welcomed him. In the center of the room Lana sat on a pillow, waiting.

"Good evening," he whispered.

Lana's dark eyes glowed in the light and her cheeks flared red with blush. "Hi," she said, her eyes pointed at her feet.

"What's wrong?" he asked, setting his pack on the ground. He walked over and sat next to her, leaning down to give her a brief kiss on her forehead. Lana hugged him, almost forcefully.

"I'm sorry," she whispered.

Spurious stiffened, taking a step back just in time to hear the clanking of armor behind him.

"DON'T MOVE!" a muffled voice screamed behind him.

Spurious grabbed her shoulders softly, chills running through his body. He held her gaze for a second before he felt the butt of a rifle smash into his spine. He screamed in pain and collapsed onto the ground, reaching for his back in agony. His mind was spinning with confusion.

He turned to see his attacker towering above him with a rifle aimed at his head. The Knight's blue goggles glowed eerily in the sparsely lit room.

"Don't move. Stay where you are," he said, his booming voice muffled by the breathing apparatus.

"Lana, what have you done?" Spurious yelled, trying to crawl across the floor towards her.

"I said, don't move!" the Knight yelled, bringing the butt of his gun down on Spurious' right leg.

He screamed again, reaching to calm the fire of pain shooting up his leg.

"Don't hurt him! Please, you promised you wouldn't hurt him!" Lana yelled from her hiding spot.

"Take him away," the Knight said, as another soldier entered the room.

"Lana, what have you done?" Spurious yelled again, crying in agony.

"I'm sorry, Spurious! They captured my family a month ago. I had no choice. They said they would deport us all to the Wastelands!"

The pain of the truth hurt more than the fire spreading through his injured body. She'd set him up. It was planned all along. The bruises on her neck in the courtyard the first night they spoke weren't from Varius, they were from the Knights. Varius never threatened her. He never showed up at her house. It was the Knights all along. She traded him for her family.

How could I have been so stupid?

The sadness and shock quickly turned to rage. His head shot up, his eyes meeting Lana's for a split second before she turned away to run out into the other room. He turned again and watched the Knight approach him cautiously, the barrel of his rifle aimed towards Spurious' head.

"No!" Spurious screamed, jumping to his feet and charging towards him. The Knight took a step back and pointed his rifle at Spurious again.

"I'll shoot!"

Spurious only made it a few feet before his first attacker threw an armored punch. The metal connected with his head, blood exploding from his mouth as he sailed to the floor.

Spurious lay on the ground, curling up and feebly wiping his mouth clean of blood. He blinked, his eyes burning in pain. He watched the two Knights reaching down to grab him, wondering if he was feeling the same fear his parents did so many years ago when the Knights came for them.

Deep down he knew the Knights would eventually come for him, but he never imagined Lana would lead them there. His head spun, fueling the confusing agony spreading through his mind like a wildfire.

One of the Knights tugged on his shoulder with an iron grip and his mind returned to his attackers, rage boiling inside him.

"Hold still!" the Knight yelled, his armored fingers digging into Spurious' back.

He blinked again, desperately hoping it was all a dream, but the shattering pain from the armored fist of the Knight was too visceral to be anything but real. He wasn't stuck in a dream. He was stuck in a nightmare.

Time: 12:05 a.m. February 24, 2071.

Location: Abandoned Apartment Building. Rohania, Tisaia

"That's it, that's the place," Leo said, pointing at a crumbling brick building.

Obi stared at the torn CRK poster hanging loosely in the cold wind.

"Are you sure this is it?" he asked.

"Damn sure, and I'm willing to bet the man you want is up there right now."

Ajax, Obi and Leo stood at the edge of the street, peering up at the white stone, half expecting to see a face looking down at them from an old broken window, but there were no windows anymore: the CRK made sure of it.

"Show us the way," Obi requested.

Leo hustled across the street, his scrawny body hunched over like a praying mantis as he slyly made his way into the alley next to the old apartment building. Ajax and Obi followed cautiously, their hands gripping weapons hidden within the confines of their large coats. They were both aware of the possibility of an ambush, something Obi always prepared for.

As the small group made their way into the building, they picked up the faint sound of voices muffled by the thick wood of the buildings walls. Leo stole a glance at Obi, who stood positioned in the exit door of the hallway, his rifle drawn.

"It's the room half way down the hall on the third floor," Leo whispered. "I need to leave now, there isn't anything else I can help you with," he continued apologetically.

Ajax grabbed Leo's skinny right arm and pulled him towards the hallway wall, glancing back at Obi.

"Let him go," Obi said.

Reluctantly Ajax obeyed, scowling at Leo before releasing him.

A scream broke through the silence, prompting Ajax and Obi to point their weapons up the dark staircase simultaneously.

"Get out your night vision," Obi whispered.

Both soldiers reached into their coats and pulled out their goggles. A cool orange glow warmed the staircase and the two quietly made their way towards the sound.

Another scream rang out above them. Obi halted, changing his night vision to infrared. He wanted to pick up heat signatures so he knew how many people they were dealing with.

"You go in first and I'll follow; if Spurious is in there with Lana, be careful. I don't want either of them harmed." Obi said, nearing the top of the staircase.

"What do we do with her?" Ajax whispered.

"Not sure, just move."

The two soldiers crept down the hall slowly like hunters, trying to tiptoe over the creaky wood floor. At the end of the passage, underneath one of the doors, a blue glow flowed into the hallway.

"Stop, Ajax."

"What's wrong boss?" he whispered.

"Tin Cans. Ahead. I can see the glow from their night vision goggles."

Obi removed his glasses and knelt, reaching for his knife in a sleeve on his right leg. Ajax hunched down next to him, resting his massive frame against an apartment door. They knelt and strained to hear the conversation coming from down the hall.

"Sounds like someone got to this Spurious before us," Obi said.

"What are you thinking?" Ajax asked.

"We need him. If the Tin Cans want him, then he is obviously valuable."

Ajax groaned heavily. "I don't like this. We're gambling with our lives."

Obi checked his clip and put his goggles back on. He was picking up at least four, maybe five heat signatures in the room. With only their pistols, they were going to need some more fire power to take out two or three Knights.

The ringing of heavy footsteps shattered the silence. Quickly Ajax followed Obi into an open apartment, hiding in the shadows. They waited, their chests both heaving in and out their eyes watching the blue glow of a Knight's goggles flooding the hallway.

Ajax pulled out his knife, revealing it to Obi with a single finger over his mouth. They waited patiently for the light to pass before Ajax peeked into the hallway to confirm the presence of another Knight. The man stood guard at the doorway where Spurious was being interrogated, his armored back facing the hallway.

"He has his back to us. We can get out now," Ajax said, turning.

"Can you take him from behind?" Obi entreated.

"Are you fucking kidding me, boss? There is an entire squad of them in there. It's suicide."

Obi shot him an angry glance, his orange goggles staring back at him. "You take out the guard, grab his gun, and we'll kill the other Knights together," he paused to take in a deep breath. "That's an order, soldier!" Obi hissed.

He pulled a new clip of armor piercing rounds from the bowels of his jacket. They were custom made, tipped with plutonium. The last of their kind, and he had been saving them for a special occasion.

"And make sure Spurious isn't harmed, or his girlfriend, if she's in there too," he said, inserting the clip into his pistol with a click.

Ajax nodded, clicking off his goggles to examine the hallway one more time before he slyly slipped into the darkness. He crouched, heading towards the guard with his knife drawn.

A minute passed and Obi watched anxiously from behind, waiting for Ajax to make his move. The Knight remained frozen, standing in the entryway of the room, no idea he was about to die.

Ajax stopped less than a yard away from the guard, bringing his knife inches away from the unsuspecting Knight's armor. He aimed it at the gap between the neck armor and helmet. With a quick jab, he jammed the sharp blade into the back of his neck. Ajax barely flinched, indifferent to the spurt of blood that exploded onto his face. He had the guard's rifle within seconds, shoving the Knight who clawed vainly at his neck. Obi rushed into the room, his gun spitting hot lead at the other two Knights, who were attempting to drag Spurious' body out of a bedroom.

The barrage of bullets from Ajax's assault rifle went high, tearing into the wall, and sending a shower of splinters into the air. Both Knights fumbled with their weapons, but it was too late, Obi's armor piercing rounds ripped through their armor. 30 seconds later it was over. All three Knights lay in pools of their own blood. Ajax checked their vitals, firing a single shot into their goggles to ensure they were dead.

In the center of the room, Spurious lay curled up in a fetal position, moaning in pain.

"Check him!" Obi shouted, rushing over to Lana, who was huddled in the corner.

He pulled the drape of hair out of her face, revealing a frightened set of eyes.

"Are you ok?" he asked.

She rocked back and forth, her knees pulled up to her chest and her wild eyes locked on her feet. She was catatonic, in shock from the gun fire.

"We need to move, boss!" Ajax yelled from across the room. "Reinforcements could be here any minute!"

"How is Spurious?"

"He's hurt, bad. We need to get him out of here fast."

Obi glanced down at the girl with concern in his eyes, knowing he shouldn't be wasting time on her. "Are you okay?"

She stared back at him blankly. Her eyes were clouded with fear and she was slipping into shock. Obi left her and ran over to help Ajax who was bending down to pick up Spurious.

"Help me get him on my shoulders."

Obi snagged one of the dead Knight's rifles on his way, throwing the strap around his shoulder.

The two soldiers rushed out of the room, just as one of the dead Knight's radios blared to life.

"This is Delta Base. Report. Over."

"Friede, what's your status? Do you have the package?"

"Shit. Let's go!" Obi yelled, turning one last time to check on Lana. Miraculously, she was standing in the corner staring back at them. "Well, are you coming or what?" he screamed at her. She froze and then reluctantly walked over to Ajax, placing her hand on Spurious' unconscious head.

"Boss, we aren't taking her with, are we?" Ajax asked scornfully.

The radio blared back to life again. "Friede, we're sending another squad to your location. ETA five minutes. Over."

A chill ran down Obi's back as he locked eyes with Ajax. No words needed to be exchanged. The two soldiers knew each other well enough to know it was time to move. Within seconds of the radio transmission they were running down the hallway, Spurious' head bobbing up and down on Ajax's shoulders.

"We need to find a different exit. This could be another trap." Obi yelled over the clamor of their footsteps. He could see the bottom of the staircase in the distance, a diminutive yet guiding glow of moonlight illuminating the first floor hallway. He entered cautiously, his rifle drawn. There were no signs of a trap through the door they entered, but he didn't want to risk it.

"That way," Obi motioned with a nod of his head. He stood guard at the door, his rifle aimed into darkness while Ajax carried Spurious down the hallway, Lana close behind.

Obi took off to catch up with them and seconds later they were at the end of the hallway staring at a sealed door, closed off with several two by fours.

"Damn, it's a dead end!" Ajax yelled.

Obi glanced back down the hallway, scanning it for an open apartment door. Every door appeared to be sealed with two by fours as well. "Shit, the reinforcements are going to be here any minute," he said.

"Help me," Ajax said, lowering Spurious carefully onto the ground.

The two soldiers clawed at the two by fours, tearing them off quickly while Lana attended to Spurious.

"Where am I?" Spurious moaned. He peered up at Lana, blinking through the fog of stars, his brain still on fire. "Lana, was it a dream?" he asked, her face finally coming into focus.

"Oh Spurious," she whimpered. "I'm so sorry. The Knights caught me a few months ago. They said if I didn't help them find traitors, they would have my family deported."

Spurious rubbed the bloody gash on his head, staring at Lana in shock. "So this was all a lie?" he asked disdainfully.

"No my feelings were real. They are real. I love you," she whispered, placing his hands in hers.

Spurious pulled away, scooting to rest his back against the wall.

"I can never trust you again," he said.

"Keep it down!" Ajax exclaimed, looking down at him while he plucked another two by four off the door.

"Who the hell are they?" Spurious asked Lana.

"We're with the TDU. That's all I have time to tell you. Now help us get these off," Obi whispered down to him.

Spurious froze. It was the first time he had ever seen one of the rebels in person. He studied the two men as they continued to pry off the two by fours. Finally he realized this is what his parents had lived like, in constant fear. And now he was trapped in the same building they were killed, betrayed by the woman he loved.

Shocked into motion he rose to his feet, a deep pain racing up his leg. Anger gripped him, filling his body with adrenaline.

"There, stop them!" a muffled voice yelled down the hallway.

The group turned simultaneously to see a glowing set of blue orb-like eyes entering the dark hallway.

"Watch out," Ajax yelled, taking a step back and kicking the door handle, sending chunks of wood splinters in all directions.

"Go!" he yelled, turning to fire at the approaching soldiers.

The hallway erupted into chaos, the Knights returning fire. Pieces of wood and plaster rained down on Spurious. He covered his ears and huddled against the wall.

"Come with me," Obi yelled grabbing his arm and pulling him towards the doorway while firing his pistol at the Knights with his free hand.

"Get them out of here, boss!" Ajax yelled, finishing off another clip at the two Knights. He watched three of his rounds tear through the chest plate on one soldier, blood splattering onto the wall behind him. The second Knight wavered for only a moment, glancing down at his fallen comrade before returning fire.

Spurious watched Lana helplessly as Obi continuing to drag him towards the door. "Lana hurry! Run!" Spurious screamed.

She stood, hesitating before she took off towards the doorway. Spurious' eyes followed her, watching the bullets tear into the floor and walls around her.

And then everything slowed. The pain in Spurious' leg and head subsided. He watched fire erupt from Obi's pistol, blank cartridges raining down on him as the bullets zipped towards the Knight. His eyes panned to Lana who was still running for him, now only a few steps away.

She is going to make it, he thought, watching one of Obi's bullets hit the Knight in the kneecap.

Spurious could hear the man's muffled scream over the gunfire. He watched the man slowly collapse to the ground, his weapon firing wildly.

His eyes darted back to Lana, who was reaching out for him, her beautiful brown hair flowing behind her. Their eyes locked and Spurious pulled free of Obi's grip to reach out for her, just as two bullets tore through her stomach. Her eyes burned with terror as she fell, blood splattering onto Spurious' shirt. She landed in his arms just as Obi finished off the last Knight, a round piercing his goggles and burying deep into his skull.

"No!" Spurious screamed, carefully turning Lana onto her back. She looked up at him, blood gurgling in her throat. She tried to speak, but Spurious put his fingers to her mouth.

"No, you're going to be okay," he lied, his eyes quickly panning down to her mortal wounds.

She reached for his face, her fingers smearing warm blood on his skin. "I'm…" She paused, choking on her own blood. "I'm sorry, Spurious."

He watched the life draining from her deep brown eyes, her last breath escaping from her mouth.

"No, Lana. You can't die! Lana. Lana. Lana!" he screamed,

shaking her fruitlessly.

"You have to leave her," a voice said from behind him. He felt a strong grip shaking his shoulder. Spurious ignored it, whimpering, tears flowing down his face while he rocked her head back and forth in his lap.

Ajax and Obi towered above, looking down helplessly. "There could be more Tin Cans coming," Ajax said, looking over at Obi.

"I know. We need to move, but we have to give him a second."

Obi hesitated, watching Spurious hold Lana's head tightly to his chest. He saw the anguish and grief, a flashback from the past taking hold of him. The image of his father holding his dying mother crawled into his mind, an image he had long since blocked from his memory.

"Let's go," Obi said, quickly shaking the image from his mind. He motioned to Ajax with a nod, and instantly, the giant soldier grabbed Spurious and pulled him screaming towards the door. Obi stopped to close Lana's eyelids before following Ajax into the darkness.

Time: 2:00 a.m. February 24, 2071.
Location: Tunnels. Lunia, Tisaia

Spurious awoke to the rancid smell of raw sewage, coughing the pungent stench out of his lungs. His hand shot to his throbbing forehead, where a deep gash oozed blood onto his fingers. He felt a stab of horror.

Was it a dream?

"He's coming to, boss," said a voice from behind him.

Spurious tried to sit up, gritting his teeth, his eyes blinking as they adjusted to the darkness.

"Stay calm. We aren't going to hurt you," another voice said, from the corner.

"Where am I? Who are you? Where is Lana?" Spurious said,

turning from side to side, desperate to see the faces belonging to the voices. "LANA!" he screamed, before anyone could silence him.

"God damn it! You have to be quiet," one of the men said, placing their hands over his mouth.

He struggled for a few minutes before calming, his eyes coming to rest on the two soldiers who had rescued him earlier.

"Are you going to be quiet?" the larger man asked.

Spurious nodded slowly. The man removed his hand cautiously from his lips. He sat up and scooted a few paces back, coming to rest against the concrete wall.

"I'm Obi," the older man said, cracking the most sincere smile he could manage. "This here is Ajax," he said, pointing at the other soldier, who didn't bother to smile.

Spurious studied the two soldiers. "She's dead, isn't she?" he choked.

Obi nodded. "I'm sorry. There wasn't anything we could do."

"She betrayed me." Spurious said quietly. "I was going to leave Lunia with her."

"It's better you lost her now then, there is no life for State workers outside the walls," Ajax said, with a snort.

Spurious wiped a tear from his eye, scanning his surroundings. He took another gasp of the rancid air and coughed.

"We need to get moving," Obi said.

Spurious stiffened. "Wait, what? Where are we going?"

Obi lit a cigarette as he waded through the knee deep sewage. "We don't have time to explain, but soon we'll tell you everything."

Spurious hesitated, forgetting momentarily about Lana. There was something about Obi that convinced Spurious to trust him; maybe it was the conviction in his voice, the sincerity in his gaze or the fact that Obi had rescued him. Whatever it was, Spurious knew he had little choice but to follow the two soldiers.

"Will I get a chance to fight the CRK?" Spurious asked, a hint of strength present in his voice.

Through the darkness, Spurious could see a smile finally crack on Ajax's face. "You'll have a chance to fight them, likely sooner than you think," he replied.

Obi watched Ajax and Spurious wade through the muck. He took one last drag of his cigarette, blowing the smoke into the cold night air and watching it disappear into the swirling brown sewage below.

Time: 3:05 a.m. February 24, 2071.
Location: Junkyard. Rohania, Tisaia.

A weak moon broke out of the thick clouds, providing just enough light to make out the junkyard below. Nathar sat perched on the rooftop of the abandoned building in which they had taken refuge in days before, staring into the darkness.

"What do you see?" Creo asked.

Nathar swung around, annoyed. "Nothing yet. I'm not picking up any heat signatures." It was the second time Creo had asked him in as many minutes, and Nathar was getting tired of sitting on his ass and keeping watch.

"Do you want to trade me spots?" Nathar asked.

Creo stood, putting a hand on Nathar's shoulder. "No, I'll check on the new recruits. Let me know if you see anything."

"Will do," Nathar said. He turned to scan the shadows below. The work was part of his job as a scout with Squad 19. Over the years he had spent as much time silently watching as he had sleeping. It simply came with the territory, but tonight he was anxious. The minutes passed by like hours.

He listened to the sounds of the night and watched the shadows dance through the antique junkyard. Obi and Ajax still hadn't shown up and Nathar was beginning to worry.

And he didn't like to worry. It was unnecessary, getting all worked up over something he couldn't control. There was no shortage of things to worry about, with the TDU having suffered such extreme losses, but Nathar normally didn't let these things affect him.

He reminded himself he was a scout, part of Squad 19—the most revered unit in the TDU, feared by the Royal Knights and known throughout Tisaia. Members of the squad didn't worry. They did what they had to do to get things done.

A sudden flash of yellow light broke through the darkness opposite his position and disappeared into the sky. He turned quickly, zooming in with his night vision goggles, but there was only darkness. There were no heat signatures or signs of life.

A few seconds passed and the same golden light shot out again. It was too quick to be a signaling unit, but then again Obi and Ajax probably didn't have one to begin with. Whatever it was, someone was trying to get his attention. His instinct was to signal back, but something didn't feel right.

For a long moment he sat there scanning the landscape below, jumping as a cold hand grabbed his shoulder. He twisted, startled to see Creo staring down at the junkyard.

"I saw it."

"There," Nathar whispered, his right hand pointing at a pair of smashed trucks piled against a concrete barrier about 100 yards from their position.

"Three heat signatures behind the trucks." Creo whispered again.

"Should I signal? It has to be them."

Creo nodded again. "Send out the signal."

Nathar reached into his pocket and grabbed a small device from his pack. He clicked it on and a laser shot into the sky, visible only to those who had goggles designed to pick it up. It was a nifty device, one he had stolen from a patrol of Knights a few years back. The TDU engineers retrofitted it so the laser could only be picked up by Squad 19's night vision goggles.

Within seconds three figures emerged, slowly making their way towards Nathar's location.

Creo took aim with his sniper rifle, cautious of a potential trap, but lowered it as Nathar smiled. They watched the familiar shape of Ajax emerge from the shadows. Thrilled to see their comrades safe, the two climbed down the ladder and jumped onto the dirt below, a cloud of invisible dust rising into the darkness.

"Damn good to see you, brother," Nathar said, embracing the large man with a quick hug.

"Holy shit, you smell like a damn latrine!" Nathar said, laughing.

Ajax shrugged, "Not the first time and won't be the last."

"Who is this?" Creo interrupted, motioning towards Spurious. The moonlight broke through a cloud and illuminated his swollen face and clothing, lurid with blood stains.

"This is Spurious. He works for SGS. His work focuses primarily on the tunnels. And he is the key we've been waiting for," Obi said, cracking a sly smile.

Spurious turned, a confused look on his bruised face.

Obi patted him on the back reassuringly. "Don't worry. There's plenty of time to fill you in, Spurious. We have a long journey ahead of us."

Time: 5:55 a.m. February 24, 2071.
Location: The Wastelands

Obi went over the plan in his head. It sounded crazy, even to him, but he knew it might be their only chance at taking out the CRK's headquarters and, if they had the chance, the Capitol building as well. If this happened Obi was sure the commoners, immigrants and other State workers would rise to the cause, toppling the government.

Obi smiled coyly in the darkness. He had led his men to and from Tisaia many times, but never did he imagine he would be in a situation like this. Their headquarters had been destroyed, their commanders killed, and as far as he knew, he was the highest ranking TDU soldier left. This meant his life expectancy just dropped dramatically.

No one lives forever.

He laughed at the cliché, stopping to look over at what was, as far as he knew, all that was left of the TDU. He took a moment to scan the four new recruits: all young men, no older than 30, dressed in raggedy clothing and equipped with antique assault rifles.

Obi shook his head. He tried to suppress the anger he felt, but after seeing so much death it was difficult. Nonetheless he continued on, weaving around the charred skeletons of old cars and trucks. In the distance a few structures jutted out of broken landscape. He stopped, motioning for the squad to do the same.

Not two hundred yards away sat two structures, their roofs long gone from the torturous wind. He watched an old sign creaking eerily in the wind, the lettering barely visible in the moonlight. *7Eleven*, the sign read. Obi instantly recognized it, recalling the chain of gas stations from his youth. He could still remember hanging out in the parking lot after classes as a boy. Years before the bombs dropped.

"Watch my six," Obi whispered to Ajax, taking off in a sprint towards the structures. He knew it was unlikely there would be any stragglers or raiders this close to the Tisaian walls, but he hadn't lived this long by taking unnecessary risks.

Silently he propped himself up against the outside of the building and peered in one of the broken windows. "Empty," he whispered under his breath.

He flashed a quick hand signal and the squad joined him. "Everyone take five," he whispered.

They only had about three more miles to go before they reached the rendezvous, but with only an hour of darkness left, he knew time was running out. He wanted to avoid getting caught in the light, even though he knew the chance of crossing paths with any raiders at this hour was slim.

The squad trudged on cautiously down the old highway. Suddenly, Obi halted, balling his hands into a fist. He could vaguely make out the skeletons of what was once a lush forest of trees. He had been here before, years ago on a scavenging mission. From his recollection of the area he knew the silo was not far.

Obi massaged the whiskers growing on his face, trying to fight off the drowsiness. He squinted again and caught sight of the barbed wired fence surrounding the old silo. His night vision wasn't picking up any heat signatures. He craned his neck to get a better look at a mound of dirt in the center of the compound. With the naked eye it looked like nothing more than a burial site. But he knew underneath was a door—and under that door was a ladder extending hundreds of feet into the bunker of a silo. He knew because he had been the scout to cover it with dirt years before.

"What do you think, boss?" Ajax whispered from behind.

"Follow me, we are here," he said, heading towards the silhouette of the building.

Time: 12:05 p.m. February 24, 2071.
Location: Silo. The Wastelands

Spurious awoke from a terrible dream. It took a while for his eyes to adjust and for reality to set in. As soon as he saw the other soldiers he remembered. He remembered it all; Lana, the firefight, the march through the Wastelands, meeting the other TDU members and John. It didn't take long before the horror slowly began to rise within him, a knot forming deep in his stomach. He lurched forward.

"Boss, he's awake," Ajax yelled from the corner of the small room.

Spurious sat up, his hand rubbing the lump on his face.

"I hope you slept well, because we have a lot of work to do.

Take a few minutes to get your wits and then follow me to the table," Obi said.

Spurious tried to listen, but his thoughts turned to Lana. He shook his head, hoping the act would stop the thoughts from penetrating his mind. But all it did was make his head throb more. He was hungry for air, needing it like a starving animal.

Obi and Ajax veered out of his way as he made his way for the door. He glanced at John and the other TDU members, who sat around a large table in the adjacent room. The door swung open and a brief flare of sunlight hit him in the eyes, bringing him to his knees. "Lana," he whimpered, his hands shielding his eyes from the rare sunlight.

The world began to spin, pulling him into a trance. He choked and vomit exploded from his mouth before he collapsed to the dusty ground.

An hour had passed and Obi began to worry. He watched Juliana apply a warm rag to Spurious' forehead as he lay staring at the ceiling blankly.

It was just as Obi had feared. The death of Lana had taken over his mind, and his grief was too much to handle.

"Damn, boss, what are we going to do? He looks like a zombie." Ajax asked.

Obi didn't respond. He sat in the corner of the room watching Spurious. He knew if he didn't snap out of it soon they were going to have to leave him. The silo wouldn't be safe for more than a few days. And in this state, he was going to be a travel liability.

"Screw it, we don't have time for this," Obi said under his breath. He dragged his chair across the room and positioned it next to Spurious' bed.

"Spurious…" Obi paused, glancing over at Juliana and motioning for her to take a break. She smiled before retreating to the table with the others.

He leaned over Spurious and continued. "What I'm about to tell you, I have never told anyone."

Obi shot a quick look over his shoulder to make sure none of his men were listening.

"The other night, when I saw you holding Lana, I had a flashback. It was a memory I haven't had for years. Something I blocked because it hurt too much. When I was a child, my mother was shot by raiders. She died in my father's arms, just like I watched Lana die in yours."

Obi coughed and massaged his whiskers again, thinking of what to say next. "When I saw your anguish, your grief, I remembered why I joined the TDU. I did it, I think, for the same reasons your parents helped form it—for all of those people who can't fight themselves; for the immigrants, the Rohanian's, and the survivors dwelling beyond the walls."

Silence filled the room and Obi watched Spurious for a reaction, any reaction, but the young man continued to stare at the ceiling.

"Spurious, we need you. We need you to help free Tisaia and restore the dream it was formed on, the dream of freedom. I know we're asking a lot. But last night you asked me something. Do you remember what it was?"

Obi didn't realize it, but Spurious was listening to him— listening to his voice; the soft, almost fragile tone caressing his eardrums, helping relieve some of his fear.

Spurious stirred, his eyes darting over to Obi and catching his gaze. "I remember," he said, abruptly.

Obi stiffened, shocked at the spontaneous reaction.

"What do you need me to do?" Spurious asked quietly.

Obi scratched his whiskers again, silence washing over the room. He didn't dare turn to the others now that Spurious was acknowledging him.

"We need your expertise on the tunnels. Specifically, we need you to help us review some maps. And…" Obi paused. "We need you to get us access to the tunnels beneath the CRK headquarters."

"How am I supposed to give you access?" Spurious asked. Anya would have already reported him to the CRK and a team of Knights would be tearing his flat apart.

Spurious forgot about his AI and apartment as a hand tugged on his shoulder. "We know you have had extensive access to maps of the tunnels under Tisaia. Obviously, we're interested in these maps, especially those of the tunnels connecting to the catacombs under the CRK headquarters. Your SGS clearance should give you admission to these tunnels. Even if it has been revoked we can reprogram the card, plant our explosives and escape."

Spurious closed his eyes.

So this is what Leo meant.

"Once the CRK headquarters has been destroyed, the Governor will not be able to prevent an uprising. Tisaia will rise to our cause. I can assure you, Rohania is full of TDU supporters and there are hundreds of them in Lunia as well. We'll then focus our attack on the guards at the immigrant camps. Behind those barbed wire fences lays an army waiting for this opportunity, and has been for a while," Obi said, pausing to catch his breath.

Spurious gazed at Obi's face. Scars lined the man's aged skin. Dark circles rimmed his eyes. He looked broken, signs of a soldier fighting for far too long, but something in his face was also trustworthy. Maybe it was his kind eyes, or perhaps his convincing voice. There was also the silver cross he wore around his neck. It was the same shape of the cross Spurious had bought from the antique store in the East Village a few years back. Which meant Obi was a religious man, in a world where it had all but been forgotten. This intrigued Spurious. Whatever it was about the man, he trusted him and knew his parents would want him to help the plan succeed.

This was the life chosen for me.

CHAPTER 13: THE BIOMASS REVOLUTION

"Revolutions are the locomotives of history."
~ Karl Marx

Time: 5:01 p.m. February 24, 2071.
Location: Silo. The Wastelands

Obi stared at several maps spread out over a large wooden table in the basement of the Silo. The bunker was just like he remembered it; cramped, dark and rancid.

"I don't believe it, for God's sake. These are all old maps?" he asked, bringing his hand down on the table.

The room was filled with what was left of the TDU. They watched intensely from metal chairs behind the table, hope flickering in some eyes and doubt in others.

Obi paced back and forth while Spurious reviewed the maps. He tried to concentrate, but the ancient wall lights flickered, a result of the dust storm hammering the roof far above.

"That wasn't a rhetorical question Spurious. Are you really telling me all of these maps are old, and finding a route into the CRK tunnels is going to be next to impossible?" Obi asked.

Spurious studied the maps, trying to fight the drowsiness. "Yeah, these maps are all old as dirt. I mean, some of these tunnels are still there, but some have caved in, been blown up, or filled with storm water," Spurious said, pausing.

"The tunnels you need access to aren't on any maps you would ever be able to obtain. The CRK will have made sure of that. Luckily, they're up here," Spurious said, pointing at his head.

Obi gritted his teeth. "I was hoping we weren't going to have to rely on your memory of blueprints, but if that's all we have, then that's all we have."

"Where is the rest of the TDU?" Spurious asked suddenly.

Ajax jumped up and grabbed the back of his chair, swinging him around. "What's that supposed to mean?" Ajax roared, a large vein in his forehead bulging out.

"Back off Ajax!" Obi yelled. "Yes, Spurious. The men in this room and a few upstairs are the all that remains of the TDU. And that…" Obi hesitated. He pulled himself from the maps and looked Spurious straight in his eyes. "That is why we need you so badly."

Spurious took an audible breath, still shaking from being lifted into the air by Ajax.

"Right now, there are probably a dozen Justice Committee agents waiting to storm my flat. Lana is dead. My life is over," Spurious said.

Slowly he raised his head, studying the fear and desperation present in the faces of every soldier. Finally he nodded. "If you promise this plan has a chance of working, I'll be your guide."

Obi clapped his hands together. "Yes!" he yelled. "We're in business again, men!"

Time: 6:05 a.m. February 25, 2071.
Location: Silo. The Wastelands

Spurious had never been a religious man. He was more of a humanist, believing the good in people was more important than anything supernatural. But on the morning of his departure back to Tisaia, he found himself kneeling on the cement floor of the silo.

Spurious had become sick of faith. He had lost patience with it. He had seen too many of his friends die and watched them laid to rest, only to decompose in the ground from which they had come.

Now he had the opportunity to be part of something bigger

than himself and to avenge the deaths of Paulo, Lana and his parents. He was going to fight. He would fight to the end. He would create his own destiny.

As the morning sun struggled to peek out from behind the clouds, Squad 19 began gathering their belongings, preparing for the journey across the Wastelands.

Rubbing the sleep out of his eyes, John emerged from the other room. "Well, it sure was nice having guests. Good luck to you all," he said, yawning.

Obi wasn't sure if the old man knew the dire situation they were in. He wasn't sure the man was even sane, living out in The Wastelands by himself, but he appreciated his hospitality nonetheless.

"Thank you for the food and shelter," Obi said, shaking the rough man's hand before running to catch up with Spurious.

"Wait up for a second, will you?" Obi asked, following him out of the door.

"I want you to know we're not the people you have heard about in the paper or at work. In fact, whether you want to believe it or not, we follow the same principles and philosophies your very own parents preached years ago in the infant stages of the TDU," Obi said, placing his hand on Spurious' shoulder. "The innocent people who died in attacks during the past decade were never meant to be killed. Our goal has always been to take out the CRK and form a new democratic government. With your help we can finally accomplish this, but I have to ask," Obi said, stopping to look Spurious in his eyes. "You do realize that this may be a one way trip, right?"

Time: 8:09 a.m. February 25, 2071.
Location: Nuke Valley. The Wastelands

Ajax took a deep breath, watching the cloud of air disappear into the slight wind. He was on point, about a mile ahead of the others to scout. Obi had split the squad up, sending Ran and Nordica to scout the western side of the rock configuration. Tsui and Juliana had stayed at the silo to wait for any other TDU members who were late to the rendezvous, while Obi, Spurious, Creo, Nathar, and the new recruits had fallen back, waiting for word to proceed.

Ajax knelt on top of a worn rock overlooking a small valley, the great walls of Tisaia vaguely visible in the distance. He removed his goggles and wiped a trickle of sweat from his forehead before squinting in the sun. They had reached the border between the rock formations and a crater known as Nuke Valley.

He squinted again to make out the crater in the center of the valley, where decades ago a bomb had blown a depression hundreds of feet deep and thousands of feet wide. The basin around the crater was weathered by years of wind storms. With zero cover and pockets of radiation, Nuke Valley was one of the most dangerous places to cross the Wastelands.

He had made the journey across the crater once, losing a CRK patrol in the cover of night, but it had cost him. Ajax grimaced, recalling the week he spent in the med ward with radiation poisoning, puking his guts out. But the internal damage was nothing compared to the suffering his skin went through. His arms were still covered in scars where boils had plastered his poisoned skin.

Beyond the crater he could make out the skeletons of buildings, dozens of them. All that remained was their metal guts jutting out of the cracked red dirt. He remembered listening to Obi tell stories of the day the bombs fell. Obi had been there, in Chicago, the once beautiful city spanning miles and miles of what were now Wastelands.

Ajax pulled his goggles back over his eyes and covered his face with a black bandana. Obi's instructions were simple: find a safe route through Nuke Valley.

Since Ajax was the only member of the TDU who survived a trip through the crater, the choice was easy—Obi picked him to lead the way.

The rest of the squad showed up minutes later, the new recruits panting through their dust masks. Obi twisted the cap off his canteen and handed it to the youngest of the men, watching the water drip slowly down his chin. The recruit looked familiar, his frightened brown eyes peering back at him helplessly. It made Obi want to protect him the same way he protected the rest of his squad, but he knew the boy had little chance of survival. Like so many thrown into Squad 19 before him, the life expectancy for the "fillers" was not long and he doubted the boy would last the week.

"What do you think, Ajax?" Obi asked, turning his attention to the valley with his hands on his hips. "Do you remember how you got through last time?"

"It was under the cover of night. All I remember was running, but I'll find a way, don't worry."

"Okay, but I don't want you turning into a damn glow stick. Make sure you use your radiation detector at all times, you got that?"

"Yes boss." Ajax said, disappearing over the cliff and making his way carefully down the rocky trail and into the valley below.

Spurious watched him go before resting on one of the rocks, feeling the fuzziness of fatigue setting in. He brought his hand to his face, wiping the dried cracks of blood caked skin from his swollen wounds. A blast of wind battered his face with dust particles, prompting him to claw at his eyes with bloody finger tips. "God damn it!" he yelled.

The other soldiers paid him little attention and continued to survey the area.

"Creo and Nathar, you take up sniping positions over there and there. I want Ajax covered from all angles," Obi said, pointing at several rock formations.

Nathar stood, his thick brown hair whipping wildly in the wind. He had quickly become one of the best scouts, and found a suitable rock formation within seconds.

The cold wind continued its tirade and the soldiers took up their positions, while Spurious huddled inside the small hollow of a rock nearby. Obi glanced at him, watching him try and curl up in the safety of the depressed concave in the rock. He could see the fear bleeding from his frightened eyes, just like he saw in the young eyes of the new recruit. He remembered his father telling him fear was weakness. Part of which he believed, but for these young men turned soldiers, fear could also be their strength.

He had seen it before, Nathar being a perfect example. Not long ago Nathar would shake before battle, his hands quivering uncontrollably. Now the man didn't seem to worry about anything.

There were times Obi feared death, but he never let it show. As commander it was his job to remain strong, unwavering even in the face of horror. Weakness caused fear, his father was right; and he promised himself he would never let his soldiers see it in his face.

The howl of a dust storm picked up in the distance. Spurious stood and made his way to the edge of the formation, surveying the valley below. Having never been outside the walls of Tisaia, he did not recognize the barren landscape, the remains of the city below littering the dead earth. Everywhere his eyes fell, destruction and death looked back at him. He could only imagine how powerful the bomb that left the massive crater must have been, obliterating everything in its path and leaving its poisonous grip on the land.

The sound of static broke though the intermittent wind as Obi's radio blared to life.

"Commander, this is Ran, over."

"Roger, Obi here, over."

"We just spotted a group of men on horses riding towards Nuke Valley. Over."

Obi rushed over to his pack to find his binoculars. From his position he couldn't see any targets yet, just a cloud of dust intensifying in the distance. A gray sky had swallowed the sun, further clouding his vision.

"There, at the edge of the crater," one of the new recruits said, his torn gloves pointing at the swirling brown blur of dust.

Obi removed his goggles and brought the binoculars to his naked eye. "That's no dust storm," he said, waving at Creo's position.

"Creo, this is Obi. Over."

"Roger, Creo here. Over."

"See if you can use your scopes to see what's creating the dust, over."

"Sir, I have five men, maybe six on horseback. They look like raiders. And they're heading straight for Ajax. Over."

"Shit," Obi said, stomping the ground and pausing to stare into the valley below. He didn't want to risk injuring any of his men, especially Spurious, but Ajax was heading blindly into a trap. He was already at least a mile away, outside of radio range, and in another minute he would be outside the safety range of their sniper rifles. Obi knew Creo was a good shot, but shooting one moving target at this distance would be next to impossible, let alone six. He also ran the risk of drawing attention to their own location if Creo fired any rounds. If there were more raiders in the area then he would be putting his entire squad at risk.

Obi knew he needed to make a decision. He had seconds, not minutes before Ajax would be too far out of range for the protection of their rifles. A somber look crossed his face as he brought the radio back up to his mouth. He knew he couldn't risk the squad for one man, even if it was Ajax.

"Ran, come in. Over."

"Roger. Ran here. Over."

"Ran, I want you two to take shelter and wait for us to reach the spillway. We're going to find some place to hide. I do not want a confrontation, do you understand? Over."

"Roger."

"Creo, hold your fire. Over."

"Sir?" Creo asked over the radio.

"I said, hold your fire. He is on his own. Over."

A second of static rang out over the channel before Creo responded. "Understood, sir. Over."

The soldier reluctantly took his finger off the trigger and peered into his scope, watching the raiders ride towards Ajax, the brown dust trailing behind them.

"Good luck, my friend." Creo said under his breath.

Time: 8:30 a.m. February 25, 2071.
Location: Council of Royal Knights Administrative Offices, Capitol Building. Lunia, Tisaia

The burly mail carrier waddled past security and entered the busy atrium of the CRK administrative offices. He navigated through the crowd of staffers and Knights, gripping a message tightly in his pocket, feeling the warmth of the fresh wax seal on his exposed palm.

"Excuse me," he said, sucking in his gut and squeezing through two staffers talking quietly in the middle of the atrium. He was in a hurry and took his job very seriously, making every attempt to deliver his messages on time. The State had entrusted him with a great responsibility, for he carried messages so confidential they weren't sent through the heavily encrypted electronic system. Messages so important, only carriers who were vetted and passed multiple background checks were even considered for employment.

Not even the beauty of the marble atrium or the ceiling painted and stenciled with perfectly symmetrical lines could distract him. He had seen them many times before and had once marveled at the dazzling chandeliers hanging from the rafters, but those times had passed. The office was only another stop on his daily route.

The carrier darted around another staffer and entered the administrative offices of Commander Augustus. Like the grand atrium, these offices were carved from marble and had magnificent chandeliers. The room was furnished with mahogany desks and a large table equipped with an AI hub.

A petite female staffer led the carrier through the maze of desks; Knights in civilian clothes were fingering their blue screens and talking on wrist radios. The office was always busy and was staffed 24 hours a day.

The long, sparsely lit hallway came into view as the carrier made his way past the last desk. He had never been back this far, but the urgency of his note allowed him to take it straight to Commander Augustus' sentry guards.

He rounded the corner, the staffer parting ways with a small nod when the Knights came into focus. They towered above the small burly carrier.

"State your business," the Knight closest to him said.

The carrier reached nervously into his pocket for the note which he had hid deep in the bowels of his coat. Finally he retrieved it and, with a shaking hand, gave it to the Knight.

The Knight spun, his armor creaking. The carrier watched him stride down the hallway lined with statues of fallen Knights. He stood on his tip toes to see over the other guard's armor, hoping to make out the faces of the famed statues. It was the one marvel he had heard of but had never seen.

The guard rotated his head; his glowing blue goggles peered down on the carrier, who took a step back, frowning. "Is there something else you need?" the guard asked.

"No, no. I just wanted to make sure the letter got to Commander Augustus," he said, stuttering.

"I can assure you, it will," the Knight replied, rotating his helmet once again.

The carrier frowned, frustrated by the Knights continued lack of courtesy. He headed back towards the offices just before Commander Augustus opened his office door and grabbed the note out of the Knight's hand, quickly retreating.

With a sigh, he took a seat. He tore into the letter and removed the handwritten note, dropping the envelope on his spotless oak desk.

Commander Augustus,

Last night we dispatched a squad of Knights into Rohania to capture a SGS worker named Spurious Timur. Our contact gave us reason to believe his parents helped found the TDU.

Unfortunately, the squad was ambushed, leaving no survivors. Spurious escaped and our contact was killed in the crossfire. We believe the attack was orchestrated by the TDU and have found evidence of armor-piercing rounds used only by TDU soldiers.

We have several patrols combing Rohania for the perpetrators of this attack and I'll keep you updated with any new information my office receives in the coming hours.

In Honor,

Supreme Knight Morr

Commander Augustus set the message down on his desk softly, and leaned back in his chair to catch his first view of the Battle of Thermopylae for the day. He had the painting from his personal office replicated and hung on the wall of his offices at both the CRK headquarters and the administrative offices.

He stared at the image of the few hundred Spartans battling an army of thousands of Persian warriors. For the longest time Augustus had believed the citizens he was trying to protect were like those several hundred Spartans, strong, loyal and selfless. But it was when he received messages like this, he began to question if this was delusional.

State employees had everything they needed: clothing, housing, food, and relative safety. If they wanted to find a wife or husband, they could simply apply for one, and receive someone that matched them perfectly. So why did they continue to try and escape?

This was not the first time Augustus had seen a note like this, and it wouldn't be the last. And as he had in the past, he would forget this traitor. He crumpled the paper in his hand and tossed in into the fireplace, watching it burn slowly in the flames.

Time: 10:01 a.m. February 26, 2071.
Location: Nuke Valley. The Wastelands

Creo sucked in a lung full of air and held it, wrapping his hand around the end of the rifle and crawling to the edge of the boulder. The cold wind of the morning bit into his jacket, but he did not flinch. He placed his eye against the scope and glassed the valley below, searching for Ajax. The ash and dust swirled violently over the cracked red earth, blurring his vision.

He sniffled, lowering the scope and pulling the bandana down from his face, wiping a cold strand of snot from his nose. Then he brought the familiar scope back to his eye, squinting to survey the valley again.

The scope revealed familiar sights: sun bleached bones, rebar protruding out of cracked concrete, and the scattered segments of road in places where the wind had not covered the blacktop with dust, but he had lost sight of Ajax.

He maneuvered to his left to get a better view. The scope brought the lead raider into focus. Creo zoomed in further, magnifying the man in the cross hairs. An ugly-tusk like bone hung off his helmet. His naked chest was decorated with bones splintered and broken, only barely covering a scar running the length of his torso. He was a bulky man, dwarfing the other raiders with his thick frame.

Creo took another deep breath and felt the hard metal of the trigger, massaging it with his well trained fingers, wanting desperately to take the shot. It was the type of shot snipers hoped they never had to make—out of viable range, with an unpredictable wind and limited visibility. He wasn't even sure he could make it if Obi ordered him to do so.

He rotated the rifle back to the right, glassing the valley again for Ajax. He tilted the barrel up slowly, combing the last stretch of blacktop where he had seen him. His crosshairs came to a stop on the concrete foundation of an old house, rebar extending out in all directions like branches from a dead tree. He zoomed in some more, magnifying the foundation, so he could see the cracks crawling up what was left of the small wall. And there he was, resting his back against the inside wall, peering out every minute or so at the approaching raiders.

"Thank God, he *has* seen them," Creo muttered over the wind, pleased Ajax had sensed the danger following him.

Creo rotated the rifle again, taking in a breath and lining the cross hairs up with the raiders. They were on the blacktop now, about one hundred yards from the foundation, quickly closing in.

"Shit, he's a sitting duck." Creo said, lining the cross hairs back up with the pack of raiders. He gripped the rifle harder and wiped his exposed nose with his elbow.

He watched helplessly as the raiders barreled down on Ajax's location. The dust from their horses swirled behind them, mixing a collage of red and black ash into the air like a trail of dark blood. A howling wind was beginning to pick up, clouding his view of the raiders honing in on Ajax. Through the wind he could hear something else. His ears strained to hear it, but the wind was too loud. He hustled further out on the ledge, trying to get a better view of Obi's position, stumbling over the rock and climbing quickly to a new position.

The noise broke through the wind again, a buzzing sound. He paused, clawing at the sharp rock, making his way higher. The sound was familiar, something he recognized. A sound that made the hair on the back of his neck stand up at the very hum.

"Scorpions," he cried, stumbling over the rocky surface again, making his way up higher into the rock formation for a better view.

He knelt down and brought the scope to his eye again. Sure enough, a trio of Scorpions came out of the west, racing over the hard cold ground. They tore onto the blacktop, a thick cloud of dust exploding from behind their oversized tires.

The raiders weren't after Ajax. They were trying to escape into Nuke Valley.

He paused, listening to the scream of their mini guns erupt over the wind, before kneeling to watch the slaughter. The riders were quickly cut down, the CRK bullets tearing through the men and their horses, sending chunks of flesh and body parts into the air. Within seconds all of the raiders except the leader were dead. Somehow he managed to dismount his horse. He stumbled towards the foundation where Ajax was hiding, a thick trail of blood flowing from his wounds.

The trio of Scorpions surrounded the man, smoke crawling out of their silent barrels. Creo watched him totter back and forth before finally collapsing onto the dusty earth next to the concrete wall.

The Knights must want him alive.

Minutes passed and the man lay in the dirt, motionless. One of the Scorpion doors opened and a Knight stepped out into the dusty wind, pointing his rifle at the fallen raider. He walked towards the man cautiously.

Creo watched through his scope, blinking just in time to see the raider jump to his feet and face the Knight.

"What the…" Creo whispered under his breath.

The raider stagger backwards, reaching for a pistol tucked in the back of his pants. A shot rang out over the wind, loud enough for Creo to hear it faintly.

The raider fired again, and again, watching the bullets ricochet of the Knight's thick armor. Before long the pistol was empty and the raider fell to his knees, reaching in his pockets for more bullets. The Knight approached him cautiously, his rifle pointed down at the man's face.

A blast of wind hit Creo, startling him. By the time he turned back, the Knight was firing on the raider. The bullets tore through his soft flesh and bone, splattering the wall where Ajax hid with bright blood.

The raider crawled across the dirt, clawing towards the Knight. For several seconds the Knight stood there, watching until the man reached his armored foot. Just when the raider made a harmless swipe, the Knight unloaded his weapon on the man until he was nothing but chunks of red meat, splattered across the dead earth.

Creo turned. He couldn't watch the slaughter any longer. Not even a raider deserved to be desecrated.

Finally he took a long deep breath, watching the Knight climb back into his Scorpion. The trio peeled off the red cracked dirt and tore on to the blacktop, zipping away from Ajax's location.

Creo dropped the scope and rested his back against a sharp rock in relief, swiping beads of sweat off his forehead. For now the danger was over, but Ajax still had a long way to go through the radioactive valley.

Time: 4:11 p.m. February 26, 2071.
Location: Abandoned Spillway. The Wastelands

Squad 19 stood at the edge of a dam, where a dirt path met the weathered gray concrete, dwarfed by the gigantic beast. Their shadows followed them down to the ledge. Obi listened to a small trickle of water spilling over the edge, a fraction of what once poured into the long since dried up lake below.

Overhead, the sun had taken refuge behind a dark gray cloud. What warmth the sun offered was now gone and the winter wind cut into his garments like frozen knives.

The dam, which had not been used for over half a century, looked like an abandoned castle, an alien in the desolate land. A thin metal ladder snaked down the cracked concrete that once held back millions of gallons of water.

Obi stood at the ledge, his orange goggles piercing the darkness below. He studied the twisted metal extending into the bowels of the old dam. Nudging the handlebars softly with his boot, he braced himself against Creo just as a gust of wind tore into his coat.

"It's the only way down," Obi said, stepping out of the way. "Two at a time. We can't risk more weight than that. Ran and Nordica, lead the way."

Nordica nudged her way carefully through the others and tested the first step with a cautious foot before she began her decent. Ran followed anxiously, his fearful eyes locking for a second with Obi's before his head disappeared beneath the ledge.

The strain of the two scouts' weight made the ladder creak and sway. They paused simultaneously, gripping the handlebars tightly, until the rusty metal stopped moving.

"Careful," Obi muttered under his breath, loud enough to pinch the nerves of Creo, who watched nearby.

Nordica paused, peering up at Ran before continuing down the steps. After a few agonizing moments they made it to the bottom of the old lake, their boots creating footprints in mud that hadn't been walked on by humans for decades.

Obi watched them disappear into the opening of the large storm drain at the bottom of the spillway. Satisfied, he nodded at Nathar and the four new recruits. They were up next.

One by one the soldiers made their way down the ladder, joining the others in the storm drain below. The squad huddled together, anxious to be out of the cold wind.

Ajax was a lucky man; avoiding the raiders, the CRK, and navigating a safe route through the radioactive valley. This much luck wasn't something Obi was accustomed to, and he knew it wouldn't last. Luck had a tendency to dry up and disappear as soon as you got your hands on it, like a glass of cold water on a hot day.

It didn't last. It evaporated, especially in Tisaia.

Obi switched on his night vision goggles again, the warm orange glow illuminating the darkness of the small storm drain. The rest of the squad members with goggles followed suit, lighting the tunnel with a safe and tepid orange radiance.

With the fresh light, Obi examined the tunnel. It was eight by six feet. He glanced in to the darkness where their lights could not penetrate. A set of small green eyes glared back at him. It was one of the stranger sensations Obi experienced when using the device, especially when the eyes belonged to mutated creatures. In this case it was just a rat. He paid no attention to it, watching it scamper away from the squad and into a small crevice in the concrete.

"Spurious. You're up. Do you remember where this tunnel leads?"

"It should connect to some utility tunnels we can access through a ladder. They should take us directly to Rohania."

"You heard him. I know everyone is tired, but this is what we've trained for. This is our chance. Take five, grab something to eat and then we're heading out," Obi said.

He crouched and grabbed an energy bar from his pack, the orange glow illuminating the faces of the four new recruits who sat huddled together, their faces all riddled with fatigue and fear. He nodded at the youngest and tossed him the energy bar.

"Are you sure?" the young man asked, his frightened eyes peering up at Obi.

"Yeah, I'm not hungry." Obi lied, walking away to find a place to sit. He listened to his men chat and chew on their meals from a distance.

"Where are you from?" Spurious asked Creo, hoping he would be more responsive than Ajax. The question hung in the air, long enough to make him feel uncomfortable.

Creo cocked his head, chewing on a half eaten piece of bread. "I suppose it doesn't hurt if I tell. In fact, you might be interested in the place I come from."

A few feet ahead Ajax snorted; his gaze fixed on the dark skinned Spaniard.

"The land I come from is across the seas, where the sun is still as bright as a thousand fires. The bombs never fell there, but the radiation poisoned everything," he added. "I left with all the other survivors. I came by boat in the year 2043 to see this world with my own eyes. After traveling from one refugee camp to another, I finally saw the great walls of Tisaia I had heard so much about. It was here I met Obi and my other companions. I have fought with them ever since."

The story sent a chill down Spurious' spine. He heard of the refugee camps outside the quarantine zones before, but never met anyone who had visited one.

"What is it like out there?" Spurious said, nodding towards the light from the entrance of the storm drain.

Creo's eyes panned to the ground. He paused to take another nibble of bread, his eyes locked on the concrete floor. "The horrors I have seen are endless: children, mutated by radiation poisoning; their mothers, working the street corners to pay for a meal that only prolongs their suffering. I have seen shanty towns ruled by ruthless men, where stealing a can of peaches will get you death, and rape is the most common form of conception..." Creo paused, taking another bite and twisting his head so he could look Spurious in the eye. "It makes Rohania look like a five star hotel," he continued.

Spurious shook the images of the mutated children out of his mind and turned his gaze back to Creo. "I have heard of the refugee camps before. You know Tisaia denies they still exist?"

"That's because the government does not want the State employees to know the truth. If they did know the truth, they would certainly want the State to try and help those outside the walls."

The truth behind Creo's statement lingered in the stale air. Everyone in the group knew there were people outside Tisaia that could use the State's help. This was information the Governor's

Office never shared with the public and never would. Spurious was the only one in the tunnel who truly knew how dishonest Governor Felix Steppe's office really was. The confidential reports he had seen and the rumors he heard from friends working at the Capitol gave him ample information to believe the State knew.

"The State knows people are out there. They choose to do nothing," Spurious said.

"Pack it up. Time to move out," Obi said, interrupting their conversation.

Spurious stood and followed the squad down the narrow path, crouching to avoid dripping water above him.

"What I don't get is why more State employees don't question these things…" Spurious said, realizing he was a perfect example of a State worker that did not question due to fear.

"You're a fine one to talk," Nathar piped in. Spurious knew the blow was coming and shook it off easily.

"You're right, Nathar. I have been living in a world of fear my entire life. Most employees probably are," he said, dropping his gaze to the green trail of water below.

"You know, Spurious, your parents were examples of people who did not fear the State. As a matter of fact, from what I heard, one of the reasons they created the TDU was to help spread hope amongst State workers in a time when fear was becoming common. If it were not for them, we wouldn't even exist. Well, at least not in the form we do today," Obi said.

Spurious looked to Ajax and saw his scowl. For some reason, one he couldn't quite figure out, Ajax did not approve of him. He wasn't sure if it was due to a bitterness Ajax had for the State, or for him personally, but something had angered Ajax ever since they met a few nights ago.

"Ajax, how long have you been a part of the TDU?" Spurious asked, trying to include him in the conversation.

Ajax snorted and stared ahead.

"You know for someone trying to help you, I think you owe

me some respect. I've done nothing wrong!" Spurious yelled at him.

Ajax stopped dead in his tracks. He turned slowly and stared at Spurious. "I owe you nothing. You're just like the rest of the sheep in Lunia. If it were up to me, we wouldn't be using you in the first place."

"You know nothing about me!" Spurious exclaimed.

Obi frowned, realizing he would have to intervene. "That's enough, you two. I already have my hands full enough and don't need to worry about this shit!" he yelled.

Spurious and Ajax glanced at one another for one last time before they continued on behind the rest of the group.

"That goes for everyone, drop the chit chat," Obi snapped. "Now, which way do we go?" he said, staring ahead at two different tunnels.

Spurious brought a finger to his lips, trying desperately to remember. "This tunnel isn't supposed to stick out like this. I don't remember there being two routes," he said.

"Damn," Obi murmured under his breath. He didn't want the rest of the squad thinking they were lost.

"Ran, Nordica, you take the recruits and head down the left tunnel. Ajax, Nathar, Creo, and Spurious, you're with me. Keep your radio channels open so we can stay in touch." Obi paused. "Good luck, men," he said, before heading in to the darkness of the tunnel.

The abandoned camp made Spurious' stomach roll. When the small squad of TDU soldiers came upon it they found decaying bodies still being consumed by rats. The poor souls who had lived in the underground camp looked as though they had died recently, perhaps in the last month or so. A stench of rotting flesh still lingered in the cold air.

"Here," Creo said, handing Spurious a handkerchief to cover his mouth. He brought it to his face instantly, trying to relieve his nostrils of the atrocious smell.

"Move on, men. There isn't anything we can do for them now," Obi ordered. He stopped for a second to massage his temples.

A few feet ahead Spurious tried to avoid the torn tents, cooking pot, and heaps of trash covering the concrete ground. He looked back at Ajax, who walked emotionless through the death. The young State worker gagged. "This is the future we face?" he asked, trekking on through the carnage.

Obi's radio blared to life, interrupting Spurious.

"This is Nordica. Over."

"Roger, Obi here, over."

"Commander, we've reached a fork where our tunnel separates into four others. Which one do we take? Over."

The aging commander shined his flashlight in Spurious' eyes. "You heard her, which one is it?" he demanded.

Spurious mentally went over the piles of maps he studied the past few months. Within a few seconds, he remembered. "Tell them to take the third tunnel that runs east. This tunnel goes directly underneath the CRK headquarters and the Capitol." Spurious swallowed hard, realizing what he said could seal the fate of hundreds of innocent people.

Obi nodded and relayed the message over the channel. He turned to face his men, who looked on anxiously. "How long will it take for us to get there?" he asked.

The office worker looked worried. He had no way of truly knowing the distance. Trying to conceal his uncertainty, he looked back through the darkness and found his most sincere voice. "Three hours, at least," he finally said.

"We better get moving then," Obi ordered without question.

The squad continued down the platform, Spurious holding the small cloth handkerchief to his nose, trying desperately to avoid the stench of death lingering in the air.

Time: 5:09 a.m. February 27, 2071
Location: Capitol Building. Lunia, Tisaia

The citizens of Lunia slept under a blanket of darkness that held the distant gray sunrise at bay. Beneath the cobblestone streets, far under the stone and soil, soldiers moved silently through the tunnels. Slowly, they made their way towards the heart of the Capitol where Governor Felix Steppe sat alone at his desk.

It was rare for Lunia's leader to be at the Capitol so early, but something had driven Felix to make the short journey to his office. He wasn't sure if it was the sleep evading him or the feeling of uneasiness lingering inside him since the legislature passed Bill 12b.

He knew the stress was also affecting his staff. The past few days, he watched Sonii leave work paler than he had ever seen him. His Chief of Staff was his most trusted confidante, and he knew the man was suffering in silence.

To make matters worse the Governor was served his morning coffee with a note from Commander Augustus, a note revealing his own fears—the TDU were still alive and operating in Tisaia.

The sun was still hiding along the gray horizon and Felix was on his third read of the memo. His strained face hovered over the yellow piece of paper under the orange glow of lamp light. He stroked his mustache and read the third paragraph again.

Several nights ago the TDU ambushed a squad of Knights in Rohania and captured an SGS worker who is allegedly the son of the founders of the TDU. We have yet to locate the perpetrators or the traitor.

Footsteps from the hallway distracted the Governor. He placed the memo back down on his desk and removed his thick glasses, rubbing his tired eyes gently. *Sonii never ceases to be on time,* he thought, rising from his desk to greet his loyal Chief of Staff.

Sonii entered the private quarters with his head tucked into his collar. He had no idea the Governor had already arrived, and it wasn't until the politician cleared his throat the pale Sonii looked up.

"Governor…" he paused. "Uh, I did not realize you were here already."

"I had some work to do," he lied, concealing the fact he could not sleep.

"I see. Anything I can assist with?" Sonii asked, scratching the small beard lining his narrow jaw.

The Governor handed him the memo, pleased to see Sonii was beginning to regain color in his face. "I'd like your opinion about this report by the time the sun comes up. And find out why I'm just hearing about this now."

Sonii grabbed the memo from his boss and slowly walked over to the mahogany conference table. His eyes scanned the document slowly, mindful not to miss a single word.

The letter confirmed his fears. He was well aware Tisaia was still not completely safe from threats. In fact, he realized the threats Lunia faced were more real than ever before. Supreme Knight Augustus had tried to ensure him on many occasions the TDU was no more, destroyed and "eradicated" from Tisaian soil, but Sonii was no fool. He hadn't risen to the second most powerful position in Tisaia by being stupid.

Perhaps it's time for the Council to choose a new commander.

Sonii turned back to the Governor, who sat studying another document at his desk. "I'll call a council meeting immediately," he said, his words cutting through the silence as he rushed out of the office.

The Governor stood and walked over to one of the bulletproof windows, watching shadows dance in the darkness hovering over Lunia. He watched the yellow hint of sunlight on the horizon like a dormant beast rising from its slumber. If it wasn't a metaphor for the threat the TDU still posed, then he didn't know what was. He frowned, glancing quickly at his wrist watch. It was going to be a long day.

Time: 7:00 a.m. February 28, 2071.
Location: Tunnels. Tisaia

Obi sat in the cold, damp tunnel, trying to keep his feet out of the murky water below him. His orange goggles glowed brightly in the darkness. He felt safe, surrounded by his trusted team. Creo, Ajax, and Nathar had just returned with the explosives. His plan was now in its final stages. Ran and Nordica were waiting for them a few tunnels away.

"What of the four new recruits?" Obi asked.

"Looks like they bailed, boss. Ran and Nordica said they disappeared a few minutes ago," Ajax replied.

"What do you mean, *bailed*?"

Ajax took out his knife and began to sharpen the blade on the bayonets attached to his rifle. "Abandoned ship, like a bunch of cowards," he said softly.

"Shit. Maybe they were compromised and we're walking into a trap," Nathar whispered.

"No, they bailed." Ajax replied, running his knife along the edge of his bayonet again.

"How do you know that? What if the Tin Cans got to them?" Nathar asked, his voice raised.

Ajax slid his knife down the length of the bayonet one more time before pausing. "I know because I could see it in their eyes. They were just kids. A waste of money if you ask me."

Obi thought of the young man to whom he had given the energy bar to earlier. "Maybe it's for the best," he said, knowing their lack of training could pose more danger to the mission.

Spurious watched the soldiers chat and stirred nervously. He wasn't close enough to hear what they were discussing, but he knew whatever it was, it wasn't good.

"We proceed without them," Obi whispered to his men. He hesitated, "We have to presume they deserted us. Besides, if they had been caught, we would have heard at least one shot fired."

The soldiers sat huddled on the concrete platform, Obi's flashlight illuminating an old map on the cold floor. It was one of the only maps Spurious recognized back at the silo.

"Nathar and Creo, you'll enter the CRK tunnel from a decommissioned air duct that runs above it. You'll drop in and take out any guards," Obi said, pointing at the different locations on the map.

"Nordica, Ran and I will drop in after all targets have been neutralized. Ajax, you and Spurious will follow us once we've been given the all clear."

"Where's the card reader at?" Creo asked

"I was just about to get to that," Obi replied.

"The card reader is located on the eastern wall of this final tunnel," he said, pointing. "Once Spurious gets us inside, Ajax and I will plant the charges. We suspect there will be light resistance, and hopefully they will never see us coming."

"Should we expect any turrets or machine gun nests?" Nathar inquired.

"Spurious, you answer that one," Obi ordered.

Spurious cleared his throat before he spoke. "This is the back way into the CRK headquarters. As far as I can tell from the blueprints I've looked at there won't be any machine gun nests and guards will be at a minimum. The tunnel is directly under the eastern half of the headquarters so the explosives should bring the entire structure down. I don't think they would see an attack coming from this direction," Spurious said, as reassuringly as possible.

"Good. Nathar, have you reprogrammed his card?" Obi asked.

"I did when we took five a few hours ago. Should work like a charm," he said with a smile.

"Men, you all know what to do. We've been waiting for this moment for years. Once we get into the secured CRK tunnel, we have to assume we'll be facing some resistance. We just need to buy Spurious enough time to get to the card reader. He has assured me that once inside the final tunnel, we can place the bombs and escape with enough time to make it out before the entire CRK headquarters collapses," Obi said, gritting his teeth.

He watched his men, scanning their faces to gauge their reactions. He wasn't surprised to see their tense jaws tightly shut. The tunnel was relatively dark, but the men's infrared goggles easily allowed them to pick up the skeptical looks on one another's faces.

Obi picked up on this quickly, realizing it would take more to reassure them he wasn't leading them on a suicide mission. There was a reason the new recruits had left, and it wasn't because they were cowards – they knew the chance of survival was low. There was no time for any more speeches though. Every moment they wasted was one second closer to their plan being discovered. And Obi knew he couldn't count on any more lucky breaks.

Time: 9:05 a.m. February 28, 2071.
Location: Tunnels. Lunia, Tisaia

The vent was pitch black, making it difficult for Spurious to even make out the shape of his hands in front of him. For what seemed like an hour, he squirmed through the tight air duct. He knew in advance it was going to be tight, but he had no idea it would be this bad. Ajax barely managed to fit inside, and was forced to remove his chest armor before entering.

As Spurious crawled further he began to feel his heart racing inside his chest. It was finally happening; he was going to have his chance at shaping the future of Tisaia.

His thoughts drifted to Lana, trying to forget her betrayal. He had to stay strong now; avenging the deaths of Lana, Paulo and his parents was all that mattered.

He pushed through the darkness, sweat dripping down his bruised and wind burnt face, seeping into his pores. With every struggling move, he began to feel like his arms and legs were moving on their own accord. His heart continued to beat faster and faster. And just when he thought he was going to vomit, Ajax stopped in front of him. "We're here," he grumbled back at Spurious.

Spurious flattened his body against the smooth metal of the air duct, listening to Nathar work on removing the barely visible cover to the tunnel below.

For minutes he lay there, listening to the faint sound of Nathar working in the distance. He strained his ears, listening to the sound of boots hitting a concrete floor below, the echo muffled by the metal ventilation.

They must be in.

Gunshots immediately erupted below, rattling the metal duct. His excitement quickly turned to horror. It was really happening. He was really going into battle against the CRK.

Spurious placed his hands over his ears, trying to shield them from the deafening noise that was amplified by the tight metal vent. The gunfire stopped as soon as it had started and a nervous silence washed over the soldiers in the air duct.

"All clear!" a voice finally shouted from below.

Spurious sucked in a deep breath of stale air, attempting to get back in a crawling position. A wave of dizziness washed over him and he dropped back to his stomach. The ringing from the gunfire was pounding in his head.

"Let's move," Ajax growled in front of him.

Spurious forced himself onto his belly and squirmed through the final length of the air duct, trying to keep up with Ajax. He could make out the halogen light bleeding into the duct from the open hole in the center of the vent. He closed his eyes slowly and took a deep breath, just like he did before jumping into the pool as a kid, and dropped through the opening.

The brightness of the tunnel instantly washed over him. He blinked, trying to regain his vision and focus on the tunnel. Spurious felt naked, exposed in the open, not knowing exactly where he was. He rubbed his eyes as his vision slowly returned to normal.

At the end of the tunnel he could make out a large metal door and two Knights lying on the concrete ground. There were warm red puddles of blood pooled around their corpses.

"Let's go," Ajax shouted at Spurious, who stood staring.

Spurious snapped out of it, removing his key card from his damp pocket and rushing over to the card reader. "Please let this work," he muttered, stepping over the body of a dead Knight and swiping the small badge over a red key card built into the wall. He waited, but nothing happened.

"Shit!" he screamed, waving the small white identification card back and forth across the front of the reader. Finally, the red light turned green with a click, and the door unlocked.

"Get him out of here," Obi ordered Ran.

Spurious watched Ajax grab the large metal handle of the door and began to pry it open. Obi waited from behind, a bag of explosives in each hand. Nathar, Creo and Nordica all had taken to one knee, their weapons trained on the door, waiting to see what was on the other side.

Before Ajax could open the door, Spurious felt Ran grab his arm. "You heard him, Spurious, let's go. Your work is done. We need to get you out of here!" Ran shouted.

Spurious couldn't move, though; everything had slowed to a crawl, like it had the night Lana died. He stood there staring blankly at the door, Ran pulling on his arm, urging him to follow.

As Ajax opened the door, Nordica and Creo rushed into the room, their weapons at the ready. The explosion of gunfire erupted immediately.

This time Spurious didn't bring his hands to his ears; he stood there, motionless, watching the red hot blasts of white lead streak from the ends of Creo's and Nordica's rifles. Spurious could barely make out the Knights in the distance. They fired from behind two metal crates positioned in the middle of the next hallway.

Ran loosened his grip on Spurious' hand just as two rounds tore through Nordica. He screamed helplessly and watched Nordica's dreadlocks swirling in the air, her rifle firing wildly before her body slumped against the concrete wall speckled with blood.

Creo cocked his head to glance down at Nordica's lifeless body before firing several bursts at the Knights' positions. "Go to hell, you Tin Cans!" he screamed.

The rounds ricocheted harmlessly off the metal crates the Knights were hiding behind, prompting them to duck. This gave Nathar and Ajax an opportunity to rush into the room. Ajax dove, lobbing a grenade towards their position.

The grenade hit the ground and rolled to the middle of the two metal crates. The Knights fumbled with their weapons, turning to run after seeing it at the last moment.

Ajax and Nathar dove for cover just before the bright white light of the grenade flashed. The explosion ripped through the metal crates, shredding the Knights and sending chunks of concrete, twisted metal, and body parts into the air.

Ajax slowly removed his hands from his head and peered around the room, coughing from the smoke and smell of scorched flesh.

"Let's move! Plant the explosives," Ajax ordered. He rushed past Obi who was preoccupied watching Creo and Ran attempt CPR on Nordica.

"How bad?" Obi asked.

Creo removed his goggles, so he could look upon his commander with his own eyes before shaking his head.

Obi, nodded, pulling a whimpering Ran off of Nordica. "Ran, I need you to get the others out of here. Nordica would want you to live. Ajax and I will finish setting the explosives."

Ran wiped a tear from his face and nodded, heading for the vent opening. Obi watched half his team make it back to the air duct, Nathar hoisting Spurious and then Ran into the darkness above him.

A small rush of relief washed over Obi. It was a small victory, considering the mission. He knew going in there would be casualties. Even though Nordica wouldn't be making the trip home, there was comfort knowing she wanted to die in combat.

"How's it coming, Ajax?"

"Almost done, boss, let's just hope the Tin Cans didn't hear us coming."

Obi knew they were working on borrowed time. By now the entire headquarters would be alerted to their presence and squads from all over Lunia would be honing in on them. They had minutes, maybe seconds, to plant the charges and bail. He kneeled next to Ajax and trained his machine gun on the door at the end of the tunnel, waiting.

"Okay, boss. Timer's set, let's go!" Ajax shouted. "You do the honors," he said, handing Obi the remote detonator.

Obi felt the cold metal of the detonator on his fingers. In his hand he held the end to a revolution—the ability to bring the CRK headquarters and the Tisaian government to its knees.

He looked up at Ajax, a smile hidden by his five days' worth of facial scruff. His friend didn't return the smile, however. He looked terrified. Obi turned just in time to see a squad of Knights pouring into the room.

Ajax started firing immediately, back tracking through the open metal door and into the first room. Shells rained down on the concrete floor, pinging as they hit.

"Shut it!" Obi screamed.

Ajax tossed his weapon to the side and began shutting the massive metal door. White hot bullets ricocheted off the other side, but Ajax would not be deterred. He grunted, snorted and heaved with all of his might. His muscles bulged, the cobwebs of veins poking out of his scarred arms until finally the door closed with a loud bang.

But Obi's luck had finally run out. He lay on the concrete floor, squirming in pain. Ajax continued on, oblivious to his fallen comrade. He headed to the card reader and blasted the device with his pistol.

"Let's go, I'll hoist you up first, boss!" Ajax shouted, reaching down for his assault rifle. It was then his eyes finally came to rest on Obi's broken body.

"I'm not going to be making the trip home this time, my friend. You're Commander of the TDU now," Obi coughed, a red stream of blood streaking down his chin.

"No!" Ajax cried, collapsing to his knees. "You're coming with, boss, we can still get you out of here," the large man whimpered. His eyes comprehended what his mind could not - Obi was mortally wounded, two bullet holes to the chest and one in his stomach.

Obi coughed again, holding up the detonator. "I never told the others, but I have always considered you a son."

Ajax squeezed Obi's hand. He couldn't bring himself to look down at the dying commander, the man he had fought side by side with for so long. He was a man of few words, and he wasn't going to change now. Placing his hand on Obi's shoulder, he squeezed it one last time, a tear finding its way out of his neon orange goggles and crawling down his thick jaw line.

"Go!" Obi coughed, another stream of blood crawling out of his lips.

Ajax stood, gritting his teeth and wiping the tear away before heading for the air duct opening. He grabbed Nathar's hand, jumping and pulling himself into the metal duct above.

The team crawled through the air duct as quickly as they could, listening to the Knights pound the metal door in the distance. It was too late for them, though; the bombs on the other side couldn't be disengaged, and the detonator remained in the hands of one of the most loyal TDU soldiers to ever fight in Tisaia.

He lay in front of the door, motionless, the pain subsiding, his life source draining from his body. He watched Ajax climb to safety and was at peace.

Obi's blood stained lips formed a smile. He had watched Spurious grow into a man in the past few days, and knew this young State worker's destiny was to rise to greatness and lead Tisaia out of the darkness. He would have a chance to do that now.

Obi gripped the remote tighter in his gloved hand and reached for the necklace Sasa had given him years ago, caressing it. He closed his eyes and remembered her face and the faces of all those lost under his command. His eyes darted back down to the remote. This was for the departed—the ones who lost their lives fighting for justice.

The pounding on the door grew louder. He grimaced, the feeling in his legs dwindling. His body was redirecting the blood to his heart and brain as his organs slowly began to shut down. He had to hang on, to give his men adequate time. They had to get far enough away from the blast zone. He hadn't come this far to fail them now.

The banging on the door rang out again. The Knights on the other side were growing more frantic.

Obi took one last breath, memories of the past racing through his mind before he closed his eyes for the last time. With a single click he pushed the button on the detonator; a single tear crept down his face before the fire consumed him.

Time: 12:05 p.m. February 28, 2071.
Location: Immigration Camp #4. Rohania, Tisaia

Kalah sat in his small tent, surrounded by three of his closest friends. He watched his companions huddle around the small fire, chatting anxiously about the news trickling into the camp from relatives and friends in Rohania. The flames illuminated a sparkle in Kalah's normally dull brown eyes.

An hour had passed since news of the massive bomb that ripped through the Council of Royal Knight's Headquarters spread.

And Kalah was excited. Normally he would have dismissed such news, but when the ground shook and the smoke rose in the distance, he knew a change was coming. Today was the day he would rise with the rest of the immigrants at Camp #4. Today was the day they would finally achieve their freedom.

He turned to his tent mate Mulia. "How many weapons do we have hidden?"

Mulia held up his fingers as if he were counting the rifles he had hidden over the years. "About 50," he finally responded.

"Then we should have enough for almost every able man in the camp. It's time to fight. Spread the word. Today we go to war!" Kalah yelled, rising from his feet.

Time: 7:14 p.m. February 28, 2071.
Location: St. Peters Church, Rohania

Leo sat in the bowels of St. Peter's church, hiding in the shadows and watching the flicker of candle light dance across the dark room. He listened carefully to the Rohanians who gathered around a massive oak table in the center of the room. He examined the weapons, maps and pages upon pages of documents littered across the table, wondering if they were real.

Leo had helped organize the meeting immediately after hearing of the news streaming in from Lunia. The Knights' headquarters had finally fallen.

"Let us call this meeting to order!" shouted Susa Waria, a middle aged shop owner from Rohania, known for her waist length gray hair.

"I want to thank Leo, one of Rohania's oldest protectors, for organizing this meeting. Rest assured you're safe here. The Knights are busy with rescue attempts at their headquarters. That's right, the news you have all inevitably heard by now is true. The Knights have been broken," Susa said, pausing, the room breaking into cheers.

"Let us not forget, however, the window of opportunity for a rebellion is short. Knights are still positioned throughout Tisaia, and will without a doubt reorganize quickly. We must rally with the immigrant camps and strike them hard, and strike them swiftly if we hope to truly retake Tisaia."

The room erupted in commotion. Susa stood, her hands trying to quell the disorder.

"What of the TDU? How do we know they're strong enough to fight a full-fledged rebellion?" a man asked from a chair at the back of the room.

"They were strong enough to destroy the CRK headquarters," another man Leo did not recognize shouted.

"We shouldn't overestimate them, though," a woman yelled at the end of the table.

"Order!" Susa yelled at the top of her lungs. The room quieted and she placed her hands down on the table softly, scanning the room with her dark brown eyes.

"We've waited for this day for a long time now. I can assure all of you my contacts have confirmed the TDU is still intact. News has already trickled in that the immigrant camps are beginning to rise up. We've been supplying them with weapons for years, waiting for an opportunity just like this..." Susa paused and grabbed a document from the table.

"In front of you there are directions. You're all ward leaders, men and women who own shops or businesses in Rohania. These documents will provide you with the information you need to organize your wards. Weapons and supplies will be provided. What your people may lack in training they will certainly make up for in enthusiasm. The Knights will not be able to stop a full rebellion," Susa calmly reassured them.

Silence crept over the room, the ward leaders scanning through their briefs.

"If you do not wish to be part of this uprising that is your decision. All I ask is you make this decision quickly. For those of you who do not wish to continue, please leave now," Susa requested.

Leo watched the ward leaders fidget around the table, a few appearing anxious to leave, but they all remained. The darkness hid the nervous brows of these men and women, who had gone from struggling business owners to rebels overnight. Most of them had no experience with fighting, something they all lived amongst for so long.

Susa, however, was no stranger to fighting or rebellions. She had lived her entire life amongst those fighting to make the world a better place. In the beginning years, when Tisaia rose out of the ashes of war, she had been part of the TDU. She knew this experience wasn't something she could pass onto the ward leaders through words on a piece of paper. She couldn't expect them to fully grasp the task in front of them. All she could do was hope they would follow through with what she asked of them.

Susa looked around the room one more time, briefly studying the faces of each of the men and women she was relying on the most.

"Thank you for staying. I truly appreciate your bravery, and soon Tisaia will as well. Are there any questions?" Susa asked, pausing to glance around the room and study the anxious faces. Silence swept over the room and she continued. "If there are no questions, then this meeting is adjourned. Good luck and Godspeed," Susa said, blowing out a candle, grabbing her rifle and heading for the cobblestone streets above.

Time: 7:01 a.m. February 29, 2071
Location: Rohania, Tisaia

Squad 19 sat perched on the first floor of an abandoned high rise, never repaired from the nuke that peeled back its layers of metal like a doctor cutting into flesh with a sharp knife. They watched the gray dawn break on the horizon, cold and dense. In the distance flames licked the skyline, smoke billowing above the CRK headquarters and Capitol, now nothing more than smoldering craters in the ground.

The sight sent a chill down Spurious' spine, a relief so overwhelming it could almost be confused with joy. But joy wasn't the proper word to describe the destruction he saw in the distance. Amongst the lifeless bodies of Governor Felix, Commander Augustus and their army of barbaric Knights lay many of his co-workers—collateral damage in a war that spared no one.

Spurious shook the images of death from his mind. The civilians, Lana, and his parents weren't the only deaths being grieved. Squad 19 had not been able to mourn Obi or Nordica either. The time for grieving would come, but first Squad 19 had one last mission to complete.

A shrieking explosion broke through the morning gray haze as an ammo depot exploded somewhere in the city. The flash blinded Spurious momentarily. He shielded his naked eyes, but it was of no use; his vision was clouded with stars.

"Here, take these." Ran said, handing him Nordica's night vision goggles. "She has no use for them now," Ran said, a slight whimper in his voice.

"Thanks," Spurious replied.

A pair of heavy boot steps interrupted them, prompting the two to turn and watch Creo enter the room, his radio blaring to life.

"Listen," he shouted, an excited grin on his face.

"We've captured the CRK garage. Facing light resistance. If the TDU is out there we have..." a pause of static broke over the channel. Creo shook his wrist and smacked the radio in frustration, but only static hissed out.

"We have four Fox Hounds and a dozen Scorpions. Need assistance. Over."

"Holy shit," Nathar said, clapping his hands in excitement.

"Roger. TDU here, identify yourself."

Static broke out over the channel for several moments.

"This is Mulia. Immigrant from liberated Camp #4. We have captured the vehicle garage and are coordinating a counter offensive with wards in Rohania. We need TDU assistance as soon as possible. Over."

"Roger. What is your location? Over," Creo asked.

"Two blocks from the CRK headquarters, just south of the SGS building."

"I know where that is!" Spurious shouted, interrupting the transmission.

"Roger. Give us 15 minutes. Hold your position!" Creo shouted into the radio.

Ajax slung his rifle around his shoulders and took one last glance out the broken window, glassing the city below. "This is our chance. I have always wanted to drive a Fox Hound. Let's move out!"

Time: 8:11 a.m. February 29, 2071
Location: Lunia, Tisaia

"Be careful!" Creo yelled over the Fox Hound's intercom. He gripped his arm rests tightly, the vehicle tearing out of the metal garage and shredding the slightly ajar door before plunging onto the cobblestone streets below.

"Hold on!" Ajax shouted, gripping the controls tightly. He took a hard left, scraping the side of a maintenance building, a trail of sparks raining down on the tank's armor.

The tank barreled down the street, cracking the ancient bricks below its heavily chained tires.

"Any targets yet, Nathar?" Ajax asked, peering through a small slit above the control panels.

Nathar rotated into a comfortable position at his weapon station, trying to make sense of the battle blue screens connected to cameras built into the armor of the tank. The four holographic screens gave him a 360 degree view of the streets.

"Nothing yet, sir, but I'm picking up chatter over the radio." He paused, pushing one of the padded ear phones against his head and straining to listen.

"Sounds like the remaining Tin Cans are dug in at the Golden Dome and there are sporadic pockets of resistance between our location and the arena." Nathar paused again, desperately trying to make sense of the radio chatter overwhelming the channel. "I'm also hearing they have RPGs set up on roof tops a few blocks from here. So stay sharp," Nathar finished.

Creo took another glance through the scope, the empty streets emerging through his viewer.

"Keep an eye on those rooftops," Ajax shouted over the tank's intercom.

Creo scanned the skyline, stopping on an abandoned high rise decapitated by the blast from a nuke decades ago. Something in the tangled metal was moving, and then a flash of light, a black dot breaking through the gray haze, with a flaming trail behind it.

"RPG!" he screamed, bracing against the metal skin of the tank wall, his hands covering his ears tightly.

The missile plowed into the side of the tank, creating an expensive dent in the armor before exploding and rocking the tank to its right side.

Creo attempted to recover, but his ears were ringing and vision blurred. He rubbed his eyes and squinted into the scope, gripping the joystick tightly. As the outline of the two Knights came into focus, he didn't hesitate in pulling the hard metal trigger. He watched the uranium tipped projectile sail towards the rooftop; a flash of light blinding him, the floor where the Knights once stood disappearing in an orange explosion.

Creo laughed. "Holy shit!" he yelled. "I turned them to scrap metal!"

"Stay sharp." Ajax instructed. "There could be more."

Creo regained his composure quickly, firing off another shell towards a Scorpion at the end of the street where two more Knights fired a .50 cal.

He watched the white streaks of lead racing towards them and listened to their harmless pings ring out on the tank's armor. Creo couldn't help but smile. It was the first time in his life the .50 cal bursts from a Scorpion had no way of killing him.

He peered back into his scope and pulled the trigger, listening to the shell explode out of the tank's gun. The first shot went wide, shattering the foundation of a stone building and lifting the Scorpion into the air from the blast. He squinted again, waiting for the cross hairs to line up with the Scorpion, but the Knights were already retreating. He watched them peel off the curb, shredding a tire before escaping down the cobblestone street.

Creo stomped the metal floor of the tank. "Damn, missed them," he yelled over the intercom.

"It's okay, they're heading towards a pocket of Rohanian rebels," Nathar said, studying his blue screen intensely. "We're only a block from the dome."

"Creo, keep an eye out for more RPGs. A few more direct hits and we're toast." Ajax said.

"Yes, sir."

Creo took a deep breath and squinted into the scope again, observing the same empty street, a few of the buildings raging with flames. The rooftops were empty, no heat signals.

The tank reared sharply to the left and slowed, the magnificent Golden Dome coming into focus. A trail of smoke roared out of a gaping hole in the dome, sending a chill down Creo's back. On the ground, hundreds of Rohanians and immigrants surrounded the structure. He scanned the countless men and women, their faces blurry through the gray morning.

"Holy shit, will you look at that?" Ajax said. "If Obi could only have seen this."

Nathar blinked, rubbing his eyes. He couldn't believe what he was seeing. The blue screens showed the entire Golden Dome surrounded. Rohanians sat perched on rooftops, in office windows, against concrete barriers, and hidden behind trucks. The Knights were trapped.

"Guys, I'm hearing chatter that the other Knight positions have already fallen. This is it. This is the last of them!" Nathar shouted.

"Get Ran on the line. I want him to bring Spurious to our location asap," Ajax ordered.

With a deep groan, Ajax unlocked the gmetal hatch to the Fox Hound, swinging it open like a cupboard door. Cautiously he stuck his head out, barely flinching as two stray bullets ricocheted off the tanks armor.

"Damn," he said, surveying the hundreds of Rohanian rebels and immigrants surrounding the Golden Dome. He watched the small army advance in awe. They cut through the dense fog crawling across the gray field, undeterred by the sniper bullets cutting through the silence of the morning.

"Over here, Ajax!" a voice yelled from the street.

The monstrous soldier turned to see Spurious running towards the tank.

"We have the Knights surrounded and the rest are on the run. The rebels are waiting for orders!" he yelled ecstatically.

Ajax climbed out of the tank, Nathar and Creo close behind.

"Take cover!" Ajax exclaimed, ducking behind the safety of the armor. Another sniper bullet ricocheted off the metal, a ping echoing in his ears.

Creo crouched beside Spurious, his head hidden behind the safety of the tank's metal shell. "Who's calling the shots?" he shouted over the sporadic gunfire.

"A ward leader from Rohania named Susa, apparently. I don't know. Everything has been chaotic since I arrived with Ran!"

Spurious yelled.

Ajax plucked his radio from a velcro strap on his metal chest armor. "Commander Ajax here. Requesting report. Over."

A pair of voices crackled over the radio, static mixing with the unrecognizable chatter. "Ajax..." Crackle. "Ajax... this is..." Crackle.

"This is Commander Ajax. Come in. Over," he replied, shaking the radio violently to the sound of more static.

"Ajax, this is Susa. I'm leading the rebellion right now and need assistance from the TDU. We broke the assault up by wards and they're holding their fire until I give orders to advance."

Ajax strained cautiously to see over the tank, his orange goggles glowing through the transparent fog.

"Report on status of Knights. Over." Ajax said, waiting.

"We put their numbers anywhere from 50 to 75 strong. There are several other pockets of resistance, but I've already sent several wards and fighters from Camp #4 to assault those positions. The Golden Dome is their last holdout. Most of the Knights perished in the initial attack on the headquarters," Susa replied.

"Roger. I'll order my men to bombard the Dome with the Fox Hounds."

"No!" Susa yelled, interrupting him. "I want the Dome saved at all costs."

"With all due respect, I don't give a shit. Unless you want the blood of hundreds of civilians on your hands, then we're going to turn that building into a crater of ash."

"You'll do no such thing!" Susa shouted angrily over the radio. "The Dome needs to be saved. The Capitol is gone now; last I checked, the TDU turned it into a smoking cave. The Dome is the only feasible place to set up a transitional government!"

"She's lost her freaking mind," Ajax snorted, cocking his head to glance at his squad.

"This could be a very costly assault, Ajax," Nathar said, fear in his voice. "The rebels have no chance at taking that building. Not with their weapons. They will be slaughtered."

"We don't have a choice; the Knights have refused to surrender. If it were up to me, we would use the Fox Hounds to bombard the building until it's nothing but ashes, but we can't win this fight without Susa, or her army."

Another shot rang out, dropping a rebel in the middle of the field, arterial blood staining the gray dirt a bright red.

Spurious watched the rebel claw at his throat, trying to stop his life source from flowing out, but it was no use. The man twitched a few last times before he became another casualty—another statistic in the war that had already killed so many.

The sudden feeling of Déjà vu gripped Spurious as he scanned the frightened faces peeking out of the fog. He saw the face of a young man dressed in tattered clothes hiding behind a trash can, gripping a shotgun tightly to his chest. He saw the face of an old immigrant crawling towards the fallen rebel who was bleeding out in the field. He saw the face of a young woman crying uncontrollably behind a light pole. And finally he saw a man and woman holding pistols nervously behind a pickup truck. To anyone else they would have been mistaken as ordinary citizens turned soldiers, but to Spurious they were more. They were Ing, Paulo, Lana and his parents.

"NO!" Spurious yelled.

Ajax took a step back from the tank, shocked at his sudden outburst.

"No what?" Ajax asked, studying the young man's battered face.

"No one else needs to die, Ajax. We've lost too many good people. And when the smoke clears we're going to need trained soldiers to help protect our walls. There are threats in the Wastelands they can mitigate; pirates, raiders, countless other terrors. Let me offer them the chance to surrender."

Ajax muttered something under his breath. "Spurious, this isn't your call. Besides, we've offered them the chance to surrender and they won't. We have no choice…"

"What would Obi do?" Spurious asked, cutting Ajax off.

The soldier scratched his beard, recalling a conversation he had with Obi in an abandoned windmill not a month ago. "Save those you can and help those that can be rehabilitated." The words repeated over and over in his mind.

"Damn, you're right." Ajax patted Spurious on the shoulder. They both knew Obi would have done everything he could to save the Rohanians, and to find a useful purpose for the remaining Knights, who were brainwashed into following orders. Obi always saw Governor Felix and Commander Augustus as the real enemy, and believed their mindless minions of Knights were pawns in the larger chess game.

"I'm going to patch a line into the arena and see if you can talk some sense into the lead Knight…" Ajax checked his watch. "Spurious, we won't have long before our channel is shut down by the rebels, so make this quick," he said, patting him on the back again.

A scream cut through the morning, another rebel falling to the ground, the victim of a CRK sniper round.

"You have to hurry! The rebels won't hold back much longer!" Creo yelled.

Spurious nodded and grabbed a radio from Ran.

"The Knight in charge is Royal Knight Tinus. Good luck," he replied.

"That's the Knight that killed the Samoan!" Spurious shouted anxiously.

Ran shrugged. "I don't care who he is. This isn't going to work. You can't trust the Tin Can's. They will never surrender," he replied.

Spurious ignored the small soldier, knowing he was still grieving over Nordica's death. Snatching the radio, he took a knee behind the Fox Hound.

"Royal Knight Tinus come in. Over."

Static crackled over the radio for several seconds.

"Roger. Tinus here. With whom am I speaking? Over." His voice was edgy, strained from yelling.

"This is Spurious Timur. I'm a State employee with SGS. I have been authorized to offer you a conditional surrender. Over."

Tinus laughed. "If you can give me one good reason to talk to a traitor, then I'll give surrender honest consideration. Over."

Ran chuckled. "What did I tell you?"

"Shut up, little man. Let him talk," Ajax growled.

"Royal Knight Tinus. I understand how you may feel right now. Everything you have known has turned upside down within hours. Your work, dedication and loyalty to the State may seem lost, but I can assure you it's not."

"You know nothing about dedication and loyalty; you're nothing more than a traitor!" Tinus yelled, interrupting Spurious.

Spurious stiffened. "I know more about loyalty and dedication than you think. After my parents were killed in the beginning years of the revolution I was sent to an orphanage and later to the University. I became a State employee and have served the State since then. In the past two months everything changed for me. My best friend was killed in the subway attacks; the woman I loved betrayed me and was killed…"

Spurious choked, the memory of Lana's death haunting his thoughts before the crackling radio brought him back.

"It turns out everything I have known to be true is a lie. My parents were the founders of the TDU. The State I served has oppressed those it has sworn to defend. I have seen the Wastelands, I have seen the immigrant camps and I have seen the ruthlessness of both the TDU and the Knights. And on top of all of the death, misery and pain I have seen something else. I have seen a common humanity I once read about when I was a young boy. There was once a place called New York City, a city full of immigrants from around the world. They came to Ellis Island for a chance at better life. As I have traveled throughout Tisaia, the camps, Rohania and even Lunia I realized what made New York great can make Tisaia great. If we give everyone a chance to survive, Tisaia can become a just place again. You know as well as I do that we have enough Biomass and food reserves to last a century. We can help those in need. We can build a strong Tisaia, one that values righteousness."

Ajax watched the young man and smiled. "Go on, Spurious," he said.

Spurious nodded and continued. "Tinus, I ask you to surrender because the bloodshed does not need to continue. We can heal from this revolution, and you and your Knights will not be harmed. I can assure you. At the end of this, we'll need your men to continue to protect our walls. Your men will not only be safe, they will be utilized in further service to the State. These are our conditions. Surrender and you shall remain Knights…"

Time: 8:22 a.m. February 29, 2071
Location: The Golden Dome. Lunia, Tisaia

The arena was almost completely dark, illuminated only by the sporadic red flicker of blinking emergency lights.

Inside the second floor business office, Royal Knight Tinus stood in the makeshift control room, staring at an outdated map of the city. His men were still hastily setting the room up, piling desks against the windows overlooking the parking lot.

A deafening gunshot rang out from the corner of the room, the shot echoing throughout, but Tinus held steady, his face stoic. He had ordered the two snipers positioned at the window to fire every five minutes, to prevent the rebels from advancing. This would buy him time, hopefully enough to devise a plan—a plan that didn't include surrendering, the option extended to him earlier by the TDU.

"Reporting for duty, sir," a Knight said from the hallway.

Tinus instantly recognized the muffled voice. "How did it

come to this, Riya?" he replied, bringing his fist down on the table. "That wasn't a rhetorical question."

Riya unfastened his helmet, taking it off so he could run his hand through his sweat drenched hair. "Sir, it's not good. We've lost contact with all of our squads outside the building. The rebels have taken two of our ammo depots, our garage, and our headquarters is gone."

Tinus froze, his eyes finding their way back to the map. "We're completely surrounded and the rebels have Fox Hounds. There is no way out."

Riya frowned, wondering if it was finally time to reveal his true thoughts about the State. Would Tinus accept them? Embrace them? Or would he call him a traitor and have him hauled away? The old Knight took a deep breath. Under the circumstances it was a risk he was willing to take. "Sir, we need to talk. Can we do this in private?"

Tinus wiped a bead of sweat off his forehead. "Sure, there is an office down the hall. Follow me."

The two Knights exited the office and entered the dark hall, ignoring the salutes of Knights who stood waiting for orders.

"It's the first door on your left," Tinus said, pointing ahead.

Riya scanned the room and found a pair of chairs stacked in the corner. He dragged them over to a coffee table and nodded at Tinus. "Please sit."

Tinus clasped his hands together behind his back. "I'd rather stand. There is a battle going on outside, our men are dying. Make this quick."

Riya nodded and reached for his hand held radio, placing it in the center of the table. "I overheard your conversation with Spurious on the open channel. In fact, most of the men did."

Tinus laughed, his face quickly growing red with anger. "You brought me all the way down here to tell me that?"

"With all due respect sir, just look outside. We're completely surrounded. There is nowhere to run and no way to fight our way out of this situation. You're the Royal Commander now. Please think of your men and the citizens of Tisaia."

Tinus snorted. "We can still win this battle, my old friend."

"At what cost? 25 men? 50?" Riya said, interrupting Tinus in mid-sentence.

"I'd sacrifice every man if it meant keeping Tisaia safe."

Riya stood to face his old ally. "Safe from whom? From its own people? The Rohanians? The State Workers? The Immigrants? Tinus, this revolution isn't the result of one horrible law; it's a result of hundreds of bad laws!"

"What would you have me do?" Tinus said, his face flushed with frustration.

"I'd have you surrender and help restore Tisaia to the State it was meant to be!" Riya yelled, spit flying out of his open mouth.

Tinus stiffened. His eyes locked with Riya's for a split second before darting away to the wall. He took a deep breath and walked to the door. "When did things go to shit, my old friend?"

Riya took a step over to Tinus and put a hand on his armored shoulder. "A long time ago."

Tinus let out a deep breath, his chest plate shrinking back to its normal position. A flash from his battle with the Samoan slipped into his mind. He could vividly remember the crowd cheering for the refugee. Even clearer was the memory of his utter shock, wondering why the audience would request mercy for the man. But now it was all beginning to make sense. As much as he hated to admit it, Riya and Spurious were right. The State had oppressed citizens for too long. Even worse, the Governor and his cohorts had brainwashed the Knights to carry out their restrictive laws. How could he have been blind to it for so long?

Tinus grunted, and cracked a rare smile. "You're right, Riya. We should have stood up for what was right a long time ago. I'm afraid fear has been rampant for too long in Tisaia, preventing justice and equality from being served to the masses."

Riya returned the man's smile. "You're right, but it isn't too

NICHOLAS SANSBURY SMITH

late. We can still salvage this. We can help rebuild Tisaia again."

"I thought that's what we did after the Biomass Wars, but I've been wrong all along," Tinus responded, slipping his helmet back on. "Inform the men. I'm heading back to the control room to discuss our surrender with the TDU."

Riya stood at the doorway, watching the red flicker of emergency lights. The glow illuminated Tinus' dust caked armor through the darkness with every flash.

Suddenly a powerful wave of relief rushed over Riya—a wave so powerful he was forced to brace himself against the wall. He had been harboring his dissent for so long, and now it was finally over. He could breathe again. And while he wasn't certain what the future held, there was something about this Spurious that convinced him things were going to change.

Time: 9:01 a.m. February 29, 2071
Location: Lunia, Tisaia

Static crackled over the radio. Squad 19 hunched around the radio, waiting for a response from Royal Knight Tinus.

Spurious glanced up to see the Rohanian's had stopped advancing and waited in a circle around the building, news of the negotiations spreading quickly.

"Spurious, this is Tinus, come in. Over."

Spurious fumbled for the radio and quickly brought it to his mouth. "Roger, Spurious here. Over."

"First off, let's drop the radio formalities. This conversation is anything but formal. Now tell me, the Ellis Island you spoke of. Was it a good place to live?"

"One of the best sir. The men and women migrated there in search of a better life. Through hard work they achieved more than you could ever imagine and built one of the best cities in the world."

285

"This sounds like something worth fighting for," Tinus replied. "How will you ensure my men will still continue to serve if we surrender?"

"Rebel leader Obi Hepe firmly believed Tisaia was corrupted not by its soldiers, but by its leaders. With Governor Felix, Commander Augustus and the legislature gone, Tisaia will need new leaders. Righteous leaders. They will need an army to protect the walls. Your men will be pardoned and will continue to serve. This is my promise to you. I've been assured by Rebel leader Alexir Jahn the TDU will honor this pledge."

A brief moment of radio silence followed Spurious' assurances.

"A lot of good men and innocent people have been killed today. It needs to end. We will accept the TDU's conditions and will surrender."

Spurious dropped the radio to the ground, ignoring the pieces of plastic cracking on the concrete below. He couldn't believe what he had heard.

His eyes scanned the faces of the squad members, all who looked equally confused and shocked, before turning back to the building.

The fog began to part and a small ray of crimson light broke through one of the gray clouds above the Dome. Like a miracle, the gold rooftop began to radiate light. The rebels rose from the safety of their hiding places, watching the anomaly, soaking in the rare splendor before the sun crawled back behind the cloud and the gray reclaimed the land. Through the silence a voice broke out in the distance. "They're surrendering!"

Spurious turned to see Leo racing through the field. "Put down your weapons, they're surrendering!" he yelled.

Spurious laughed at the sight of the crazy old man, his arms flailing joyfully about. The rebels cautiously began to put down their weapons, erupting into cheers. One by one, the men and women emerged from the fog.

Ajax grabbed Spurious and hugged the man half his size. For a second Spurious couldn't believe what happened, but as Ajax let go, Spurious realized it was real.

"Obi would be proud of you," Ajax said, laughing.

Spurious smiled, not his half grin, but a full one gleaming with joy.

"Spurious! You've done it! Tisaia is now free!" Creo yelled.

The two embraced as more and more rebels surrounded them. "Spurious!" someone began to shout.

He turned to see Leo again, shouting his name energetically in the middle of the growing crowd.

"Spurious! Spurious! Spurious!" the old man shouted. In a matter of seconds those around him started to repeat the same. Ajax grabbed Spurious and hoisted him onto his shoulders.

By the time the Knights began to emerge from the entrance of the arena an entire crowd was chanting his name, Ajax carrying him through the hundreds of faces of civilians.

Ajax looked up at his comrade. "We've won, my friend! We've won!"

A tear crept down Spurious' battered cheek, not from joy, not from sadness, but a combination of both. He watched the crowd shouting his name and remembered Lana, Paulo, his parents, Obi and all of the others lost in the fight for Tisaia. And he smiled.

The sun finally broke through the gray morning, illuminating a new Tisaia, a free Tisaia.

EPILOGUE

Time: 1:14 p.m. September 29, 2072.
Location: Lunia School of Philosophy and History. Lunia, Tisaia.

A cool breeze rustled the leaves outside of Terro's lecture hall window. He watched the wind pluck a red leaf from a maple tree, swirling it towards the ground.

In the front of the room the professor paused, his eyes falling on the young man lost in his thoughts. "Terro, what was your take on the end of the Biomass Revolution?"

Startled by the question, Terro's eyes swiftly darted to Professor Creo. The man had taught at the Lunia School of Philosophy and History for a little over a year now. He was, in many ways, a living legend. It was rumored he fought against the Council of Royal Knights in the uprising of 2071.

"Not a lot, Professor. Mostly just what my mother has told me."

"Which is?" Professor Creo entreated.

"Well, she said, the TDU helped start a rebellion, rallying citizens from Rohania and immigrants from the old camps."

"Your mother is right. She should know; after all, she played a large role."

It was not a secret Terro's parents were both part of the rebellion. He tried to remain humble, but all of his classmates knew he was the son of one of the most respected soldiers of Tisaia.

"It's my understanding the beginning years of Tisaian history were sealed in secrecy," Terro continued.

Professor Creo placed his pencil down on the podium and began to stroll down the hallway.

"Terro is partially correct. The beginning years of Tisaian history are certainly not a time we should be proud of, but they were not necessarily sealed in secrecy, as he suggests."

Terro stirred nervously in his chair, a tint of red forming on his face. He didn't speak much in class, but when he did he liked to be knowledgeable about the topic.

"You all know Governor Felix Steppe and Council of Royal Knight Commander Alexander Augustus ruled Tisaia with an iron fist. The Governor and his allies isolated Tisaia from the rest of the world. Laws were passed to restrict the rights of Tisaian citizens. Immigrants were hunted and imprisoned in camps before they were deported into the Wastelands. The Biomass that powers the very lecture hall you sit in was hoarded and kept within the Tisaian walls." Professor Creo paused again, stopping at Terro's row.

"I'm sure you all heard I fought with the TDU. This is true. I do not normally announce this, but today's class is unique," he said with a slight grin. "Today you all get to meet Senator Spurious Timur."

At the back of the lecture hall a young man made his way slowly down the aisle. He removed his beret and carefully ran his hand through his short cropped hair, swiping a few loose strands back into place. A few students shuffled in their seats to get a better look.

Professor Creo stiffened his back as Spurious approached. "Everyone, I want to introduce you all to the man that helped restore justice to Tisaia."

The lecture hall erupted into applause, students rising from their seats to recognize the Senator.

Spurious stopped at the center of the room and stretched his hand to Professor Creo, before changing his mind and instead embracing him with a large hug.

"Good to see you, Creo. Thank you for having me today,"

Spurious said, turning back to the students. "I'm so glad to be with you all…"

The hall grew silent.

Spurious cracked a half-smile. "Being here brings back some fond memories. You know, it wasn't long ago that I too was sitting in one of your seats. In fact, I think this is the one I often sat in," he said, pointing at the chair next to Terro.

"But I digress and unfortunately I have little time today. The legislature is meeting to vote on a new bill this afternoon. Which is why I am here."

Spurious took a step forward to face the center of the hall, scanning the young faces.

"I'm sure most of you have heard of Bill 199, but for those that haven't, listen up. I've worked out a deal with our newly sworn in Governor to share 25 percent of all Biomass with any surviving communities outside the great walls."

Applause echoed through the lecture hall, with one student whistling before a peer silenced him with an elbow to the ribs.

Spurious waited for the commotion to die down before continuing. "Governor Susa has assigned Squad 19 of the newly minted Tisaian Knights to explore the Wastelands for survivors of the Biomass Wars. Any refugees will be brought to Tisaia; they'll be housed, fed and supported until we can find work for them."

Another round of applause broke the silence and Terro stood, joining the rest of his classmates. It was the first time he'd ever seen Senator Spurious Timur and he wasn't exactly sure what to think. The man was so young.

"Before I leave I have one request of you. Someday you will be the leaders of Tisaia. When you are, do not forget what Professor Creo has taught you—do not forget the revolution so many died fighting. If you remember anything may it be this…" Spurious took another glance at the empty chair next to Terro. "All governments are prone to corruption. The duty of youth—your duty—is to challenge greed and injustice when it arises, before it morphs into corruption."

The whine of a tree branch scraping the window followed the Senator's words. For a few moments the classroom was silent, the students soaking in Spurious' advice.

He reached into his pocket and pulled out a letter. Terro watched him carefully, thoroughly impressed with his speech. In the past he'd doubted the stories about Spurious' role in the revolution, but there was something about the man. He had a presence, just like Terro's own father.

"A little over a year ago I found this note. When I first read it I didn't know what to think. It said my parents, who died in the revolution, were the founders of the TDU. This was days after I was told I had the ability to shape the future of Tisaia—to restore justice," he said, his eyes shifting to the floor for a moment.

"Seeing the empty seat next to this young man," Spurious said, pointing towards Terro, "I am reminded that you are all in the same position as I was. You may not be fighting a revolution, but I can assure you, the world we live in has changed forever and safety will always need to be earned. So I leave you with the same words I was told in the streets of Rohania," Spurious coughed and placed the note back in his breast pocket before turning back to the silent room.

The young Senator cracked another half-smile and tucked his hands in his pockets. "You're the future of Tisaia; you'll shape the path of our country," he finished.

The room did not erupt into applause. Students did not stand and clap or whistle. They simply watched the Senator place his beret neatly over his hair and walk slowly past their rows and out of the lecture hall. His words continued to echo in their minds, playing on repeat like they had once done in Spurious' own mind.

A bell sounded, breaking through the stillness like a shotgun blast. Terro stood and packed up his belongings with the rest of the students in silence. They all knew what was at stake for their new government, and they all knew it would take severe sacrifices to keep the cogs of progress turning.

"Terro, do you have a moment before your next class?" said a voice from behind him. A quiver ran down his back when he realized it was Professor Creo.

"Certainly sir," he said, placing his last book inside his bag.

"You may not know it, but you are, in many ways, much like your father. I served with him for many years and he taught me to fight for freedom, tolerance and equality. He gave his life so your generation could have a better quality of life."

The student turned to Professor Creo. "Is it true, did my father really help save Tisaia with Senator Spurious?"

"Without his leadership, we would never have destroyed the CRK's headquarters."

Terro gripped his book bag tightly. He had heard this many times, but each time it sent chills down his back.

"Senator Spurious was right. You're the future of Tisaia now, son. You, like your father, will have the opportunity to change things for the good of all Tisaians, but we can save that discussion for a later day," Professor Creo said, placing his hand on the young student's back.

"I'll see you tomorrow."

"Yes, professor, have a good night," Terro said. His voice was precise, controlled, not a hint of nervousness present. He wanted to be like his father, respected and humble.

As Terro walked away he began to suspect there was more to his life than he thought. Like all young men, his dreams were overflowing with ambition. And Professor Creo's lecture ignited his excitement of the future even more.

The hallway was packed with students heading to their next classes. Some laughed and played, while others remained silent, intent on making their next class on time. Terro was like the second group, concentrating on his way to the Royal Gardens. He often studied there on his breaks between classes, especially when he needed a chance to think.

He remembered being told the center of the gardens used to be home to the first Governor of Tisaia's statue. It was said to have been removed in the uprising of 1971.

Now the gardens consisted primarily of fountains, and the single monument to his father, Obi Hepe.

It was early September and most of the hibiscus, roses and other perennials were shriveling up and dying, waiting for the spring to re-emerge. The fountains, however, were still alive and spouting clear water into the fall afternoon air.

Terro strolled through the grounds towards the statue, remembering stories he had heard of his father's time as the leader of Squad 19. They weren't just stories—they were legends, and they always made him wonder if he too could be a brave leader.

The steady trickle of running water reminded him he was close. He took in a deep breath of the fresh air as the top of his father's statue came into focus through a row of trees.

He studied the features of the man he had never met; his short cropped hair, thick jaw line, and obsidian black eyes. *I wish I could have met you,* he thought, reaching out to touch the statue's stone hand.

When he was younger he never quite understood why his father hid him away as a child, choosing to fight the CRK instead of being a dad. Sure it probably prevented his family from being slaughtered, but growing up Terro was constantly angry, never really forgiving Obi for his decision. It wasn't until Terro's first day in Professor Creo's class he finally realized why his father hid him away so many years ago. Obi choose to fight over being a father so Terro could one day grow up and live in a world where he would be able to be a father. It was the ultimate sacrifice and gift to his separated son.

Suddenly a gust of cold wind bit into his shirt, distracting him from the painful memories. A squadron of dying leaves twirled about the statue. He cocked his head to look at the sky and watched a pair of dense storm clouds moving in over Lunia. The wind began to pick up and a soft drizzle began. *Change is coming,* he thought, gazing back up at his father's statue one last time.

If what Senator Spurious had said was right then change would be something his generation would see often. It would be his duty to help stop corruption.

"You're the future of Tisaia now, son. You'll have the opportunity to change things for the greater good of all Tisaians." The words of Professor Creo echoed through his mind one more time before he stood to pay his final respects to his father.

"I'll serve Tisaia, this is my promise to you," he whispered, stopping in the middle of the stone path to watch a pair of dark storm clouds creep over Lunia. Taking in one last lungful of the rain scented air, he picked up his bag and headed for the school. "Change is coming indeed."

Liked the Biomass Revolution? Read the new short stories chronicling the lives of Squad 19 and the Royal Knights before the events of the Biomass Revolution, now exclusive to Amazon.

Look for Book II
INTO THE GRAY WASTELANDS
Coming winter 2013.

ABOUT THE AUTHOR

Nicholas entered the whirlwind of self-publishing in 2013 with the gripping dystopian thriller, The Biomass Revolution, a coming-of-age story set in a post-apocalyptic future after fossil fuels have vanished. Two prequel stories that detail both sides of the revolution—Squad 19 and A Royal Knight—followed shortly after. His second novel, Orbs, is a terrifying and suspenseful sci-fi account of a science team working in a Biosphere that finds they are suddenly cut off from the rest of the world. When the blast doors hiss open they enter the horrifying aftermath of a cataclysmic cosmological event (anticipated release in October 2013).

His writing consistently addresses topical issues such as climate change, immigration, fossil fuels, religion and war by adding the intriguing twist of science fiction. His motto as an author is, "Forever writing something different," and he strives to create unique concepts.

When Nicholas isn't writing he is more than likely attempting to find innovative ways for his insurance company to take away his life insurance. An adrenaline junkie at heart, Nicholas exploded onto the triathlon scene in 2012, consistently finishing in the top 10% of his age group in short distance races. In 2013 he decided to up the ante and completed his first Half Ironman in Galveston, Texas and Full Ironman in Coeur D'Alene, Idaho. In September he will compete in the Hy-Vee 5150 National Championships in Des Moines, Iowa. Check out his blog at nvrstoptriing.tumblr.com for fitness and health tips.

An honest gentleman and humanist, Nicholas is known for his compassion. A vegetarian and animal lover, he started the not-for-profit 2RRacing in 2013 with the idea of running a dog in races across the Midwest to raise money for animal welfare. Look for him and his dog on the race scene in 2014 and visit them at 2RRacing.org.

He pays the bills as a project specialist with Iowa Homeland Security and Emergency management where he helps communities recover from natural and man-made disasters. He has undergraduate degrees from the University of Iowa in Political Science and American Indian Studies, and a graduate degree from Drake University in Public Policy.

Nicholas lives in the Middlesex historic district in his hometown of Des Moines, Iowa with his dog Bella.

For more info, follow his trail of spilled ink at:
http://nicholassansbury.com